HER HUSBAND'S HOUSE

Her Husband's House

BY CATHERINE POMEROY STEWART

AUTHOR OF "SO THICK THE FOG"

New York   CHARLES SCRIBNER'S SONS   1946

AUTHOR'S NOTE: All the characters in this novel
and all incidents and situations mentioned are ficti-
tious and do not relate to any persons living or
dead; and any possible coincidences are accidental
and unintentional.

TO

ALAN COPELAND COLLINS

1:

*T*HERE IS an Italy hidden behind and among the mountains to the south. An Italy where ancient road posts point down a deep mud-rut to Philadelphia or Athens; and where along the way small treasured shrines implore Minerva, her laurel wreath but recently converted to a halo and her name Maria. The greater spinal column of the Italian railway system extends beyond Naples to the tip of Reggio Calabria. It clings to the western coast, winding through narrow mountain lands from whose high places Scylla and Charybdis can be seen. If you would travel eastward across the Sila to Catanzaro above the gulf of Squillace, or farther south to the temples where the Greek adventurers worshipped, and where the olive trees are large as oaks and older than three generations of man, you must change over to a local which will twist and turn and carry you the small distance in many hours. As for the interior of Calabria, there is no choice but to travel by car over roads that are steep and tortuous. And farther, you will pass through a country so wild and abandoned as to give instant rise to the illusion that you have stepped back in time into the magic land of the Druids, where a few miles were a very great distance, and the hour was eternity,

The ancient Calabrian bandits fled Ferdinand of Naples to this place. So successful were they in waylaying and slaughtering the troops which the great king sent after them that

Ferdinand considered, and, crossing off certain of the more
desolate stretches of campagna, the blackest of the forest jun-
gles, he named them sanctuaries and risked no more of his
soldiers. This was Alessandro Cavalierre's land.

One of the main roads in Calabria winds down the hill from
Catanzaro, to straighten when it reaches the gulf of Squillace.
Following the curve of the waterfront, it stretches to Crotone.
There are still steep hills to be climbed and descended, but
such a road is straight, in Calabria. Five miles beyond Crotone, a dirt track bends away from the macadam road. It
ambles through miles of citrus groves, across a plain of wheat
fields; then, turning and twisting, it climbs through the thickly
treed olive hills until, in dead earnest, it commences the ascent
of the mountains. Here it doesn't go fifty feet before it bends
back on itself in hairpin turns. Here the olives give way to
chestnuts, and, later, to firs and pines. Once it clears the forest
to discover a high valley among the mountains, where it follows, for a way, the shores of a lake so desolately uninhabited
as to conjure up thoughts of Walden, or of that "ultimate dim
Thule" of which Poe dreamed. Beside the lake are the half
overgrown ruins of a black stone castle, Valombra, once the
home of the Cavalierre family. Past Valombra, the road goes
up the mountain to Nimpha, perched like an eagle's nest at the
very top. Orange and olive, chestnut and pine, desolate lake
and mountain eyrie still belonged to the Cavalierre family.
Though they had, many generations since, gone to Rome to
live, they were nourished and clothed and had their being from
the fruits of Valombra.

Once a year, when the other lords of Calabria gathered to
look into the well-being of their estates, Alessandro Cavalierre
would go to Crotone where he would meet his agent. Eventually, he would go to Nimpha to look into matters more care-

fully, to see for himself that his people were well, and his trees and his hogs and his mules. Alessandro Cavalierre was a good landlord, and a careful one. If he lived in Rome, he still knew his people and his land, and to this end he brought his son to spend a part of every year at Crotone. On each trip to Nimpha he took the young Gian Franco to run and play with the village children while he himself discovered the tempo of the village. He talked, and he listened to talk. There was the roofing, there was illness, there was the malaria in the valley, there was the grafting of trees, the pressing of olives and grapes, the breeding of stock and the butchering of it. No Cavalierre yet had lived on the milk of the land without paying the good price of it. And Alessandro intended that none should.

2: **"Viene! Viene il Barone!"**
"Viene Don Alessandro." As though a strong wind had
whipped across the village square, men, women and children
commenced to run in every direction. There was a clatter of
hobnailed boots and the pad-pad of bare feet across the cobbles and up and down the steep, narrow streets that radiate
like so many dark stairways from the square. A few children
were captured and dragged by unwilling ears to have faces and
necks scrubbed. Above the village a round and fat white cloud
sat like a benign halo while, all about, the sky was blue.

"A good day, a blessed day for a wedding." Padre Pasquale
folded his thin hands neatly and watched the scatter and
scurry about him. The church of the Holy Virgin of Nimpha
was built on the ruins of another Cavalierre castle. It surmounted, and seemed almost larger than, the village that
circled downwards from its steps. Padre Pasquale stood at the
top of the steps and listened to the distant whine of a motor
which could be heard, now coming towards, now going away
from Nimpha as the car changed direction with each hairpin
turn. Beside him, Odilia Tregatti, wife of Pancrazio, quivered
with excitement so that her whole fat body shook and the
whisper of her black taffeta gown was unpleasant to Padre
Pasquale's ears. It was her daughter, Rosa, whom he was about
to join in holy matrimony to Giuseppe, son of Francesco the
head goatherd.

"Is it really the Barone?" Odilia's voice came shrilly from between her fat lips. "Will Donna Lucia really come?" With the rest of the villagers, Odilia gave the Cavalierres the inaccurate but descriptive title of Baron. There was no title in the Cavalierre family, though they had been lords of Valombra for a matter of fifteen centuries. When the Calabrian says "Barone" he intends "Lord" and he also intends to say "a great man, and one I can admire." So that the villagers made no mistake when they called Alessandro Cavalierre "Barone."

Padre Pasquale said, "Mateo has said that they will come." He did not look at Odilia as he spoke, having a great distaste for her. Odilia Tregatti was fat, and sometimes she was complacent, but for the most part she behaved as though she were prey to a terrible boiling from within. Her desires, her greeds and lusts rode her, as she in turn rode the people about her. Upon occasions she would confess and Padre Pasquale would admonish her severely and order her to pray and to diet. Within his own heart he had small hope that even this would help her to pass the boundaries of Purgatory.

"They will be here in half an hour," he said. "Go and see to your house and to Rosa." Now he looked at the woman, his pale brown eyes cold and disgusted. "If she has broken her fast I will not marry her," and he turned away into his church.

Inside, he moved with ease and great grace, so that his thin body seemed no longer gaunt and unlovely but an exact and beautiful symbol of his church come to life. He knelt before the altar and prayed for his soul.

Padre Pasquale found that he had more often to pray for his own soul than for the souls of his flock. There were times when, despite his religion and his faith in redemption, he found himself hating his people. There were even times when he found himself thinking that Mother Church did great harm and great injustice in demanding confession. He knew too much about people, and because he was an aesthetic man he could not always bear his own knowledge. To know that Odilia Tregatti had given bed-room to half the able-bodied men in the village and that her sixteen children were mostly of parentage uncertain even to herself! To have to know this! To have to know the pettiness and greeds and the small, unclean vices that grew about him. He prayed, believing that if he had been a pure man these things would have been nothing to him, that only his own hidden desires could produce such hatred as that which these people were able to stir within him. He knew that he alone in the village sinned, for he alone knew his sin. The others were children. They satisfied their physical and their biological needs and then, because they could not live on bread alone, they came to him to confess and to repent.

In the piazza before the church a car drew up. Padre Pasquale bent low until his head touched the altar steps, then he crossed himself and, feeling pure again, went out to meet Don Alessandro and his lady.

Don Alessandro was a tall man, thin and hawklike. He was a man Padre Pasquale liked to look upon, for he had a stern, clean look and his face and bearing were not unlike the portrait of an early Medici cardinal which hung in the college where Padre Pasquale had studied for the priesthood. Donna Lucia was different, a foreigner. She was taller than any woman he had ever seen, and more beautiful. As she crossed the paved place and came up the church steps, he saw that she moved with the ease of a peasant woman but more gracefully, swinging her long legs straight from the hips, not rolling as the peasant does. He saw that her skin was as brown and her cheeks as ruddy as a peasant girl's, but without being coarse. Her eyes were different too, not somber pools of black, as a peasant's are. They were black, to be sure, as black as the wings of the Mourning Cloak, but afire with so many lights and so much joy that even an unhappy village priest was for an hour made the happier. The boy, Gian Franco, was like his father, with the wonderful gift of his mother's eyes.

From the village below them the men and women and children came. Their movements made a murmur, for the women and girl children were dressed in padded black taffeta, while the boys and the men were stiff in their Sunday best. Padre Pasquale inclined his head without bowing and said, meaning it:

"You are welcome, Don Alessandro, you are welcome, my lady, you are the very welcome one, my little lord," and he made the sign of the cross in the air, to give blessing to their meeting.

When they had answered his greeting, Lucy Cavalierre smiled at him and said:

"Father, please tell me who the lovely blonde child is whom we saw in the valley by the lake."

Padre Pasquale was suddenly aware that Odilia was again by his side, and Rosa and Maria Pia, mother of Giuseppe the bridegroom. Knowing that they would take it as an ill omen that the girl's name should be mentioned at this time, that they would probably disgrace him by making the sign against evil, he had no choice but to answer. So that when he spoke, his voice was heavier than he would have intended.

"The girl is Pia," he said. "She is without other name, as she is a bastard child."

The three women on the church steps crossed themselves hastily, and Odilia Tregatti surreptitiously pointed her index and little finger. The priest scowled. She should have fifteen days of skimmed milk for that, and a good fifty stations on her rosary. Lucy looked her surprise but she said no more and presently she stepped back and allowed Alessandro and the priest to precede her into the church. The ceremony was about to take place.

By the lake of Valombra, Pia stepped out of a ragged chemise, clutched the piece of soap she had stolen from Margherita, the baker's wife, and climbed down the rocks into the water. The floor of the lake was stony and would have been hard on a gentler foot, but Pia was accustomed to rough ground, and her slim, straight body did not waver for an instant. She reached a place where the water came up to her waist, and commenced to lather her body. When this was done, she plunged under the surface and, where she had been, white foam circled like a huge lily pad. She came up in a different place and now she went to work on her hair, soaping it and scrubbing it, and twisting and rinsing it again and again. Presently she finished, and waded back to the shore, where she threaded her way through the thick brush that grew along the lake.

Above her, among the rocks where she had dropped her clothes, another child moved. A stone clicked against another. Pia hesitated, listening. There was no other sound. Then, clearly on the sunlit air, came the high lilting song of a pipe. It was so sweet and pure a song, and in so wild a spot, it might have been the great god Pan, "spreading ruin and scattering ban."

Pia raised her head from among the green branches about her and a rare smile danced across her face. When the song was done, she went out from her shelter to the place where she had left her clothes. Sitting on a rock beside them she found a short thick boy.

"Ave, Leone!" she called. "Would you like to have my soap?" She stood before him, her hair plastered like seaweed to her body, and the water running in pools to her feet. Sunlight glittered on the wet gold and white of her, and she was fair as a forest is after a storm.

"Ave, Pia!" The boy Leone was short and broad without being fat. He had strong hands and a beautiful head. Pia thought that his neck was like the trunk of an oak tree and that his head was God sitting on top of the tree. He scowled at her, and said:

"I have bathed already and have got on my Sunday best, if you'd trouble to look. But haven't they given you anything better than these rags for the wedding?" He stirred the despised garments with his feet. Pia grabbed them quickly.

"I'm not to go to the wedding. But I shall, of course." She slipped into her chemise. "Why aren't you there?"

"I came to find you."

"Well, you'd better go back, if you want to see them in the church." She sat on a rock beside Leone and, leaning over, spread her hair in the sunlight to dry. "Because I'm going up to the house to hide in the loft, and I'm not coming down till they all get good and drunk, like the pigs that they are."

Leone grinned, but he looked at her doubtfully.

"Donna Lucia is there. Do you think they'll get drunk with her there? They'll be too scared."

Pia snorted and for a moment she was silent; then with her fingers she pulled the curtain of hair aside and peered up at the boy beside her. In the shadow of her hair her green eyes looked gray and wistful. She said softly:

"Santa Maria, but she is beautiful! Are all the Americani so big and beautiful?"

Leone shook his head. "I don't know. Some day I shall go and see."

"You will! You! How, Leone? Tell me. How?" Pia's head had whipped around at his words, regardless of the hair which fell tangled and wet into her lap. Now her eyes were suddenly green and alive with excitement.

A dull red crept up the fine oak tree that was Leone's neck and a scar on his cheek turned livid; his finger went to it quickly, for the blood made it itch. Pia was eight years old and Leone was thirteen, but already she had the ability to stir the man blood in this child and make him conscious of himself. It was a power she was to have over many.

He said quickly, to cover his embarrassment, for the scar which he touched he had of a fight for Pia, who was called a witch:

"I shall go, it doesn't matter how. I won't stay here to be a blacksmith. It is well enough for my father—he doesn't want anything else. But I shall go to America, where I can be anything and as rich as I like." With his words the blush had died slowly from his face.

Pia said gently, "Like Titto Scalpi from San Giovanni Marina." They were silent, thinking of Titto Scalpi who had gone away to America and come back with a big shining car and a portable radio and enough money to build himself a fine cement house at San Giovanni and to marry his old sweetheart, who was without a dot. Pia's eyes widened and she said:

"Will you come back?"

Leone fingered his scar. As though a secret thought had

come to bother him, he could not speak. Then, taking up his pipe, he commenced to play a merry tune.

Pia spread her hair in the sun again. From the dark cavern that it made for her face, she whispered:

"I wish you would, Leone. I shan't have a friend, without you."

For a moment the piping faltered, and then it fell into a shepherd's chant, two-toned and mournful. Leone did not know how to answer. His warm brown eyes were as sorry as his tune. Beneath her hair, Pia wept.

For the first eight years of her life Pia lived among an ancient people, and the mark of wildness which they put on her was never to leave her. Its roots struck deep and had to do with the fact that she belonged to none of them. They clothed her, very much as a scarecrow is clothed in the field, for a purpose and with rags which will not in any case be missed. They fed her, very much as a hound dog is thrown a meatless bone or a sop of stale bread soaked in water. They baptized her in the church, and admonished her to walk in the ways of God. When they could lay their hands upon her, they slapped her and bade her mind her manners. They were as night chasing day, for they were people of black hair and dark eyes and sullen looks. Pia's hair was platinum gold. It hung to her knees, and it shone like a streak of fire in the dark village. Pia's eyes were green; like a cat's, they said. They were wide, slightly slanting eyes that sometimes seemed almost blue, but the transparent green-blue of the Aegean Sea. Pia was neither godly nor good, nor sufficiently unhappy. She could, and did, weep; but laughter always spilled hard and fast upon her tears, and such easy tears leave little mark.

Every country in Europe has known the invader. And though he be victor, carrying off sheep or wine, gold or silver, besides not a small number of lives, in his quick wild forays, the invaded have their own subtle, ageless revenge. For they steal the blood of their enemy and incorporate it into their being even as a wild beast who has consumed his prey. The sons of Alexander, of Saracen lord, of Viking and Spaniard, the children of Cæsar and Barbarossa are not in their high places but are eternal prisoners in the lands their ancestors despoiled. So it was at Nimpha, where Saracen and Spaniard and hot-blooded bandit glared from the dark eyes of the Italian women at the unwanted Viking in their midst.

Pia was a bastard child. She was not illegitimate; in Nimpha they had no law about such things. There was no lawyer in Nimpha to have told them. The church called her a bastard, a love child, a child of God. So, bastard she was, although she was given somewhat less of a welcome than a child of love and a child of God might have had the right to expect. The villagers had their own excuses:

"Just look at her hair; you didn't know where you were at with blond people."

"Straniera!"

"And probably a witch. Look, then, at the eyes!"

"Child of God, indeed; she'd need to be mortified, that one, before ever she was brought to the ways of God."

Pia had her own ideas of whence their small love of her was born. She would dodge a slap and, tossing her white mane, would stamp her foot on the cobbled square and shriek at the incensed village:

"My father was the devil over on the hillside, and I was born out of his left horn and the fire of his tongue, and one of you was with him and I know who it was! I know who!

I know who!" She'd dance away up a narrow street and scream to the skies, "I'm a bastard, but somebody's going to burn in hell."

Behind her, the village would tremble almost visibly. Neither man nor woman nor child but believed what she said. They called her a liar. They chattered like magpies among themselves. But they crossed themselves quickly; and twice, in her eight years among them, they caught her and locked her up for twenty-four hours without even the little food to which she was accustomed. When they considered that she had fasted sufficiently, they dragged her before the stregona, a yellow-skinned and toothless hag. Whether the stregona was a witch herself, as she looked, or a witch-enemy as she claimed, it was she who wove spells for the needy and she who cast out devils. Pia was thrown to the ground of the dark and sunless hut. They who brought her stood by, a grim bulwark, while the old woman chanted and swayed and jerked through the hours of the night and the day. When the devil commenced to escape from her own body in noisy, gusty yawns they crossed themselves. And they fell on their knees and thanked the tender baby Jesu and the sweet Virgin when that moment came and the devil, able to endure no more, wrenched himself free from Pia's frail body, leaving it unconscious on the cold floor. Then they carried her out and laid her on the cobbles in the sunlight. Or if it were night, they took her into a kitchen and laid her before the fire to dry out. When she awakened, they gave her bread soaked in goat's milk and said they hoped that now they would have no further trouble with her. These, then, were Alessandro Cavalierre's people.

3:

*P*IA DID not weep for long. She was not entirely sure why she wept. Soon she dressed and, combing her still wet hair, let it fall down her back, where it felt heavy and clammy. Leone watched her and, when she was ready, he got up without being told and together they climbed through the rocks to the dusty road. They knew that they had plenty of time, for the wedding party would stop first for a toast at the house of Odilia and Pancrazio. Then they would have the long walk down the mountain and across the valley to the house which the goatherds had built for Giuseppe and his bride. Pia and Leone would be there well before them and have time to sample the food and wine as well.

The new house was made of straw, with a roof that looked like a haystack. It comprised one room and a small loft. Two windows were curtained with goat's hide. It was a summer house such as the goatherders all lived in. In the winter, Don Alessandro's flocks were driven from the pastures into sheds in the village, and those which were the property of the goatherd himself wintered in the home kitchen.

There was nobody at the new house when Pia and Leone arrived. The middle of the room was occupied by a bed. On the left was a charcoal stove, and on the far wall, by the ladder to the loft, a rough table was well laden with wine and fruit and great egg-and-yeast bread-cakes. Pia sampled the wine from the jug. It was heavy and sweet. Satisfied, she poured a mug for Leone and one for herself. Then she set the jug back on the table and eyed the cake.

"Do you suppose they'll be drunk enough not to notice, if we break it?"

"They won't be drunk, I tell you; not with Donna Lucia there."

"Well, they won't be sure who started breaking it. Besides, they will get drunk; you just wait." Pia's green eyes stared out of the open door prophetically, and she broke into the nearest bread-cake without waiting for an answer.

The two children took their cake and sat on the big bed to eat it, for there were no chairs in the house. They ate quickly. They were hungry and the cake and wine tasted good to them, and they could not consume them fast enough. They had barely finished before they heard the first distant sounds of laughter and song that raced on ahead of the wedding party.

Pia said, "We'd better get up." She smoothed the bed, making sure that there were no crumbs left on it. Then she filled their cups again and, handing Leone's to him, she followed him up the ladder. The loft was low and hot and, for all of its newness, it was heavy with dust. They settled themselves comfortably, with their heads at the opening, and waited.

Children surrounded the wedding like a nimbus. They hopped and skipped and ran before it, they clung to its sides, they straggled behind. Rosa and Giovanni headed the adults, arm in arm, red-faced, laughing and expectant. Behind them were Don Alessandro, Donna Lucia and the priest, and behind these were the bridal parents, aunts, uncles, brothers and sisters and other mixed relatives, which comprised the entire population of Nimpha. They trooped across the fields and when they came into the small house they all threw money on the bridal bed, to well wish and start the young couple off, as was the custom. From their point of vantage Pia and Leone watched and saw that they were indeed not drunk.

"Madonna!" Pia whispered, her eyes big as cheeses as she saw the hundred-lira notes Don Alessandro and Donna Lucia each put on the bed, the little Baroncino following with a silver lira piece. Below, there were cries of wonder and admiration and thanks. The Saints were called down to witness the event, mugs were filled with the bubbling red wine, and the drinking began. Pia grinned; in a little while there was going to be fun. Not quite yet; in a little while. She rested her head on the hot boards and the red wine in her tingled pleasantly. She closed her eyes for just a moment, and whispered so softly that Leone, had he been awake, could scarcely have heard:

"Close y' eyes, Leo, an' y' c'n see th' feelin' inside."

After a second round of toasts and good wishes, Alessandro and Lucy Cavalierre called Gian Franco and Mateo, the agent, and left; but Pia did not see them go. Nor did she hear the swell of laughter and good cheer that grew with the day. By evening, the laughter took on a shriller and more raucous tone. The children were corraled and pushed out of the house and the long roll of rawhide which served as door was lowered to the ground. The men, excepting the thin priest, who had long since gone back to his church, prepared somewhat unsteadily to assist Giovanni in his toilet. On the other side of the bed, a robust band of women seized the suddenly reluctant Rosa. Above the struggle and the cries of protest no very subtle jokes were tossed from one side of the room to the other, and not a few suggestions. Two of the older men, who had not weathered the wine too well, left off their services to the bridegroom to peer through the bulwark of skirts for a glimpse of the fair, plump Rosa—an occupation at once remarkable and suggestive of the unplumbed powers of the lively fruit-juice which they had imbibed, for not one of the men present but had bathed with Rosa in the lake without feeling a particular urge to look upon her more than on any other woman. Rosa's status was new, but her figure was as yet unchanged. The attempt, in any case, was thwarted by Signora Odilia's fat elbow, and in a moment a side show of interesting proportions was set up. The young couple were put to bed with a show of great reluctance on their part. But no sooner were the covers thrown over them than Giovanni gave up the struggle for freedom and proceeded, with no little vigor, to pursue his legal and religious rights. Rosa screamed, whether with fright or delight, and clawed at the choice of her heart, drawing blood in four fine lines from forehead to chin. The women giggled appreciatively and then the party filed out, pulling the rawhide flap decently into place behind them. In the loft, Pia and Leone slept, the thick wine and the heat of the confined place paralyzing their young limbs, and they were helpless prey to violent and unaccustomed dreams.

Pia was the first to awaken. Her head was blanketed in pain, her breath was coming in short gasps, and beneath her belt her stomach turned. She raised herself cautiously and felt for Leone. His body was hot and relaxed. Pia crawled closer and shook him a little. But Leone would not be roused and Pia had no great strength to spare. The heat clung to her like some vital thing that would have suppressed her and held her down. Without looking into what dangers there might be awaiting her, she lowered herself over the side of the loft and stumbled down the ladder. For a moment, the darkness below seemed cooler, and then the heat swirled about her again. The window flaps were down and there was a heavy scent that drifted above the odor of the wine and the food and perspiration, and made the small room seem smaller. Pia gasped.

She moved closer to the bed, intending to pass it quickly and run for the door. Giovanni snored loudly and loosely and there was a bubble in his voice as though he had not complete control over it. Pia giggled a little, forgetting her stomach for the moment. Her eyes were accustomed to the dark now and she could see that the covers had been flung off from the bed. Giovanni lay on his back and Pia thought that he looked bigger than he had ever looked before, and beside him lay Rosa, not snoring but breathing deeply, and her body had a look as though all of the bones had been pulled from it. Suddenly, Pia grinned and, pointing at them, said quite loudly:

"Your first-born shall have cross-eyes."

Then, her stomach claiming her, she ran quickly from the room and was neatly sick on the grass outside.

4: *7* HE MOON rose to her high place in the sky. She was small and round and white, but her pearls were beyond price and she cast them abroad freely. One rope fell and, slipping down the shaft of a fireplace among the ruins of Valombra, tangled in the fair hair of the sleeping Pia. There were pearls in the fields and in the forests and, where the desolate lake waters lay, pearls floated on the surface, to sink with a gentle rocking motion and glisten dimly from the depths. Along the white dust roads there were pearls, and beneath the pale waters of the bay at Crotone heavy ropes of them twined about the submerged columns of a Grecian temple where Pythagoras once paced and, perhaps, gave wondering thought to the immeasurable distance the great lady could throw her gems.

At Villa Falconierre, a white marble house on the bay, jewels floated through open casements to sparkle on glistening floors. Beneath a canopy of gold cloth Lucy Cavalierre moved, uneasy in her sleep. She dreamed of a child who cried for help. A child sinking rapidly in a morass of fair hair. While the hair sucked, strangling and smothering the child, a horde of women stood by and crossed themselves. Nobody gave a hand. Minutes are not to be measured in sleep. The dream was brief, but when morning came, there were circles under the dreamer's eyes and Lucy Cavalierre was more fatigued than she had been upon retiring.

She lay for a moment with her eyes half open, listening to the sounds from the bathroom. Alessandro was having his bath and Lucy thought that it was the one thing about him that did not go with his leanness, for it was the bathing of a fat man, full of splash and brrr! and snatches of song. She rang for Fortunata, the maid, to bring her a ewer of hot water and a cloth and towel. When she had washed her face and combed her hair, she slipped into a bed jacket and sent for her breakfast. By the time Alessandro came into the room, she had a tray on her knees and was peeling a peach with great care.

"Well, my lovely," he took his tray from the desk and arranged himself beside her, "you look as though the cares of the world had not agreed with your sleep."

Lucy cut her peach with knife and fork and ate it in small neat mouthfuls.

"It was the wine," she said, "the original Bacchus brew."

"Too much for you?" he laughed.

"Worse than too much! How in Heaven's name do they survive it? And they were giving it to the children!"

"It's the pure drink. They trample the grapes with their feet and pour it into hogsheads to ferment, and they don't refine it. Would you like me to have some sent up?"

"Certainly not. Feet! I'm glad I didn't know that was still being done. I though that was prehistoric."

"No, the peasants prefer it. And, in fact, scientifically speaking, the bacteria are helpful."

"Sandi! That's repulsive. It was bad enough. I felt as though I were drinking Syrup o' Figs strongly diluted with wood alcohol. And now I have to hear about the bacteria of peasants' feet!"

"And what, may I ask, is Syrup o' Figs?"

Lucy smiled at her husband and thought, as she had never grown tired of thinking, how handsome he looked, how frightfully austere, and what fun he was. She said:

"It was a sticky sweet ghastliness we were given as children, for a laxative. Substitute grape for fig, lace it good and strong, and you have Nimpha's favorite beverage. I wonder if it has the same powers!" Lucy stopped smiling, suddenly, and turned her brown eyes to her husband. There was in them all of the misery she had known during the night.

"Sandi, the child! That is what is worrying me. I had the most awful dream about that child."

"What child? Not Gian Franco; he had only a sip of wine. It won't do him the least bit of harm."

"The blonde child. The lovely, unreal little girl sitting on the rocks by the lake. She was all alone, and she never turned up at the wedding."

"But, my dear girl!"

"When I asked about her I'm sure that Padre Pasquale didn't like it, and those three vulturous females crossed themselves. I saw them."

"But that's silly; it's not reasonable."

"That's why it worries me, Sandi. Will you ask Mateo about her?"

"You are a continual source of surprise! I don't know what I should have done for stimulant if I had not married an American. However, I will ask Mateo." Alessandro put his tray on the floor and took the morning paper and a cigarette from the table beside him. Lucy pressed a button that was fixed in the side of the bed. In a moment, there was a knock on the door. She called, "Avanti," and when Fortunata came in, she said:

"We're through with the trays, Fortunata. And I am ready for my bath."

"Si, Signora. Immediately, Signora." Fortunata took one tray to the door and handed it to someone outside. Then she came back for the other. Lucy watched her curiously.

"Who've you got there?" she asked.

"It is my cousin's brother-in-law's daughter, Signora."

"Oh! And how did she get here?"

"She walked, Signora. Her mother brought her."

"Her mother! How old is she?"

"She is ten. With the Signora's permission I will teach her the service."

"Well! We shall see. Now, about my bath."

Fortunata went out quickly and Lucy threw back the covers. "It would seem," she said, "that we're about to have a slavey. And I should not be at all surprised if Fortunata worked her to the bone and received a fee for training her, as well. Fortunata was well named."

Alessandro grinned. "It is done." He looked up, and now his expression clouded and he looked back at his paper and didn't speak again.

Lucy, unconscious of any change, stood pinning her hair up. She had slipped into a robe of Chinese brocaded silk. It was red, patterned with the sign of good luck, and it became her tall and well-proportioned figure. It seemed at once to lend lights to her melon-brown hair and even greater darkness to her eyes.

Though it served well to set off his wife's extraordinary beauty, it was a robe for which Alessandro had little love. For it reminded him of an old jealousy, and it was a source of humiliation to him that his emotion had meant so little to Lucy that she could still treasure its symbol. Lucy had had the robe almost eight years and she still wore it in preference to any other. Alessandro had once said, half-angry and half-sullen:

"The Chinese are great craftsmen and I haven't a doubt that that garment was made to outlive us both."

Lucy had only laughed at him and he had never spoken of the matter again.

The Chinese robe had been given to Lucy by an American friend, in the first year of their marriage. Alessandro had at first been cool enough, and yet disturbed that any explanation of his feelings was necessary. He did not like to see her possessing, let alone wearing, anything that had been given her by any man other than himself. Lucy had laughed, pointing her slim Anglo-Saxon finger at his Latin ways: jealousy had no place beside love! And as long as she loved her husband, so long would she dare to wear another man's present. With an Italian wife, Alessandro would have acted simply; destroyed the robe—or given it to the cook. Instead, he had taken his anger and his hurt away on a business trip which was not at that moment strictly necessary.

To have his emotion dismissed as Latin was not to cure it. He closed himself in a hotel room and smoked innumerable cigarettes and drank innumerable bottles of wine. Alessandro was twenty-five and Lucy eighteen. She had been a secretary at the American Consulate for five months when they met and three months later they had married. Alessandro's family had not approved. The girl was a foreigner, she was young, it was too hasty an affair altogether. In his hotel room, Alessandro remembered their warning and pulled himself up short. Lucy was apparently not going to lend herself to understanding him. She was his, just the same, and no one lived to whom he'd give the right to say, "I told you so," or even to shake their heads. He remembered how they had said that Americans were different and that marriage could only be successfully built on sameness. Dozens of unsuccessful international marriages had been quoted, and he had said proudly:

"You ask me to class myself with gigolos and fools? With men who seek money, and Lucy with women who seek titles? So! 'Go to bed with dogs and get up with fleas.' It is another thing, I promse you. Lucia has no dot and I have no title. We have what these others omitted to consider, love and intelligence. You'll find quite a few international marriages successfully rooted in the same soil. But you'll have to look; they aren't the marriages you hear about."

He'd give them no chance to remember his words. He would go home and see if the thing could not be mended. America, with all of its ill ways, had only had Lucy for eighteen years. He would have her for the rest of her life. The work of so few years should not be hard to undo. With this thought, he commenced to forgive her. It was no fault of hers that she had been brought up badly. As an American, she knew nothing of the passions that can ravage the human heart. She was not naturally cold, and Alessandro thought that he could find ways to teach her. He threw the most recent bottle of wine out of the window and went home.

Lucy had received him with a certain un-Anglo-Saxon display of warmth. He thought that the business trip had worried her, and he was pleased. But she only asked him primly if the trip had been successful. He said, Yes, that it had, and thanked her for her interest. They understood each other well, though they made no sign. The next morning, Lucy put on the robe.

The following year, the summer of 1926, Gian Franco was born. And still there was the robe. And still, now, in the year 1933, it was there. The giver had been forgotten; Alessandro

could scarcely have named him; it was the robe itself that
Alessandro hated now, thinking of it as a symbol of Lucy's
independence of him, her untouched Anglo-Saxonism.

For Lucy, the old story was done with. She had forgotten.
If Alessandro was moody upon occasions she did not link this
with the days she put on this particular robe—he was a man
of moods. Lucy loved her husband and she was a woman of
deep sympathies; she could have given a great deal if he had
asked for it, but she was not one to trespass. The integrity of
another human being was to her a sacred thing.

She pinned her hair up and went into her bath and, in a
short time, she heard Alessandro leave, taking Gian Franco
with him. She called out that she would meet them for an
apéritif on the Corso. When they had gone, she allowed the
soap to slip to the bottom of the tub and lay back in the hot
water to think. There were so many things to think about; she
closed her eyes and tried to sort them out.

Zia Margherita would be down in two days, and she could
be counted on to make them all miserable. She stood in the
place of a mother to Alessandro, who was an orphan, and
Lucy thought that she was not greatly pleased with Alessandro's wife. Lucy didn't mind particularly. She respected Zia
Margherita for an efficient, well-ordered tyrant, but she had no
love for her.

Lucy sighed a little. Before the old Borgia came, there
would have to be some scurrying—if only Sandi weren't so
thin! There were going to be some acid comments on that
score. Well, one couldn't put fat on a man in two days and
there were plenty of other things to worry about—the new
linen for the servants, the lock on the wine closet to be repaired, the oil to be removed from the new wine and a talk
with Franco's governess. Miss Tooley was not going to like

the idea of teaching Franco some new piece of recitation. She did not believe in teaching for an occasion. Well, then the silver had to be cleaned too. It was outrageous to be made to feel this way, like a child before examination day! But the Zia could be counted on to get into everything. Let's see. She ticked the day's work off on her fingers: get fresh lavender—the Zia liked it for her bed-linen—also look up menus used before to see what she had liked. But what Lucy really worried about—and now her eyes were open and she rescued the soap and commenced to wash briskly—was that strange child!

Lucy stepped out of the tub and wrapped herself completely in a turkish-toweling sheet. It had been like seeing an American child out in that wilderness all alone. None of those black-minded people could possibly understand a child like that!

5: *W*HEN LUCY had finished dressing, she went back into the bedroom. The bedclothes were on a chair by the window airing, and Fortunata and her little slavey were already at work with dustcloth and mop. Fortunata asked quickly:

"Shall we come back later, Signora?"

"No." Lucy went over to the child. "What is your name?" she asked.

The girl was small for ten years, with a thin face and too shiny black hair. She stammered, her brown eyes dumb. 'Beautiful eyes,' Lucy thought. 'Be they never so homely, they always have beautiful eyes. If the eyes are truly the "windows of the soul," the Italian people have a corner on the market.'

Fortunata answered for her. "Her name is Louisa. She's going to be a good girl, eh!" Louisa nodded dumbly, and Fortunata grinned. Fortunata was an ugly woman, short, with thick shoulders and a squat face which gave the impression that too many features had been crowded into too little space. She had a sparsely toothed grin, which she was in the habit of stretching from one prominent cheekbone to the other.

"You must be happy here, Louisa," Lucy said kindly. To Fortunata she said, "We will talk about this later. In the meantime wash her hair, and don't keep her in the house all day long."

"Si, Signora." Fortunata grinned again and Lucy went to her desk. She took pad and pencil and a ring heavy with keys from a drawer and went out of the room.

Villa Falconierre was a two-story building covering perhaps half an acre of ground. The rooms were large, with high ceilings and marble floors. The family living quarters, the kitchen, and other service rooms were all on the first floor. The second floor, by virtue of several balustraded terraces, was smaller and given over entirely to the servants' rooms. Two hallways quartered the house: the one, a wide foyer, connected the entrance of the villa, on the land side, with the living room overlooking a terrace on the bay. The other hall was narrow. It cut across the foyer like a street, dividing the master rooms on the bay side from the kitchen, scullery, laundry and wardrobes on the street side of the house. It was down this hall that Lucy made her way to the wardrobe.

She found Maria, the cook, and Emma, the laundress, fighting over the ragged condition of the servants' linen.

"Madonna!" Maria shrieked. "How can you expect to preserve the linen if you will use so much acqua raggio? If you would do a little work instead——"

"Are you telling me how to wash, you dirty, badly educated cook!" screamed Emma.

"Dirty, badly educated! Cook! Accidenti!" the incensed cook hurled back, and as Lucy came into the room she turned supplicating hands to her. "Donna Lucia, did you hear? Dirty! Badly educated! Cook! It is not to be borne, no, no, to be defiled by pigs and drunkards and slaves of lazy washwomen. I go! From such a house I assuredly go. On the instant, precipitously!" and she paused to hear some word of supplication, or apology. But Emma screamed, "Go, go, go!" and Lucy said, sternly:

"Go to the kitchen, Maria. I will be there in a little while," and when she showed a disposition to remain, Lucy turned her back and commenced to talk to Emma.

"Dirty, mal-educato, cook!" Maria mumbled in great distress, and slammed the door after her.

Lucy frowned: "Emma, you and your sister will have to make up your minds to get along better or you will both have to leave. I won't have this screaming in the house any longer."

"But, my lady—" Emma started excitedly.

"I don't want to hear any more about it—you work it out with Maria. But I warn you, if you can't work it out peacefully out you get. Now the laundry."

Lucy selected a key from her ring and opened three cupboards which lined one wall of the room, revealing as she did so household linens of every description, neatly tied and stacked. At her back, Emma was removing fresh piles from hampers on the floor and laying them on the padded ironing tables. As she worked she mumbled to herself, "Too much acqua raggio! Telling me how to wash!" Lucy turned back to the table and together they counted the laundry, separating it. The masters' linen, the servants' linen, the children's linen, each tied with its own color in stacks of one dozen pieces. The servants' linen had to be gone over carefully to see how many replacements would have to be made. Those articles which could be repaired were put aside for the seamstress, while others were folded away for cleaning cloths. While they worked, the child Louisa came asking for the day's linen. Lucy counted it out to her: sheets and pillowcases, bath towels, face towels and wash-cloths. When it was done, she closed the cupboards and locked them. Instructing Emma to take Don Alessandro's personal linen to his dressing room, she went in search of Maria.

In the kitchen, Maria sulked. Emma was her sister, and younger than she. It was quite wrong of her to speak as she did. The fact that Emma was married, while Maria was not, that Emma was the mother of fourteen children and still bearing, while in Maria life had stopped with herself, did not in any way excuse Emma from the necessity of some respect in her manner towards her elder. In fact, though she scarcely realized it, these were points which goaded Maria's distemper, making her even more conscious of the disrespect. Emma was married and she, the elder, was not. Emma was anything but good-looking, and by no means so good a wage-earner as herself. Common sense told Maria that her state was no fault of her own. Emma had married poorly, while Maria had saved her dot with a view to augmenting it and doing better by herself. She might even marry a shopkeeper some day. Also, Emma had married young, which is the only time for homely women to marry. Be the face never so square, with broad nose and small pinched eyes—features which the two sisters, in varying degrees, shared—when the peasant body is young, it does exude a certain desirability. Emma had married at sixteen, when the curves of her short body were round and rosy. Childbearing had alternately puffed her up and deflated her. But childbearing has not the way of disfiguring that sterility has. Emma was still a buxom woman, while Maria, at the age of forty-five, was as flat as though she had been run over by a herd of mules. Waiting for her shopkeeper, Maria's distemper grew on her and she became more quarrelsome all the time. Now she recalled that Emma, who always used to ask her when she would make up her mind and marry, had for some time ceased to do this. And Maria suspected angrily that Emma hoped she would never marry but would leave her fortune to Luigi, Emma's eldest. In Crotone, he was talked of by many as an heir. Maria grew harder to keep peace with every day.

When Lucy came upon her she was sighing gustily.

"Ah, Signora," she said, "the time you give to that ill-mannered slut. I have been waiting here on your orders to find out what the Signore is to have for his dinner, but of course that is not so important as that—" She veered suddenly. "You are not ill advised to watch her like a hawk, for she would steal the thread out of the seams if you did not. Yes, yes, I understand now how it is."

Lucy found the key to the storeroom and opened the door. "Come, Maria," she said, "I know you are fond of your sister. Why must you always make so much trouble? Would you really like to have me send you both away?"

Maria cried, "Send us away?" as though she had entirely forgotten her own threat. "Holy Mother of God, Signora, Donna Lucia, you would not do such a cruel thing! Would you turn the poor master's shirts and his unhappy stomach over to some wretched Calabrian bandit who will in no way know how to iron round the buttons without breaking them off, as Emma knows, or how to make the soufflé as fine and light as the clouds around the blessed Virgin's own halo, as Maria knows! Oh—ooh! ah—aah!" and Maria lifted her voice until Lucy thought that the jars on the shelves nearest the ceiling must presently shatter, spilling jams and jellies and preserves about their heads.

"Shut up, Maria," she said hastily. "Whether you go or stay is up to you. I want no more of this screaming in the house. If you and Emma can get along, that will be fine."

Maria ceased abruptly. "What does my pretty lady want for dinner?" she asked in a matter-of-fact voice. Lucy smiled, but managed to swallow the laughter that was in her throat.

For eight years she had been managing an Italian household and for eight years she had been struggling to discipline the laughter in her. She had no very sanguine feeling that the fights in kitchen and linen room would now be abolished. But things would be quieter, for a few days. At the next sign of outburst, she would turn Alessandro loose on them. Alessandro understood them and, though they adored him, they lived in terror of him. Certainly he was harsher with them than she, and yet he gave them something which Lucy knew that she could not. To Lucy, her servants were people with certain rights and certain dignities. They earned their living in the manner in which they were best able. To Alessandro, they were children. They served because this was what they were born to do. By serving, they earned in return no little devotion, the right to be disciplined and the shelter of his protection.

Together Lucy and Maria planned the day's meals. Then Lucy gave out what measure of sugar, flour, oil and vinegar was needed for the day, as well as the allotment of wine for the servants. The family wine had not yet been decanted, a task for Gerolamo before lunch. Maria carried her stores into the kitchen and Lucy locked the storeroom and went in search of Gerolamo.

Gerolamo was a small man who had not been graced by many hairs either on his head or face. He had the disposition of a rabbit in the parlor and of a wild buck hare in the kitchen. Maria and Emma and Fortunata would have walked quietly in his presence, had they known how to walk quietly. As it was, they hastened to be a step ahead of him, waited on him hand and foot, and were just as noisy about pleasing him as they were about fighting among themselves. Lucy found him cleaning the silver. She told him to finish his work and then come to her for the keys to the wine room. The wine had to be decanted. Gerolamo bowed and Lucy returned to her own room to see to the mail and to go over Maria's marketing accounts. Accounts first, because Maria would be wanting her money in a little while and Lucy liked to know what had been spent the previous day before giving her more. It never varied much, but you had to keep in touch just the same or it would begin to vary. Not in dishonesty; Lucy had come to realize that the Italian cook who took more than the usual amount of squeeze from the market money took it out of contempt and disrespect for a housewife who was slovenly and who cared so little for her husband's money as to disregard accounts. And Lucy sometimes felt that she worked harder for her servants than they did for her.

6:

$\mathcal{I}$T WAS noon before Lucy was free to read her mail. After the accounts there were the keys to be given and taken from Gerolamo, who had to be looked in on at least once while he was at work; Emma had to be lectured on a pair of ruined gloves and instructed in how to clean them; the seamstress arrived and had to be settled and given her work and instructions; Fortunata had to be told to prepare the guest room for Zia Margherita; the gardener had to be advised about keeping his goats away from the flowers and, finally, Miss Tooley had wanted to argue about teaching Franco another multiplication table in two days. At last it was all over and Lucy saw that there was a letter from her mother under a stack of inconsequential mail.

She took the square blue envelope in her hand and held it for a moment, enjoying it. Her mother didn't write frequently, and to Lucy everything about her letter was to be savored. The envelopes were always blue and square and she loved them to be so and felt that this blueness and squareness was important to her. She looked at the stamp, which was blue too and had become strange to her. She looked at the black waves that cancelled it and tried to make out the postmark, which was blurred. She read her name in dark-blue ink: "Mrs."— Mother never could be persuaded to write "Signora." Well, what did it matter? "Mrs. Alessandro Cavalierre." That always made Lucy smile, thinking how puzzled the postal authorities would be at the "Mrs. Alessandro," for in

Italy the wife did not take the husband's Christian name, another custom to which Mrs. Storey would not bend. "Via delle Tre Madonna 3, Rome," in the same round, carefully formed hand, had been crossed out when the letter was forwarded and the Crotone address had been supplied in purple ink, in a fine spidery hand. But the most important thing about the envelope was the back. Lucy turned it over slowly, holding her breath. Then she sighed, unconscious of doing so. The same address, "Cherry Hill Road, Genesee, Pa." She took up a paper cutter and slit the end of the envelope carefully. Everything was all right.

When Lucy had finished reading her mother's letter, she sat back and looked at the strange room about her. The little things her mother said always did this to her. Strawberries had not been good that year, so they had not put any up; it didn't seem as though any of the berries were going to be good. She had made new curtains for the kitchen out of a heavy net that was being put out, red—they were very pretty. Her rheumatism had been troublesome, but she was trying a soda-and-lemon cure and it seemed very good; there were new people next door—you couldn't tell yet but they seemed nice. Roosevelt had been in office only five months but he certainly had things hopping; you'd scarcely believe the changes. She didn't say what the changes were. Her mother never had a great deal to say or anything of much importance, but Lucy always finished reading her letters feeling strange and as though she didn't quite know where she was or how she had got there.

At home she'd had a white bedroom, dotted swiss ruffles and flounces with pink bows at the windows, and pink-and-blue shaggy rugs that her mother had made, on the floor —a warm, safe little room. Lucy let her glance travel slowly about her: the great 'matrimonial bed' almost as big as two double beds. It was covered with gold damask and, while is was innocent of a foot or head board, it was surmounted by a half canopy of damask, giving it the look of a baldachino and lending, Lucy decided, an air of benediction to their married life. There were two bedside tables, inlaid and with marble tops; there were two bureaus, not matching but beautiful pieces of honey-colored marquetry. The desk was cinque cento—a fine one, big and square, but a lady's desk, and with green morocco leather inlaid on the top. It was a family piece that Alessandro had had done over for her. The smell of jasmine drifted in through the window beside her, while from the other side of the room, through a wall of French windows, the sun glittered over the aquamarine bay to dance on her marble floor. There were no rugs on the floor, and the only other furnishings in the room were a heavy gilt-framed mirror which hung over one of the bureaus, and a small portrait of Madonna and child by Mattia Preti which hung over the other. A chaise-longue, well supplied with small cushions, was drawn close to the doors, where it commanded a fine view of the terrace, the umbrella pines and the bay. The chaise-longue was Lucy's most treasured possession. The chaise-longue meant a siesta.

Lucy put her letter in the pocket of her dress and got up. There were so many things to be done before the afternoon: get the car out and go downtown to see about the servants' linen; take Alessandro's new shirts and the handkerchiefs which she had bought for her mother to the convent to have the initials embroidered on them—a small, neat initial on the pocket of the shirt, a fine, flowery initial for her mother; meet Alessandro and Franco at Bolatti's, where they would have apéritifs, and then home for lunch at two o'clock. Lucy put on a large straw hat before the mirror. After lunch, everyone in the house would take a siesta, a custom in which Lucy took great delight. Now she picked up her purse from the desk and went out of the room.

Alessandro and Franco were at a table with Lawyer Tocci. Lucy passed them in her Ballila, and waved. There were two other cafés before the street widened into a piazza, and she nodded to several friends and acquaintances sitting at the sidewalk tables. Lucy knew herself to be the center of not a few fabulous tales in Crotone, due partly, Alessandro and the Toccis had told her, to the fact that she drove a car. It was six years since she had been coming to Crotone and they were still not used to seeing a woman at the wheel. This sensation of being a creature from Mars was not entirely displeasing to Lucy, who liked to be sharply distinguished from Italian women. While she respected and admired not a few of them, she found them on the whole inferior to their men. She knew that it was a conscious part of their education that they should be so. She parked the car and walked back along the paved Corso to Bolatti's. Francesca Tocci had joined the party since she passed them, and they were all having vermouth. Franco had a small lemonade. The men stood up and drew up a chair for her and Franco pushed it in. Lucy ordered vermouth and smiled admiringly at Signora Tocci.

"Francesca, your hat is—but so chic! Straight from Paris."

"Do you like it, Lucia! Ah, it goes then."

Lucy said, smiling at her friend's round pretty face, "You are being silly. It goes if Signora Avvocato Tocci wears it, to begin with!"

The avvocato said: "Donna Lucia, you were born with the Italian tongue. . . ."

Lucy wanted to say, "We call it Irish," but she did not, for she saw that she was complimented. Instead she murmured, "Thank you." And, remembering again what she had had on her mind all day, she turned to Alessandro:

"Did you remember to ask Mateo about that child at Nimpha?"

Alessandro frowned. "Yes," he said, "I'm glad you brought it to my attention. There is something wrong there, undoubtedly." He explained to the Toccis, and went on, "Mateo says that the girl is a foundling. Ordinarily, in these cases, the village takes care of them and there is no trouble. In this instance, it seems that the superstitions in the people have been stirred"—he shrugged—"because she is blonde and different? I don't know why, it doesn't altogether make sense—perhaps she is strong-willed and they are incensed because they cannot manage her. In any case, Mateo, while he insists on the one hand that she is no good, is not at all sure that she is well treated. He tells me that they have dragged her to the stregona to be exorcised, at least once, to his knowledge, perhaps more often!"

"Alessandro! But it's not possible!"

"Quite possible, my dear," his voice was grim, "but we will do something about it."

"Ah, the poor little thing." Francesca Tocci looked as though she were about to cry; her face puckered, the rosebud mouth drew together and her brown eyes were soft and warm. Lucy thought, involuntarily, that she would like to see her cry some day, perhaps to find out if she could, for this verge-of-weeping was as far as anyone whom Lucy knew had ever seen her go. Alessandro was asking the lawyer what the legal situation was, who was responsible for the child, and whether he could do anything about it.

"Do you mean, remove the child from the village of Nimpha?" Lucy watched Lawyer Tocci's face for some sign of his thoughts or feelings, but the little man was perfectly fended and hedged from such surprise. He had round eyes with more white than seemed a correct proportion, and small, piercing, pale-brown irises. Beneath them, the dry, yellow skin hung like empty bags.

Alessandro said, "I don't know. I'm asking your advice."

"Well, of course, if you want to help her she would have to be removed. But it is a grave responsibility. She is, by natural law, a ward of the state." He explained the technical details involved but Lucy was not listening to him. Her eyes were suddenly on her husband and she was thinking of the gold-bright hair and the wide-apart green eyes. The hair would have to be cut a little bit, it was too long; beautiful, of course, but ungroomed; it wouldn't do, not around the house. She said, almost dreamily:

"We are going to be late for lunch, my dear."

Alessandro nodded and signaled the waiter. Lucy said to the Toccis, "You will come Thursday night? We'll have some bridge."

"Is it true that the Pontella really prefers poker?" Francesca asked.

Lucy nodded. "Our new first lady is all new! It is a change. We will play poker, perhaps, and let the men play bridge."

They all laughed and, after a few more exchanges, they parted, the Toccis going north on the Corso and the Cavalierres going to the Piazza where they had left their cars.

Through the remainder of the day, Lucy carried her secret thoughts with her, wondering a little at herself for keeping them secret. She planned what she would tell Alessandro, and how. It was so simple, and yet—! While he slept after lunch, she lay on her chaise-longue and alternately looked out across the bay and back again at the sleeper. He was strong and he was tender, the tenderness growing out of his strength so that it had a firm quality, and Lucy felt that his strength was the greater for this. He was good to her. Lucy remembered having written her mother this once and the outraged answer she had received: "Indeed, and how would he not be!" But he could very well *not* be. That was something Mrs. Storey could not grasp, even as she could not accept "Signora," or that Lucy was "Mrs. Lucy," not "Mrs. Alessandro Cavalierre." Lucy knew; she knew so much. Sometimes she felt like a person who stood on a high place and could see both sides of the mountain. Something of her still belonged to the house of the hand-made shaggy rugs and the dotted swiss flounces, and that something wanted to take a homeless little wild child into her home and make her her own. But, like Persephone, she had eaten the pomegranate and something of her belonged just as deeply to the baldacchino and the bay and the glistening marble floor, and that something kept its secret. Alessandro had never refused her anything, he had never objected to anything she had chosen to do.

Lucy's eyes rested for a moment on her husband's dark head; in sleep the look of austerity was always enhanced. Suddenly she remembered the robe. She turned again to the bay. He had forgotten that, soon enough. When he awakened, she would speak. But she did not. At four, Alessandro went to his office. Nor did she speak at dinner or after, though the thought was ever uppermost in her mind and the words forever near her lips. She heard Gian Franco's prayers, she kissed him good night, she sat through dinner absently, chattering but not giving great thought to her words. For the picture had grown in her mind. She would have a daughter, a lovely blonde daughter. They would make the second guarda-roba into a bedroom for her. They'd have to take out all those great cupboards; they could go—oh, up in the servants' quarters. Lucy wondered if the child would like dotted swiss. Tonight, they would talk.

Once in bed, Lucy was no stronger than she had been on her feet. Some secret fear had grown up to protect her dream. Well then, tomorrow morning. In his black robe, with the soft, white silk of his pyjama collar making light shadows and giving the hollows of his throat a dark look by contrast, Alessandro was like a dry-point etching.

"You are every shade and nuance of black and white." Lucy smiled at him, a broad, big smile, as though to hide her sense of guilt at having a secret from him. However broad her smile, Lucy was one of the rare people of the world who never grinned. Everything that a grin is, lovable and warm, coming as it does from the deepest places in the human heart, Lucy's smile was; and more, for it was beautiful as well. When she smiled, her small brown eyes, which were at all times alight, commenced to sparkle and dance and became, for the onlooker, as personal and dear as an old and well-loved song. Then from somewhere a light came, settling on her face, so that the fair, brown hair that framed it seemed of a sudden possessed of fires that had not been there before, and the pale, olive skin grew rich and golden. Though they had been married eight years, Lucy had only to smile to make Alessandro forget other things and give her his full attention. He stood looking down at her where she lay in bed and his thoughts were so transparent in his dark eyes that Lucy's lips quivered a little. She said softly:

"You look like a Medici about to run a dagger through his lady's heart."

Alessandro mocked her. "Is that what you think of the Medici, then?"

"Weren't they like that? I'm sure I couldn't quote you cases—it's an impression, though."

"Perhaps, and why not? Yes, I think that I could run a dagger through your heart, my dear. Sometimes you are too beautiful, and then I must have the soul out of you. Lucia, mia bella, it is great danger you are in. If some day you should deny me your soul, there would be nothing left for me to do but send it back to its Maker."

"But it's sin, to possess another person's soul; besides, I don't think one ever can—" Lucy's eyes had widened.

"No?" Alessandro smiled inscrutably. "But then, you cannot understand. How could you?"

"Oh, Sandi," Lucy smiled quickly, "I do. Why else should I have let myself be born all over again in a place like this where there is nothing and no one whom I understand? It is just that the idea of the soul is somehow inviolate. And yet I don't want to be free of you in any sense. I would hate it, darling. So, go ahead and 'paint the lily.'"

"Paint the lily?"

Now it was Lucy's smile that mocked him, but gently, as though she were pleased with him too. She quoted softly:

> " 'To gild refinèd gold, to paint the lily,
>   To throw a perfume on the violet,
>   To smooth the ice, or add another hue
>   Unto the rainbow, or with taper-light
>   To seek the beauteous eye of heaven to garnish,
>   Is wasteful and ridiculous excess.' "

"Ah, then," Alessandro took her hand from the cover where it lay and kissed the finger tips, "let us by all means be ridiculous."

7:

$\mathcal{I}$N THE morning, Lucy told him, letting her arguments race one against the other and, by some instinct, afraid to pause in her speech:

"The child needs love and protection," she said. "She would be a playmate for Franco, and—I had never thought it before—but I should like a daughter—" Oh, there were any number of good arguments.

At first, Alessandro did not seem to understand what she was asking. But when she used the word "adopt" he stared at her, aghast.

"Lucia mia, you are entirely mad! But you don't know what you're talking about."

"Indeed, I do. Oh, Sandi, I've thought it all out."

"If you want a daughter," he said, "you can have all the daughters you want, that come to you naturally."

Lucy said desperately, "But this child is in need. We have so much; there is no sacrifice called for—I don't see how you can hesitate."

Alessandro flicked his cigarette over an ash tray, and blew out a screen of smoke. When it had thinned and almost disappeared, he said:

"The sacrifice that we would make would be nothing, if it were a sacrifice. The child is the only one who would suffer. Think, Lucy! You must know us well enough by now. As a child she would be loved, Gian Franco would play with her, even as he will play with the girl Louisa or with any servant's or villager's child. His friends and, in general, the children into whose class you would force her, would do the same. Then she will grow up." He paused to take another breath of smoke. "Perhaps she will remain beautiful—perhaps not. The odds are that she will develop ugly, square lines."

Lucy exclaimed, but he raised his hand impatiently. "We will examine this thing logically, since you have no instinct for it," he said. "Look at the peasant women! You've seen too many of them to be fooled. Fair hair will not help her when her body thickens and her skin coarsens. Pia is a peasant's child, the devil notwithstanding! But, Lucy, if she were to remain as beautiful as a dream, she cannot have any friends or any place among people of our kind. They will know that she is a peasant and look down on her. And no matter how large a dot I gave her, nobody but some money-loving gigolo would marry her. Do you think that Pia would thank you then?"

"But, Alessandro, it is awful to have to admit that the society we live in is so superficial."

"Perhaps; yet it is so—and there is good reason for it."

"No—it is, rather, entirely unreasonable."

"No man who is proud of his line wants his sons to have any cause to be less proud. The peasants can offer great physical vigor, and some of them are astute enough. But intellectually they are more apt to be lacking than otherwise. Apart from the social stigma, no man wants to risk half-witted children."

Lucy said: "I don't believe that they are any duller than half the people you meet in the salons in Rome. Besides, they have not much opportunity to polish their wits."

"Lucy, that has nothing to do with it. I am not propounding a general social question. Most peasants may only be dull because they have led a hard life or had no education. But no young man of Pia's choice is going to think that way. He is not going to consider the question of the hardships or rights of the peasant. He is going to think, Shall I bring peasant blood into my family? He would father sons by her quickly enough, but not sons of his name. And there is another thing. With her peasant instincts, you could never give her sufficient inhibitions to protect her."

"Well"—Lucy put away the tray that was on her knees and rang the bell—"I suppose you're right. But it seems so wrong."

"Would you like to have her here, like the girl Louisa?"

Lucy looked at him quickly, but she could say nothing, for the disappointment was too bitter in her.

Fortunata knocked at the door, and when she and Louisa had taken the trays, Alessandro got out of bed and went towards the dressing room.

"I'll see Tocci today and find out what can be done," he promised.

While he dressed, Lucy had her bath and then the day commenced. Outside, the sun was bright, making everything seem white except the sky and the bay, which were as blue as poster paint. Sunlight streamed through open windows and doors, giving to all the rooms a look of gold aliveness. Lucy moved through the day feeling gray and heavy and constantly aware of her disappointment. There was nothing that she could do about it, and she did not doubt that Alessandro was right. But she had built up something in her mind that was so gay and friendly, and so desirable, that it was not easy to let it go. She thought of the child, Pia, and wondered where she was and what she was doing. And whether she would really have done her a harm.

8: *A* GROUP OF men and women were gathered in Odilia Tregatti's kitchen. In their midst stood Pia. Her bare feet were planted on the stone floor, with the toes spread wide as though to give herself a running purchase should she indeed have a chance to run. Her skirt was torn and soiled and she wore a blouse that was too big for her and kept falling off at the shoulders. They were all talking at once and, in turn, they told her that she was fortunate, that she did not deserve what was being done for her, and that she was also greatly to be pitied. Who could tell now where they would take her or what they would do with her? The Barone was, of course, just removing her from Nimpha because she brought bad luck to his land. There were those three men who had camped out in the orange groves. Who was it, if not Pia, who had sent the gray devils that moved by night, so that the men sickened and died? Pia could not know about malaria, and her white skin turned whiter and her eyes seemed a shade greener. Padre Pasquale came through the open door and strode across the floor angrily.

"Enough," he stormed at them, his voice as thin as ice. "I have told you a hundred times, these things have nothing to do with Pia. She is going to the Barone because he wishes to see her grow up with a trade. It is a fine thing, Pia." He laid his thin hand on her hair. "Go, my child, and forget your devils. God will help you, if you ask Him."

Pia looked at him distrustfully, but still she said nothing. In a moment the people about her moved. Through the gap they made, Pia saw the children crowded about the door, and she saw Leone, his throat and cheeks red with anger and distress. She said slowly, watching him, not the grown people who were near her:

"Well, I will not go. I will stay here."

There was a stunned silence and then the fat Odilia cuffed her ear suddenly and hard. "You will not go? The Barone has sent for you and you will not go?"

There were cries of outrage and astonishment, and another hand reached out to match one ear with the other. Padre Pasquale caught the woman's hand in his own surprisingly strong one.

"None of that," he said sternly. "Pia, you have no choice, my child. The lawyer Tocci, from Crotone, has come with papers from the state, and they have been signed and returned to the government. You are bonded to the Barone as a maid servant until you have reached eighteen years. You are a very fortunate girl. You will earn money that will be put in the bank for you every month, and you will learn service. So that when you are grown you will have a way to earn your living, and a dot to marry on. Here you will have nothing."

A dot! Pia did not speak, but again her eyes sought Leone and, as though a cloud had slipped across the sun, the angry, sparkling green of them faded away until they were the gray-green that field stones sometimes have, soft and mellow. Pia was only eight but she knew what it meant not to have a dot. Not many men had enough money when they were young to set up a home by themselves. Girls like Rosa, who had a little dot, enough to match the money of a goatherd, well, they married goatherds. While a girl like Giovanna, the daughter of Mateo, the agent—why, she would marry a shopkeeper, without a doubt. And Pia would marry no one—unless Leone came back, as Titto Scalpi, of San Giovanni Marino, had done. Slowly she turned her head from looking at Leone and looked up at the priest. She would go. In any case, Leone would be away in America for a long time, and she would not want to be here without him.

They all heard the car as soon as it entered the village, and Padre Pasquale said, "Come, then; Mateo is here." He took her hand and went with her, and all the village followed behind. As she passed Leone, Pia turned her head away. She could not look at him now. She thought that he spoke to her and then she did look, but Leone's eyes were on the ground and his head bent sullenly, so that she could tell nothing. Then it was too late. Mateo was lifting her, as though she were so much thistledown, into the car, and in a moment the motor was going. Pia was frightened. Although there was no noise, there was a feeling about her as though the car had come to life. She crossed herself quickly and commenced to pray. She didn't hear the shouts or see Mateo's wizened face break into a reassuring grin, and she didn't feel the car move until it commenced to bump across the cobbles of the piazza. At once, Pia ceased praying and revolt took the place of fear. She would jump out of this maledetta thing on wheels. She would run. Pia clutched the door of the car. In her mind's eye she could see herself running down the winding road, with her hair streaming out like a cloud behind her. Perhaps now, at last, her father, who had deserted her for so long, would come out of his fiery regions and save her, turning her hair into two golden wings so that she could go faster, much faster than the car. Down the road, off and away! Pia tensed, ready to leap, and her eyes moved wildly from the driver to the swiftly moving landscape. If she could just get out! There was a place where she could go. Across the rocky goat pastures to the falls at the head of the lake. There, on a wide shelf half way up the mountainside, was a small cave made by the roots of a giant oak tree. Leone could come and bring her food and she would live in the cave and drink the water that gushed from the mountain to fill a deep blue pool and then spill over into the lake below. The roots of the oak were big, and two of them clutched like talons over the edge of the shelf and grew down the cliff to disappear in the lake. And these were as good as a ladder for such as herself and Leone, who knew how to climb. Yes, it would be good, and when Leone went to America she would go with him.

As though he read her thoughts, Mateo put a hand on her, gently; so he would have touched a frightened mule.

"It is a good house, Donna Lucia's," he said simply, and even as a mule would have been calmed, Pia's fear died in her, for Mateo had a natural hand with wild things. She let go of the side of the car and the tears came like pain to her eyes, making them close. She wept quietly and like a blind man. She could not understand what had happened to her or where she was going.

9: *W*ELL ENOUGH! Well enough! A lady like the Donna Lucia could have a soft heart. What was another mouth in such a house! Maria thought that the girl would be of no use, eight years was too young. Emma said that Maria knew nothing about children and what they could do. They screamed at each other for half an hour while, on the flat roof above them, Fortunata and Louisa were busy killing the lice on Pia.

It took time. It took patience, and more than patience—fortitude.

When Pia arrived at Villa Falconierre, Donna Lucia met her at the door, smiled, took her hand and said in stilted Calabrian:

"You are very welcome, Pia. Come now and I will show you your room and you shall meet Fortunata, who will help you with your bath and your new clothes."

Pia went without a sound. This house was beautiful and this Donna Lucia was beautiful, but Mateo had gone and Pia was frightened again. She thought of Leone and the cave and she thought of fat Odilia, who had said:

"And who can tell now where they will take you or what they will do with you?"

Fortunata, with her wide grin, was reassuring. She looked a little like Margherita, the baker's wife, from whom Pia had stolen too many times to be afraid of her. Louisa was nothing. Pia barely gave her a glance. When Lucy had gone, Pia felt more comfortable. She understood now what was going to happen; she would be washed and her hair cut and she would have new clothes. That was all right. She stepped out of her old clothes happily and followed Fortunata to the bathroom. Inside the door, she let out a piercing scream, turned and bolted, knocking Louisa over in her flight. Fortunata screamed for her to stop and ran after her, treading on Louisa as she went. Louisa, who had been silent with surprise, now raised her voice in lusty protest, and from their various parts of the house Maria, Emma, and Gerolamo ran screaming, "What is the matter? What is the matter? What is the matter?" without pause or let-up.

Lucy, caught in the midst of a telephone conversation with the Signora Pontella, wife of the Governor, and a person who gave minute observance to the rules of etiquette, excused herself as soberly as she could, knowing that she would never be forgiven, and fled to the stairs.

In the upstairs hallway she found her entire staff, lacking only Cato, the gardener. Lucy hesitated a moment, trying to hear through the excitement what they were saying, but the only words she could discern were Maria's repeated "Jesu, protect us!" She pushed through them and saw that their fingers were pointed, and that they were crossing themselves. In the corner, backed as far away from them as she could go, her thin body white and her neck and face red, Pia spat words at them.

Lucy stamped her foot. "Enough," she shouted, and then blushed angrily for having had to shout. They quieted gradually, like a tide going out, the waves of sound going and coming. As they quieted, she could distinguish what they were saying. It was so incredible and outrageous that it was some time before she discovered that it was also funny. Pia, never having seen a tub before, had immediately jumped to the conclusion that Fortunata intended to cook her in a cauldron. She would probably have been satisfied with flight. Cornered, she had turned on the unfortunate Fortunata and the arriving household and horrified them with every manner of curse and bedevilment, ending with an unexpurgated rendition of her own genealogy and conception, which left them with little doubt as to who and what she was.

Lucy told them that they were fools, without in any way convincing them. She sent them about their business and then she ordered Fortunata to bring two chairs and place them in front of the bathroom door.

"Louisa," she said, "get your clothes off and go in there. Fortunata is going to give you a bath and we are going to watch. Be a good girl, now. We want Pia to see that it doesn't hurt."

Fortunata grabbed Louisa's hand and muttered angrily, "Louisa's all right, but don't ask me to touch that little hell cat. Send her away, Donna Lucia, she'll bring a curse on the house if you don't."

"Shut up, Fortunata, and get busy." Lucy squatted down beside Pia, who was stiff with trembling.

"There are no such things as witches and devils, Pia," she said, "and no one is going to hurt you. We are going to love you here. Now, look!" She took Pia's hand. Pia pulled back a little, and then let it be. While Lucy talked to her the red slowly left her face, but the trembling didn't stop and her green eyes never for an instant left Fortunata.

Lucy said, "I saw you bathing in the lake at Valombra. Did you go often?" Pia didn't answer.

Lucy tried again, "Here there is no lake and in the gulf the water is salty. You can't bathe there, because the soap won't lather. Here, we have to bathe in the house and so we have big tubs to bathe in. You watch Louisa get washed and you will see how it is."

Slowly Lucy drew Pia to the chairs before the bathroom door, and together they sat and watched Louisa having a bath. While they watched, Lucy talked, and she talked as much to Fortunata and Louisa as she did to Pia.

When it was over, Pia took her bath. She wasn't talking about the devil any more and Fortunata wasn't talking about witches. They were sullen, and Louisa was sullen, and Lucy was feeling tired, but triumphant too. She would love this child; there was so much to win. Suddenly the expression on Fortunata's face exploded into a grin and she sat back on her heels and cried with no little delight:

"Well now, witch maybe—who knows?—but you've got bugs just like anyone else!"

Louisa said, "Ha!" and ran downstairs to tell the kitchen. Pia surprisingly began to cry. Lucy wanted to take her in her arms, to lift her out of the tub and comfort her, but now Fortunata pulled the child's hair wide like a fan, and against the light Lucy could see the clusters of eggs. Her skin prickled and she turned away.

"Can you get rid of them?" she asked.

"But rest secure, Signora! Fortunata fix."

Pia continued to cry, the tears running down her face and sobs shaking her thin body. Louisa came back with a large bottle of larkspur and she too was smiling.

For the rest of the day, and most of the next day, Pia sat on the roof in the sun, her head done up in a towel and wet with the larkspur. Sometimes Louisa came and talked to her and sometimes Gian Franco. When they were not there she looked down at the terrace where flowers grew in marble pots, and across a narrow strip of beach to the gulf. The waters of the gulf were a transparent aquamarine and sparkled in the sun, and the sand on the beach was coarse and yellow and here and there it flashed with infinitesimal specks of gold. It was beautiful and quiet. Beneath her, the house was astir with the noises that go with the living of a house. A window was opened, a blind raised or lowered, there was the faint click of shutters being adjusted, there were footsteps and running water and now and again voices were shrill. When Louisa came to the roof, she came because she had been told to. She squatted on the ground beside Pia and stared at her and had nothing to say. Once or twice, she tried. She said, "I had lace on my communion dress. My mama made it." Pia didn't answer. At Nimpha the children wore fine, white dresses for their communion too, and some of them had lace. Pia had worn a good dress. It belonged to Odilia's Rosa, and Pia had it only for the day. Louisa said:

"On Sundays, my mama comes for me and I go home for dinner and I have ice cream and wine too. Here, Donna Lucia won't let me have wine."

But Pia had nothing to say to her. When Gian Franco came, it was different. She liked Gian Franco. He too squatted down beside her but his face wasn't dull and he was not stupid.

"Are you really a witch, Pia?" he asked, and his black-brown eyes were excited. Gian Franco looked like his father, with the same black hair, the slender, sensitive face, and proud, eagle look of the nose. Sometimes Gian Franco had this haughty look on his little-boy face, but now his expression was sweet and sensitive and ready to believe almost anything. It was as though he thought that Pia was the loveliest and the most exciting person he had ever known.

Pia thought of Leone, who fought the other children when they called her a witch, and she said "yes" very sadly.

Gian Franco said, "I'm glad," and he jumped up and hopped about the chair that Pia sat on. "I never met a witch before. I'm very, very glad." Then he squatted down again and stared up at her expectantly.

Slowly, something in Pia commenced to warm. Gian Franco wasn't at all like Leone; she didn't know what to say to him. But he was glad. No one, not even Leone, had ever been glad about her being a witch. Gian Franco was all right and it really didn't matter so much about the bugs, and Louisa, and Fortunata laughing, and Donna Lucia turning away so that she wouldn't have to look. It really didn't matter about anything, because she was a witch and somebody was glad. Pia wished that Leone were there. She wanted to tell him.

In the afternoon, Fortunata and Louisa came with cotton and more larkspur. They took the towel off, and first Fortunata cut the hair to shoulder-length and wrapped the fallen ends in paper to burn them. Then the two of them worked, wetting the cotton and pulling it through strand by strand of hair, until there was not an egg left, not a creature. Down in the kitchen, Maria and Emma argued.

At her desk, Lucy wrote in a letter to her mother:

"—they were ready to make life miserable for the child, and for the rest of us as well, because they thought that she was a witch, and now because she has bugs she has become quite human and acceptable."

Lucy picked the letter up and tore it across slowly and a little wistfully. Her mother would not think that funny. She wouldn't understand and she would be disturbed. It would be better to tell her something else: that Cato had planted the corn seed she had sent from America, and how they were looking forward to corn on the cob, and how Gian Franco went every day to see if it had grown. That was better; that would please her.

10:

$\mathcal{7}$HE CAVALIERRES went to Rome in the fall, and Pia went with them. She went to the public school, where Gian Franco was in the third class and she in the first. After school, they walked home together to the pink stucco house on the Street of the Three Madonnas. Sometimes they played in the garden and Pia would teach Franco games that he had never heard of before, and sometimes it would rain and they would play indoors. Then Pia would tell Franco stories of witches and warlocks and babies born with the evil eye until Franco would feel the skin on his scalp move with fear and delight. But a good many afternoons Franco was away, learning to ride or fence or play the piano. Then Pia was left alone and she would wander around the house dumbly, as though she were looking for something.

She would stay close to Fortunata or Maria, doing little things for them if they were nice to her, or casting spells at them under her breath if they were not. She was not afraid of the people in the kitchen, for she had seen at once that they were no different from the people of Nimpha. But she cast her spells quietly none the less, for there was Don Alessandro in the house. He was a great lord and never smiled, except when he was with the Donna Lucia. Pia would not willingly have displeased him. As to the Donna Lucia, she was a princess and a saint, sometimes a very militant saint with anger in her eyes and a flaming sword in her mouth. As passionately as a man full grown, and as blindly as an infant, Pia had fallen in love with Lucy. Her love, in the presence or within the hearing of its object, lent her a fear that was akin to terror. She dreamed haunted dreams, she yearned, she crouched outside of Lucy's door, and when the handle turned she fled. And whenever Lucy came upon her, or spoke to her, she looked down at her feet and was dumb.

Lucy had been kind to her, at first, watching the seamstress make her clothes and fitting them here and there herself, helping her to braid her hair and showing her how to fix it at the ends with small bits of ribbon. And always smiling at her with a special smile that made Pia feel, for the first time in her short life, that she belonged to somebody. But since they had come to Rome, it had been different. Lucy still smiled, but she was not at home often and when she was she had no time for Pia. In Crotone, Pia had been put to sleep in the nursery with Gian Franco; here, she had a room on the top floor where Maria and Fortunata and Gerolamo had theirs. Once, standing in the shadows of the front hall, waiting to watch Lucy pass, Pia heard Alessandro's voice and he was saying: "Leave Pia alone, and stop worrying about her; you will only harm her." And Pia had slipped away to her room to cry into her pillow, not quite sure why she cried, or what the words had meant, but feeling as though a blight had fallen upon her.

For a while, Pia clung close to the kitchen quarters. She couldn't fathom what 'harm' Don Alessandro had referred to, but she was too much a witch herself to like the word. In her fertile imagination, it could have meant anything. When two days had passed and nothing had happened, she crept back to the halls from whence she could watch, her love too great for her fear.

From her point of vantage, Pia watched also the people

who came to the house. When Franco came home, she would tell him what she had seen. They would crouch at the top of the back stairs, eating cake or a plate of cocktail appetizers which she had stolen from the pantry, and Pia would identify the visitors, sometimes by name and sometimes by a gesture, a flutter of the hand or the quick twist of fingers twirling an invisible moustache. There were two visitors whose names she knew but whom she never mentioned. One was Zia Margherita, who Pia was convinced had the evil eye.

The Zia came frequently. Sometimes she came with Don Graziano, who was Alessandro's brother, and sometimes she brought Aurelio, who was Alessandro's nephew. Pia hated two of them and disliked the third. The Zia because she looked down her aquiline nose at everything that Lucy was or did. A child could see the displeasure which the older woman took in her nephew's wife. She hated Don Graziano, for another reason. He was unlike Alessandro, as brothers sometimes are, being fat where Alessandro was lean, and gross where Alessandro was as fastidious as a monk. Don Graziano was a man who liked women, whatever their age. Once, he had come into the hall unexpectedly and discovered Pia peering through the crack of the door at the people in the living room. He'd run his fat hand over her body and then pinched her bottom, and laughed. Pia had spat at him quickly, jumping away. Then she had run to hide on the stairs and had spent the rest of the day thinking of curses and bedevilments and things that she would like to turn him into. After that, she began to notice that he looked at her mistress in a special way and she hated him even more.

Aurelio escaped Pia's hatred by a fine margin. He neither sneered at Lucy nor fawned on her, so that Pia was willing to accept him as merely unpleasant and nothing to her. Aurelio was a year older than Pia, being nine, and like Franco he was delighted to meet a witch. Unlike Franco he held her witch-craft as a weapon over her head and when he had the chance he would push her into dark corners and tell her tales of Hell, where witches went. Once, he brought her a print from a collection of his father's. It was the work of Dürer and it depicted Hell as even Pia's active imagination had not been able to depict it. Pia cried so loudly in her sleep that night that Maria went in to shake her up. Hearing of what manner of snakes and fiends and tortured souls she had dreamed, she lectured her on the spot and advised her to see the priest on the following day.

The Zia Margherita was one of those of whom Pia would not voluntarily speak and the other was Captain Nero. Captain Nero came to the house frequently and, when he was not beside Lucy, he was watching her. Whether he talked with the Zia or Alessandro or the other men and women who frequented the Cavalierre salon, his bold black eyes were always restively in search of one person. Pia, with the sensitiveness of a wild thing that loves for the first time, knew that he pursued the Donna Lucia, and was, without recognizing the emotion, passionately jealous.

Captain Nero was as broad as a bull, not quite tall enough, but otherwise compellingly built. His hair was black and his dark skin, where it did not shine over heavy muscles, lay close to his bones. He wore the black-shirted uniform of the Fascist and carried a white-handled dagger in his belt. Pia hated him whole-heartedly. Every time that her mistress smiled on him, or called some pleasantry across the room to him, her hatred grew a notch. And presently she saw something that she might otherwise have missed: Don Alessandro hated him too. Once, Franco said:

"I don't think Papa likes Captain Nero, but Mama says he's fun."

"He carries the devil in his pocket," Pia told him darkly. Franco had looked at her in some surprise.

"Papa said he didn't want him in the house, but Mama just laughed and, anyway, they didn't say anything about the devil."

Pia was glum. "Everybody doesn't know about the devil," she said; "you watch."

But watch how they would, the devil did not manifest himself. That summer, they went back to Crotone. Captain Nero came down, once for a week end at Villa Falconierre, and twice to visit Centurion Fornelli, who was the Federal Secretary of the Party at Catanzaro. In July, Aurelio came for a visit.

11:

*L*UCY BRUSHED the ends of her hair around her finger, where they clung like tendrils. Then she slipped her finger out and the hair lay, a soft roll of shining melon-brown, down the side of her face and low on her neck. She fixed a small comb to keep the wave from her forehead. She studied herself for a moment in the mirror; then, satisfied, turned and went out of the room. The Toccis were already in the living room. A moment after she had greeted them, Prefetto Pontella, the King's Magistrate, and his lady arrived. Despite the six years that she had known them, Lucy still found them exacting and stuffy. But she was fond of them too, and enjoyed the evenings which they spent playing bridge or poker. Alessandro came up as the Prefetto was saying:

"I hear that that rogue Nero is back; he must enjoy our climate."

With a sudden flash of insight, Lucy thought, 'Why, he thinks that the man's in love with me,' and she turned to Alessandro, smiling, as though she would have said: 'Thank heavens, you are not like that.' But Alessandro did not smile.

"Who is going to play poker," he asked them, "and who bridge?"

Captain Nero, who had just come in with Centurion Fornelli, said, "Poker, by all means," and then he greeted them, kissing Lucy's hand formally and looking into her eyes a little too informally, she thought. She turned to the Centurion, whom she had not yet welcomed. He was a tall man, with fine classical features but not, Lucy thought, as attractive as the more homely Captain.

The Pontellas and Fornelli chose poker, as did Lieutenant Russo, who had come bringing his small, rather ugly and entirely charming wife. Lucy and Emanuella Russo and the Baron and Baroness Corte played bridge.

Lucy liked the Cortes, whose estate was south of Valombra. The Baron was a small man who wore an old-fashioned goatee and an old-fashioned manner; he had married a young wife, to whom he was entirely devoted. The Baron had a passion for foreign cattle, which he had imported from Holstein in herds, only to watch them die off under the ignorant care of his peasants. Once, Lucy asked him why, when he spent a fortune on the cattle, he did not bring in a Swiss or German manager to look after them. The Baron had scowled, saying:

"And is a cow something mysterious which an Italian cannot keep alive?" And he continued importing his animals and letting them die of neglect.

In Calabria, an evening of cards can last until morning. The Cortes left close to midnight, for the Baroness was with child and easily fatigued. After that, Lucy and Emanuella Russo moved to the poker table. Emanuella sat beside her husband. The men had all risen to make place for them, and Alessandro and Captain Nero each found a chair for Lucy. She looked across at her husband and smiled, but she took the chair which the Captain held out for her.

When she chanced to look up from the hand that had been dealt to her, she saw that Alessandro's brows were drawn in a straight, black line and she wondered vaguely whether he had been losing a good deal.

When the night was over, she remembered to ask him. He said that he had not, but Lucy thought that his look had not changed.

She said, seeking to lighten his mood, "I met the Pontella on the Corso this afternoon. I was wearing slacks, and I wasn't sure for a moment that she was going to speak to me."

Lucy knew that she caused a great deal of talk by her habit of going in the sun without a hat, her legs bare, with painted toenails glistening through open-toed sandals. For, in the Italian provinces, women are careful in their dress, never allowing themselves to be seen on the street except in their best black silks, their most formal hats, veils and kid gloves.

Alessandro did smile now, but his eyes still held a look that searched her. "Did she?" he asked.

"Oh, yes, but she kept trying to find excuses for me—" Lucy shrugged. "Had I been to the beach? Was I going to the beach?—When it seemed that neither of these was so, I'm sure she wanted to add—'Ah, well, a crazy American. Poor Don Alessandro!'"

Alessandro ran his fingers through her hair and pulled her suddenly to him. "Poor Don Alessandro! I sometimes think so myself," he said gruffly, and when he let her go she saw that his mood had passed. So she did not ask him the question which was on the tip of her tongue to ask, fearing to bring the mood back.

Captain Nero and the Federal Secretary called, the following day. They drank vermouth and they talked of city life and provincial life. The Captain announced his intention of prolonging his visit to a fortnight. Alessandro, who had been friendly and casual, the black mood dissipated, said coldly:

"One would have thought that the Captain would find Calabria over-dull, after the season in Rome."

Lucy looked surprised but, before she could speak, the Captain had cried gallantly:

"Ah, much duller places than Calabria would be made brilliant by the company one finds here."

Lucy smiled, thinking that for a man so broad and virile he talked like a seventeenth-century French fop. She looked across at Alessandro, who frowned for a moment and then shrugged a little and accepted the compliment, laughing and addressing the Centurion:

"Donna Lucia and you and I, Federale, would choose Rome, I am sure, however brilliant the society elsewhere," and then, as though he did not wish to discuss the matter further, he said, "Have you heard anything more about the rubber experiment?"

"Nothing. They will keep trying, of course. But, at least, there are no negative reports."

Lucy said, "It's so hot here, I can't think of any good reason why they can't grow rubber—and think how rich we'll all be."

Captain Nero said, "If rubber can be grown here, il Duce will find a way to do it."

They talked of the possibilities for a while, and then the Centurion and the Captain took their leave. After that, Captain Nero called frequently and, more than once, he came alone and at time when he must have known that Alessandro would not be at home.

Upon one occasion, Lucy came onto the terrace to find him leaning across the balustrade, watching the children on the beach below.

"They look cool and happy, do they not?" Lucy asked.

The Captain kissed her hand and murmured a greeting. Then he said, "I was watching your little peasant."

"Isn't she lovely?" Lucy asked, leading him towards a group

of chairs under the marquee. They sat down and Lucy smoothed out the lines in her linen dress with her long thin fingers and thought that watermelon was a cool color and that she would like a dress of the same color for Pia. The Captain was saying:

"—But she will not always be so lovely; you can see that too."

"Men are impossible—how can you know what she will look like or—" she hesitated "—what she will be?"

"It is all there, written," he gestured eloquently, "in the breast that is beginning even in one so young, in the line of the hip, in the short legs and the big mouth. Perhaps she will even be ugly. But she will be voluptuous! This I can tell you from experience."

Lucy shrugged distastefully. "She is a strange child," she hastened to say. "I wanted to make friends with her, but it's been almost impossible to approach her. I don't believe that she likes me."

"Then you have not seen her watching you. The girl is in love with you, and of course she is afraid, even as I am," and he leaned towards her and reached for her hand. But Lucy suddenly found a wisp of hair to tuck away and she laughed, sitting farther back in her chair.

"Captain, you alarm me. I had not realized that I was so terrifying a person."

"Donna Lucia, do not jest with me," the Captain said, now in deep earnest. "I do not understand women of your race. I have declared myself to you. I love you. I am wild with the desire of you. An Italian woman would call the servants to put me out of her house, or she would invite me into her bedroom."

"In the middle of the afternoon?" Lucy asked innocently.

"Ah, no!" The Captain looked shocked, and then he jumped up from his chair angrily. "You are laughing!" he cried, clapping his hands to his hips and unconsciously fingering his dagger.

Lucy thought that he looked very dramatic and she would have liked to tease him a little to see what he would do, but she said with quiet dignity, "I am laughing, Captain, because I pay you the compliment of believing that you are flirting. If it were otherwise, you would deserve to have the servants throw you out. You must know that I love my husband."

"And now you talk to me of your husband!" Captain Nero was still angry, his dark face suffused with blood. "American women are heartless, then?"

"Undoubtedly!" Lucy said, and then as they heard the front door slam she added, "though I imagine it is all in the point of view. That is probably Alessandro arriving, why not ask him?"

The Captain looked at her, scandalized. "With your permission," he said coldly, "I shall not do so."

Lucy shrugged, still smiling. They waited, but Alessandro did not come. In a few moments, the Captain took his leave. Lucy gave him her hand and said softly:

"Come to see us again. Alessandro is generally in by six or seven and will be delighted to see you. And give my regards to the Federale."

Captain Nero gave her one half-angry, half-pleading look, bowed stiffly over her hand, and left.

She watched him go, not sorry that he should do so. When she heard the front door close a second time, she went into the house, through the open living-room door. As she passed the library, a small sound of paper rattling caught her attention.

She paused, surprised, and then turned and went in. The room was darker than the living room, shuttered against the heat of the day. As she stood in the doorway, Alessandro's voice called her name and she started slightly. She turned towards his desk, where he sat, and went to him.

"I didn't see you," she said. "You did come in, after all."

"Yes, about fifteen minutes ago."

"But why didn't you come out? Captain Nero was here." She saw that he was smoking and that his brief-case lay on the desk, unopened before him.

"I know. I had no desire to see the Captain."

"Oh, Sandi," Lucy cried impulsively, "didn't you want to see me? You're looking as black as thunder—and I love you!" and she slipped her slender arm about his neck and stooped to ruffle this hair with her lips.

He pulled her to his lap, almost roughly. "You don't say that often enough," he said and kissed her hand.

When he let her go, she said softly, "But I think it, Sandi. I think it all the time."

Shortly after that, Captain Nero went back to Rome and Lucy was glad that he was gone. Though, even from the distance, she was not rid of him. Twice, he wired her roses, two great boxes of unnumbered white roses. Once, he sent her a large bottle of Arpège, a perfume which he had once spoken of, saying that it was an especially exquisite perfume not for the jeune fille or the innocent burgeois matron. Lucy sent the perfume back without mentioning it to Alessandro. The flowers she put about the house, for they were beautiful. When Alessandro scowled, she scolded him gently, saying:

"We've entertained him; there's no reason why he shouldn't have sent flowers."

"Do you think that he sent any to the Federale?" Alessandro asked, caustically.

"But they are so beautiful."

"There are too many of them," he said angrily and went out of the room.

In July, the Zia came for a visit, bringing Aurelio with her. Lucy was concerned to see that Franco and Pia avoided Aurelio, running off to play by themselves. She spoke to Franco, but he only looked down at his feet and said:

"Aurelio likes to read better, anyway." And he would not say anything else. Nor was Alessandro of any help to her, saying only that children were best left to work out their personal friendships alone.

"It is not just a matter of friendship," Lucy protested. "I am afraid that Aurelio is up to some unpleasantness."

Alessandro shrugged. "I should not be surprised. Let the children avoid him, then. Aurelio has bad ways, but he will outgrow them."

Lucy wondered a little whether this was the way to handle the boy. She remembered an occasion when she had wanted to see an old-fashioned belting administered. Aurelio had found a large spider, which he kept in a box, feeding it flies. Because nobody watched him carefully, or knew what he was about, it was not discovered until too late that he had pulled the legs off the spider. He kept it for days this way, forcing food on it and watching its reactions through a magnifying glass. He said later that it made funny faces when he poked it. One day, on the terrace, he held the magnifying glass so that the sun struck it and in a moment the spider shriveled up and died. Lucy thought, 'He did outgrow that phase without a beating,' but she thought that a beating would have done him good just the same. She said:

"Do you know, I think that I understand how the servants felt about Pia, when they found that she had bugs. Aurelio is an unnatural child and I'd feel much better towards him if he had bugs too!"

Then, one day, the witch song was revived. The household was in an uproar, and Lucy was reminded that there was a stranger in her home.

Mateo came from Nimpha to see Don Alessandro, and Pia ran out to meet him.

"Ha, little one!" he cried, pulling her taffy-colored braids. "You're a different story now."

He put his arm about her and walked back to the kitchen, Pia skipping beside him, asking questions and not waiting for the answers. In the kitchen, Mateo put down several parcels. In one was a pink ribbon for Pia's hair. Fortunata arranged it in a bow on top of Pia's head, to the delight and admiration of the entire kitchen. When it was done, Mateo said:

"Now you should come to Nimpha and let the old fat Odilia have a look at you."

"Oh, and Leone!" Pia cried. "I do want Leone to see me."

Mateo shook his head. "Didn't you know?" he asked. "Leone has gone to America."

Pia's smile stayed for an instant on her face, while the life went out of it. Then she said quickly:

"But he couldn't—he is just a little boy. He wasn't going until he got big. You are fooling me!"

"He has an uncle in America who wanted him. His father was willing to have him go, so Don Alessandro sent him," Mateo said. "Don Alessandro is a fine man to his people."

"Ah, good as an angel," Fortunata and Maria cried together.

As they chattered about Don Alessandro's goodness Pia, who had at first turned quite white, commenced to regain her color and then, in turn, to grow red. Her green eyes were black with the size of the pupils and the tears that were ready to spill. Without another word, she turned to run from the room. As she slipped by, Maria put out her bony arm and caught her, and seeing the look in her eyes she cried out, coarsely but kindly too:

"Well now, and if the baby hasn't lost her lover!" She laughed, pulling the girl towards her. "Never you mind, witchling, you'll have ways of getting him back, though maybe the water between you is his good luck."

Pia, whom Lucy worried about because of her quiet and ghostlike ways, whirled on Maria with her claws and her tongue. Maria, in her anger at this unjust turn of affairs, let out a cry, but still held on tight to the little demon to whom she had tried to be kind.

"Unmarried stomach of a goat," Pia cried. "I'll witch you a man with a frog's belly to come and get all your money away, and then, don't think he'll marry you! I'll witch him to spend your money on Fortunata. I'll——"

What further damage she might have done they were all left to guess, for at this moment an adroit kick on the tender bone of Maria's leg so unnerved the cook with pain that she loosened her grip and in a flash Pia was out of the room. Through all of this, Fortunata and Mateo had maintained a shocked silence. Now their angry voices joined Maria's, and soon Emma, Gerolamo and Cato, the gardener, were in the kitchen, all angry, all declaring the girl must be got out of the house if they were any of them to survive.

"Being good for a year doesn't mean a thing," Maria declared between crossing herself with a rosary and pointing fingers after the departed Pia. "The witch never dies. Donna Lucia was a foolhardy woman to take her in."

"She'll be sorry, sure!" agreed Emma, all the time watching her sister. She added, with no little delight, "The girl certainly knew what to say to get you riled."

Mateo said, "Oh, be quiet—the girl was all worked up— she wasn't half as bad as she used to be, at that. But I'll speak to Don Alessandro if you like."

They accepted his offer gratefully. And they waited to see what would happen. Any day now, Pia would be sent away. Two days went by, and then three, and Pia was still there. Had Mateo not told Don Alessandro, or was it possible that Don Alessandro was not impressed with the dangers that confronted them all?

Around noon of the fourth day, it was discovered that a whole week's pasta had been ruined by hoof-prints pressed into the dough while the dew made it soft, and now baked hard in the sun. The pasta was always dried on the upper terrace and there no hoofs, except a very famous pair, could have climbed. Maria destroyed the pasta quickly to avoid bringing a curse on the house—a gesture well appreciated by the kitchen, who had no wish to see such unholy evidence.

With screams and angry eyes she returned to the kitchen where Gerolamo was having a plate of spaghetti and a glass of wine, and Pia and Louisa were preparing vegetables for the stove.

"Witch!" she screamed. "Witch! Cursed with the evil eye!"

Pia looked up, and old memories stirred. At Nimpha, she had learned how to defend herself. In an instant, the loves and the fears that had kept her in check so long were as though they had never been. Her eyes sparkled and a slow grin spread across her face.

"Ha, ugly one!" She slipped out of Maria's reach and tossed her head so that the two braids danced in the air. As she jumped to one side she crashed into the table, spilling the spaghetti and the wine into Gerolamo's lap. Now Gerolamo's own brand of curses joined Pia's on the noisy air, but still Pia's wild words could be heard above them.

Lucy came upon them to find Gerolamo, his white coat stained with red wine and tomato sauce, while the whole group cried in their various dialects, flailing their arms, their faces writhing with expressions of anger and of fear.

Gerolamo, in something that was enough akin to Italian for Lucy to understand, repeated over and over again:

"Be silent, women of Satan!" His chest was arched with anger and his face and ears were as purple as the wine on his coat. But, for once, his women forgot to go in awe of him. In a corner, Pia crouched and her mouth was made enormous by the grin that stretched across her face, while her eyes were deep with delighted lights. Lucy had never seen her so and she had a sudden moment of thinking, "She's not going to be beautiful at all. I believe she will be homely, just as Alessandro said she would."

When they saw Lucy in the doorway, they all turned upon her and broke into Italian without changing one beat of tempo or one shade of tone. Pia fixed her eyes on Lucy and the light went out of them and she looked frightened.

"All right now, one at a time. Gerolamo, please?" she turned to the butler, granting him the prestige which his position deserved. The two women ceased talking as suddenly as though a switch had been touched to turn them off.

Gerolamo clasped his hands in a gesture of despair.

"Signora, my lady," he cried, "just look at me—this girl—these women—it is not to be borne. Make them all go!—Out of this house!"

"But, Gerolamo, you must tell me! What is this, how did it start?"

"Ah, Signora," he lowered his voice, now that the women were silent, "it is these females, cursed creatures with the tongues of asps. They fight about this, about that—the sauce of the pasta is not hot enough; the table linen is not white enough." Maria and Emma mumbled angrily but Gerolamo glared at them and they subsided. "The girl," he pointed an unfriendly finger at Pia, "has the devil, her father, prancing around the roof at night, leaving his prints all over the new pasta. Ha! She'll bring trouble, that one. When Maria accused her, what did she do but upset this whole table and, furthermore, she made the woman mad by saying that she would have a better temper if she would get a man; that she knew from a woman called Signora Odilia of Nimpha that a woman's organs dried up from disuse when she did not have a man, and that her disposition soured."

Lucy stared at him in horror. Maria started to scream again.

"Madonna!" she cried. "This house! What I have to put up with! Everything! And now a witch to insult me! I tell you, Signora, my beauty, you get rid of that devil's child."

Lucy said, "This is ridiculous, Maria, and very stupid. Here, Pia, you come with me and we will talk. The rest of you get back to work and, if I hear any more of this, Don Alessandro can talk to you." And she took Pia by the hand and led her away.

In her bedroom, she sat back in the chaise-longue and made Pia sit down on the end. She looked at her for a long time, wondering how to begin, how to approach the girl. Finally she tried:

"You are a pretty girl, Pia."

Pia's eyes widened with pleasure but she said nothing.

Lucy said, "Wouldn't you like to grow up to be a lady?"

This was forbidden ground; Alessandro wouldn't like her talking to the child this way, but Alessandro's way hadn't worked. Pia only looked at her blankly.

"A lady?" she asked.

"Of course. Anybody can be a lady, who is kind and gentle and well mannered. But you have to try, Pia; you have to be willing to learn."

Pia said, a little sullenly, "I couldn't be a lady. I will marry Leone and Leone wouldn't marry a lady."

"Who is Leone, then?" Lucy tried.

"Leone is just Leone. He has gone to America, but he will come back." Pia looked defiant, and Lucy was afraid for a moment that she was going to cry.

"Of course he will," she said quickly, and then she went on more slowly. "Pia—there is going to be a new child in the house. I am going to have a baby—would you like to help take care of it?"

"Oh, Donna Lucia!" Now Pia's eyes were pools of delight, all anger and fear and curses gone from their green depths. "Oh! Donna Lucia, could I really?"

"If you will do something for me, Pia."

"Si, si, Pia will do anything, Signora."

"Forget about the witch, then."

Pia said, "A little baby for Pia. Pia won't make any more curses at all, Signora—promise!"

12: $\mathcal{T}$HE CHILD was born in Rome. They called her Clara for Lucy's mother. Lucy saw at once that she was not going to be a pretty girl. Holding her close, she knew a feeling of gladness that this small ugly child was hers.

"Never mind, darling," she murmured into the red little ear, loving the child and knowing that she would be loved by her, and wondering a moment whether, if she had had her own way about Pia, who was beautiful, she would have felt this same tenderness. "Pia is hard to reach," she said aloud, half to the child, half to herself. "Perhaps because she has never belonged to anyone—she doesn't know how—"

When Alessandro came in and found her murmuring she smiled at him and said:

"I was just wondering whether perhaps we all have to be what we start out to be—no matter what happens to us, or who tries to change the pattern."

"That borders on the sacrilegious." He smiled, putting his hand on her head.

"Oh, I don't think so," Lucy said. "Besides, it's your idea."

"Mine!"

"Remember what you said about Pia, about not being able to change her, of only hurting her if you tried?"

"It's not a matter of changing her superficially—her habits or manners or way of life—but her nature and her tendencies. That's what I meant."

"I know. I am beginning to understand."

They were close in that moment, and Lucy was sorry when dinner came to interrupt them.

Captain Nero came the next day, laden with flowers and bringing a silver amulet to put on the child's crib. He looked at Clara critically and said:

"It is well. I was afraid that she would take after you."

Lucy raised an eyebrow. The Captain turned his back on the crib and went to stand by the bed where Lucy lay looking white and thin but very lovely.

"A copy is never worth anything, and a duplicate of Donna Lucia is not possible!" he said formally.

Lucy smiled. It amused her that the Captain always managed to insinuate a certain degree of intimacy and always in the most formal manner. She said:

"You're very sweet," and thought, 'he is living in the wrong era. He is really mediaeval. He should be allowed to use his beautiful dagger, to poison his enemies and make love in verse to princesses leaning out of locked towers; he should be allowed these things just for the sake of his looks.'

The Zia came while the Captain was still there, and sat stiffly on the edge of her chair, her austerity denying every courtesy that he directed towards her. When he had gone, she said:

"You should not receive that man when Alessandro is not here."

Lucy shrugged impatiently. "He is a friend," she said, and then quickly, to change the subject, she asked, "Do you like my hospital, after all? Isn't it pleasant here?"

"It is nice. But in an Italian hospital Alessandro could have stayed with you. I am sure that it must have hurt him that you did not want that."

"It wasn't not wanting that," Lucy said coldly. "And, in any case, I'm sure that Alessandro was not hurt."

"Well, if you are sure——"

They talked of other things, until the Zia left. Lucy thought, "In her Italian hospital I would probably have had her living with me too."

Alessandro came shortly after, and Lucy told him that the Zia had been there.

"She thinks that I've neglected you, running off in this dissipated manner and having a baby all by myself."

He smiled. "It's a very surprising thing, in her eyes. I don't suppose that she has ever heard of a married woman going to a hospital alone—unless her husband was a very hard and unfeeling man."

"I don't think she believes that I love you."

"You don't try to understand her, my dear. She is very devoted to her family, and I think she is unhappy because you do not let her feel that she is at all important to you. Take some of her advice—and let her know that you take it and find it good. You needn't follow it much—just give her the feeling——"

"It's not easy."

"No, of course not."

She frowned a little, thinking of it. Then she said:

"She didn't like Captain Nero's being here."

"He was?"

"Yes. And, you know, I was thinking that we might ask him to be Clara's godfather."

Alessandro looked so displeased at this suggestion that she shrugged.

"I don't really care. *You* choose someone," she said. "I just thought he'd be fun. Besides which, he will undoubtedly still be the Beau of Rome when Clara is a young lady; and think what an advantage that would be!"

Alessandro said shortly, "We must ask Graziano to be

godfather," and he took no notice of the face that Lucy made.

From the time that they went back to the house on the Street of the Three Madonnas, Pia worked in the nursery, helping to take care of Clara. And Pia commenced to grow. She had definite duties now. She stopped school and she wore an apron. Though she still played with Gian Franco and Aurelio, when he came to the house, she considered them children and had not much time for them. Pia was ten that spring and thought herself old. She even tried to make peace with the kitchen. For long periods she forgot that she was a witch and once or twice when she was scolded she took it so meekly that Maria ordered her to bed and told Donna Lucia that the doctor should be called.

The olive season had been bad that year and Alessandro decided that they would go down to Calabria for a year. It would save them money to live in the province, and it would give him the opportunity to supervise certain improvements which he had in mind for Valombra. Instead of one winter they stayed two and a half, liking it well and only going to Rome for short trips. The colony at Crotone was small, but there were always enough for an evening of poker or bridge. And their ranks were constantly swelled by visitors from Rome and Naples. Lucy found that life was as gay as she could want it to be. In the fall, a great many people came for the hunting season. They went in large parties, sometimes to Valombra and sometimes to the Corte estate, and sometimes farther into the mountains, where the country was even wilder. And Captain Nero was always there. At his best, Lucy thought; for he was a man who could handle a gun and who belonged in the open. She enjoyed being with him in the field, and forgot the things he had said. When he took the biggest boar of the season he had the head mounted and sent to her, and she did not refuse it.

"It brings good luck, Sandi," she said, kissing the black look from her husband's face. "We can't refuse good luck, can we?" And she stood away to look at the great tusked head and so missed the searching look that Alessandro gave her.

Zia Margherita was with them at the time. She looked at the boar's head and her pinched face grew still and she said somberly:

"Good luck is not always compatible with well-being." And she went out of the room without letting them answer.

Lucy turned to Alessandro quickly, and now it was her eyes that searched. But she was too late and there was nothing in his face to answer her.

"If I thought—" she started, and then she shrugged. "But it's silly—if you didn't want me to take it you would say so, wouldn't you!"

But Alessandro said nothing and the head was hung in the foyer with a little silver plaque under it, "Shot by Captain Ernesto Nero at Valombra, October 27th, 1937. Presented to Donna Lucia Cavalierre as a token of good fortune and esteem."

The Zia had come for the month, bringing Aurelio with her. Lucy was half amused and half sympathetic to see Pia sulking and angry at the new duties which the Zia forced upon her. For the Zia never appeared before eleven o'clock and between nine-thirty and eleven she had to be attended. That she bathed herself and got into her own underwear, Lucy was sure. After this modesty was attended to, she had to be powdered, laced, buttoned and hooked into place. Her hair had to be brushed and combed. Fortunata had once had these duties to perform and, if she had not liked them, she had not minded them overly. Pia was another story. Pia sulked in the

Zia's presence and used her thumbs for fingers. Behind her back, she stormed, spitting anger at every word. The Zia was exacting. When she appeared, she must look just so. She knew precisely, to the last hair on her head, how she must look. In Pia's opinion, she sought an effect which God alone could produce for her.

Aurelio watched Pia's tantrums with interest, but without sympathy. In his eyes she had no rights, but her wildness aroused something within him that was precocious, that should not have been there. Pia was still not full grown but her breasts had commenced to swell and when she was angered he thought that they would burst through her dress. Now and again he would nudge Franco and whisper in his ear. Franco, who did not understand, would look at once surprised and uncomfortable.

Lucy saw this and she was both anxious and disgusted. But Alessandro refused to worry, saying:

"Aurelio is unclean. I'll speak to Graziano about him. But I would not be troubled about it. He is not here often, and Franco is a healthy child. He won't take any hurt."

Lucy said, "I would rather not have him here any more."

Alessandro shook his head. "That is impossible. He is, after all, my brother's child." And the subject was closed.

The boar season had just opened when the Zia came, and the month of her stay was gay. The house was full of guests and the officers from the garrison at Catanzaro came and went frequently. The Zia sat through the festivities like a stiff and unrelenting specter. And she watched Lucy's gaiety with her friends with an expression that was at once bleak and suspicious. She left for Rome before the season was over; but before she went she called Alessandro to her.

"Your happiness is close to my heart," she said, "and I ache to see you make the mistake that you are making."

Alessandro said, "I don't know what you are talking about."

The Zia's eyebrows were black and heavier than a woman's should be. She raised them now and her thin lips drew down at the corners, lending her face a look of censorious disbelief. Then her expression relaxed and she said firmly, "I am not going to tell you exactly what I have heard, because I do not choose to repeat gossip. But I think it is well to remember that there is no gossip where there is not some seed of cause. I think, Alessandro, that you would do well to refuse to receive this Captain Nero who is here so much."

Alessandro scowled, but he did not speak, and in a moment she went on, "Lucia is so lovely. And the man is, obviously—well—" she hesitated. "I should not have to tell you! Americans are independent, they have their own ways," she concluded, "and nobody knows what they are."

Nothing more was said. The Zia had finished and Alessandro did not speak. It was morning when the Zia had sent for him. Soon after, she left, taking Aurelio with her. When he had seen them onto the train, Alessandro sent a message to the house that he would be away for the night and turned his car towards Valombra.

He spent the night in Padre Pasquale's narrow house, glad of the priest's quiet company. He would not let himself think in words that were thoughts; but all of the time that he talked with the priest of the small secular things of the village, or the spiritual things of life, he was conscious of a deep sense of fear and of shame. Despite himself, his mood was dark.

The next day, he went to the olive groves with Mateo, going on horseback and riding many miles into the heart and through to the outer edges of the groves. Some of the trees were young—slender, gray saplings planted but a year or two ago. Some were middle-aged trees, their trunks thickened and their leaves coarsened. And some were as old as three hundred years, and these were as big as oaks. Their massive limbs bulged and twisted, as though too much tree had been poured into one bark. Mateo knew each tree and what manner of fruit it gave, and his hand on the trunk of a tree was the hand of a lover. They sat their horses before a tree whose branches reached high above them.

"She has ceased to yield," Mateo said sadly.

"Take it down," Alessandro said absently, looking at the great tree and thinking of other things—a boar's head, a house full of white roses. "When the ground has had a chance to recover, put in a sapling."

"But, Barone," Mateo cried, shocked, "she is the grandmother of the grove. My great-grandfather said that his great-grandfather did not know when she was planted. Some say that she started the grove, without the help of man. No one knows about her, Signor Barone, or what ill chance will come to the grove once she is gone. She brings luck, Signor Barone; there is no doubt about that."

Alessandro touched his horse with his heels, and moved away from the tree. "I am sick of this talk of luck," he said impatiently. "She is not bearing; cut her down." Unconsciously, he had adopted the peasant's pronoun and spoke of the tree as of a person.

They rode on in silence, Mateo's lined face grim with displeasure. He shook his head from time to time, but he did not speak of the tree again.

Nor did Alessandro. But Alessandro was not thinking of the tree. He was remembering a host of little things, and the Zia's words of the day before. Alessandro had never suspected Lucy's good faith, though he had been jealous before. The nearest he had ever come to blaming her was that her independence sometimes put her beyond his reach. He thought that a state of mind could be as great a rival as another man. He could not suspect her now; he would not.

And yet, there were the Zia's words, words which fell in with his own knowledge. Lucy was independent, she was different. She could not be ruled, she would not be told on whom she might and on whom she might not smile. He saw that he had no way of knowing whether she was capable, or again incapable, of infidelity. It was not possible—and yet, was it? For all of their years together, for all of their love, she was still the foreigner, and he could not tell about her.

For their lunch, Mateo provided black bread and two flagons of wine which he had carried in his saddlebag. They sat their horses and ate the bread, and drank from the bottles, as they went along. When they reached the end of the grove, they came down across the hills and cut back towards the road through the orange groves.

Alessandro's car was by the roadside and the blacksmith, who had driven it, had waited to ride his horse back to Nimpha.

Mateo said, his hands gentle on his horse's mane, "Will the tree be cut down immediately, Signor Don Alessandro?"

Alessandro looked up at him; their eyes met for a moment. The peasant was the first to look away, his eyes going towards the olive hills.

"She is an old lady," he murmured, and there was a deep sadness in his voice.

Alessandro got into his car. "The yield of one tree can make no difference," he said. "Leave her, since you care so much."

As he drove off, he thought of a man who could sorrow for a tree. "I am a great fool," he said to himself, not speaking the words aloud.

13:
*L*UCY UNDERSTOOD her husband's moodiness as he did not always understand it himself. In time, she had come to see that a man who has great self-control is more moody than a man who is merely temperamental. Such a man can be displeased and yet wish to give the other person a chance to prove his or her way the right one. During this time he would hold in his temper, waiting. The mood would only lift when he was sure that either he, or the other, was right. Once sure that he was right, there was no more moodiness; quite simply, then, he had to have his way.

After the Zia and Aurelio left, Lucy breathed freely, as though she had postponed living while they were in the house. At first, she did not notice that Alessandro watched her and was at once angry and unhappy. It was late November and had commenced to turn cold. The mountains at their back did not so much protect them as they served to chill the winds that had started warm from Africa to blow all winter, without let-up, at their door. All about, the ground was bare and bleak and hard with cold. In all Crotone, there was not an evergreen or a holly, not a glitter of fine frost or a single coat of snow to lend the winter a festive air. Even the olive groves were bleak, the summer's layers of dust so ingrained that trunk and leaf alike were gray, and what had been refreshing and cool to the summer eye was sad and dreary now. No house in Crotone had an adequate furnace. What heat the furnace at Villa Falconierre gave out was quickly dissipated between marble floors and high ceilings.

Her first winter in Calabria, Lucy had sent to Sears, Roebuck for a pot-bellied stove. It had only arrived in time for the second winter. Unlovely as it was, it held the place of honor in the library, with armchairs grouped comfortably around it, and it was the joy and pride of all Crotone.

Quite suddenly, Captain Nero was no longer there among the groups that gathered before the pot-bellied stove for an apéritif of vermouth before dinner or, afterwards, for a night of poker and bridge. Once or twice, when Lucy knew that he was in town, she spoke of his absence. But Alessandro only shrugged. And now Lucy commenced to realize that Alessandro was displeased and she waited for him to tell her what was wrong, thinking, as she did so, that few people could be attractively angry, and that he was one of these.

When a week had passed and he had said nothing, Lucy spoke to him, thinking that there might be trouble of some sort at Valombra. For answer, he looked at her long and steadily. While he looked, the frown died away for a short moment and there was a look of pleading in his eyes. Instantly it was gone, and he evaded her question, saying:

"I hear that there is some correspondence between Mussolini and that German."

"Ah, politics!" Lucy sighed a little. "But why should it trouble you?"

Alessandro shrugged. "Call it prejudice. I do not like the Germans."

Another week passed, and another. Shortly before Christmas, Lucy commented again on Captain Nero's absence and suggested that they ask him to the villa, for Christmas.

Alessandro stood with his back to the pot-bellied stove and considered her, his face gone suddenly white and the muscles at the sides of his mouth hard.

"Do you suppose that something can have happened to him?" she asked.

He removed a long, black cigar from his mouth and said with studied courtesy:

"And why should I suppose any such thing?"

"Well, after all—we've asked him at least twice for dinner, and I've never heard a word from him."

Alessandro looked at her evenly. "He never received the invitations."

Lucy frowned. "That seems rather strange. In any case, why hasn't he phoned then?"

"He has."

Lucy said, "I'm afraid that I don't understand. Is anything wrong?"

"You should consider it so——"

"I—Sandi? What are you talking about!" She hesitated. "He has got into some trouble?"

Alessandro crushed out his cigar in an ash tray and then, with his hands behind his back, stood tensely before her. She felt as though the still hands that she could not see were holding down some anger in him. And again she thought how it suited his austere looks to be angry. The black eyes of a Medici or of a Borgia would have glared from behind just such a high-bridged nose. Just such a fine-drawn mouth, a little sensuous in the lower lip, would have been pressed tightly; and then the angry Prince would have turned to flick a finger in careless gesture to his court poisoner. Only, with Alessandro, it would not have been poison, ever. A jewel-studded knife for the heart of his lady!

"You should realize," he said, "that I would, naturally, intercept the invitations and give orders that you are not receiving the Captain."

"But, Sandi, I haven't heard anything. What has he done?"

Still the constraint, the body that looked as though it wanted to tremble and would not.

"Is it nothing to you, then, that he is in love with you?"

There it was, but it was not a thing which you could understand easily. It was too sudden, too unexpected.

"You're not joking," she said, "but you should be."

"No, I am not joking."

The icy feeling that seemed, for no reason, to start in her toes and in her fingertips and in the roots of her hair, that converged at a creeping pace upon her heart, was anger. With twelve years in this country, she had learned so much. There were husbands who loved their wives and yet were not true to them; there were wives who did not love their husbands and yet submitted to them, in the interval between lovers. There were women like Lucretia, the frail homely wife of Count Morgano. She was permitted legal abortions, and she had had two a year for four years now. Always they followed the brief bi-annual visits which her husband made her when he came to Calabria to collect from her estate. He never waited for the abortion. While he collected the money, he used his wife like a prostitute and then went back to Rome, or Paris, or London to enjoy himself. Lucretia remained, with her misery, and awaited his return in the most unrelenting poverty.

There were tales everywhere. Some of them were true and some were not, though for all of the talk they might as well have been. Oh, she knew so much! But she, Lucy Cavalierre, had never been touched, and she never would be. She was an American, clear-cut and free; these things did not happen to Americans. Nor to such men as Sandi. There were things about him which Lucy's mother would not have understood; but he was good none the less, and he was different, and he was her husband. The anger seeped away and she said gently:

"Look, darling, this is very silly. I did know the Captain was in love with me. What difference does it make?

There've been others, you surely knew, but it never disturbed you."

"You are depraved," he snapped angrily. "I should have known. The Zia has been right. I have trusted you as no Italian woman has ever been trusted, and you can admit this to me——"

Now the anger, which had once started so slowly, so icily, flushed quick and hot upon her. Lucy was not pretty in anger. Her eyes were small under a scowl, her skin burned unpleasantly, and her lovely mouth became a thin hard line. She sat silently, as though every nerve in her body had been paralyzed except her long fingers, which moved convulsively. She bent the cigarette in her right hand so that a hot ash fell to the rug and tobacco spewed from the other end of the butt. When she spoke, her voice was quiet:

"You are saying that I am not to be trusted! You dare, Alessandro, you dare!" She stopped, because protests and anger and reason made a jumbled confusion in her mind and she could only think, "It's not true, not of us!"

"He is in love with you—and now you say that there were others. Yet you never told me. You did continue to welcome these men to my house, you encouraged them—do you think me a fool then, Lucia?"

"Yes," Lucy said between her teeth. And after Alessandro had gone quickly past her and out of the room, she said, "Yes," again.

Outside, the night was hard with cold, and in the room the stove glowed, and a thin string of smoke rose from the cigarette that had fallen to the rug. Lucy leaned down to pick it up. She ground out the glow of hot ash, leaving an ugly, brown spot on the rug. She heard the motor in the garage, then the car roared out of the drive and she straightened up.

Midnight came and went and still she sat there. Slowly it

came over her how alone she was, for the first time since her marriage. She was sorry, less for herself than for Alessandro, for she saw that she had failed him. Looking back, she thought with a sudden flash of understanding that in all of the little differences they had ever had Alessandro had tried harder to forgive the foreigner than she had. And she thought, with a sense of bitter reproach, how the Anglo-Saxon will laugh at a stranger who speaks his language with difficulty, and how when the shoe is on the other foot the Italian will listen with courtesy and kindliness, be the accent or the arrangement of words never so funny. She pushed a strand of hair from her forehead. "He needed to be told that I love him," she thought, "that Nero means nothing to me. I've been arrogant and heartless—and Anglo-Saxon!"

Now she wanted Alessandro. She moved restlessly about the house, planning how she would admit that she had been wrong, how she would erase what had happened with the proof of her love. They would talk, they would understand each other. Alessandro would be gentle again, accepting her good faith. It would be a beginning, for now she realized what she had done and she knew that she would not be arrogant with the foreigner again.

The hours after midnight went and still Alessandro did not return. Something in Lucy's heart commenced to grieve, wondering why he stayed away so long, whether anything could have happened, or whether she had lost him entirely. Perhaps he would not let her begin again.

A terrifying sense of aloneness swept over her, and she went to Franco's room to reassure herself. But in his sleep he was a young Alessandro. The gay lights in his eyes, the sometimes impractical but oh, so pleasant ideals that shone through his every waking expression were hidden away. He was Alessandro, dark and austere and, in this moment of sleep, a little defenseless. He could not reassure her. In Clara's room she found even less that was hers. For there, against every rule, was Pia, curled up on the floor beside the small girl's bed. Lucy loved her child. But in this moment she saw only that she was dark and strange, her ugly, chubby little face flushed in sleep, with a Mona Lisa smile subtly tilting her small fat lips. While, on the floor, Pia was white and pink and fair.

Perhaps, after all, if Pia had been hers—if she could have begun from the first day of her coming to make her her own—perhaps it would have worked, and now she would have had something to cling to, to reassure her. For Pia looked like home. While she slept, the witch slept too and she was the kind of little girl who takes an apple to the teacher every Monday. On Cherry Hill Road, they would approve of Pia.

At three o'clock, comfortless and frightened, Lucy went to bed. Despite her anxiety and her pregnant grief, she slept at once.

When the light went on beside her bed, she stirred, opening her eyes. It was Alessandro. The blood beat in her heart and she was wide awake. She called his name softly, eager to bring him back to her. He did not answer and she sensed suddenly that he was strange. Behind him, through the slats of the Venetian blinds, the world was gray with dawn. He commenced to undress, still standing there and looking at her. She thought, with a strange thrill of understanding—'He is hoping that the light hurts my eyes.'

She told him quickly, wanting to change him back into the Alessandro who loved her so simply and understandably, to the Alessandro for whom she had been waiting all these hours. She told him what her thoughts had been. She told him that she loved him. He kept looking at her; with a sense of horror she saw that he did not believe her, and so she told him again, her breath quick in her chest.

"Ah!" he said. "Well, I am sorry, my darling." His voice was cold and the word was no endearment.

He sat down on the side of the bed and removed his shoes and socks and then he stood up. He was not sorry; he was, in some indefinable way, some uncivilized way, glad of her hurt. In his voice, in his silence, in his cold tall silence, he hungered to see her hurt.

Lucy gasped, unbelieving and shocked. As he came to her she drew away, crying out:

"No!—not now—don't you understand——"

But he would not speak to her. When she would have risen, quick with outrage, he thrust her roughly back, tearing at the shoulder that turned from him.

Black as the ink of the octopus, feeling surged through her and out of her and around her until the room was filled with it. Now she lay quiescent and the long waiting grief broke in her. She wept for her loss and her guilt and for the ugly thing that had happened to them. The tears wet her face and her neck and trickled cold and clammy into her ears. She knew instinctively that the stranger Alessandro had become found satisfaction not of her body but of her despair.

In the morning he was gone, and Lucy's whole body ached as it had not in twelve years of marriage. She was glad of the pain and let it occupy her whole mind so that there was no room for thought of how she had come by it.

14:

IN ROME, Alessandro went to the theater. Not only was his displeasure with Lucy unabated, it had subtly increased. Lucy had in some way placed him in a position which made him displeased with himself. For days he had brooded, and now he sat through three acts, still too intent upon his own thoughts to see the performance. Before the final curtain, he sent for the manager to ask whether a young lady whose name appeared on the bill as Minervina del Arno would care to have supper with him.

The manager saw before him a man of wealth—a great lord. Minervina was, undoubtedly, very hungry. In his experience, artists were always this way.

Minervina, who was blonde, though not from the roots out, was in fact hungry. Also, she was gay. For a while, Alessandro forgot. After supper, he went to her apartment, where he ceased forgetting. The doubt came again, like a small pain growing in his heart. You couldn't tell with Americans, and he had never completely won her! The hidden elements in Lucy's nature tortured him now. To know that a man was in love, and to smile upon him, meant only one thing to an Italian. From conversations which Alessandro had heard between Lucy and Franco he had gathered that purity was of great importance to Americans. But was it pure, then, to encourage if you had neither desire nor intention? Alessandro thought it depraved. Confronting these doubts was the haunting fear that Lucy might actually have desired these men, and it made no difference that he now believed her quite innocent of adultery.

Minervina was prettier dressed than undressed. Alessandro was not attracted. But he thought that he had not had to leave Lucy to sleep with a beautiful woman; he was not looking for prettiness or even for pleasure. He knew it now—he was after revenge. Some living ligament of his ego had been torn and it must be mended.

Alessandro stayed with Minervina the next night and the next, but the conviction had gone out of him. The fourth night, he dined with Zia Margherita.

Minervina, Alessandro had decided, should move to a more comfortable apartment and he would come to her once a month. In the meantime, he would keep Lucy in Crotone for a third winter—perhaps for good. He was not very happy about his decision. Nothing in the situation gave him satisfaction. He thought longingly of Crotone as he sat down to the heavy luxury of his aunt's table.

Lucy had once said that Zia Margherita's house was too solid. There was a look about it of having been there forever and of intending to remain there forevermore. Alessandro, who had grown up here, could understand what she meant. There was too much heavily carved furniture, too many tapestry-draped walls, too many somber portraits of long dead Cavalierres. Even the table silver was too solid, massive with its crest. At the head of the table, the Zia was as aquiline as Alessandro himself—but with no lightness, no joy beneath the surface. Graziano, also, had the family features, well overlaid with fat, and he was as ponderous of temperament as he was of body. One day, Aurelio would be like him. Lucy had seen that too, and now Alessandro saw that it was so.

Zia Margherita said, a smile loosening her thin lips, "You are being a naughty boy, Alessandro," and added quickly, as he scowled—"one hears things! But it is doing you good."

Graziano wiped grease from his lips with a damask napkin. "Good time," he said. "You've been a damn fool long enough." And then he guffawed loudly and mirthlessly.

Alessandro signaled the butler that he would have more wine. He continued to scowl, but he said nothing until Aurelio, his eyes bland, asked whether his Aunt Lucia would be in Rome that winter. With a sense of physical shock Alessandro realized that the boy had understood, and a great surge of shame swept over him for them all.

"We are all coming up after Christmas," he said quietly and, as soon after dinner as it was polite for him to do so, he left. It was almost a week since he had come away from Crotone in such anger and such hurt, and he had not yet sent Lucy a word. Now he remembered that she had tried to tell him that she loved him.

He went back to Crotone without another thought of Minervina's apartment. He was ready to confess and repent— Lucy had been wrong but, well, he felt himself in the wrong— though, in all logic, he had done nothing to make him feel so. He found Lucy very quiet.

After dinner, they went to the library for their coffee. It would have to be now. It was not pleasant—while he hesitated, Lucy said suddenly:

"Don't tell me, Sandi, I'd rather not know."

He turned to her then, stirring his coffee with a quick, nervous gesture. "Do you want to stay here another winter or shall we go to Rome?"

Lucy took her glass from him and sipped it. She said, "I want to take the children to America for the winter."

"Well, of course, some time—but not this winter."

"Why not?"

Alessandro shrugged impatiently. "I can't have you go this winter—next, perhaps."

Lucy didn't answer. In a few minutes she got up and left him, and when Alessandro came to bed she was already asleep, or pretending to be. He undressed in his dressing room. When he came in, he slipped between the sheets quietly so as not to disturb her.

This became their routine, night after night, for Alessandro would not touch her until she gave him some sign that all was well between them. Their days were as they had always been, pleasantly even, even gay. No one but them could know. At night, Lucy slept early, or pretended to.

15:

$\mathcal{I}$N JANUARY, the family prepared to return to Rome. Lucy was glad, feeling almost as though in going back to Rome she would go back into the past, that things would be made easier for herself and for Alessandro and that they would be able to step into the old relationship, to find each other again.

Lucy knew no way of telling Alessandro how she felt, how lost she was, for he made no sign of wanting to hear. She thought that she could have humbled herself before anything but his lack of generosity, his unwillingness to forgive her. She thought him unrelenting, and she was never without this knowledge. Why else should he sleep in her bed, night after night, without ever so much as putting a hand on her arm. She thought that what he felt must be worse than hatred. She had heard, once, that an Italian would use a wife he hated, because he considered it their biological and religious duty to lie together. And she believed that this was so. But if his anger had burnt something out of him and he no longer had need of her—what then? She could not give him any sign, for fear that this was so.

Captain Nero was not mentioned again, nor Alessandro's trip to Rome. They packed in silence. On the terrace, Pia and Louisa squatted, watching the graceful baby tumblings of Clara. In the schoolroom, Gian Franco pointed out to Miss Tooley that his model aeroplanes would have to be done up more carefully. Lucy looked in the door and said:

"Pack them yourself, Franco. Miss Tooley has other things to do."

In the kitchen, Maria and Emma were screaming. Emma didn't go to Rome with the family and whether it was Emma, or Maria, who was jealous of the other's life it was not easy to determine. Gerolamo conferred with Cesare about packing the servant's car; they conferred over a glass of wine in the pantry. From an upstairs window, Fortunata threw slops into the vegetable garden, a step-saving device which was strictly forbidden. From behind a hedged-in compost heap Cato appeared, brandishing his fist. He told Fortunata that she was unclean, of accidental birth, and a pig of specific antecedents. He also asked her to give up going away and to marry him. Fortunata only laughed and picked up another pail of slops.

The family went by train. For the first time in her short life, Clara was turned over to Miss Tooley. Pia, crushed and not a little angry, was left to follow with the servants. It was not a pleasant trip.

Gerolamo and Cesare sat in front with the smaller packages, while Maria and Fortunata were held firmly in place by the heavier luggage and boxes. Pia, whose growing thighs had not been taken into consideration, sat where she could. They progressed slowly, for Maria suffered from car-sickness, and frequent stops had to be made for her. Other stops had to be made for wine and refreshment. All in all, they took their time in getting to Rome. When they did finally arrive, Maria had almost lost an eye; Cesare, who considered himself different, had lost his temper; and Gerolamo had three times fired and rehired the entire staff. All because, on top of a hard day and several hours perched on a slanting seat, while the edges of two boxes refused to yield to the wigglings of her lower spine, Pia had been told that Clara was an ugly child and would have to have a heavy dot with which to find her a husband. Pia remembered words which no one who had not lived in Nimpha would have understood. They had mostly to do with genealogy, a subject on which Pia was well informed. To illustrate her words, she descended like a bird of prey from her high perch and did everything in her power to remove Maria's eye.

Maria and Fortunata were helplessly entangled, wedged in as they were, and attacked from above. Only their voices were free to range, and these were permitted no little leeway. It took the concerted efforts of Cesare and Gerolamo to disentangle the flailing heap of feminine teeth and talons. Apart from hauling Pia off bodily, they also joined Maria and Fortunata in returning her Nimphian words to her unimpaired. When she had finally been threatened with a dousing in the nearest river she quieted, and for the remainder of the run she sat on her high box, her white-gold braids flopping in the wind, her green eyes at their angry greenest, smoldering like half-extinguished embers.

Once established in Rome, the unhappy conditions of the journey would have taken their place, unnoticed and forgotten, amid the lifetime of quarrels which the servants were given to, had not Maria's eye become infected. Pia's nails, it would seem, had been dirty. Maria had to go to the doctor, and to wear a large and unattractive bandage for a good two weeks. As though her discomfort were not obvious enough, she talked about it incessantly in that nasal whine which is so mistakenly considered by the sufferer an inducement to sympathy. Pia was genuinely sorry.

In fact, Pia wanted to make amends. While she was doing the bedrooms with Fortunata, she consulted.

Miss Tooley had taken Clara to the Villa Borghese; Gian

Franco was in school. The day was brisk with cold, and Fortunata and Pia were polishing the parquet floors. Fortunata liked being consulted. She gave Pia the cloth to wipe up the floor under the bed and she herself sat in a chair eyeing the girl's buttocks while she considered.

"Being a cook," she said at last, when the rounded lump of Pia's buttocks had stopped wiggling and was backing out from the bed, "there isn't anything she would want. You couldn't give her a present of something to eat, and you couldn't give her a present of something to drink. What with wages and the squeeze she gets at the market and from selling off bits of supplies whenever Donna Lucia isn't looking, she has more money than any of the rest of us. What else is there?"

"Maybe a rosary!" Pia squatted on her haunches; her square little hands smoothed at her hair. "Or I could burn a candle for her eye?"

Fortunata looked disappointed. But she nodded; a candle was always a good thing. Pia got up now and went around to the other side of the bed. She had used to be able to do the whole floor under the bed at once. That was before she began sticking. The first time she got under and couldn't get out it had taken both Gerolamo and Cesare to lift the bed off from her. The second time, they made her stay there a good half hour before they rescued her. After that, Pia worked from the edges, never going in farther than was easy. Little by little, the distance that she could go grew smaller as Pia's hips grew larger. At twelve and a half they were broad and fat like a woman's and she had no taste for the job, for her breasts hurt her when she lay on them. Now, she sighed rather lustily and said:

"Imagine having everything you want, except maybe a candle or a rosary!"

"She's got a rosary, and I don't guess she'd change it for another—it's blessed. But the candle might do"—Fortunata snorted a bit—"unless you could find her a man."

Pia emerged from the other side of the bed and considered this solemnly. Her wide, candid eyes looked into Fortunata's and she rubbed her breasts gently where they hurt. She said:

"Gerolamo doesn't like her——"

"Gerolamo is a capon."

Pia said, "A what?"

Fortunata only grinned and wouldn't explain. Pia stored the word away, like a nut, to be used when she needed something mysterious to say.

"There's Cato."

"She can't have Cato," Fortunata said flatly. "Cato wants to marry me."

"But I thought you didn't want him."

Fortunata shrugged and grinned again. "I do and I don't," she said; "I do and I don't."

"Well, if you do, you do," Pia said impatiently.

"Oh, no; it's not that way, little one. You'll see, one day. There's the dot. One thousand lire he would get, that I have worked hard to save, and my salary he would likely collect, and I'd be keeping his house and cooking his meals as well."

"All right, then you don't."

"Well, but that's not so easy, either. He's a good man and active. He has a fine way with him too, and he knows just how——"

"Just how what?"

"None of your business," Fortunata snapped. "Get on with your dusting, girl, and don't be asking such questions."

Pia looked at her sidewise. Small flecks glinted like foxfire in her eyes. She took up her cloth again, and her voice was disgusted.

"I know you go to bed with him. I was there once."

"You were," Fortunata screamed out and aimed a sharp slap at Pia's ear. Pia dodged, tripped backwards and fell over the corner of the bed. The older woman was quick to take her advantage. She kicked twice with vicious strength.

"Maledetta little bastard," she screamed, and as Pia tried to drag herself back, she kicked again. Then, quite suddenly, the anger went out of her and she let the girl up.

"Well, you can see how it is!" she said, philosophically. "I've got Cato and I've got my money too, and no extra work."

Pia rubbed her thigh sullenly. "Yes, but you haven't really got him. Maria might sneak up on you some day."

"No"—now Fortunata grinned again—"I keep him used up."

"There isn't anyone else," Pia said hopelessly; "Cesare is in love with Miss Tooley."

"Cold little English fish. He is a fool. He'll never get her. The English aren't the way we are."

"No? How are they?"

"Well, I'll tell you another time. It isn't nice."

"Well, I guess it will have to be a candle."

"Yes—unless you want to advertise."

Pia clapped her hands, and now her eyes sparkled and her braids danced as she tossed her head back. "That is the thing. I'll advertise for a husband for Maria. Then she won't care about her eye, even if it doesn't get better."

So it was decided. As they worked together, pushing the heavy wax mops over the floor, they talked it over. When the floor was finished they went to Lucy's desk, and with

the paper and pen which they found there Fortunata labori-
ously scrawled—"Magnificent cook to lordly family," she
spelled aloud, "requires husband. Young man with passionate
disposition and good nature preferred. Handsome dot, salary,
and extras. Apply service entrance all day. 3 via delle Tre
Madonne."

Fortunata said, "Now you only have to get the money."

"Money?" Pia looked crestfallen.

"Sure. Do you think the papers will print it for nothing?
—And don't ask me for any."

"Do you think Maria would pay for it?"

"No, I don't. Besides, you're supposed to be doing this. You
can get some money from Donna Lucia."

Red crept up Pia's neck and she said, "No," very flatly.
Then, suddenly, the red washed away again, leaving her white.
"Fortunata," she said softly, "Leone will send me some money.
In America, there is lots of money. Maybe he is already rich.
You must write to Leone for me."

"Well, maybe you better make it a candle," Fortunata said
dubiously.

"No, write to Leone. He is assuredly rich. We will send the
letter to his father at Nimpha. He will know how to send it on
to him."

Fortunata shrugged. "You might just as well wait for him
to come back. But then, I don't care. We'll do it when we
finish the dining-room floor."

16: IA PERCHED on the edge
of the kitchen table and dictated.

"Say, 'Dear Leone, I need some pennies to advertise a husband for Maria because I scratched her eye and she thinks it
is going to come out and nothing else will satisfy her except
maybe a candle which is not as nice and I am sorry and I
would like to give her a husband anyway because she has a bad
nature.'" Pia bit the edge of her finger thoughtfully, "Tell
him is he having a good time," she said at last, "and when will
he come back and if he will send me some other pennies I will
burn a candle for him. Oh, and tell him Titto Scalpi's wife
has three children and they are getting another in December—
and what else?"

Fortunata still wrote diligently, her face two inches from
the paper and the muscles of her right arm taut in her effort
to control the pen.

"That's enough, God help us," she said. "But you have to
say 'respectfully yours' and put your name at the bottom."

When it was done, Pia put it in an envelope and Fortunata
addressed it to Leone Pontevecchio, son of Oreste Pontevecchio, Blacksmith of Nimpha, in Calabria, to be sent by the
father to the son in America. Pia thanked her and put the
envelope away in the pocket of her dress. After lunch was
served she went with it in search of Donna Lucia. She found
her in the salon having her coffee alone, for Don Alessandro
had not come home for lunch.

"Signora, Donna Lucia," she said, bending the letter in her hand, "I have need of some stamps, if you please."

Lucy put down her coffee cup. "Why, of course, Pia. How many stamps do you need?"

Pia shook her head, raising her eyebrows a little.

"Well, then, where is the letter going to, and perhaps I can tell you?"

Pia smiled shyly and said, "It is a letter for Leone which I send first to his father in Nimpha who will send it to him in America."

"I think we had better put a foreign-mail stamp on it, then."

Pia said, "Oh, yes, Signora, that will be nice."

"Well, then," Lucy smiled, "put your letter on my desk and I will see that it is properly mailed for you." Then, seeing the girl's crestfallen expression, she said kindly, "But of course you'd like to do it yourself. Come along, Pia," and she led the way towards her room.

In the hall, she slipped her arm about Pia's shoulder and then drew it quickly away as the girl cringed at her touch. She wanted to say, "Why are you afraid to be loved, Pia? Is it that a peasant's child is so afraid of losing her personal freedom?" But she could not talk this way to the child, even had Alessandro's ban not stood between them.

In the bedroom, Lucy went to her desk, weighed the letter on a small silver scale and took stamps from a leather folder. She handed stamps and letter to Pia, saying:

"Is it the first letter that you have written to Leone?"

"Yes, Signora; he is far away."

Lucy smiled," "All the more reason to write him, then. When people are far away, they like to have letters from home. Is Leone not the boy who you told me would come back and marry you?"

"Oh, yes, Donna Lucia." Pia was blushing now and suddenly the words came tumbling out, one over the other. "He is beautiful as Saint Sebastian, Donna Lucia, and strong and good, and he is my friend. Sometimes at night, when I think I am asleep, I am not, for I can hear the sound of his pipes. His same pipes, for up in the mountains, when even the goatherds are far away and the lake is alone with just the two of us, the pipes make a special sound. It is as though all of the angels were listening. When there are people around, the pipes are different."

Lucy looked at her gently, her brown eyes soft. She thought, "I have never heard her talk this way. I had no idea there was anything like this in her——"

"And you have heard Leone's pipes?" she said quietly, accepting the fact of it.

"Yes, Donna Lucia, and if I went to bed sad, in the morning I was not sad any more," and her small, lovely face shone as though some light had been kindled behind it.

Lucy wished suddenly that she too could hear pipes in the night. "You're almost thirteen, Pia, aren't you?" she said.

Pia nodded. "I shall have completed my thirteenth Saint's-day in three months' time."

In the days that followed, Lucy's thoughts went back many times to their conversation, to the thought of a piping in the night-time that the angels listened to. She told Alessandro and she thought for a moment that he looked at her oddly, wondering why she had told him. If he had asked her, she thought of the words she would use. She would say:

"Pia is free to hear Leone's pipes in the night because she is sure, in her simplicity, that he is her friend—and that she is his. You—no, perhaps not you—I am no free person, but a slave to my own complexity. I have no way of being sure of you. There are no songs in the night for me—oh, how can there be?" And she wanted to cry. But Alessandro looked away and did not ask her to explain.

The year that Pia was fourteen, Lucy took her and Franco to the opera to hear "Parsifal." She worried a little that it might be too strenuous an experience for children; at least where Pia was concerned she need not have. From the opening bar to the last note, Pia sat like a little stone figurine except when, at times, her square little hands clasped and unclasped. She sat on the edge of her chair, leaning forward; and her face was white and her eyes were bright as stones. Franco fidgeted from time to time and when the intermission came he was glad to move around. And when the matinee was over he was glad to go home, and he talked all the way, while Pia was silent.

Her fourteenth Saint's-day was considered a great celebration, for, though she was not yet legally of age, Pia was now considered a woman. Lucy gave her a dress for the occasion. It was a light-weight blue wool, with flowers embroidered on the pockets. Pia cried when she saw it, and then brushed her tears away and laughed. She kissed Lucy's hand and Don Alessandro's hand, the top of Clara's little head, and Franco, quickly and easily, on the mouth. Lucy frowned, surprised. And then she smiled; it was an occasion.

Don Alessandro had put an extra month's wages in the bank for Pia, and Miss Tooley gave her a sweater which she had knitted herself. Franco gave her an aquamarine ring which he had saved his allowance to buy. And Pia, who had never owned a piece of jewelry, ran up three flights of stairs to her room under the eaves to cry over it. At first she wouldn't wear it but kept it under her pillow. Then, gradually and quite blandly, it became her engagement ring to Leone. She wore it constantly after that and was pleased with it in a way that delighted the unsuspecting Franco. Soon, she almost forgot from whom she had it.

It was an unpleasant spring, wet and cold. Then, within a week, it became hot and the family prepared to return to Crotone. This time, Pia was to travel by train. There was much talk of war, and Miss Tooley had decided to go back to England to her family.

Before she left, Cesare, who had read the classics and knew how a gentleman should behave, went to Don Alessandro to ask for her hand in marriage. Alessandro explained that Miss Tooley would not expect such formality—would, in fact, not understand. But Cesare stood on his rights. It was Alessandro's duty, as master of the household, to inform Miss Tooley of Cesare's request, and to vouch for him. If Cesare's intentions had been less honorable, he would have known how to handle the situation by himself.

It was a position from which there was no escape. With a little inward smile Alessandro succumbed. As he had expected, Miss Tooley was outraged.

She said, firmly, "I do not believe in international marriages." Then she blushed to the roots of her hair, so that the pale, yellow freckles faded from her nose; and her mouth, which was small but nicely shaped and never painted, faded into the blush and could not be distinguished from it. In agony at her lack of tact, she stammered till Alessandro interrupted her kindly:

"There are many of your opinion, Miss Tooley, and it is not to be made light of. I understand, then, that you do not love Cesare, and that you are not interested in a marriage with him?"

"Yes," Miss Tooley looked at him gratefully. "Though I am sure he is a very fine young man, and I have enjoyed his friendship and his kindness to me." Suddenly, her formal tone broke and, to the surprise of them both, she wailed—"Oh, dear, I didn't know!" and, jumping up, she ran from the study.

Lucy came in, a few minutes later. "What have you done to Miss Tooley?" she asked. "It scarcely seems credible, but she is in her room howling like a baby."

"It has taken her eight years to discover that Cesare is in love with her," Alessandro answered, running his long, thin fingers through his hair, and looking, Lucy thought, really disturbed, "and then she had to be told. I cannot understand it—why didn't she know?"

Lucy shrugged. "She is too nice, I think." They were talking in Italian, but Lucy used the English word "nice."

"But quite nice people marry—" Alessandro smiled.

"You don't understand," Lucy put her hand on his arm. "I really came to tell you that lunch is ready. Nice," she went on, "is so overworked; but it's the only word I can think of for this."

"Do you mean that she is sexless?"

"Oh, no. I'm sure that she thinks that she wants to marry, and has all the desires that the rest of us have—but if it came right down to the actuality she wouldn't think it very 'nice.' In self-defense, she doesn't think of it at all, and I don't suppose Cesare has been more than a piece of furniture to her."

"It's a wonder," Alessandro said, "that the British reproduce at all."

Lucy laughed. "They're not all like Miss Tooley."

They went into the dining room and Alessandro said, "I am glad that she is leaving. It would give me gooseflesh to have her in the house, now that I know how virginal she is."

"Alessandro!" Lucy frowned. "That's not nice."

"Ah! nice, nice, nice," he mocked, and they both laughed.

Miss Tooley's departure brought the feeling of an imminent war more closely home than the newspapers had been able to do. The newspapers were something that you grew accustomed to—there was Ethiopia, there was Spain, there was Albania. Of course there would be another world war; it was self-evident—if you walk in one direction long enough you will come to water. But the Cavalierres, and their friends, were certain that this time the Italians would stay out. This time, there was Mussolini; he was strong and he would spare them. No, since Italy was not to be involved, the enlightened were complaisant enough. It was a black cloud that hovered over Europe, and Italy denounced it excitedly, but this was still on an intellectual basis and not personal. Other people's war is not really war.

Now, as in a game in which each side scurries to get behind its safety lines before commencing to play, Miss Tooley had gone back to England; and the entire household was conscious of a feeling of taking sides.

In Crotone, the feeling persisted. Lucy spoke of going to America. This time, Alessandro did not talk of "another year." He said:

"One cannot tell where America is going to stand in this. I cannot have you and the children going at this time."

There it remained, despite anything that she could say. And

it stood between them, a spoken symbol of that other disunity which had grown out of a moment of jealousy and misunderstanding.

In July, Aurelio came to stay. He had not grown tall as Franco had, but he was looking well. His olive skin was burnt to a deep mahogany by a month at the beach, and his muscles rippled from a year's new interest in athletics. He kept his black hair slick to his head, and Lucy thought, watching him at a game of tennis with Franco, "I believe that he oils himself to make his muscles shine—" and she was immediately ashamed and conscious of being unjust. She tried to excuse herself, watching carefully and seeing that Aurelio played too perfect a game. It was not good, hard tennis, but a precise and graceful game. Franco had not the form, but at least he hit the balls hard and did not spare himself. Some day, he would make a good player. That was as much as one wanted from a boy of thirteen.

At the back of the court on which Aurelio played, Pia and Clara chased balls.

17:

THE SUN beat down on Villa Falconierre. The marble balustrade of the terrace was too hot to touch, and the water in the bay rippled in the hot sirocco and was as warm as a bath. Pia lolled on the sand, watching for flecks of gold, while Clara dug holes. From the terrace above them Franco shouted. Pia waved, and in a few moments he joined them. Clara said distinctly:

"Giafo!" and threw a handful of wet sand in his face.

Pia said, "Naughty baby," smiling at her.

"Naughty baby! You do that again and I'll eat you up," Franco stormed, wiping his eyes. Clara gave him a startled look and commenced to cry, climbing quickly to the protection of Pia's arms, who scolded and petted and dried her tears. Franco watched. Suddenly he said:

"Has Aurelio been bothering you?"

Pia set Clara down and said, "There, dig Pia a castle."

Franco frowned.

"Aurelio's all right."

"I want to know, Pia." Franco dug his hands deep into the sand and he looked as though he would like to follow them with his whole body.

Pia turned around to him. Her eyes were wide and clear. "What do you want to know for? He's not bothering you, is he?" She stopped and then smiled slowly, and looked at him.

Neither Pia nor Gian Franco were conscious of what she was doing. Pia had thought of something, and the thought brought a quality to her smile and a look to her eyes which were mere reflexes. They had no way of knowing that it was at once sensuous and maddening. Gian Franco twisted his hands under the sand. Pia said:

"You too—" softly. But she had no time to finish, for Franco had jumped to his feet and was running towards the water. He swam for a long time and when he came out, he ran past Pia without speaking to her. She shrugged and poked windows in Clara's castle.

Pia thought that Franco was being silly. In Nimpha, she had not had a bed of her own but had slept about the village with one family and another. Most of these people had only one bed. With the children of the family, Pia had lain and watched the begetting of yet other children. Or when the elders slept at last, she had seen how the bigger brother and sister played in the dark, exploring and inquisitive.

Pia built another castle for Clara, and showed her how to make a road between the two. She stretched her body in the sand and thought of Aurelio and Franco. Something stirred in her and she could not drag her mind from the things that she knew of. There was the girl Celeste, who had married when she was only thirteen. Pia remembered how she had cried and how her father had beaten her with a cudgel, so that her body was like pulp and she couldn't move for a week. Celeste hadn't been pretty and, after the beating, she was ugly and never walked straight again.

Late in the night, her father had awakened and found Celeste and her brother locked together in embrace, and it was then that he had beaten the girl and thrown the brother out of the house for the rest of the night. The next day, the priest came and there was fasting and repentance and prayers to be said for a month. And Padre Pasquale had said, "Get her married; she has eaten the apple and you will have no further peace with her."

The law was strict; it was the law of the cudgel and it knew no mercy. An unmarried girl found with a boy was married to that boy, whenever it was possible, and when it was not possible to cleanse her with this, or with any other husband, she was thrown out of the village. With Celeste, it was different: she could not marry her own brother. Her name was evil now for having slept with him, for was it not a cardinal sin? Her father brought Zeppe to the house, and Padre Pasquale was called to marry them. Pia shuddered, remembering. Zeppe was half-witted and old. His teeth were decayed, and the pores of his skin gaped like black caverns. He made no living, but slept in a dark hole under a stairway and ate what other people threw out, or what they gave him on feast days. And Celeste went to his dark hole under the stairway to live with him. People said that he did not sleep with her, that he did not know how.

The Signora Odilia had said, "And who cares? He keeps her used up in other ways. And I for one have no interest. So long as she has no strength left to lead the good children of this town into trouble and evil—it is well."

Celeste's hair had fallen out and, in time, her teeth, and her constant whimper had become an accustomed sound on the streets, so that like the shrieks or laughter of children at play, or the unending cooing of the mourning-dove, one scarcely heard it any more.

Celeste's brother had married, and was respected and happy. "You can't blame the boy," they had said. "A man's nature is that way." And thus they kept the women in line with cudgels, and they were fanatical that this should be so. But nobody beat the married woman who met passion behind some hay-stack. Unless, of course, her husband found out. The rest of them shrugged and snickered. If her husband could not keep her used up, whose concern was it, then?

Pia thought that at Villa Falconierre it was better. At Villa Falconierre, there were no cudgels. At Villa Falconierre, no one concerned himself with the ways of women.

It was a hot summer and constant wind made them all nervous. Franco was irritable and he never stopped watching Pia, so that even Lucy noticed it. She wondered, uneasily, if Pia were up to some foolery with her witchcraft. Once, with an unaccustomed flash of insight, she said to Alessandro,

"The children are growing up—I probably ought to talk to Pia."

He looked at her in astonishment. "Pia was full grown when she was twelve," he said. "Do you mean to say that you have never talked to her?"

"No—but of course not; after all, there was no need. But now—well, perhaps she ought to be told."

Alessandro stared at her blankly and then, suddenly, he threw back his head and laughed. When the laughter had gone out of him, he said to her gently:

"Tell me, am I right? Is it that you think you must explain about sex to Pia?"

Lucy said stiffly, "Of course."

"Ah, Lucia," he said, "you Americans are amazing to me. Have you no eyes to see! At the age of six, the girl knew more about sex than you know now. There is only one thing for you to tell her, and very likely it will have to be told with a whip before the thing is done with, and that is that she may not exercise her knowledge until she is given in marriage. And this is a thing you should have been telling her since the day she came here."

Lucy frowned. Then a memory came to her of a child who heard pipes in the night, of a child who had a friend of her own. "I don't think you understand Pia," she said.

"I understand Pia well enough," he said shortly, "but I'm not sure that I understand you."

They didn't talk again of Pia, and Lucy let the matter drop, for she had other things on her mind. Alessandro was away a good deal that summer or he would have seen what was happening and taken matters into his own hands.

Franco continued to watch Pia and Aurelio unhappily. He had little curiosity himself, for his own questions had always been answered simply and honestly. And the natural forces within him were immature and not ready to ripen. But they were there, so that he was unhappy in the face of the thing that was growing like an invisible and unclean tentacle out of Aurelio, and threatening to encircle Pia. Pia belonged to everything that Franco loved. She belonged to tales of fairies and witches and charms that worked by the full of the moon. She belonged to the pink stucco house on the Street of The Three Madonnas, and to the beach and to the shiny marble floors of Crotone. She belonged to Valombra, which was a place his forefathers had taken from a wild people fifteen hundred years ago, and made their own. And who belonged to Valombra belonged to Franco; this was in his blood. Pia was his. Franco, with a certain amount of innocence and a certain amount of knowledge, hated Aurelio for looking at her.

Aurelio's point of view was quite different. He had no such feeling for Pia, nor any knowledge of how Franco felt. His own education had been carefully supervised by Zia Margherita and his father. What they had not told him he had got, in distorted versions, from certain boys at school. To Aurelio it was an exciting new world that was unfolding, and a highly secretive one.

Pia, six years distant from the cudgels of Nimpha, felt no sense of secretiveness. And because ideals are the outgrowth of words, such words as had never been whispered to Pia, she had no sense of a faith to be kept with Leone. She had no philosophy with which to sort out her feelings and only knew that something within compelled her, and that there were no beatings in Donna Lucia's house. And she knew no shame, for this was the way she was.

Aurelio followed Pia with his eyes, at first. Then he commenced to wait for her in the halls and to whisper to her, or touch her, as they passed. Pia would giggle, and sometimes she would run from him.

Then, because the moment must come between them, it came. They were on the terrace and Aurelio's ever-inquisitive eyes were washing Pia with a look that fitted her body, flowing into places no normal look could have penetrated. Seeing this, Pia instinctively arched her back. Her breasts were pushed forward so that, while they were big enough, they looked bigger. Then, with a giggle, she collapsed and this brought her hips forward with a jerk. Aurelio said:

"Madonna, you've got a front like a wet-nurse."

Pia slapped at him, and her hand was hard.

"Shut up, you dirty pig," she said, but her green eyes were interested.

In his pocket, Aurelio felt a coin. Suddenly, he laughed and pulled it out and tossed it at Pia, so that it struck her throat and fell down between her breasts and, almost instantly, it clicked on the pavement and rolled away.

Aurelio opened his eyes wide. "Madonna!" he exclaimed. "Don't you wear any underclothes?"

Clara scrambled for the coin, and Aurelio looked off towards the beach. He said, casually:

"Let's go for a walk."

Far along the beach, where the cliffs rise to throw shadows on the bay, Clara dug her castles in the sand. She tunneled her castles and allowed them to collapse. She built up others and poked windows in them herself, while in the shadows Pia and Aurelio looked upon the face of nature.

They walked home slowly. From time to time, Aurelio smoothed his hair. He never once glanced at Pia but, for all his small size, he looked out over the world as from a great height and Pia was, for some reason, the smallest of the small things about him.

On the terrace, they found Gian Franco. Gian Franco was tall for his age, and slender. Lucy sometimes laughed at him and said that he was knobbly-jointed, for his feet and his hands and his knees were big, with the joints protruding and supple. Now he said sullenly:

"Where've you been?"

"Oh, places!" Aurelio sat down on the balustrade, still managing to strut.

Pia giggled. Clara crawled on her hands and knees in pursuit of a beetle. Franco's eyes were dark and unhappy. He didn't say anything, and presently Aurelio said, with a smirk:

"Why don't you take Pia for a walk; there's time before dinner."

Franco looked from one to the other, at Pia first, then at Aurelio, and then his eye fell upon his sister, whose dress had taken advantage of her position to fall over her head, and whose pants were sandy.

"I suppose you had her with you," he said, and the blood commenced to burn in his face. Aurelio shrugged and Franco turned suddenly to Pia and said, "Get her and go into the house."

Pia said, "What?" dully, and didn't move.

"You heard me." His voice cracked, and if it stole from his dignity it added ferocity to his words. Pia moved back quickly and Aurelio slipped down from his perch. He said reasonably:

"Don't get so worked up, Franco. Clara's all right—she's too little to understand. And Pia's nothing but a peasant—you've got to begin some place. Why else do you suppose Zio Alessandro has her here? Papa says it's so you'll have someone to learn on—well, I've got to learn to—I——"

Franco hissed, "Blood of God, but you're rotten."

Aurelio shrugged, impatiently, "And you're a prude—that's what you get from having a mother who——"

He had no time to finish, for Gian Franco was on him, clipping him an inexpert smack which, though aimed at the jaw, landed on the side of the neck. If it had been expert, it could not have been more effective. Aurelio's arms flailed out and he reeled backwards, crashing across the balustrade. For a split second he seemed to balance there, his body jerking to re-establish itself. As Pia and Franco jumped to grab at him, he went over.

The terrace was twenty-five feet from the sand. At that, Aurelio might have escaped with a few broken bones, had he not fallen on his neck. He was dead before anyone could reach him. Pia and Gian Franco ran to him, taking the terrace steps two at a time. They found him with his head doubled under him. Pia's screams pierced the air, with scarcely a breath to separate them. Gian Franco turned away and was sick. Then the household arrived and Clara whimpered unhappily:

"What's 'Relio doing?"

18:

AT THE request of Prefetto Pontella, the family's position and their great grief, and the nature of the accident, were taken into consideration, and an informal inquest was held at Villa Falconierre.

Colonel Venesco, Colonel of the Carabiniere, came from Catanzaro with the Prefetto and took the head of the table, with the Questore, Colonel Tarde, at his right as head of the police, and the Prefetto, representing the King, at his left. Centurion Fornelli, Federal Secretary and head of the Fascio for the province, sat next to the Prefetto and next to him was Captain Ganno, the local Secretary of the Fascio. Two clerics took notes and Avvocato Tocci was there to represent the family. They sat about the dining-room table. Alessandro and Graziano, Lucy and Zia Margherita sitting opposite the officials, while Gian Franco and Pia stood between Alessandro's chair and Lucy's. They were in black, with the rest of the family, and their faces were pale with the subtle alabaster white that the olive-skinned have.

Colonel Vanesco was a man of girth, a man who knew good wines and good food, and who at once satisfied both his wife and his mistress, and knew that he did so. He was also a man who worked hard and gave great love to his work. The Carabiniere, who are picked men and who, in taking the oath of their office, swear not to stop even at the ruin of their own blood, their own child, should it fall foul of the law, were proud of him.

For once, the Colonel was not happy in his work.

"This," he announced, "is pure routine—we must ask questions. You understand?" His thin, gray mustache bristled as he pulled his lip in, and a dull red showed through the single layer of hair on his head.

"Come now, Gian Franco, tell us from the very beginning." The Colonel's sculptured and almost hairless lids were half lowered, but beneath them his eyes were kind. "What was this quarrel about?" he asked.

Gian Franco was silent, his shoulders stiff and straight, his eyes unwavering on the men before whom he stood.

The Prefetto spoke suddenly from his place beside the Colonel, and Lucy, hearing the undertone in his voice, was grateful to him. "We are friends here, Giovan Franco," he said. "I held you at your christening, Colonel Vanesco went to school with your father, and the Questore and the Federale and Captain Ganno have known you all your life. This is a serious inquest none-the-less, and you must answer when you are spoken to." He looked about him and the others nodded approvingly.

Gian Franco looked down at his hands now, but still he was silent.

Alessandro said sternly, "Speak, Giovan Franco."

Lucy said, "Franco, please."

The Avvocato said, "Come now, my boy!"

Alessandro, who was angry now, said, "I command you."

The Colonel and the Prefetto, the Questore and the Federale, Captain Ganno and the clerics all commenced talking. Above it all, Pia's voice could be heard. She yelled at them, stamping her foot, and her face was red. "Leave him alone. I will tell you."

"Ah!" They were silent. But now Franco turned on her.

"You shut up," he said between his teeth, and he would

have sounded fierce had there not been in his voice the struggle with tears.

"Well, *you* do, or *I* do," she said; but she said it in a whisper and she looked frightened and white again.

The tears settled back in Franco's throat and he swallowed. Pia meant it. Anyone could see that. Well—maybe it would be better if *he* told—there was no telling what *she* would say. Still, knowing that he could not help it, he did not want these people to know about Pia. He addressed himself to the Prefetto, saying:

"I was angry with Aurelio, Excellency, because of some unclean things that he said—but I did not mean—I hit him—I did not want him to fall. Please! I did not mean him to fall."

"Of course you didn't," the Prefetto said.

"What were these unclean things?" the Questore asked.

Gian Franco was white and his teeth clipped the words as he spoke, and it was as though he were chattering with cold, "He spoke of Pia—and of my mother——"

There was an uncomfortable silence and Zia Margherita hissed, "I don't believe it."

Aurelio's father stared dully. Gian Franco looked at the uniformed men at the other end of the table and said, his voice defiant:

"He said that Zio Graziano said that Papa had Pia for—for us——"

"Well?"

"He said that she was just a peasant—that's all she was good for—" his voice broke and the tears came spilling out of his eyes and he went on angrily—"he said that my mother had not brought me up right—and so I hit him."

Zia Margherita alone broke the silence.

"You are a wicked, wicked boy," she cried, and collapsed

back in her chair to weep into a large black-bordered handkerchief.

Colonel Vanesco was unexpectedly gentle. "Not a good boy, your cousin. Now, Giovan Franco—I understand you—but you have not been very explicit, and this is necessary for the records—" he hesitated and his eyes shifted to Pia. "Perhaps we can fix it this way—Pia, was Aurelio ever, er, unpleasant with you?"

Pia's eyes opened wide, and they were as clear as the bay in midsummer. "Aurelio was all right," she said.

The men in the room were watching her, and now Lucy commenced to watch. She saw the skin over the girl's cheekbones tighten involuntarily, pulling her beautiful eyes slightly, so that they were elongated and had a look of speculation. Zia Margherita sniffed. Centurion Fornelli shrugged and laughed suddenly.

"You might just as well ask her whether they co-habited—you wouldn't get a better answer, Colonel. The girl doesn't understand your language."

The Colonel's face cleared. "Of course," he said heartily. And he asked Pia in a way which she would understand.

Pia said, "Yes," and looked surprised. Her eyes remained clear of any guilt, and they hooded slightly as though with a thought that had come to her. The flick of black lashes cast a shadow, lending them greater depth.

The Prefetto sat back with a sigh. Centurion Fornelli laughed again. Lucy's eyes went from Franco, who looked as though he were physically ill, to Pia. She felt as though she were seeing the girl for the first time. Alessandro had been right, then!

The frail beauty of the hungry little urchin whom she had found in the mountains was gone; and Lucy had not even noted its passing. Pia was a peasant, stocky and mature. She was short, with the full curved hips that French and Italian postcard artists like to depict on some half-clad woman sprawling, amid lace and crushed roses, on a divan. Lucy saw that her waist was thick. As though it had happened overnight Pia was no longer lovely, and yet she was not ugly. Even in her thickness, there was something appealing. It was as though in her woman's body she hid a child. The child looked out through her eyes, through the quick, clean little gestures of her hands that were short, square-fingered and stubby. And in the same body she hid a dynamo. The dynamo radiated through her wide, friendly mouth and through the fullness of her body. Lucy looked again at Franco and her heart tightened within her.

Aurelio's father was saying, "You couldn't blame Aurelio." And he, too, was looking at Pia. He was looking with open speculation, as though Pia's feelings couldn't matter—if, indeed, she had any.

The Colonel shook his head disapprovingly.

"There is nothing further to be said—we will write this down as an accident. A most unhappy one. You have, all of you, my deep sympathy. However, I cannot let this matter drop without pointing out to those of you who are responsible for this tragedy just what your crimes have been." He eyed them all sternly, and then went on, his voice official. "Your son, Don Graziano, may, or may not, have been a naturally bad and degenerate youth. There is not any proof to help us. There is merely proof that he was extremely badly brought up——"

"Ah!" Zia Margherita sucked in her breath.

The Colonel went on firmly. "He not only took advantage of a servant in his uncle's house, but one who was a child and a dependent. And, according to his story, he did this at your instigation——"

Don Graziano cleared his throat hastily and cried, "No—indeed no—the boy misunderstood me—I may have said something in jest—I meant no such thing—it is preposterous."

"It was preposterous to jest about such a thing in front of a growing boy," the Colonel said and the men beside him nodded their heads in quick agreement. "It should have been more important to you that he learn the behavior becoming to an Italian gentleman than that he learn how to become a lover.

"And you, Don Alessandro," he turned quickly, "you too are responsible. You have a ward of the state in your care, and it cannot be said that you have given her sufficient protection."

Beside the Colonel, the Prefetto puffed out his cheeks and looked disturbed. "Upon my word, yes, Don Alessandro!" he said.

The Colonel gestured towards Pia. "I cannot understand you," he said. "One of your own people—you know them well enough!" He left it there, shrugging his shoulders and signalling to the clerics that the inquest was over.

Alessandro stood up. "You are right, gentlemen," he said. "Your Excellency," bowing towards the Prefetto, "I shall know how to arrange things. In future, Pia will be protected."

The death of Aurelio was accounted for. Now vermouth was brought, chairs were pushed back and officials became friends, men who had, some of them, grown up together, all of them hunted and played cards together, who knew the story of each other's lives, and knew from what blood each one had come. They talked of the piping of water to Sicily, of the possibility of war in the north. Lucy left them, barely touching her own vermouth to her lips before she shepherded the children and Zia Margherita out of the room.

The Zia was weeping with renewed grief and it was as though, with the Colonel's words, Aurelio had died all over again.

19:

THE ZIA'S mourning was a terrible thing to watch. For three days, while Aurelio's young body lay in the house, she sat stiffly on a hard-backed chair and received her friends. Lucy saw that it was a form which she demanded of her world, and of herself The woman who had always taken an hour and a half or two hours for dressing and had made the life of the maid who attended her miserable, who had been so precise and exacting in every well-arranged instant of her daily life, had changed overnight. It was still the Zia, but there was a sagging of the old manner. She would have no attendance, and she was in her chair at ten in the morning. You could not touch with a finger where she was changed; but it was there, a crease where there had never been a crease, a hair where there had never been a hair, a bleak face where there had been unrelenting asperity. Pity welled in Lucy for this woman, whom she still could not love.

Lucy and Alessandro and Graziano received with her. In the far bedroom, Franco knelt at the foot of his cousin's coffin, keeping vigil. No food was prepared in the house for a three-day period and the servants were required to keep the days' fast with the family. All day long the mourning went on. Guests and family and servants kept a running chant alive, the virtues and the beauties and the crushed hopes of Aurelio. Once Lucy got up abruptly, her handkerchief clutched to her mouth, and ran down the hall to her room. Alessandro found her, face down on the bed, choked with hysterical laughter.

He took her in his arms and let her laugh until the laughter turned to sobs. When she was still again, she pulled away from him and said,

"I am sorry—it's that terrible chanting. Do you listen to what they say, Alessandro?"

"No, you mustn't listen—empty your mind or think hard of something else, or count the beads of your rosary."

"How wonderful he was! How beautiful he was! How young! How beloved of God!" Lucy's voice was growing hysterical again. "Old Carmelita Meldrano kept singing, over and over again, 'Did you ever see him on horseback? Oh, he was so beautiful on horseback! Oh, how much better had he been thrown from a horse than to die the way he did!'"

Alessandro shook her suddenly.

"Stop it," he commanded.

"I'm sorry," she said, quiet again. And then she whispered, "But he was never even on a horse—are they crazy?"

"It's just the old custom. Go to bed now, I will make excuses for you."

"No, I'm all right now." And she went back to the living-room with him.

During the daytime no food was eaten, but when the visitors had gone the boxes and baskets which they had left were opened and laid out in the dining-room and first the members of the family and then the servants came and helped themselves. The Zia dried her eyes and sat down to a complete meal. Lucy turned away from the table, nauseated, and went to bed.

The Zia mourned her great-nephew and the house was hers;

and she mourned in the way of her people. But Lucy thought that it was terrible. She would not have had such mourning in her house, but she was helpless to prevent it. She lay on the bed, with her eyes closed, and felt alone and frightened. For a moment, that afternoon, she had felt close to Alessandro again; he had been tender with her. The feeling was gone now, for she saw that he belonged to all of this; if it was not his choice in behavior, still it was in his blood; he understood it. She alone, of all these people, could not understand. She alone, of all these people, was alone. She thought of her mother. She thought that she would like to go home. Then, with a sick feeling, she wondered whether she could. She got up from the bed and turned on the light. The rest of the house was dark. They would sleep heavily after such a repast, such an orgy of nerves. There would be candles in Aurelio's room. Franco had been sent to bed and Alessandro was keeping vigil.

Throughout the entire house there was the smell of the strangeness that was with them. It was a cold smell, a smell that evaded the immediate olfactory sense to fasten upon the nostrils of the soul. Lucy wondered whether it was in fact unreal, or merely something to do with the undertaker's work. She went down the hall to the door of Aurelio's room and stood looking in for a moment. Alessandro and the two nuns knelt in prayer, and they did not move to look at her. Lucy stepped across the threshold. Aurelio lay banked by flowers. The undertaker had touched his face with color and between each finger, clasped piously across his chest, was a miniature porcelain flower. As she looked down at him, she knew a feeling of sacrilege. They had done this to him in life, and were not satisfied, but must follow him in death with the superficial and the unreal, making a travesty of a young soul. Suddenly her dislike for Aurelio was gone, leaving in its place a great pity and a great contempt: pity for the child who had started life no differently from Gian Franco, contempt for the adults about him who had given him so false a perspective. And Lucy wondered whether she too were not at fault. She had been satisfied with disliking him, with condemning him—a child. Never once had she tried to help him.

There was a movement behind her. Two nuns came in, their heads bowed. They went to the foot of the coffin and waited until the first nuns had finished their prayers and crossed themselves. Then they lit fresh candles and took the places of the first nuns, who went out of the room without looking at Lucy or giving so much as a glance at the child who was dead. Lucy clasped her hands convulsively and her black eyes looked tormented with the feeling of guilt that had come to her. She was not praying, she was thinking, 'Prayer won't do it; one has got to be better—one has got to remember this.'

In a way, she did remember. The feeling could not always be there. Aurelio was buried and the mind busied itself with forgetting, but somewhere, deep inside her, there was a sadness and the memory of her own words. And the words mattered long after Aurelio had ceased to matter.

When the funeral was over, Zia Margherita and Graziano went back to Rome. Lucy had every shutter flung open, every door and window wide, and let the soft salt breeze from the bay play through her house as though to cleanse it of the last remnant of death. Then she went to Alessandro and said as kindly as she could, but firmly:

"We shall have to decide about Pia now. We'll have to send her back to Nimpha."

They stood near the entrance to the living-room. Alessandro had his brief-case in his hand, for he had just come in from the office. He nodded and led her across the room where the gaily-flowered curtains billowed in the breeze and the sun lay on the marble floor in precise rectangles. In his study, he put his papers away and then he joined her on the small, stiff sofa and took her hands in his.

"I know how you feel, Lucia, but you cannot send Pia away."

Lucy drew back and her eyes hardened. Within her mind she was remembering, 'You mustn't condemn, you mustn't condemn.' She said carefully,

"I am not blaming her, Alessandro—perhaps it was my fault. But she is dangerous—for the children—surely we can provide for her—we needn't just send her back without any-thing——"

Alessandro shook his head. "It's not that. Pia is a respon-sibility that we took on voluntarily. She is a child, and bonded to us—she cannot leave us, no more can we desert her. Besides," he took a cigarette now and lit it, "she is no different than when we took her—she is a peasant—the time has come for her to mature, that is all. Now she will have to be watched."

"Watched!"

"Of course. She will not be permitted out of the house alone, and at night she will be locked in her room."

Lucy looked at him in horror. "You can't mean it, Alessan-dro—why, it's—it's degrading. For us and for Pia too— We can't have any one in the house whom we have to lock up——"

Lucy thought automatically of her mother—how horrified she would be—how horrified anyone in Genesee would be!

Alessandro shrugged. "What do you suggest?"

"I suggest that we send her away." Lucy looked at him, reading his expression and knowing that she could not move him. "Well," she said at last, "I'll try talking to her."

"Certainly, I think you ought to. But her room will have to be locked at night, just the same."

"No——"

"Yes——" Alessandro frowned at her now. "In her normal environment Pia would be living so closely with others that she would not be able to get away with anything. If she tried, she would have a father with a heavy staff to see to it that she did not succeed. Here, Pia is virtually unprotected. Don't think for a minute that now that she has commenced to grow up she will have learned her lesson and end the thing. Aurelio was handy—the next time it will be the garbage man——"

Lucy said, "There is something else, Sandi—something which you have not taken into consideration."

"Gian Franco."

"You know?"

"But, of course," Alessandro smiled. "He came to inform me very seriously that he intended, one day, to marry Pia."

"And you still can keep her here?"

"Ah, now, my dear, you are being ridiculous. Even if he were not a baby, there would be nothing to worry about. He cannot marry without consent until he is twenty-one. By that time, you may be sure that if he has not outgrown any puppy feelings which he now has for our little peasant—tradition will take care of the rest——"

"You count a great deal on tradition."

"He will not marry a peasant. And I am not going to worry myself about this further. You have filled the boy's head with notions about freedom and equality, and like Ulysses you have to combat the seed you have sown. But you will see, Lucy; it is not so difficult. Even in your country, these nice things you talk of are only words. Look, you discover it yourself now because you don't think Pia good enough for

Gian Franco. In time, Gian Franco will make his own discoveries——"

"And in the meantime?"

"In the meantime, Gian Franco will go away to school and we will watch Pia."

"Oh, no, Alessandro—please—it's too early for him to go away—and not good at this time. You forget, it is a terrible thing for him—all of this——" Lucy gestured vaguely, "he needs his home."

"He needs discipline more. He is a good boy, Lucy; I am not doing this to punish him—an accident has happened and this has nothing to do with it. But it has shown me that Gian Franco is growing up, a fact which I had failed to notice. He needs school now and the discipline that other boys are having. It is not a reflection——"

"But it is. That's just what it is, whether you mean it that way or not."

"Well, then, that cannot be helped."

Lucy stood up. She couldn't answer now. She would wait until her mind was quite cold and clear.

She did speak of it again, and again, and again, coming back to it each time incredulous that Alessandro would not see how right she was, how important this thing was for all of them, but particularly for Gian Franco. As with the visit to America, she came up against a solid front. Alessandro was all that was courteous, considerate and patient—he had infinite time to listen to her. But he could not be swerved one iota from his path. With her new anxiety, Lucy forgot Pia.

20: *W*HEN IT came, war in the north was, after all, not so impersonal a thing. Mussolini, who had been the great leader, who had shown Hitler the way, proudly, as a master a disciple, had become, in some obscure manner, tied to his pupil's chariot wheel. If the world at large understood what had happened, such people as the Cavalierres, who made up the unofficial world in Italy, did not. Il Duce had something up his sleeve, undoubtedly it would all work out satisfactorily. In the meantime, they eyed with a strange combination of fear and contempt the big blond men who had commenced their infiltration of the country. There was a stillness over Rome, for all of the official bustle. It was the stillness of knowing that you were headed for calamity, without knowing from which side it was coming, or why. They could only pin their faith blindly, and wait.

Lucy found that she was, after all, not sorry to have Gian Franco at school. Something which had been growing in her home for a long time had commenced to take shape. Between herself and Alessandro the coldness which was as old as their quarrel about Captain Nero grew with their difference over Pia and Franco. On their return to Rome, Lucy had Alessandro moved to the guest room and, having done it, was immediately sorry. In some indefinable way, she knew that by so doing she had put him out of her life. She had done what no Italian woman would conceive of doing, no matter what the provocation. Alessandro would not easily forget. She wondered a little whether he would take a mistress now. Except for the one time when he had left her in such anger, Lucy was sure that he had been undividedly hers. Surprisingly, since she had made the move for independence, she was unhappy at the thought.

Alessandro was called for service with his regiment, and Lucy threw herself into Red-Cross work, so that when they met at home they were both tired and both willing to escape in formality from a situation which neither of them knew how to work out.

In the kitchen, there were changes too. For now the men were called up. Cesare was warlike and eager; Miss Tooley had left him with a bitter taste in his mouth as regards the English. For Gerolamo, it was another thing. He shrugged and went, but not without announcing to the staff at large that nothing good could be expected of the future.

"The Germans," he said, standing with his hands in a rabbit-like pose over his stomach—"the Germans eat raw meat. It is a fact which I have from a cousin who is butler to the German Consul General."

Maria looked properly horrified. "God!" she exclaimed. "What barbarians!"

Fortunata said, "I heard it too. They say that the Duce has stomach ulcers from eating with them too often."

Gerolamo scowled and said, "You talk too much." And then he bid them each a formal goodbye and was gone. Fortunata said:

"Who do you suppose will wait on the table now?"

Maria shrugged. "You and Pia, certainly not me. I have my work cut out as it is."

Fortunata grinned. "You watch. Donna Lucia won't let Pia."

"And why, I am asking you?"

"For no better reason than the way the men guests look at her."

"I don't see what they see."

"Some nice fat handles." Fortunata laughed coarsely.

Maria looked sour and the corners of her mouth tightened. She slapped a sheet of pasta down upon the marble-top table and commenced to spread a layer of meat for ravioli.

"I shouldn't think that she would want that little witch anywheres in the house."

"Oh, I don't think that she's really a witch. She's a good enough girl and not afraid of work."

Maria laid down another layer of pasta and began to cut out little triangles, pinching the upper and lower layer of pasta together as she did so. "How do you suppose she gets out of her room at night, if she's not a witch?"

Fortunata looked surprised. "You don't say!" she exclaimed.

"I do say! I met her coming up the stairs at six o'clock this morning—before I had opened her door."

"Accidenti! What a little cat!" Fortunata laughed again. "It's a good thing she doesn't have a father; he would have the skin off her and pin it to the wall."

"She's got a father all right," Maria said, with a significant hiss, "but his kind don't make any objection—how do you expect she got out?"

"Did she tell you?"

"On a broom-stick!" Maria hastened to cross herself.

Fortunata said, "I don't believe it—will you tell Donna Lucia?"

"Certainly. Now maybe she will believe me and get rid of

the little piece of bad luck. Everything's been wrong since that girl came. Look, then," she pressed a triangle viciously, "Aurelio gets killed, Gian Franco goes off to school, Donna Lucia and Don Alessandro aren't sleeping together anymore—and now Cesare and Gerolamo are going to be soldiers—and all of the time that devil's spawn just gets fatter and witchier every day and spends her nights God knows doing what!"

Fortunata had to admit that it looked bad.

While they were talking, Pia was with Clara in the garden. She made her a crown of white chrysanthemums to set on her black curls, and she called her queen of the sprites.

"If you leave your crown in the middle of the grass overnight, Your Majesty," she said, bending low before the child, "tomorrow very likely there'll be a magic mushroom in the center of it, pushed up by the fairies."

Clara clapped her hands and cried, "Let's hurry and have night."

Though she was fourteen, Pia was not permitted to take Clara out of the garden. Well, it was a nice garden, if not particularly exciting. Pia knew it well. At the far end, beyond a clump of bushes, there was a small wrought-iron gate. It was locked but, after all, one could see through it, and seeing into the street could sometimes be as exciting as being in the street. There was always something different. Today, there was a bersagliere sitting on the curb, with his bicycle propped beside him. It was a warm day for fall and he was mopping his face with what looked like a dirty rag. Pia called solicitously,

"That's the dirtiest handkerchief I've ever seen."

The soldier turned around and looked at her crossly. "What's it matter to you?" he snapped. Then, having looked at her, he looked again. Pia giggled. The soldier took in the wall and looked down the street to the front of the house.

"You live here?" he asked. Pia nodded mutely. The soldier eyed her as carefully, as speculatively, as he had eyed the wall and the house. "Well," he said at last, "you're a swell hunk of a doll—and now go home, I'm resting."

Pia said, "Oh, I haven't anything to do."

The soldier got up and sauntered over, to lean on the gate. He was tall, with a red face and a thin body. Pia thought that he had the biggest mouth she had ever seen. It was bigger than Fortunata's, and she told him so. The soldier leaned close to the bars and grinned at her.

"I've got something else that's even bigger," and he grabbed through the bars at her. Pia ducked quickly. At a safe distance, she stormed:

"You dirty pig!" Her eyes flashed in the sunlight, and she dared him to speak to her again.

The soldier shrugged. In a moment, he turned away and picked up his bicycle. As he prepared to mount, Pia came back to the gate.

"Don't go," she called a little wistfully.

The soldier scowled at her. "You're no company," he said, and added, "for a man."

Pia said, "It's lonesome here. Stay a little while."

"And be called names? No, thank you."

"I'm sorry." Pia clung to the bars, looking as though she really were. "But you *were* a pig," she added——

The soldier dropped the bicycle back to the curb and stretched out his hand. "Well," he said, ignoring her last words, "we'll shake on it." Pia put out her hand. The soldier took it, then he pulled her suddenly and hard against the bars, so that she cried out with the pain. Before she could speak, his mouth was on hers, sucking her lips apart, his thick strong tongue pushing between her teeth. Pia had never been kissed

by a full-grown man before. When he finished, she stood looking at him dully; the fire that ran in her blood almost blinded
her, and her hips were weighted so that she could not move.
The soldier said,

"There seem to be a lot of bushes over there——"

Pia nodded and the soldier came over the wall.

Clara, who had been collecting pebbles under the bushes,
made way for them, but after a while she got bored and
wandered off.

The next day, Alessandro returned to find Lucy white with
rage. Pia was confined to her room on a diet of bread and
water.

What Lucy could not understand was that Pia could not
understand! Alessandro went through the kitchen and up the
backstairs. Maria and Fortunata looked at each other significantly. They waited until they heard his boots commence the
second flight before they made any comment, then Fortunata
said:

"She's in for it this time, poor little one."

Maria shook her head glumly. "Not likely. She's got a
charm against trouble, that one—except for other people."

On the third floor, Pia was not thinking of charms. Faced
with Don Alessandro, she was trying to think of words. Her
eyes were rimmed with red, and her hair had not been brushed.
She had not changed her dress since the day before, and it
was soiled and rumpled. She was thinking desperately of
Leone, as she always did when she was unhappy, wishing that
he would hurry up and get back from America and take
her away. For the beautiful Donna Lucia had gone mad and
did not love her any more, and here was Don Alessandro
ready to do Heaven only knew what to her. What words

she may have thought of, Pia could not bring herself to utter.

Alessandro did not spare her. He said:

"Pia, you have turned into a very sinful girl. You have disobeyed God, and you have disobeyed Donna Lucia and me." He stood with his hands behind his back. He scowled down at her, and Pia knew the half-formulated thought that a visitation from God would not be quite so terrifying. She whimpered a little.

"Also, you have put yourself in great danger. This thing that you find so easy to do could give you a baby." He watched her closely. Pia smiled now, tremulously, as though the idea was not unpleasant to her. Alessandro went on quickly and his voice was deep and earnest, "It could also give you a very horrible disease."

Pia looked at him dubiously.

"Would you like to have your hair fall out? and your teeth? and have your skin turn black with blotches?" He elaborated and Pia commenced to turn white. "Furthermore— it is a criminal offense for any man whatsoever to do this thing with you—if I had been here yesterday, instead of Donna Lucia, your soldier would have been in prison."

While he was talking, Lucy had appeared in the door, and now she said,

"Look at her face, Alessandro. She doesn't understand."

"Well, Pia?"

"Well—" Pia looked down at her feet, she wished that Donna Lucia were not there. It made her sad all over to have her look like that.

"What is it——?"

"Well, oh, everybody else does—" perhaps if she explained it, Donna Lucia would stop being mad.

Lucy's face darkened and Alessandro said quickly,

"When people are married it is different—this thing is for marriage, Pia. When you are older, you will marry and then you will understand."

There was Fortunata and Cato, and there had been Signora Odilia. But Pia could not think of how to say it. She stole a secret look at Lucy and thought that perhaps being a lady and a gentleman made a difference. She remembered that Lucy had said once that she, Pia, could be a lady too. Remembering this, her face cleared. That explained everything—they wanted her to be a lady. Lucy saw the look and misunderstood it. Alessandro looked pleased.

"Well, now," he said heartily, "just be a good girl and everything's going to be all right."

"Yes, Pia—but, until I am sure you are going to be good and stay good, Clara will have to have another nurse."

They went out of the room, leaving Pia to burst into tears, not quietly but loudly, wailing about her misery, so that her words followed them downstairs:

"Poor little Clara, she needs her Pia," the girl wept, and "Pia wants her little saint, her little heavenly baby of the blessed virgin." Lucy laughed, a little uncomfortably, and said,

"All that devotion isn't good for Clara anyway—and I certainly can't have her exposed to another experience like that. Oh, Sandi—send Pia away and have done with it." She turned to him impulsively and Alessandro took her hand. His black eyes searched hers, softening as they did so, and at the same time begging her to understand.

"It's not possible—come, my dear, you must understand."

Lucy pulled her hand away and went on down the stairs without looking at him again.

21:

*L*UCY TOOK off her small cap and went to lie on the chaise-longue. It was six and she was just back from the hospital. Alessandro would not be in for two or three hours, if he came in for dinner at all. At home, in America, they ate at six, or at seven o'clock, at the latest. Lucy thought of how hungry she used to get, when she was first married, and how impatient that people always seemed to choose this hour to call. Somewhere in the house, Pia was singing: "Bimba t'amo tanto da morir."

It was a lovely voice, as simple and clear as her mountain pipes. But song and voice were unhappy, and Lucy was sorry.

Alessandro came early, as she lay there. She heard him in his room and called to him. When he came, she was shy and did not know what to say:

"I think I was lonely," she confessed, "I was glad to hear you."

Alessandro was tired. In the past months, his brows had seemed to grow in one straight line. Now, his face cleared for an instant. Lucy made room for him and he sat down beside her.

"I've been listening to Pia," she said. "It's strange that she can have such an exquisite sense of music and—oh, other things. The fairy stories she tells Clara, the way she arranges flowers, the way she talks of her Leone—and yet she's such a little beast."

Alessandro shook his head. "That is where you fail to understand Pia. If anything, she is purer than you or I."

Lucy stiffened. "You've no right to say that to me—I hope —about either of us."

He went on as though he had not heard her. "Because she is simpler. Her biological directness is the outcome of experience. You've never seen the things that she has seen, neither have I. The things that she has seen she has had to arrange in her mind by herself; she has had no one to direct her thoughts, to suggest at ideals. So she has taken the simple way. You and I, without the same knowledge, have been shackled and chained and hemmed in on every side with another kind of knowledge which has come to us second-hand through generations of talking and thinking and writing, through religion and ritual. We've learned to say, 'This is right,' and 'This is wrong.' But we are a complex pattern of too much second-hand knowledge and, within ourselves, we are not sure."

Lucy said, half wistfully, "It sounds logical—but words always sound more logical than the facts—and the facts are that Pia is bad. Oh, you were so right, in the beginning. I think of that often, that it is my fault that she is here at all."

The long black line was back and Alessandro looked tired again. Lucy said:

"No, I'm not asking you again to have her leave. I know you that well at least, to know when it is useless."

"If, only you wouldn't—" he started, and then he got up, shrugging.

"If only I wouldn't what?"

"Be so sure that you are right——"

Lucy looked at him angrily now. "I'm not alone in that, you know."

When he had gone, she was sorry and she thought unhappily that every time they approached friendship it ended this way. She thought bitterly that it was, a good deal of it, her own fault. But knowing it did no good; for when the moment came again it would be the same; something within drove her to feel as she did.

There was nothing that she could do but to meet each day as it came. As though to expiate a sin, she threw all her energies into her Red-Cross work and was glad to be tired out at the end of each day.

She went early in the morning; she came home for a light lunch, and went back to work until late in the afternoon. If her household was not neglected it was because the habits of many years were too deeply ingrained to be easily disrupted. Maria continued to cook food that was the envy of Lucy's friends, and to steal perhaps a little more, now that the larder was not so carefully watched. Fortunata and Pia and Emilia, Clara's new nurse, kept the house as clean as ever. The laundry and dry cleaning and general care of the wardrobe were in the hands of a great mountain of a woman who, contrary to all the laws of probability, went by the name of Bambolina or Little Doll. Little Doll was fat without being jovial. At one time she must have earned her name, but now her tip-tilted nose, her small eyes and rose-bud mouth were embedded in flesh, while her chin was marked by a deep dimple, kept immovably in place by a second chin so vast that one wondered that she could lower her jaw to let out words or to take in food. As a matter of fact, she both talked and ate sparingly and worked as energetically as though she had been mere skin and bones.

In the kitchen, the talk continued. They talked about food and work, and sometimes about Mussolini and the war, but largely their talk was about personalities and about biology as they knew it. Their own biology was simple. They had their sense of humor and they laughed loudly at a joke or a prank, but sex made them giggle. From Maria, who was sour and desiccated, to Pia, whose green eyes hooded readily, they were frank and they were practical, and yet they giggled. Even the austere Little Doll, who could not be coaxed into good humor on any other account, was ready to break into a surprisingly high-pitched giggle at the mere mention of her "man." The subject that interested them even more than their own biology was the mysterious situation that existed between their master and mistress. If the servants of Casa Cavalierre were practical, they were also highly romantic and had boasted for many years that their master and mistress were great lovers. The word went around: The Signora Baronessa had taken a lover! They were not such fools as to believe in the Red Cross. The Signore—well, his regiment was very real to them, that was the occupation for a lord—still, he had time for, not one, but many mistresses.

Pia alone held out against them. The Signore—well, of course, you can't expect a man to sleep alone. But the Signora was not made like the rest of them—only look how she talked to Pia! Donna Lucia was a St. Agnes, a Santa Cecilia, a lamb of God. She was chaste—a state which Pia revered without envying.

Over and above the talk and the bickering, the work and the pilfering, there was the bitter rivalry between Pia and Emilia. Clara, who was homely, but had always had the charm and the gaiety that only a well loved baby can have, lost weight and became whiney with nerves. Emilia, though she was as red-cheeked and buxom as a new wet-nurse, had no temperament for children, nor any love or loyalty like Pia's. She had a suitor, who called for her and went with her when she took Clara for long walks in the Villa Borghese. If Clara was a nuisance, if she importuned too much, with her whiney:

"Let's go on, Emilia," or "Let's go home, Emilia," or "Let's run, let's skip," or "I want Pia," or if she came spying and sneaking into the bushes, when she had been told to sit still on the bench, then she got her ears boxed. Later, just before they went home, Emilia would hug her and pet her and bribe her with candy not to say anything. For Emilia went in fear that some day Don Alessandro or Donna Lucia would discover she had slapped the child. She never meant to, she was always taken unawares by her temper.

In November, Gian Franco came home for the All Saints' holiday. He whirled Pia off her feet, took Clara for a joyful series of piggy-back rides, and set the kitchen in an uproar with his demand for food and service and his fantastic descriptions of the starvings and beatings which he had received at school. By the time Don Alessandro came home, he was met by a sobbing mass of feminine indignation, begging him not to send the poor little saint back to that purgatory of a school. The poor little saint and Pia crowded behind the folding doors of the dining-room to watch through the cracks, holding their mouths hard to bottle up their laughter.

During his vacation, Franco put himself to work on Pia's long-neglected education. He lectured her by the hour, telling her about Plato and Aristotle and Socrates, telling her about the Greeks and their democracy and about modern democracy. He would end by saying:

"You see, Pia, all men are equal—and so are you and I."

And, later in the day, Pia would serve Gian Franco while he sat at the table, and she would clean his room and shine his boots. Easily, as a duck's back sheds water, she shed his talk. Pia took naturally what the day brought her, and in the future there was Leone. It was enough. Life was full of little dreams that were no farther off than tomorrow, and for Pia it was both vital and exciting. A chance to spy on Little Doll and her little man, or to do Emilia an evil turn, a smile coaxed from the Donna Lucia, a song heard across the garden wall, an afternoon stolen with Clara, or a glass of wine from Maria, all these kept Pia from thinking of the far-off times. One day Clara would be a young lady and married, the Donna Lucia and Don Alessandro would be happy again, and Leone would come for her and build her a fine cement house at San Giovanni Marino, and they would have lots of babies and a radio.

On the week-end of All Saints, while Gian Franco was still there, one long-forgotten dream came true—a letter from Leone. For Pia, a letter was an event. She had never received one before. Fortunata and Maria and Emilia dropped their work and gathered around. Even the Little Doll left her iron and waddled in to demand in a surly voice what had happened. The letter passed from hand to hand, each exclaiming as she touched it and turned it over not once or twice but many times. At last, Pia was prevailed upon to open it, only to find that none of them could read it. It was in American, no doubt.

They were impressed. American! That was something, now. They studied the letter carefully. The bold, big letters meant nothing to them, but they understood the enclosed slip of paper printed in more than one language, with words in Italian announcing it to be a money-order for thirty lira! Pia's eyes sparkled; Fortunata grinned her widest and her voice screamed above the din of the others:

"Well, now, and I never believed he'd do it—see, Pia!" She pointed to the signature and then to the money-order. "It's from Leone, it's the money for Maria's husband."

"For what!"

Pia stamped her foot. "There you go and spoil it. Now how can it be a surprise?"

Fortunata pursed her lips unhappily, so that her whole face crumpled together. She clasped her hands in a gesture of despair and cried, "Oh, che peccato, che peccato! Forgive me, Pia, I forgot——"

Maria and Emilia continued to wring their hands and cry: "What is it, what is it?" and "Are you crazy?"

In the kitchen, they never spoke in what the rest of the world considered normal voices. Sometimes they hissed for emphasis but, for the most part, they screamed, each trying to be heard above the noise that the others were making. Now Pia clasped the letter and tossed her head so that her thick braids bounced in the air. "You explain," she shouted angrily at Fortunata, "I'm going to find Gian Franco," and she twisted her hips as she ran from them so that her skirt flared insultingly. Let them carp, she was somebody now!

Gian Franco sat back until his chair balanced on two legs, his own spider-long legs bridging the distance between chair and nursery table. Equilibrium thus secured, he permitted himself an occasional rock.

"I'm translating literally, you understand," he said to Pia, who against all rules was cuddling Clara.

"Yes, yes, go on—you are slow as a tortoise."

"Well now, let me see," he pursed his lips. "He says, 'Dear Pia, I was gratified to receive your letter and to hear that you are well and happy. I think of you often and I hope you think of me. I am sending you this money to get something for yourself. Advertising for a husband, even for somebody else, is most un-American-like.' " Gian Franco paused to say, "He can't expect you to be American-like, now, can he? Or isn't he very clever?"

Pia snorted, "Go on."

"He then says, 'I am going to public school. I can learn Italian in my school if I want to. Can you learn English in your school? I hope so, for we will speak English together when we are married. Please give my obliging respects to the Barone and his family. I am your obedient servant, Leone Pontavecchio!'"

"Well!" Pia cried. "He's got very American, hasn't he?"

"Since when did you plan to marry this—er—emigrant?"

"'Emigrant'?" Pia giggled. "Well, I guess he is—only he's coming back. That's when we will marry." She hesitated, but the dream of the cement house was too precious to be shared even with Gian Franco. The cement house was Pia's retreat, and some instinctive fear told her that she would lose it if she shared it.

Gian Franco looked cross. Then he shrugged. His conception of democracy did not encompass his considering a peasant seriously as rival to Gian Franco Cavalierre.

Pia said, "I don't know what he wants to talk English for, in America."

Gian Franco laughed. "Because that's what the Americans talk. When they first went to America, they were so busy chopping down trees and killing savages they didn't have time to invent a language, so they copied the English."

"I don't believe you," Pia said disdainfully, and reached for her letter. But Gian Franco held it away from her. Suddenly, he grinned and, jumping clear of his chair, he bounded for the door. "Come and get it," he called over his shoulder.

Pia set Clara down carefully. "Devil take him," she screamed. "Pia will fix that boy!" And her braids flying, she whirled out of the room.

22: *M*RS. STOREY died in November of 1939 while the house still wore mourning for Aurelio. Lucy received the news numbly at first, not quite understanding it. For some time now, she had wanted to go home. For some time she had felt the need of the solid familiarity of her mother's house, with her mother busy about it as she had always been since Lucy could remember. Where she could be herself without apology, and understand the ways of the people about her without being assailed by constant doubts. Now it was too late.

Though she had not seen her in almost fifteen years, Lucy's mother had been as warmly real to her as though she had lived across the street. If the people about her became too hard to understand, she turned to her mother, and courage, if not understanding, grew out of the knowledge that her mother would have thought as she did. Most of her communion with her mother had been in her mind, in this way. For she had left her life out of her letters home, thinking that many of the things that troubled her would trouble her mother too, and that it would help neither of them to share this.

Now it was over. Where her mother had been, a vast unhappy emptiness stretched. She turned to Alessandro and said, her face still blank with the numbness:

"Sandi, I must go."

He said: "Of course; we'll see. I am sorry, my darling."

And his voice was deep and gentle and his arms went about her, protecting her.

But Lucy stiffened and the numbness commenced to run out of her, slowly and steadily as the sands from an hour-glass. He had said, "We'll see—" She thought, with a wave of unreasoning terror, 'He will try to stop me.' And suddenly she knew that her instinctive desire to go had been right. She had to go. Her mother could not have vanished like that— there would be something left, some fragment of the solidity to fall back on. People did die; you had to expect it. Your mother died; you grew up with the knowledge that she would. But nobody ever prepared you for the vanishing. People didn't prepare you, because it didn't happen to others.

Lucy pulled away from Alessandro and ran to her room where she closed the door and leaned against it. The tears were bitter in her eyes, burning them, and the sobs in her chest were solid things, choking her. She blamed herself for letting Alessandro stop her from going, before, when her mother was still alive, and she blamed Alessandro. If only she had been there! Her mother might have died, but she would not have lost her.

The next day, Zia Margherita called on Lucy. It was the first time that she had entered the house since Aurelio's death.

"I have not been well," she said, folding one black-gloved hand over the other

She made no gesture to remove her gloves and Lucy saw by this formality that the house, or she as mistress of the house, was not forgiven. She knew that Alessandro had seen his aunt. She thought that perhaps the Zia was glad of a foreigner in the house on whom to focus the blame.

Lucy said, dutifully, "I am sorry. What has been wrong?"

"Ah, I am not as young as you. I cannot recover from my sorrow so easily."

"Yes, I am sorry."

"And now you have lost your poor beloved mother. Well, it is a vale of tears indeed and we are born to suffer."

Lucy said, "Yes," searching her mind frantically for something to say, to pass the time of this visit, which by all the rules could not be short.

She said, "I shall have to go to America now."

The older woman's eyes were suddenly on her. "Have you spoken to Alessandro?" she asked.

"Yes, though we have not discussed details."

"Ah," the Zia smiled now to Lucy's surprise. "You must let me know in what way I can be of help. I will come and see to the house and the children for you."

"No!" Lucy said suddenly, loudly, and then she added, "I mean, I am taking the children with me, of course. After all, it is their grandmother—they are half American—they should see their mother's country."

The Zia stood up. Her black eyes snapped. "I will leave you," she said coldly, "you must have a lot to do."

"Oh no, please!"

But the Zia would not stay. She kissed Lucy formally on either cheek, her expression hard and unrelenting. When she had gone, Lucy rubbed the spots that she had touched, with either hand, as one scrubs away the faint touch of a cobweb.

It was early in the day. Alessandro wouldn't be home till night. She moved restlessly about the room. She wanted to have it out with him, she wanted the decision made. She made up her mind quickly. She would go down to the American Express and find out what boats sailed and when she could get passage. It would be good to know such solid facts. The mere knowledge was a bridge to her going.

She took a carriage just outside the house. As she rode slowly through the streets, she looked at them as though she were seeing them for the last time. In the Via Boncompagnie a company of bersagliere came running towards them. The carriage pulled to one side to let them pass. Lucy looked almost sorrowfully at each familiar detail about her, seeing how coldly the sun slid down the arms of the leafless trees that lined either side of the street, how quiet the houses were. It was a street of fine villas, the palaces of the nineteenth century. Their façades, always austere, were so still now that it was hard to imagine any normal stir of life behind them. The skeletons of mimosa trees leaned over the walls and the dead gray wood of wistaria was on everything. The bersagliere had scarcely passed when a troop of boy soldiers came sharply around the corner. When they had gone by, life was resumed on the frozen street. Men and women went their way; a bus roared into gear, expelling a cloud of noxious gas. Lucy's driver clucked and the old horse ambled on. The wooden wheels went smoothly on the tar road and the horse's hoofs clopped pleasantly. Presently, the clop became a sharp click as the carriage turned into a cobbled street leading to the Piazza di Spagna. The wheels rumbled now, and the carriage shook. A queue of school boys crossing the street held them up. They were dressed somberly in black, with black-visored caps. Lucy's eyes followed them. They were from San Anselmo, Franco's school. Franco was not with them, though if he had been he would have given no sign of having seen her. That was part of the school discipline. She watched them cross to the fountain in orderly file, then cross the far side of the piazza and turn into the via Condotti. There was a sameness about them that made them look right in a queue, a pale, thin, pinched sameness. It was a good school, known for its high scholarship but giving little thought to any place for athletics or to the value of fresh air and sunshine. Lucy thought that an outing along the narrow shadowy streets of Rome to spend their pocket money in a candy store could hardly come under the heading of fresh air and sunshine. And she was quickly glad that she was taking Franco away.

The American Express promised her a sailing within three weeks. They would have to fit her, and the children, in somewhere, and couldn't tell her yet on what ship it would be. Traffic was heavy with Americans going home. Lucy was satisfied to leave it that way. She had still to talk to Alessandro.

23: *W*HEN HE came into her room that afternoon, Lucy saw that Alessandro knew. His face was white and his eyes were cold.

"Zia Margherita sent for me," he said.

She got up from the dressing-table where she had been fixing her hair and went towards him.

"She talked to you about my going?"

"Of course, what did you expect?"

"But you knew! Why are you angry—why are you surprised?"

He unbuckled his sword now and flung it across the bed where his hat and gloves lay. He had come to her directly and he was in street uniform. "I did not count what you said in a moment of grief—I suppose that I did not believe you. And then, nothing was said about the children."

"I've wanted to go for a long time. I wonder if I can make you understand. I need to go home. I need to take the children. To get my bearings. To have familiar things and people and thoughts around me. And the children—it's partly not wanting to be without them—but mostly because I want them to see and understand what I came from, what is, after all, one part of their blood."

"This is your home, and theirs," Alessandro said stolidly. "Look, Lucia!" He reached out and took her hand and led her like a child to the window. "There are the familiar things."

In the garden beneath them was Clara's sand-box; a bright blue bucket and a large kitchen spoon lay half buried in the sand, awaiting another day. It was an old sand-box. Pia and Gian Franco had played there six years ago. Across the garden wall were the wide avenue and other villas. Beyond, ancient Rome, with its towers and domes, its palaces and slums swarmed about the greater dome of St. Peter's. The sun had newly dropped, leaving the city a deep blue or green where the darker shadows clung, as though the ravine-like streets were hung with moss. Where the sun had been, a bright halo crowned St. Peter's.

"You have lived almost as long here as you have lived in America," Alessandro said, "and you have the rest of your life to live here."

"No!" Lucy drew away. They stared at each other, conscious of the implication in her words. "Of course! I didn't mean that," she said quickly.

He let her go. For a moment, he stood looking out of the window, then he turned, without moving from the window, and said,

"You are married, Lucia. I wonder if you begin to realize what it means—no—don't interrupt, I want to talk to you. I should have done this long ago. Do you remember once, telling me that you were sometimes embarrassed because you came to me without any dot?"

Lucy nodded, frowning.

"You were not embarrassed with me, because we understood each other perfectly, but with the world. Because you felt that it was known, and that people here could not understand your father's attitude, and that they criticized him. Of course, they did. They granted that this is not the custom in your country; but you were marrying into a country where it is the custom. They argued that any man can afford some sort of a marriage portion for his daughter. He must be a niggardly man, as well as stubborn and unfeeling, to put the customs of his country before the possible discomfort, or even unhappiness, of his daughter."

"You never cared, Alessandro—why do you say this now——?"

"Because it is a concrete example of something which you have never learned. Why do you think the marriage settlement is the custom here? It is a symbol that the man and the woman who enter the state of marriage give, not equally perhaps, but everything that they are in possession of, towards the building of one home. Certainly they give equally in spirit. While in body the woman has the burden to bear, and the man in finance. A dot is rarely enough to support a home. Sometimes it is necessary towards establishing a home—sometimes it is merely the symbol. I am trying to tell you, Lucia, that marriage is a state of giving, entered into without reservations. If you would stop reserving yourself, you would not be so unhappy!"

Lucy looked past Alessandro at the darkening panes of glass. "Perhaps," she said a little wistfully, "we have both needed to do that."

"No." Alessandro's voice had grown gentler as he talked, now it was unrelenting. "If you will think this over, you must agree that I have done my share. If I have been wrong, it has been in going too far your way. Now that is all over."

As his voice hardened, Lucy looked at him squarely and now her own face hardened. "Yes," she said, "now it is all over."

"But not quite in the way you think."

"I am going." She shrugged. "If you won't give me the money, I can get it from the Consul, but I am going."

"You misunderstand me. If the knowledge that I want you to stay won't stop you, then I won't keep you from going. But the children stay here." And he went out of the room and left her alone by the window.

She turned back to the window and watched the yellow lights of the city come on, dimming the pale light of the sky. To leave the children was no little thing. Clara was so small still; she couldn't leave Clara. And Franco. He was older, he was more independent, he was away from home. Still, he was hers.

"No," she thought suddenly. "That's just what I'm afraid of—he's not quite mine, he never has been, nor Clara. None of this is mine, none of it is real to me."

And she thought that that was why she wanted to take the children; in America they would be hers. There was a decadence in the very air in Italy that was not good for growing children. In this way she excused her determination—it wasn't good for them! In Italy they shrugged at war, at falsehood and immorality, and said disdainfully, "You must be practical!" And Lucy thought that they were not so much practical as they were decadent.

When dinner was announced, she was still standing there. She sent a message that she had a headache. She went away from the window and lay down on the chaise-longue. In a moment, Fortunata was back.

"The Signore says he will wait," she said.

Lucy went, saying to herself, "He is right. I am being childish."

They talked through dinner. They talked of a new piece of

music and of a new material for dresses, made of a fine wood fiber, and of the rumors that rubber was to be planted in Calabria. But they talked without looking at each other. They had coffee in the study, and Lucy took hers standing and moving restlessly around the room. When she had finished, she set her cup down and went to her room, saying "goodnight" casually.

In her room, the bed was already turned down. She lay for a long time without sleeping. There was much in what Alessandro had said that was right and true. Still, however she looked at it, she needed to go home now. She was infinitely tired of the continual seeking to understand the things that went on about her, of seeking to translate them into terms of her own people, of continually comparing. In America, Pia would have been properly adopted and properly brought up, so that she could not have turned into such a little tart. If she had, she would have been sent away. In America, Aurelio would have been a nice little boy, and there wouldn't have been the accident. Gian Franco wouldn't have gone away to school until he was older. Alessandro would not have used her so callously. Oh, there would not have been gossiping, bickering servants, and gossiping, bickering friends, spying on one another and carrying tales. Presently, Lucy forgot what Alessandro had said, and only knew that she must go back to America, and as quickly as she could find passage.

To Alessandro, alone, she had given no thought. Yet it was Alessandro of whom she dreamed, an unhappy dream that made her sad and sorry, then slipped from her grasp as she awakened in the morning to find him standing by her bed.

He said, "I am glad that you are awake. I wanted to talk to you before I left."

He was in uniform, with his sword buckled at his side.

Lucy thought, 'He can't still be pale from last night—it must be that he has become pale and I had not noticed.' She thought of how strong and brown he had been and, surely, should be, with his work with the regiment. Suddenly she felt guilty, as though she were personally at fault.

"Of course," she said gently. "Let me ring for my breakfast and then we will talk."

He nodded and stood aside for her to go into the dressing-room. When she was settled in bed again, with her tray over her lap, her face and hands bathed, and her golden-brown hair brushed smooth and done up with a ribbon to keep it off her face, he pulled up a chair beside her and said:

"Lucia, I am doing something which you will find difficult to understand. I have thought the matter over carefully and I am making no mistake. I owe this to my family, to my children, and to my name. How you or I feel, personally, has no importance. The individual is not important in time—only the family——"

Lucy had not touched her food. She stared at her husband, a small devil of fear stirring deep in the nerves of her body. She said, "What are you talking about?" and her voice sounded quick and impatient in her own ears.

"Just this. I have written a note to Salucci to attend to financial matters for you, see to your passage and in every way make things easy for you. I did not tell you last night, but I am leaving with the Regiment for Piemonte today."

Lucy put her tray aside hastily. "You should have told me. I didn't know—I'll wait, of course."

"No, it's not necessary. I shall ask the Zia to come to stay while you are away."

"I don't understand—what it is that you are warning me about—what about the children——"

"That is it. The children stay. If you make any attempt to take this into your own hands, I shall have you stopped at the frontier."

She looked at him for a long minute and then she said helplessly, "I thought last night of going without them—but perhaps, after all, there's no need of my going——"

"No," he spoke gently now, "you are wrong, but you will never know until you have gone."

He took her hand and kissed it and went without saying any other good-bye. Lucy turned her head into her pillow and wept.

24:

*7*HE ZIA called again. The Zia's friends called, older men and women who had worn the Pope's black for so long that they had not known how to break mourning when the Pope, after fifty years, came out from his Vatican. Lucy's friends came and Alessandro's friends and brother officers.

Lucy served vermouth and thanked them for their sympathy.

—Yes, she would have to go to America now.

—Yes, there was the estate to be seen to.

—No, the children would not come—it was, after all, a hard trip, and times were bad—there were Gian Franco's school and Clara's lessons to be considered.

The older women eyed the vermouth, scandalized. Death was an occasion. It was the greatest occasion of life, and you met it accordingly. They understood that she must go to America. They were sympathetic with her bereavement. When they left, they shook their heads. Donna Lucia Cavalierre was a hard woman, and unfeeling. She had lost her mother and she did not weep. She did not speak of her mother, extolling her virtues, mourning her loss. She did serve refreshments. Even in a foreigner they felt that this was poor taste.

The younger women cared nothing for these things. They were not greatly sorry for Lucy, for they, like their elders, thought that she did not mourn. They were excited about the trip that she was about to take. Don Alessandro was letting her go alone. Of course, he was an officer, he could not go with her at such a time as this. Still, it was a long way; not many men would let their wives go such a distance from them. When the older people had stayed their time and gone, Lucy's friends and Alessandro's gathered around her and talked excitedly about the trip. America was a fabulous place, by all accounts. Some of them had been there and they too said that it was fabulous. They gave her commissions to carry out, they envied her. The men stood back a little, admiring her. But in their expression she read that they were puzzled too.

They left her tired and she went to see about her packing without great enthusiasm. She made lists of the things that she would need and went through her closets, throwing things that she should pack onto the bed. While she worked, her mind was free and she wondered if she were right to go. Perhaps if she gave up the struggle, if she threw all of herself, "without reservation," as Alessandro had said, into this life, into being Italian, she would find happiness for all of them. Perhaps in time she would win back Alessandro's love as it had been—before Captain Nero, before Aurelio and Pia— especially before Pia—and oh! before the Zia with her unrelenting demands that Lucy live thus and so, that she mourn this way and give birth this way, that she bring up her children so and listen to the advice of her elders. Lucy thought, 'She would have advised me on how to make love, had she known anything about it.' And she remembered, in fact, the Zia's words when she was newly married:

"You must eat oysters, Lucia; they are good for the bride. They aid towards conception."

Lucy shuddered. She couldn't become Italian. And yet she

loved an Italian. For, whatever their misunderstandings, their different ways, she knew that she loved Alessandro.

She dropped the things in her hand and went slowly to the window where they had stood the night before and in her heart she said the things she wished she had said then.

'I love you, I do love you, Sandi—but you won't let me. And I can't crawl back to you; you have to show that you want me. You have become so courteous and cold. A lot of it is my fault—I've never known how to say the right things at the right time. But you have never let me say I was sorry—you never seemed to care. Perhaps there is a way, and perhaps I shall find it—but you see I do have to go now.'

In her heart, his voice answered her and she heard him say again, 'You are married, Lucia. I wonder if you begin to realize what it means?'

Her shoulders sagged and she put her hands to her face. Would that be the only answer that he would have for her? 'He's an Italian,' she thought wildly, 'he can never understand me.'

That night a note came from him, written from the station. He said:

"I am afraid that I have made you unhappy and I am sorry. Though I have not been wrong and there is nothing that I can apologize for. I have tried for years, and I continue to try, to mix oil and water—the culture of my country, which is in my blood, and my love for you, which is in my blood. If it were any different, I should not let you go. But I find that I must have integrity from you, a duty to yourself which you must recognize by yourself and give freely if it is to have any meaning for either of us.

"Gian Franco will have to remain in school. But take Clara with you. Come back as soon as you can."

A small, exultant laugh sprang unbidden to her throat.

"I was right," she said, half aloud, "we shall find each other again this way." And she read his words over, her eyes lingering on the one sentence, "—and my love for you, which is in my blood."

The week before she was to have sailed, Gian Franco was sent home with measles. Lucy cancelled her passage and unpacked her smaller bags. Pia, who had been going around like a whipped puppy ever since the first bag was brought down from the attic, recovered as rapidly. Maria baked a cake *a l'Americano* which, as it contained no baking-powder, was flat and heavy. Fortunata walked all the way to Porto San Giovanni to buy fresh lavender to put with Lucy's silks. Only Zia Margherita showed her disapproval, saying:

"It could have happened after you had gone, Lucia. There is no point in changing all your plans like this. We will take good care of him." Her tone said, 'We do not need you—we do not even want you.'

Gian Franco's was a light case; but Lucy stayed as close to him as though he had been seriously ill. The moment he was up, she called the American Express to get her another passage. She was not at all sure that she still wanted to go, but some instinct urged her, and it no longer mattered whether she was right or wrong. She kept Franco at home until it was time for her to go. For, now that the moment had come, all her love for Alessandro welled up in her and found expression in her love for Franco, who caused no conflict in her and was hurt at her going. She ached for him and for herself. He was so young. He was so defenseless in his still untried ideals.

The day before she was to sail, they went for a walk. Lucy said,

"I've been thinking of some of the things we've talked about. The ideals of one race of people and the ways of another. I'm afraid that I've often tried to explain things to you which weren't plain to me. I was wrong, my darling. We have to work these things out as they come to us—and when they come to us. One day you will see how it is."

Franco took her arm and they walked down the avenue from their house to the Pariole, where they turned, going away from Rome. They went past the stadium and past the review grounds, over a wide stone bridge, where the Tiber was a muddy stream beneath them, and on into the Campagna. A half mile up a small dirt road, they turned into a field. At their right was a peasant's straw hut, with raw-hide at the windows. While above them, on the hill, was the Villa Madama, where Raffaelo had frescoed the walls, and the horse-stalls of whose stables were said to be inlaid with lapis lazuli. Behind the villa, on the crest of the hill, was a grove of cork trees. To this place Lucy and Franco climbed. They stopped at the edge of the grove to catch their breath. The trees were short, with slender trunks and branches that spread to meet and intertwine, making a neat ceiling overhead. Winter let the sunlight through to fall in a crazy pattern on the bare ground. In spring and summer the grove was a dark place, like a room shut away from the light.

From here, Rome was visible, not always below them, but rising on its own sovereign hills, whose final slopes spread toward other hills by the sea. To the north and south, its more modern roads and buildings ate like a great ripple into the heart of the Campagna. To the east, it was ancient and narrow again, straggling along the gaunt line of the aqueduct. The old melted into the new, and neither was so beautiful alone as they were together. Lucy's heart stirred within her;

this was a thing which she loved. She pulled off her hat and a cold breeze rushed up the hill to slap her hair across her face and then fling it wildly on high, a bright, brown spirit, desperate to escape the earth-bound head. Blood tingled in her cheeks, and her eyes felt hard and clear. Suddenly Lucy knew why, above and beyond her reason for bringing Franco here, she had come—what she had come to see. She said slowly:

"I wanted to show you something very simple, Franco. I thought I could illustrate it for you. Look down at the villa— and then——"

"At the hut?"

"Yes. What do they mean to you?"

"A rich man and a poor man."

"More than that, Franco. The Villa Madama means that the Italians are a highly developed civilization, born to create beauty. And the hut, with its raw-hide and straw and its dirt floor, means that Italians lack integrity and self-respect.

"When England was still a horde of barbarians, eating with their hands and thinking of nothing much more than the next fight and the next feed, Italy had her temples, her mosaics and intricate friezes, and especially her patriots and philosophers——"

Franco watched her, his expression puzzled. Lucy pointed to the villa first, and then to the hut—"In England—in all of England—you won't find another Villa Madama, but also you will not find such a hut, or any man whom you will dare call peasant. Always remember, Franco, that your blood comes from both sides. Be proud of both, and be the best of both."

The sun, for all its brilliance, lay softly on Rome, washing it with yellow and gray and shades of blue and green. Only the Victor Emmanuel monument gave back glitter for glitter, standing out like a gold tooth in an otherwise pleasant face. Even the glass in the city had a dark flash when the sun struck it, whether from age or dirt or the one ingrained with the other. Lucy said:

"This is why I have to go, Franco. I hope the day may come when you will understand. Whether you stay or go, this is important, that you understand."

Over the roofs of the villa and the hut she swept her arm toward Rome. "It is so beautiful," she said softly. "As beautiful as death."

"But, Mommi, you love it," he cried, puzzled at her voice.

"That has nothing to do with it."

"But that's important."

"No. Not even that. If you made a ship model, Franco, more beautiful than any you had ever made before, an exquisite, a perfect little model. Then, if Clara threw it on the floor and broke it—what would you do?"

"I should spank Clara!" Franco said, so indignantly that Lucy laughed.

"What would you do with the model? Would you leave it in the middle of the floor? Would you try to mend it? Or would you make a new one?"

"A new one, I think—it would no longer be perfect if it were patched up."

"Then you would leave it where it had fallen, and make a new one?"

"Mommi! Of course not—why should I leave it there?"

"Because this is what Italy has done—Italians, who were Romans, who were Etruscans and tribesmen before them. For three thousand years things which their great spirit of beauty gave them to create have been permitted to fall into ruins and to lie untouched in the center of a living city. Streets and buildings have gone around—sometimes over—but without so much as clearing the ground. This is decadence, Franco. It is unclean—the worm at the heart of something beautiful—and this and this alone will ruin Italy. Men with vigor and ideals do not permit their dead to lie in the streets in this way. London is almost as old as Rome—but there are no such ruins in London. The fallen places in England are out of the way—in the country, where they are out of the way of the living."

Franco's eyes were on the city. The breeze played with his hair, lending him a blue-black halo. He frowned uneasily. Lucy put her hand on his arm.

"They're just words, Franco. They'll always be 'just words' until they mean something to you."

"When will you come back?" he asked suddenly.

"Soon. This summer, or in the fall—it depends—" she said quickly, afraid that she had already said too much, that she had already threatened some security which was necessary for him to grow on. Partly for his sake and partly for her own she was afraid to let him see farther into her mind. When the time came, he would understand. Now, she could only talk of such things as fallen buildings—she couldn't explain. She couldn't tell him about the little things, the living things, that spelled decadence to her.

She couldn't tell him why the Princess Aristede wore a black chiffon handkerchief about her arm. That every time she was complimented by another man her husband took her home and twisted her arm so that the skin was burnt and torn. And it was said that, as she was a beautiful woman, the flesh had not had a chance to heal in fifteen years. She could not tell him that she herself had seen a friend of theirs lean over and burn his wife's hand with a hot cigarette, because she flirted casually. There were women who had been put into convents and others who had been locked in their homes. It was not only in their own class. The peasants beat their women and, even among the stolid bourgeoisie, there were such men as the little banker in Crotone, an established business man, respected by everyone. His wife was almost eighty and in sixty years nobody had seen her, except upon rare occasions the family doctor. The banker saw to the marketing himself, and when he left the house he locked the door and affixed a postage-stamp to the keyhole. Whether to make sure that no other key went in, or that no one tried to look in, Lucy had never been sure.

There were a thousand little stories. Lucy had seen and heard so many of them. But she couldn't explain to Franco.

He turned to her now and something within her hurt as though it had been physically bruised. He was as tall as a man, and in that instant he looked as though he wanted to cry. As she thought 'I cannot leave him—I won't!' she saw him grow up.

His face stiffened a little and then she was in his arms.

"Come back soon," he said, holding her tightly.

Their hair mingled like light and shade and the breeze played around them and the grove moved slightly, crackling like ancient bones.

"Oh, I will, darling, I will," Lucy whispered in his hair. And then, arm in arm, they went down the mountainside.

25:

ALESSANDRO knew when Lucy had gone even before he had word from her. He knew by the token that all men sense when they rap on the door that a house is empty. Loneliness invaded him. He would have stayed away from Rome, but in January he was called back, to be given, at the age of forty-two, a permanent post there, his regiment turned over to a younger man. It was not easy for him to go home. He thought of taking an apartment. Then he knew that he could not, for this would be to say to the world that Lucy was not coming back. So he went back to the house, and when he had done so, the habit of it fell on him like a dark cloak. And he gave no more thought to freeing himself from it.

Graziano had moved to Milan for his firm, and Zia Margherita came to the house to stay. Slowly the place that had been Lucy's became hers. Shutters that had been flung wide to sun and air were closed, "to keep the curtains from fading." Vases that had been full of flowers were empty, for flowers were an extravagance which Zia Margherita would not permit herself. And gradually the friends who had been Lucy's and Alessandro's went too; in their place were Zia Margherita's friends, Black Romans who frowned on the world and talked of Judgment Day.

Alessandro saw what was happening, and did not care. The changes within him matched the changes about him. He knew that it was not mere things that could make a difference, but only Lucy herself. As long as she had gone, let her be gone entirely. Something austere, which Lucy had always felt to be there in Alessandro, rose up and made him embrace his darkened home. He made no move to push back the shutters, he asked for no flowers, he received his aunt's guests as courteously as a prince the dignitaries of another land. If they bored him, he cultivated boredom as an antidote to his own unhappiness.

Morning melted to noon and noon to night, while the night itself was a chimera before the dawn. As a wheel that rolls, the cycle of days rolled on. At Easter, Gian Franco came home. Like his father, his discontent matched the house and he made no attempt to change it or to protest. For a day or so, he prowled about uneasily, watching his father, watching Zia Margherita. And then he gave it up and went out to the kitchen to find Pia.

Zia Margherita watched him, her thin lips closed to a tight line. She heard them running in the corridors overhead, she heard them rough-housing and tumbling about. She heard the long silences, that were not like the dark silences of her domain, but were contented silences, companionable and as real, by contrast, as any noise. She saw them start out on their frequent walks. Once, she sent Maria to follow them. Maria came back tired and disgusted and out of temper. They had spent an hour wandering through the zoo. There they had fed the seals with pieces of fish which she was sure they had stolen from her kitchen. They had gone out from the zoo, across the Villa Borghese, and had chased each other five times around the water-clock on the Pincio.

What they had done after that Maria didn't know, for she

had left them there and gone home, mumbling as she went that the Signora Zia was an ill-conditioned old woman and that she would do no further spying for her.

Zia Margherita listened to Maria's report in silence, then sent her back to her kitchen. She was not pleased with what she heard. She reasoned coldly, as Aurelio's father had, that Pia might have her uses. But friendship of this sort was not one of them.

The Zia was not unkind in intent. She loved all the members of her family and she considered that she had made every attempt to love Lucy, and to welcome her, as a stranger in her family as well as a stranger in her country. Zia Margherita had been ready to advise and to guide. But Lucy had not been willing to accept her offer of friendship and of welcome, so that what could have been love had grown back on itself. And how hard she had tried not to disapprove! The struggle was over now. Lucy was gone and Zia Margherita was free to pick up the pieces in her own way. She remade Lucy's home into what she felt a home should be. Alessandro was morbid just now, but there would be ways to cure him. Only Franco really disturbed her. Whenever she felt that she was about to touch him, he escaped to something that was his mother within him. If he would only explore, with Pia, those facets of nature which a boy facing manhood must, Pia would in time have played her part and be of no further use to him. But these races, these games! The communion that was born of such little things as stealing from Maria to feed the animals at the zoo! The hours spent playing checkers or reading aloud things which Pia could not be expected to understand! And, twice now, Franco had spent his pocket money and taken Pia to the opera. Afterwards, they had sung together the different arias; from the top floor to the ground floor their voices were all over

the house. This was something that frightened Zia Margherita. This was something that had to be handled.

While Franco was at home, she did nothing. It was after he had gone back to school that the solution, which was there of its own making, came to her. To close the shutters of the house was not by this simple act to shut Lucy out. So long as she was in Alessandro's mind, she was there; so long as she was in Franco's heart, it was her home and she would come back to it. And the Zia did not want her back.

She commenced to watch Alessandro and, as she did so, she noticed how Pia hovered over him when she waited on him at table, how solicitous she was, offering him more food than he ever wanted, and always a jump ahead of his wishes. Once, when he had gone to the telephone, leaving the two of them alone in the dining-room, the Zia had said, her voice low and soft:

"You are fond of your master, are you not, Pia?"

She had surprised the girl looking after him, her green eyes gentle. "Oh, yes." Pia said. "He is so sad, and I am so sorry."

The Zia looked at Pia speculatively.

As plainly as though a voice had spoken to her, Zia Margherita saw the answer to her problem. What Alessandro needed was another woman to free him from Lucy. What Franco needed, and quickly, was disillusionment. She believed that Franco was in danger of ruining his life. She did not blame Pia, as Lucy did, or disregard her, as Alessandro did, but she understood, as neither of them had, what Pia meant to Franco, what danger Franco was in. Now suddenly she saw that Pia was the tool that would accomplish her end. Once Alessandro was persuaded to accept another woman, any woman would do for him. And once he had taken Pia, Pia would not do for Franco.

It might not be easy, but it could, she thought, be done. One night, she had stood in the door of Franco's room. Pia and Franco were on the floor doing a puzzle and Pia was humming.

"Donna Lucia is like that," Pia had said suddenly. "Like the music in the opera, sometimes very sad, but mostly very laughing. Don Alessandro is like this—" and she had pressed both hands to her breasts, as though to keep the music inside, and had sung a resonant chant. "Like after the Mass," she said. "It's very sad but very strong."

Remembering the look in the girl's eyes, Zia Margherita thought, 'It won't be hard; she's half in love with him as it is.'

Zia Margherita set Pia to waiting on the table, to waiting on Alessandro. His morning coffee, his bath, his clothes, the nightcap that he took before retiring: every service by which he could reasonably be approached, Pia was assigned to. Over a long period of time Zia Margherita watched and talked, suggesting, but so subtly that when the words were spent on the air the suggestion might have been imagined.

Pia was neither sophisticated enough nor sufficiently educated to enable her to understand more than the simple fact of what was happening. Zia Margherita saw to it that these facts were plain to her. She said nothing at first, but laid her foundation. Then, when the cool dampness of spring had given way to the hot dampness of approaching summer and all of the fresh glory of mimosa and wistaria, that sprang like a myriad fountains in Rome, had withered to the same brown husk and fallen upon the June gardens and streets, when the spring semester was almost over and Franco was due to come home, Zia Margherita spoke to Pia:

"Your master is a vigorous man; he has been without his

wife for a long time now and he may be for a great deal longer, for she has business to do with her people in America. It is not a healthy thing for a man of such vigor to go for any length of time without a woman. I talk to you, Pia, as to a member of the family, for I am worried about your master and I know that you, too, must be, for you are under great obligation to him."

And Pia understood, as she was intended to understand. Pia's eyes grew dark and hooded, as they did when she thought of some soldier, or of the gardener's boy, or even of a stolen moment with Little Doll's "man." But she turned pale too; for she was more than a little afraid of Alessandro. The excitement of the things which Zia Margherita had so pointedly left unsaid mingled with her own fears and gave birth to something new, which grew in her, generating and regenerating within itself. Excitement became desire, and fear terror. She would offer herself to Don Alessandro, she would go to him in the night when she could not see him or he her. She wondered if he would be as other men. Here her terror took hold and she thought that he could not be, but, like a dark vampire, would suck the life out of her. No, she would not go to him. Sometimes she hid in her room, and sometimes, driven by some subtle word of Zia Margherita's, she went down to haunt his threshold only to flee in terror at the first sound of his approach.

Zia Margherita was exasperated, but afraid to show her displeasure. If Alessandro was alive to her suggestions he did not show it. And Pia had only become unmanageable and unpredictable. The night before Gian Franco was to return, Zia Margherita decided that she could wait no longer. When Alessandro had had his nightcap and Pia had gone to her room, when Fortunata had locked up the house and she and Maria had gone to their rooms, Zia Margherita went to find Pia. She went into her room without knocking and turned on the light abruptly. Pia slept heavily, her hair a tangled mass on her pillow, more silver than gold in the glare of the light, her body outlined beneath a rumpled sheet.

"Pia!" Zia Margherita shook her. Pia stirred uneasily, twisting her head as though to avoid some unpleasantness. "Pia," Zia Margherita touched the girl's shoulder again and then, with a swift and merciless gesture, she ripped the sheet from her body and Pia started up, her eyes blinking, a cry of fear in her throat. In the harsh light, her nakedness billowed. Zia Margherita eyed her with a look that said plainly, "It is obvious what you were intended for—" and the Zia's angular body seemed to grow an inch, as though distaste flattened into height what little breadth she had.

"Get up," she said. "The master has rung for you twice—he wants a pitcher of water. Go and take it to him." Her voice was like a whip, her eyes were cold and determined. Alessandro, who had not sent for water, would think that Pia had invented this as an excuse and, being a man, would not hesitate further. If Alessandro took her tonight, he would take her tomorrow night while Franco was here, and the next night, and the next. Alessandro would forget the need of Lucy, and Franco would see what, and what alone, Pia was good for.

Pia whimpered and tugged futilely at the sheet which the Zia still held. The Zia threw it at her scornfully and said again, "Get up."

Whether by her tone of voice, or by some look in her eye, the Zia stirred a memory deep in Pia, and the whimper died in her strangely, making a sound that was neither human nor animal. In her eyes an old, green fire sprang.

In the years since Pia had come to Casa Cavalierre she

had at times been punished for some wrong, she had been lectured and admonished, she had been locked in her room and known cold disapproval, but never before had she been looked upon as something bad, something which was even unclean. The skinny little waif of Nimpha knew the look. The hot, witch blood remembered and stirred in her, and was as pride is in other women, who have no such memories. She threw away the sheet and jumped out of bed, no longer ashamed.

"I will go," she said slowly, the words trembling with hate, and then she said, distinctly, mouthing each syllable, a word which sent the blood from the Zia's face, leaving it yellow and giving to the lines on her cheeks a withered look.

With, first, the front of her hard, thin hand, and then with the back, she struck Pia, not across the face, but flat across her breast, so that the girl cried out with pain. An angry red sprang up beneath the white skin, and from the soft dimple of a collar-bone to the brown circle of a nipple a deep welt followed the path of Zia Margherita's diamond ring.

"Now go— No, wait." Zia Margherita went out of the room. When she came back, she carried an old, red silk robe over her arm. "Put it on," she said, and something that was soft and malicious had crept into her voice.

Pia took it, recognizing it. It was an old one that Donna Lucia had put away in the wardrobe long ago. It was too long for Pia. She gathered it tight about her and held it up to keep it from trailing on the ground. The circular Chinese signs of good luck that were woven into the silk lay against her skin like seals.

She went, forgetting about the drink that she was to carry with her. She went into Don Alessandro's room without knocking, just opening the door and slipping into the darkness before her, then with a sharp click closing out the faint light of the hall. She knew why she had come, and now she forgot the Zia. The beautiful, strong, sad Don Alessandro needed her and she was faint with excitement. A soft rustle came from the canopied bed, and then all was still.

What fear or courage, what desire or half-sensed loyalty born of a wild and desperate moment had driven Pia to come here, deserted her entirely. She turned, clutching at the door. In her haste, she knocked the handle so that it clattered loudly. She cowered from the noise, and in that moment a light went up. Pia sobbed and turned again, quickly, as though she were afraid to be seen without seeing.

26:

*P*IA COULD neither speak nor move. However urgently she wished that she might drop dead upon the floor, she stood there at the height of health and consciousness. Then her eyes, which were wide with fear, began to absorb the picture of Don Alessandro, clad in a pair of green- and rose-striped pyjamas, sitting bolt upright in his bed. The fear subsided and a giggle bubbled nervously to her lips, only to die with a sob as he sprang out of bed and came menacingly towards her.

Although his pyjamas may at first have seemed to rob him of dignity, making him, for Pia, no different from other men, Alessandro was not a man to be thus leveled. Lean to the point of gauntness, he towered over Pia like a Savonarola, his aquiline face as haughty in his anger as the great monk's might have been. There is a dignity that no motley can mock. Confronted with it, Pia crouched, no longer seeing a man in pyjamas but rather a personification of anger which would reach out in a moment and destroy her completely.

"You rang, Signore!" Her own voice startled her with the suggestion that she had not thought to put into it.

Alessandro said nothing, and the way of his silence was terrible, even as the stillness of his body. For it was as though an icy will held back something that was ugly.

Pia had no words of her own to use at such a time. The men or boys with whom she had slept had not needed words. They had lain together without talk. The words of love or desire or need were not of their world. The agonized "to be or not to be" belonged to another stratum of mankind. Pia had no philosophy nor any instinct for words. But the words of others she had: the words of Zia Margherita, of Fortunata and, out of the past, the words of the Signora Odilia of Nimpha. The silence was like a vacuum about her and the great suck of it drew the words out in an unconscious torrent of meaning——

"I thought—the Signore is a man—the Signora Donna Lucia —well, a man of vigor cannot sleep alone—the Signore—the Signora—well, in Nimpha it was the custom—the Signore has many beautiful, fine ladies away from home—but if he wishes —maybe he wouldn't always feel like going out——"

What Pia said had neither beginning nor end. She only stopped when the disjointed words had run out. When she stopped, Don Alessandro slapped her across the mouth and the strength of the blow knocked her against the door. Her hands flew up, as though to ward off any further blow.

"Get back to your room," he said, his voice harsher because it was soft than if it had been loud with anger.

Pia turned quickly but, as she turned, the robe that she was no longer holding billowed, exposing the deep curve of her thigh. Silk and skin played at contrasting each other, and the one was fair as alabaster, while the other was bright and soft as if it had been spun by a magic hand, of human blood.

As though he saw her for the first time, Alessandro clutched her shoulder, spinning her towards him.

"Where did you get this robe?" he cried. Then, not waiting for an answer, he ripped the silk thing from her back and flung it to the floor behind him.

"You are vicious and bad," he stormed. ' You are without honesty or loyalty. Your mistress did what no one would have done for you—she gave you a home, she gave you people, she clothed you and fed you and gave you her love, until you yourself chose to destroy it—she gave you a decent life to look forward to, a profession and a dot, when you would have been the village prostitute, beaten and run out of town even by men who had been glad to make use of you."

While he talked, his eyes held hers and only when he had finished did they let her go, and his eyes then traveled downwards. Pia had developed as a woman without having grown greatly. She was short and her shoulders were small, but her breasts were big and, beneath them, from a small waist, her hips sprang, many inches wider than her shoulders. Her legs, below the knees, were disproportionately short, not heavy, but shapeless, with no diminishing of size at the ankle, and her thigh and her legs were covered with a thick, golden down.

"So you are now trying to repay your mistress!" he said coldly; his eyes sought hers again, and his look tried to shame her. "You steal, and dare to come to me dressed in her robe." He stopped again, but Pia had no words. "What did you come here for?" As Pia still did not speak, he grabbed her shoulder, jerking her back into the room, so that they stood near the bed— "Did you think that you would be allowed to lie on her bed!" He twisted her arm and she cried out. "Well!" But still Pia did not speak, and with a cry of rage he flung her to her knees and in the next instant he had seized his belt from the chair where it lay. He brought it down across her back and, as she screamed and struggled to escape, he raised it again and again, and over her screams his own hurt cried out:

"I will lie with you," he cried, "when the day comes that I and Italy are as depraved, as lost, as she thinks we are—but not on her bed—" his words came in grunts now, detached and soft with breathlessness—"on the floor, Pia!—in the gutter!—in the mud!" He flung back his head, and as he did so his eye caught that of Lucy in a photograph across the room. The belt dropped from his fingers and he stared in horror at his hands and at the crouching girl. Pia was still clutching her ears and screaming. He had to yank her to her feet before she would stop and, when she did, she continued to sob.

"Go to your room," he said, his voice quiet now. "Tomorrow we will see what to do about you." He opened the door and thrust her into the hall where Zia Margherita and the servants were gathered, whispering in agitation and wringing their hands. He pushed her towards them, not caring that she came from his room naked, with thin streaks of blood running down her back, her face swollen with tears. He was angry with all of them. He slammed the door on their whispers and her sobs.

He walked back across the room, kicking aside the pool of red robe on the floor. At the desk, he took a cigarette and lit it. Then he crushed it out and fell on his knees before his wife's picture. Tears, that were as hard to come as though they had been stones, crept from his eyes, and his face was broken by deep lines. Ugly sobs shook him, and he thought, 'She was right to go——'

27: *W*HATEVER anguish Alessandro had felt the night before, the morning only brought cold logic. He knew that if he had failed anyone, he had failed Pia by not having administered this beating long ago. He gave instructions that she was to spend the day in her room on a diet of bread and water. The following day she would resume her place and no more would be said or thought about the matter.

Zia Margherita made little tchking noises at breakfast, stealing looks at Alessandro as though to see how much Pia had told him. Seeing immediately that the girl had not had the wit to defend herself, she smiled her tight smile and said:

"It is well that you punish her, although you can never punish sufficiently to correct nature. It was apparent when she brought on dear little Aurelio's death, and should have been handled then. It is late, but I am glad that you see the wisdom of putting an end to the thing now."

Alessandro scowled over his coffee. He had been sure that Lucy was wrong, that Pia was merely a simple mechanism, reacting as nature demand that it react. A little peasant, but not as Lucy thought, bad. Now he saw that she had become another thing; for whether she dared to come to him for her own need, or had doubly dared to comfort him, she was no longer the simple peasant. Yet he could not send her away. She had to remain for three more years. He was determined that those three years should be chaste ones, if he had to whip her every day to make them so.

Zia Margherita "tchk-ed" again. "The convent of The Good Shepherd would be the best place. They do very well in correcting girls."

Alessandro put down his coffee.

"No," he said. "I have said that I will not send her away, and I will not. We will do what correcting is necessary ourselves. Today, she will think; afterwards, you will see we shall not have great trouble."

"Think!" Zia Margherita snapped. "With what, her uterus?"

Alessandro smiled. "You will see." And the subject was closed.

That day, Alessandro did not come home from the department until late, and Franco was already there, excited and happy to be home for the summer. They greeted each other warmly, the constraint of Lucy's departure dissolved in their old affection. With his arm still about Franco, Alessandro led him into the study and said: "You may have a small apéritif with me, if you like."

Franco grinned, and Alessandro said quite seriously, "Vermouth or Dubonnet?"

"Well, vermouth, I think."

"Good." He poured a small glass for Franco, a larger one for himself. They settled in comfortable chairs and Alessandro said, "Now. How did you make out?"

"Well in mathematics, Latin and Greek and English. Not so well in history. Pretty badly in literature and composition."

"You will have to make them up this summer."

"Yes, Papa."

"What would you like to do this summer?"

Franco shook his head. He had never been anywhere in the summers except at home. Crotone was where he wanted to go, yet, without his mother, and without Clara tumbling about in his wake, and with Zia Margherita closing all the blinds to keep the curtains from fading, it would not be home.

"The Sila, perhaps? You could go up there with the Toccis; they have invited you."

"Where will you be?"

Alessandro lit a cigarette and sat forward, watching his son. "I shall remain here. We cannot avoid this war much longer —though—" he hesitated for a long time, and Franco watched him curiously, "it could have been avoided. Do you remember the fable of the peasants and the three wishes? A peasant was granted his first three wishes, in return for some great kindness. The peasant wanted to wish for a fine farm with animals and implements, but his wife wanted a kingdom, with jewels and riches. They argued so long that they became hungry, and the peasant, without thinking of what he was doing, wished for a bit of sausage. It appeared immediately, and the wife commenced to scream with anger, saying that he had wasted a wish. The peasant, losing patience said, 'Oh, I wish the damn thing were on your nose!' And there it was, immediately, on the end of his wife's nose. There was nothing left for them to do with the third wish but to wish it off again. So that they were back where they had started from.

"Italy could have anything—but I think she is about to wish for the sausage."

Franco grinned a little, taking the words literally. Alessandro glared at him, not seeing him, and said angrily:

"It is incomprehensible. I am no statesman—I am a soldier and a farmer—and yet even I can see this war, allied with Germany, as a disastrous thing for Italy."

"But perhaps it won't come, Papa. Nobody wants it."

Alessandro shook his head. "Did your mother talk to you before she left?"

"But not about war."

"About the people—that we are, Franco—about a people who will see something wrong and do nothing about it because it is too difficult?"

"She talked about making beautiful things and then letting them decay—or no, if they were destroyed, not trying to rebuild, to clean up and start anew."

"Yes, well, she was talking about this too—but she does not understand. We are an old people, we are tired. It is easy enough for her people to be indignant and outraged when they see something that is wrong. It is easy for them to make a clean sweep—to crusade. They are young and they are also ignorant. And this is something that your mother cannot understand; knowledge and ignorance are not always of the mind; there is a point where they are of the blood. The crusader must believe, and Italy can no longer believe. Many thousands of years of wars, of tribal wars, of imperial wars, of holy wars, of civil and political wars, have given her this knowledge, that wars, no matter under what banner, are fought for gain alone —and that wars cannot be avoided. With this knowledge tucked beneath our belts, we fight when we are told to and whom we are told to, no matter what our sympathies. If we don't like the ally and we do like the enemy, we shrug and make little jokes about everything, including ourselves. But we won't struggle. We won't even fight very hard. The Italian soldier could be a great soldier. He has almost inhuman endurance. He can live for days on a crust of black bread and a little water. He is almost immune to disease, and can stand up under any amount of pain, fatigue and discomfort. But he will lie down on the job and not even care that he is called a coward and a weakling!"

"But, Papa, this is terrible." Franco looked honestly shocked.

"Good. I am glad that you think so."

"But can't we do something?"

Alessandro stared at him for a moment and then he leaned back and shouted with laughter, while Franco watched him, sullen and a little hurt. "Do something!" He stood up and towered over his son. "Go wash your hands and don't worry too much—it looks as though I had done something by breeding a little new blood into the race. You marry an American too and see how it goes. That will help. Not as fast as rabbits perhaps, but there is time, plenty of time."

After dinner, a call came for Alessandro to report to his office. Zia Margherita suggested to Franco that he might like to go to a movie. Franco said, "Yes, maybe—I'll go see if Pia is back. She might like to go."

Zia Margherita said quickly, "But Pia is not away, she is in her room."

"Is she sick? Why didn't someone tell me? I went up and the door was locked and she didn't answer."

She looked at him speculatively. Her plan hadn't worked—but perhaps it could be made to work—perhaps it was not too late.

"Come with me while I have a cup of coffee and I will try to tell you—I am afraid that you should know." She spoke so gently that Franco, already half way to the door, turned and came back to her.

"What is it? Has something happened?"

"Come. You must be brave and grown-up. I am going to tell you."

She sipped her coffee, sitting very stiff and upright. And she told him in the way she wanted to, sympathetically, excusing Alessandro.

"You cannot understand yet," she said, "but for a vigorous man who has not the habit of continence—it has not been very easy for him to remain alone as long as he has—whether he called Pia or whether she understood and went to him—!" she shrugged. Inventiveness grew in her like a fever of words, each pushing to get out before the other. "I can't tell why he beat her—some men do that sort of thing as part of their lust, but he is not like that; she must have done something indecent—depend upon it—suggested some indecency. If she had lain with him obediently and gone away it would not have happened, you may be sure."

She stopped only when she saw that Franco's face was bloodless, the cords of his neck standing out, and his forehead wet with sweat. She started quickly to talk again, afraid, for she saw that she had gone too far. But Franco would not stay to listen. He looked for one instant as though he were going to strike her, and then she was alone. She heard him slam the kitchen door and pound up the backstairs, two at a time. Half way up, the pounding ceased and, after a moment's silence, he came down slowly and went out of the house.

His father had always been something special for Franco; he loved him and, over and above his love, he thought of him as a king or a general, someone strong and infallible. And his mother was as pure and irreproachable as his father was strong and infallible. Only Pia he had loved humanly, knowing her faults. Pia was sensual and greedy and immoral, she lost her temper easily, and told a lie as quickly as she told the truth. But Pia belonged to him, just as his box of soldiers had belonged to him when he was a little boy. Scratched and damaged, broken or glued back together again, they were his and he treasured and loved them.

Now, in the course of a few moments, under the magic of a few spoken words, his father had become a monster of evil. And Pia and his mother alike were hidden behind a cloud of shame. He dared not let his thoughts look at them, for fear of what he would find. He thought that he would like to kill his father; he thought that it was even his duty. He walked across the Villa Borghese, by the old water-clock on the Pincio, and down the hill to the Piazza del Popolo. He walked towards the heart of Rome and through the narrow, cluttered streets of the Campo Marzio, across the Ghetto and the slums, to the banks of the Tiber. He chose his weapon and he ran his father through the heart. The blood that spurted out was not red but brown. As it flowed, it changed, the brown becoming redder and redder until it was as bright and clean as fire, and the crime which his father had committed had been expiated, so that they could all go back to what they had been and be happy again.

When Franco could scarcely carry himself any farther, he turned and commenced the long walk back. He couldn't kill his father, but he could hate him. He would never speak willingly to him again, he would take away his friendship. This he could do. Too tired to feel horror or anger any longer, or to separate the hurt in his heart from the fatigue and the ache of his body, he went home.

It was late at night when he arrived, and the house slept except for the Zia, who had waited for him. She let him in, saying nothing to him but letting him go to his room. In the morning, when he awakened, his father had already left for his office.

That day, Italy declared war on England and France, and

Franco did not see his father again for almost a year. A messenger arrived in the afternoon, saying that a party of officers were leaving for the South that night. Franco was to go with them as far as Cosenza, where the Toccis would meet him.

Franco said good-bye to his aunt stiffly, he embraced Maria and Fortunata, shook hands with Little Doll, gave one quick look at Pia, and went out of the house. In a second he was back again, grabbing Pia, who was wailing like a demon, kissing her on both cheeks, and then running from the house. There was still a scowl on his face, yet he was somehow relieved of a tenseness, leaving the air behind him happier.

28:

$\mathcal{T}$HERE WAS fruit on the table for breakfast. There was fresh baked bread: Sofia, the Toccis' cook, had been up at five o'clock in the morning to put it in the oven. There was coffee, burnt black, and they drank it in tall cups half filled with hot milk. The Avvocato and his wife did not come down for breakfast, so that the Avvocato's nephew, Nino, and Gian Franco had the breakfast table to themselves. They ate like young wolves, hungrily and quickly and without looking away from their food. When they were done, they grinned at each other and talked of the day ahead.

The Mountains of the Sila lie, like the backbone of a whale, down the length of Calabria. They are the wilder because they are not great mountains, deep from one end of the year to the other in lifeless snow and ice. Instead, they are covered with dense forests, with lonely lakes and streams. The small scattering of peasants who cut the wood in the forests, who till some high, wild field or mind a flock of sheep or goats or turkeys in the rocky pasture lands, only make the place more desolate. For they are few, and they are an inarticulate people, steeped in their aloneness.

The sound of war in the north found no echo here. But Gian Franco and Nino were aware of it just the same.

They left the breakfast table and went onto the terrace. The Toccis' cabin sat on a high place at the edge of a forest and looked across a great cup of land formed by a ring of mountains. In the bottom of the cup a lake glistened flatly, like a mirror set among bits of evergreen for a table decoration. Nino said: "Let's fish today."

But Franco shook his head. "No, let's go up the mountain. Remember what the old woodcutter said?"

"The wildcat! Still, it would be nice on the lake today. We could swim, too."

"But if we got the wildcat, Nino——"

"You always want to go shooting," Nino said sullenly, thrusting his hands into his pockets and still looking towards the lake. He was short for his age, and dark, with eyes that were round and soft as a gazelle's. His face was small, his nose and chin were buttons, and a dimple came and went in either cheek. When it was there, he was a pixie, and when it was not, he was heavy and sullen, for there was no light in his eyes but only softness.

Franco said, "Yes, and you should, too. This war's going to be long enough so we can fight. I'm going into the Grenadiers. And I'm going to be good!" he boasted fiercely.

"Oh, all right. Let's get going."

Sofia gave them rolls and salami, cheese and fruit and a square of chocolate apiece to take with them. They would find their own water at some spring or brook. They went up the winding road from the cabin for three miles before they branched off into the forest. After that, they went slowly, marking the trees from time to time with their hatchets so that they would have no difficulty finding their way home. There was little undergrowth for many miles, for the peasants cut it down, using it to kindle their fires, year in and year out. Towards noon, they reached the beginning of the undergrowth, and still they had seen no sign of the wild-cat. Nino threw himself on the ground beside a small trickle of water and cried: "I am sick of this. The old man lied. I don't believe he saw a cat at all."

"And why not? It would be much more likely that he would rather than we, with you trapesing through the woods like a wild elephant."

"Well, how do you expect me to go? Like a bird with wings?"

"Hush! Let's listen, maybe——"

They lay still for a while, their eyes wide and their ears alert. The pine and spruce towered like giants over them and, beside them, the small stream clicked and stumbled over pebbles or ran with a sound that was sweet and soft over a bed of pine-needles and moss. Sunlight, white-hot, slid where it could through the thick foliage overhead and, like a feather falling, settled now here, now there, as a breeze moved the tops of the trees. A beetle climbed to the crest of a stone by Franco's head and stayed there a moment, rubbing its front feet together as though satisfied with some deal it had just put across. Then it scurried over the side of the rock and was soon lost in the tall grass.

Nino broke the silence. "If we are quiet like this for about an hour, we might see a snake or a wood rat. If we are quiet for another hour, we might see a deer. I should like to see a big buck myself."

"Would you shoot it?"

"Well, I don't know. Maybe you'd have to—if it came after you. But if you missed, it would kill you surely."

Franco laughed, "I bet you'd climb a tree."

"I bet I wouldn't."

"Well, then, let's wait your two hours and see."

"It's too long." Nino sat up and stretched. "It might not come, after all, and then there we'd be, with two hours wasted. Besides, I'm hungry. Let's eat and go up the stream to see where it comes from."

They ate and they lay flat on the ground and drank from

the stream, putting their lips to the surface and sucking the clear water into their mouths. Franco said suddenly, almost violently: "Nature is so perfect. Why is it that only man is ugly?"

Nino laughed at him. "You're crazy," he said.

Franco was silent. He folded the paper that they had carried their food in and put it in his pocket, leaving their few scraps on the ground for the animals to find. They started up the stream. In a little while, Franco said: "Do you like women?"

"Some," Nino said. "Zietta Francesca, and Donna Lucia and——"

"I mean the other kind," Franco interrupted impatiently, "I mean—did you ever—did you ever sleep with a woman?"

"Oh, well, no—but my grandmother said that I could. She asked my mother's maid if she would have me and she said that she would."

Franco made a face. "I'm glad I don't have a grandmother," he said.

"You have Donna Margherita."

"Oh, I don't think she would do anything like that. My mother wouldn't like it."

"My mother didn't care. But Papa was very angry. He said he'd see that I had all the experience that was necessary, when the time came."

Franco thought suddenly of his own father and his face was white. "I'll be glad when school starts," he said, slashing at the bark of a tree viciously with his hatchet. "I'll be glad when next summer comes and then school starts again, and then next summer and I shall be old enough to go to war."

Nino laughed, "You mean, then you'll be old enough for your papa to give you someone to sleep with!"

"No!" Franco shouted, and then he said between his teeth, "I'll never sleep with anyone, never. I mean war."

"Oh, you're crazy." Nino shrugged and they climbed on, over rocks and up a steep incline down which the stream came tumbling.

They didn't find the source of the stream, for it commenced to get late and it was the rule that they must be at the cabin by seven o'clock. They went back quickly, not stopping to listen for animals, disillusioned in their search for the wildcat. Once, Franco shot at an eagle soaring in a blue break above the treetops. But he couldn't sight it well, for all the foliage, and he brought down no feather.

"Devil a soldier you'll make," Nino scoffed and aimed his gun at a lark that had started up at the sound of Franco's fire. But Franco grabbed his arm and the shot crashed into the branch of a tree, making the bark spatter like wooden spray.

"You, fool!" Nino cried. "What did you do that for?"

"A lark! Shame on you, Nino Tocci."

"Well, better than taking nothing home."

"Did you ever eat one?" Franco said unexpectedly.

Nino shook his head.

"Well, I did—with Pia once, at old Mateo's house. It was at the festa of San Mateo. We had hot fresh-baked bread, broken open and covered with garlic-seasoned oil and new red peppers. Hot! Whew!" Franco whistled and shook his hand from the wrist as though the memory burned him. "They had a hundred little birds they'd caught in snares. They were crammed onto spits, and roasted."

"And they were good?"

"Sure, they were good. You had to eat them in your hands and chew the smaller bones. Pia said that it was like eating songs and so it had to be good." He laughed. "Just the same, I wouldn't kill a songbird—leave that to the peasants."

They were late getting home and they were scolded. But the next day they went out again, and the next, and the next, and more often than not they were late. They would be tired and hungry and Francesca Tocci and the Avvocato had little heart to make the scoldings severe. They were young and there was war in the world and these were the ones who would bear the brunt of it. Let them have their pleasure while they might.

When the summer was over, the Avvocato drove the boys to Cosenza and put them aboard their train. His dry, yellowed face broke into worried lines when he saw that the train was already overcrowded with German soldiers coming up from Reggio Calabria. He found the conductor and took him aside, pressing a large bill into his hand.

"These children," he said, "are for Rome. One of them is the son of a colonel—see if you cannot find seats for them."

The conductor looked unhappily at the bill in his hand, bending it back and forth. Then, quickly, he thrust it back towards the Avvocato. He shrugged his shoulders desperately and clapped his hands to his side. "I would if I could, Barone. I would gladly if I could."

There was a sound as of tears in his voice and his big, red face was crumpled: "These Pigs—" he made a half gesture towards the crowded train—"don't give a damn for any Italian, whether he is a colonel's son or a prince of the royal blood."

"Well—" the Avvocato thought a moment and then he pressed the bill back into the man's hand, "keep an eye on them. Perhaps you can take care of them at Naples."

"Depend on me, I will do what I can." The conductor touched his cap and swung back onto the train.

The Avvocato shook his head, but he let the boys get aboard and watched them climb onto a heap of dufflebags on the platform. They grinned at him and waved, and yelled last-minute thanks and messages for him to take home.

The boys had not been on the train an hour when a group of soldiers going from one carriage to another stopped and ordered them off the dufflebags. They got down sullenly and made their way slowly through the train until they found a corner where civilian luggage was stacked. Here they stayed until they came to Naples.

"I wish the train would turn over and kill them all," Franco stormed angrily.

"And us too— No thanks. Anyway, they're the allies you're so crazy to go to war alongside of."

"I can't choose who I fight alongside of, can I? I don't regard them—I fight for Italy."

They were silent. The train rattled and swayed, jolting their young bodies until they were limp with fatigue and discomfort. They slept intermittently and, waking, were silent for long stretches. Franco's mind was ahead of him in Rome, wondering what news there would be of his mother's return. Wondering how he could avoid his father. Wondering how Pia would be, how she would look, how it would feel to see her.

Actually, he did not see his father at first, and then only for a moment after he had been home for several days. For Alessandro was rarely at home, taking all his meals, except breakfast, near his office and only coming to the house late at night.

Pia he found unchanged. She threw herself on him, gay and glad to see him. And he was strange to her embrace, his body stiff, resenting that she should be unchanged.

"Holy Mother," she cried, "you're like a black man. It is plain to see that you never wore a hat in the sun."

Maria and Fortunata threw their arms about him too, laughing loudly.

"The house was not the same without you," Fortunata cried.

And Maria cast her eyes in the direction of the salon, where

Franco had gone, the very first thing, to greet his aunt. "It was a mausoleum, a very mausoleum," she whispered sibilantly.

They had news for him, too, for Maria was to be married. Her homely face creased in an unaccustomed grin and she turned quite red. "Pia saw to it," she said, "that money that Leone sent her. We all forgot about it, what with the Donna Lucia going away and all. Then, come summer, she advertised."

"No, Pia!" He laughed shortly, glad of a subject that let him escape his own unhappy curiosity.

"Yes, yes—and I waited for all the answers at the back door, and when the right one came—in he came."

"And what is he like?"

"Ah, a little ugly—and old."

"But it is well," Fortunata laughed a little spitefully. "He's had twelve children already, he's not interested in Maria's side of the bed so long as she gives him his spaghetti and mends his clothes and is there to talk to in the evenings!"

"Certainly he is not a fortune-seeker," Pia said complacently. "I saw to that. He is a workingman, a barber."

"His wife died and he is lonely," Maria said. "His name is Ricco Polanzari."

Franco said, "Maria, I felicitate you! When is the wedding?"

"Ah, the banns are published now."

"Good, I will come to it. Now I am going to unpack." He went out and Pia followed him and he strode coldly ahead of her, knowing that she was there.

He let Pia unpack. He sat on his bed and chewed the end of a pencil and watched her as she moved about from trunk to bureau.

"What has happened this summer?" he asked at last, interrupting her gay chatter about the coming wedding.

"Nothing—oh—did they tell you about the Donna Lucia?"

"Go on," he said quickly.

"Oh, there were cables and cables, and the Zia talked and talked, and the Signor went around looking very white and angry. The Donna Lucia wanted to come home at once—" she wrinkled her brows—"that was about when you left, I guess, when the maledetta war commenced. And all summer the cables. But Don Alessandro says it is not safe to travel. And the Signora Zia said once—" Pia looked towards the door nervously—"'She went of her own choice, now you must make her wait until the war is over.'"

The blood had gone from Franco's face, leaving his skin the color of brown ash. "What did Papa say?" he asked.

"I don't know." Pia looked at him curiously. "I didn't hear."

"It's going to be a long war," he said hopelessly. His eyes met Pia's and he thought, "It hasn't made any difference to her—she can talk about him perfectly naturally, even kindly." The thought brought its own illness, and he was at once revolted and hurt. He got up suddenly and went out of the room. "Let her be what she is, a servant. Some day some Nino's grandmother will go begging her services for the boy of the family."

He was sorry then and went back to her, the old love pulling him. He knew Pia. You couldn't blame her. With her songs and her wildness and her funny ideas that were always earthy and not infrequently sweet and childish, you could only love her. The Italian in him understood her nature. She had to follow her nature. It had been his father's duty to protect her, instead of outraging her as he had done. Franco's mood was kind and dark at once. He hated her, and he loved her. But he was sick with hurt and shame for his mother, who would feel the outrage as Pia could not.

That winter at school was a hard one. Franco was glad of it and made every excuse not to go home, throwing himself into his studies as he had never done before. The year slipped away, and part of the next. The war was joined against the United States. Now Franco ceased studying. He sat long hours, staring at the page before him, not seeing it at all.

Across the ocean, as far away as myth could make it, as distant in space as a thousand years in time, was a land where people loved each other and treated each other, with mutual respect and courtesy, as equals. There, any man could say what he wanted, or think what he wanted, worship what gods he owned, do whatever work he was able to. And no matter how different, even how opposite the words and thoughts, the prayers and work, they were equally respected by all men. That was democracy. He thought now that his mother had gone back because she could not stand the way the people of Italy thought, their approach to life. With the coming of America into the war, Franco felt as though he were asked to fight against his own mother. He was sixteen, there was no question of his fighting yet—but war was not all shouldering arms. War was hatred and war was loyalty: hatred of something he instinctively loved, the America that was partially in his blood and wholly in his heart; and loyalty to something he had come to hate, an arrogant, overbearing and contemptuous ally.

Lucy had written Franco regularly. Now her letters stopped coming and he commenced to read over her old ones. And he found that they had new meaning for him.

Once, when she had first arrived in America, she had said: "I am missing you and Papa more than I can ever say. We talk about home, Clara and I. Here, everything and everybody is in a hurry. I don't suppose that America is any noisier than any other country, but even the noises seem to be in a hurry, saying 'Hurry up,' 'Come on,' 'Get out of the way.' So now, Clara and I are hurrying too. When you are not used to it, it makes you tired and nervous. I think with amazement how the same number of hours in Italy took so much longer to pass, and passed so simply, without leaving this mark of strain. How was it that we had time to talk, you and I, to walk across to the Villa or to the Zoo, and yet none of the mechanics of life ever suffered? I sometimes think that even the sunlight there was slower, a little older, a little yellower, and much much more peaceful. It was there to warm the idle hours, for, whether you were busy or working, the atmosphere was idle. Here the sun is bright and hard and a constant reminder that there are only so many hours in a day."

In all of her letters that followed, she did not speak of Alessandro again, but gradually she ceased saying "Italy" and commenced to talk of "home." Once she said, "I sometimes think of the village priest at home, and how concerned he was for every growing soul in his community. I remember how terrible I thought it when he spoke to me of a young man whom village gossip branded a virgin. As this young man showed no vocation for the priesthood it could be only presumed that he was unhealthy, or forming unhealthy habits. I was outraged, not that a priest should speak of this, but that he should encourage unclean gossip and that he, whose province was the soul, should be willing to look for something ugly where there might well have been beauty. But I am beginning to wonder whether he was not right. The young man in question doesn't matter, but the attitude of the priest who cares enough for his people to look into the soul of any young man is actually a fine thing, and something which I miss over here. Here, a young man is no one's concern but his family's and his own, unless he should become the concern of the police."

And once she said: "Do you remember our talk above the Villa Madama that day? The things I said were true; I feel them still, but somehow they are no longer quite so important. Whether from the perspective of so great a distance, or merely from fatigue of too much thinking, the point has got lost. I am like Alice in Wonderland, who was first too big to go through the door and then too small to reach the key to open the door. Do you remember how the little Alice swam around in the tears she had wept when she was big, and how several of her fellow creatures were almost drowned? Like Alice, I am regretting my tears. Still, when you come up against a little door, you have to go through it. There may be nothing of any importance on the other side, but if you don't go through it you'll never know and its importance will grow in your own mind until it has power to ruin your life and the lives of those who are dear to you."

Always she said: "If only you were here! When I have finished a letter to you, I feel as though I had written a lecture. And yet I do the same thing all over again. There are, it seems, so many things I want to tell you and to talk to you about. One of them is the idea which, I am afraid, I have given you about America. Have I really told you that this country is so perfect? Or is it that you want to believe that some place is? Because, of course, no place is. People here don't go around loving each other and doing for each other and respecting each other's creeds. There is as much prejudice, racial and social and religious, as anywhere else. In the course of time, an unbelievably beautiful state has been evolved in America, but it's largely on paper. You need to come here to see it, particularly since you have such an admiration for America. For the one thing that is admirable about America you miss from such a distance—not her perfection, but her awareness that such a state is desirable."

She continued to speak of Italy as "home," but always, when she spoke of people, Italians or Americans, she spoke of them as "they." It was as though she stood apart and had no being in either country, no identity that made her a basic part of either community.

Franco didn't know what letters his father had had. At first, there had been letters and during the summer, while he was away, there were cables. Between school and the fact that even during vacations his father worked hard and for long hours, Franco saw little of him, and the hurt that he had received went unchallenged. Franco knew that his father had never had a chance to defend himself and that he never would have the chance, for he, Franco, could not give it to him. So the hurt grew to hatred. His mother and Pia had been outraged! Without knowing when the thought had come to him, or how it had grown, Franco believed that his mother had not left to settle his grandmother's estate, or because Italy, with its decadence, affronted her ideals but, rather, because his father did this. He became sullen, talking in monosyllables and keeping to himself. He watched the war eagerly, praying that it would last long enough for him to fight. He hated the Germans, but he had no great feeling against fighting alongside of them. Franco's was not a warlike nature. The war had become for him a dummy on which he could vent some of his unaccustomed venom. He felt that he wanted to kill and to be killed, and that there could be satisfaction in dying violently.

Only with Pia could he be natural and even gay. For Pia never changed, and you could not be old or hurt or tragic with her. She was as young and happy as though nothing had happened. Life was never dull for Pia, for she peopled it with love and hatred and the sauce of intrigue.

She had got Maria a husband and she promptly set about seeing what he was made of. But she soon saw her mistake.

Ricco Polanzari was not one to be fooled with. He chased her around the kitchen table with a stick one night and, when he caught her, he trounced her roundly while Maria and Fortunata and Little Doll looked on and laughed. The next day, he invited her to the opera. Maria was furious, but Ricco was not being used, one way or any other, by women. He shut her up firmly and told her to mind her own business and her manners, and Maria was meek.

At the opera house, they climbed ten thousand stairs and stood behind the railing close to the dome. They listened with rapt delight and, during the intermission, Ricco Polanzari gave Pia a salami sandwich and a small flagon of red wine, unwrapping a similar provender for himself. While they ate, he admonished her:

"Attend to your work," he said, "to music and the Holy Mother. And wait patiently for that Leone to come home, and you will have a happy life."

Pia nodded dutifully, her mouth too full to speak.

"Work and music and God," he reiterated, "it's all that matters."

"That's queer," Pia wiped her mouth, "and you a man! Of course, Don Alessandro is like that, but then he's a lord."

"That has nothing to do with it. You learn—or you don't—that's all. It took me twelve children to learn. Maybe he learned from a bad wife."

Pia's eyes flared. "Shut up," she cried, "you don't know her. You've no right to speak so. Donna Lucia is a saint."

Ricco looked at her in surprise. "All right, all right!" he soothed, and then he grinned wickedly and his small eyes were embedded in the wrinkles of his grin. "But I'd hate to be married to a saint."

Pia snorted. "Don't worry, you aren't." Then the orchestra walked into the pit, commenced to take their places. She took the sandwich away from her lips, and presently her arm dropped to her side, and presently the sandwich dropped to the floor and lay there unheeded.

When they reached home, the house was astir with excitement. Franco was home, in uniform, for it was the day of his pre-military training. Don Alessandro was with the Zia, who had had a fainting spell, and everyone was running around. Franco met them and he pulled Pia aside into the hall, where the light fell on her face, and told her quickly:

"My mother is coming home. She has given up her American citizenship and she is coming on the boat with the diplomats." And he scowled down at her, wanting to say, "I dare you ever to tell her; I dare you on your life. For, however much I love you, I will grind you into the dirt if you do."

But Pia threw her arms around him and cried excitedly, "The saints be praised"; then, "Oh, the blessed Holy Virgin be praised! Oh, Pia is so happy!"

Franco pushed her off to look at her again, and then he laughed and said, "Oh, all right, be glad. There's no accounting for a Pia."

In his own heart, Franco was afraid to be glad. He had not been able to understand why his father had not let his mother come home sooner. He was too young to believe the best, and he thought that his father probably had his reasons. He was afraid of what his mother would discover. He looked for her coming eagerly, and was half sorry that she came.

29: *7* HE EARLY morning light, like the ghost of a day struggling to rise from its grave and haunt the world, crept into the railway station. Tattered shreds of ectoplasm floated between earth and sky, and unseen fingers of cold touched everything, so that the stone floors and marble pillars and the great engines in their stalls broke into a fine sweat. Lucy stepped off the train and her eyes ran down, along the guarded platform, to the gate. Her eyes swept the heads of the people gathered there, for Alessandro always stood out in a crowd. Clara tugged at her hand and whimpered: "You're hurting me, Mommi, you're hurting."

Lucy let go of her hand quickly and said, "I'm sorry; walk by yourself, dear."

At the gate, she kept looking, and now the people pressed about them and Clara caught hold of her hand again. He would be there, there wasn't any doubt of that—there could be no doubt. Still, there were the cables, there was the fact that he had not wanted her to come back. With a cold fear growing in her, Lucy lived over the hour in which she had given up her citizenship in order to come back—against his expressed wish.

Suddenly, there was a cry and Pia was there. Unmistakably Pia, with her fair hair now up in a crown upon her head, and her green eyes swimming in tears. She kissed the hem of Lucy's skirt and she kissed both her hands and stopped to throw her arms about Clara.

Then she straightened up, talking excitedly:

"This is Ricco Polanzari, Maria's husband." She introduced

the short red-faced man who stood quietly with hat in hand behind her. He bowed and said, "Welcome, Signora, we come to be of service."

"Thank you, Ricco, you are most kind." To Pia she said, "The Signore?"

"He sleeps, Signora. The Donna Zia sent us, and there is also a Signor 'Tenente and a soldier we have lost somewhere." She craned her head about, and then she shrugged and went on, "The Signor 'Tenente's car will take you home. We will stay and find him and see about the bags. Maybe he is already seeing the military."

Lucy gave her checks to Ricco, and they took her to the car.

Back in her own room on the Street of the Three Madonnas, Lucy stood at the window and looked down into the garden. The sun was up and fell in generous splotches on the world outside, making the morning gay and clean. She felt as though something were missing from the garden. She studied it seriously, concentrating on each detail, as though to hide from herself the coldness and the unhappiness that was in her.

Alessandro still slept. The Zia had explained, kissing her coldly on either cheek. His light had burned all through the night. She, herself, had gone into his room early and drawn the shades and had countermanded his order to be called. He worked hard. He needed his sleep. She had sent Pia and Ricco and Alessandro's aide, who was to have gone with him in any case to attend to the military details of Lucy's arrival. She had known that Lucy would understand. Of course she understood. She stared out of the window, trying to feel as though she had come home. The sand pile was covered with a tarpaulin. She saw that it was neatly done, as taut as over the hatch of a ship. She knew then what was missing, for it used to be open, with buckets and bright-red spoons protruding like banners from the sand. She remembered looking at it when they had talked of her going away. She remembered how Alessandro had said: "This is your home," and pointed over the top of the wall to Rome. He should not have pointed farther than the sand box.

She turned away. She had gone to America too late to find any remnant of her mother. Had she come back too late to find any remnant of her home? In America, her old friends were glad to see her; but less, she had been made to feel, for love of her than out of curiosity. To them, she was a foreigner. She had eaten alien bread and borne alien children. From the fortress of their own families they peered at her.

She lay down on her bed, waiting for Alessandro to awaken. And as the doubts crowded in upon her she prayed, as she had prayed for the past months:

"God, let him want me back. Let him show me that he wants me, for without that I am helpless. I went away against his will and I have come back against his will—but I can't ask him to love me."

Across the hall, in the old nursery, Clara and Pia, Maria and Fortunata were making love. Cooing and exclaiming and calling the saints down to witness the hour. Clara had grown, in the two and a half years that they had been away, and she was not as homely as she had been as a baby. The baby fat that had made her face gather, like the bottom of a pear, in a continual pout was gone, and the shape of her face showed more clearly. Her small nose curved gently. It was the Cavalierre nose but neither so high nor so proud as Alessandro's and Franco's, nor so forbidding as the Zia's. She was as a dove among hawks. Her eyes were long and her cheekbones high and rounded, as though she carried plump crab apples beneath the flesh. Her looks were more Slavic than Latin, like her temperament, for Clara was a quiet child, and serious.

While she listened to the sounds across the hall, Alessandro came in. They looked at each other for a moment and panic rose in Lucy and she thought: 'He is a stranger, a complete stranger!'

He came towards her and she jumped up from the bed, trying to smile and hide her unwonted embarrassment. He took her in his arms then and she could feel his body trembling, and her own commenced to tremble. She laughed shakily and thought, 'Our bodies know each other and our minds do not.'

"I was sorry you were not there," she said, and was sorry that she had said it, for it was not what she had intended to say.

"Lucia! But they explained? I would not have had it happen for worlds."

"Oh, of course. It doesn't matter."

They stood away from each other. They had so much to say to each other. And yet, they had nothing. Alessandro's austerity, which long ago Lucy had loved and taken lightly, because she knew herself well loved, frightened her now and she could not surmount the barrier between them. He was gentle and courteous, but proud too and without enthusiasm.

"Franco?" she asked quickly.

"He is fine—his pre-military class is away on maneuvers. He will be here in three days."

"I was afraid—of course, I knew his time would come."

Now Alessandro smiled. "His time hasn't come," he said.

"Of course—but, I meant, it's there."

"Yes, it has always been there." And his look bored into her as though he wanted to ask, "Is this why you came, then?"

The Zia usually had her breakfast in bed, but this morning she came to the dining room. She took her place at the foot of the table and only when she had been served did she apologize, saying that she had grown absentminded, that Lucy must, of course, have her own place! Making a fuss until all of the plates had been changed and she was seated at Alessandro's left. She sat stiffly, taking small graceless mouthfuls as though she found no pleasure in her food. Lucy thought her thinner than she had been, and harder. She had a look of having been carved from one bone, instead of being a mass of bones joined supply and intended, beyond their practical use, to express the human body. The Zia said:

"We are all so happy that you are back, my dear. I shall leave at once, of course. You will want your home to yourself."

Alessandro looked quickly at Lucy, waiting for her to speak, and Lucy said, "Nonsense, how could you say such a thing!" And even while she said it, she wondered, 'Is he annoyed because of the confusion? Because he is being delayed in getting to the office? Or is there something else he wants me to say? Would he be glad, or would he be angry, if I said as I want to, "Yes, go, for Alessandro and I want to be alone"?' She saw the waiting look fall away. She almost thought that he shrugged, though he hadn't moved. He took her up at once and said:

"We should be lost without you, Zia. You mustn't think of going."

So the matter was settled. Zia Margherita would remain in the guest room, while Lucy and Alessandro would use the room which they had not shared since the winter of Aurelio's death. Lucy's heart sank. She had come back against Alessandro's wishes because she had to. Because the war had brought her a consciousness of her exile, of her need for her family. With war, a certain contempt for everything Italian had found expression in America, and Lucy had discovered herself constantly on the defensive, explaining things which she had never thought to sympathize with or to understand. And while she explained, she came to understand a little herself.

"His way is different from mine, but he loved me just the same and I let myself be too conscious of the difference and too little aware of the love." So she had come back, feeling that it must be different, that she would make it different, for she had new eyes to see with. Instead, the old terrors attacked her. For Alessandro was a stranger. She thought that he would come to her if he wanted her, but she could not ask him to come. She thought, half hysterically: 'He will not let me come back. I must sleep with him, and it will be like sleeping with a stranger, and one who does not particularly like me.'

They looked at each other across the table and talked of the ocean crossing, and compared the foods that one was able to get in America with those that one got in Italy. Lucy ached for Clara too, for the homecoming had been a stiff and shy one for her. Alessandro had kissed her on her upturned cheeks and put his hand quietly on her head while he told her that she had become a very pretty little girl. Lucy was sorry for both of them, remembering how constantly Clara had talked of her father, how excited she had been. Remembering, too, that Alessandro had never been cold toward his children.

When breakfast was over, Alessandro left for his office, the Zia went to her room and Clara to her nursery to rediscover her books and toys. Lucy wandered from room to room, putting off her unpacking while she too rediscovered.

Coming back to Italy in wartime was not an easy experience. The small hardships which Italians had gradually grown accustomed to were unexpected and shocking to her. In America, there had been enough of everything. It was hard to understand that bread was so precious that you could not go to a dinner without bringing your own, wrapped in a napkin.

It was hard to go without tea, to drink boiled burnt barley in place of coffee. Cigarettes, butter, soap were not to be had, and they were warned that there would be little coal the coming winter. Perhaps hardest to understand was the unaccustomed atmosphere of hurry in her household. The servants, who had to spend much of the day standing in line to get food for the house, had, therefore, to rush their work at home in order to get it done at all. And to add to the confusion, the Zia had acquired the habit of giving them wool to make into sweaters and knitted-wear for the soldiers. Then, there was Alessandro, whom Lucy remembered going to his office late and coming home for a siesta in the afternoon. Now he left the house early and returned late. They had dinner at ten o'clock and sometimes he came home early enough for an apéritif, and sometimes he did not. After dinner, he smoked one cigarette and went to bed, to fall asleep immediately.

Franco came home three days after her arrival. Lucy knew the moment he came into the house. The front door slammed and there were feet pounding up the stairs, two at a time. At the top of the stairs, the feet were still for a minute and then came on more slowly. Lucy did not wait to wonder at their slowness but flung her own door wide and flew out to meet them. When she had wept on his shoulder, for Franco was now taller than she was, she stood back to look at him. He was thin, as he had always given promise of being, but beneath his drab olive shirt his shoulders were broad and his muscles well developed. She led him into her room, laughing, though her eyes were still wet with tears.

"I am not making sense," she said. "It is so good to be with you again that I want to laugh, and I must cry; and I want to cry, and I must laugh."

Then, before they could talk, Clara burst into the room and Franco caught her up in his arms and buried his face in her hair. He looked up suddenly and Lucy caught her breath.

"He's glad to see us," she thought, "but he is as morose as his father." And she wondered if he were unhappy. Later, when she asked him, when she took his hand and her eyes begged him to tell her, he shook his head.

"You can't be entirely happy with war," he said, and Lucy breathed a sigh of relief.

"Sooner or later, of course, you'll have to face it," she agreed, "but not yet a while."

"It's not that, Mommi—it's—well, just war." He shrugged, at a loss to express himself. "I am going to the pre-military camp this summer."

He ran his hand through his hair and Lucy thought that even his gestures were like those of his father. "Do you have to go?" she asked slowly, half ashamed of herself for asking.

"No."

"Ah, well——"

"But I want to. Oh, Mommi, I am sorry." Suddenly his expression was young and pleading, like a child who begs to be forgiven for a misdeed. He came to her, taking her face in his two brown hands and, for the first time since he had come home, his eyes looked deep into hers. "I know it's America," he said, "but Italy is my country. I'll have to fight, in another year and a half. I want to. Not because I love the Germans, not because I hate the Americans, not because I understand what has happened. Just because I love Italy. Now, I have to go and learn how. I am sorry, Mommi."

"No," she said softly, "not sorry, Franco. Proud. Be proud; I am proud of you."

Lucy had come home in May. In June, Franco went to his

camp, after a brief week's vacation at home. There was no question of the family going to the country that summer. Alessandro had to be in Rome, and Lucy did not want to leave him again. She shrugged when he suggested that she go, saying:

"It will be lonely there, without either you or Franco. Besides, I must see if I can't do something. Red Cross, perhaps."

"I am afraid not. There have been new regulations since you left."

"Oh, do you mean they won't have me?"

He nodded.

"Because I'm a foreigner?"

"Because you are not a member of the Party."

Lucy looked at him, shocked. "But it's volunteer work, Alessandro. It has nothing to do with the Party."

"It's a war-time regulation. To insure solidarity, I presume."

They sat in the library, waiting for dinner to be announced. It was the one room in the house that had not been touched during her absence. Lucy looked at it now, thinking that the rust-colored satin curtains were faded and that she must have new ones made. And she thought that it was a peaceful room and that she would not like to see it changed by even so little a thing.

"I have to do something," she said at last—"I mean, something that is useful—and I would rather do the hospital work than anything else."

"Undoubtedly there is a greater need there," he agreed simply.

"I could join the Party."

He got up, nodding to Pia, who stood in the door to announce dinner. "You must decide that for yourself," he said, hesitating a moment before he went on, "but I would prefer that you did not——"

Lucy nodded. "Of course!" she said, and was glad that she had, for Alessandro smiled at her and pulled her arm through his as they went in to dinner.

The month went by, and another and yet another. Lucy joined Maria and Pia and Fortunata and the Little Doll in knitting, and gradually she took back the reins of her house. She threw open shutters and filled the rooms with flowers; she cleared the tables and mantels of the little statuettes and ormolus, the host of small silver and gold and leather boxes, of cloisonné objects, of miniatures and souvenirs. Zia Margherita frowned with displeasure, and kept the door of her room closed, to accentuate her feelings. Lucy commenced to order her own meals and to draw her own friends back about her. Though Alessandro continued to live coldly at her side, her first disappointment passed and she watched him more kindly, thinking that the past could not, after all, be irrevocable, and that he must come back to her before long.

When the Americans bombed Civitavecchia, Lucy became a member of the Party. It was no indication of her sympathies; it was a simple need. Alessandro only nodded now, seeing that she must do it. The hospitals were packed with wounded and dying, and there were too few nurses and doctors to care for them. Still, they persisted that only Fascists might work in the hospitals. So Lucy joined the Party, and after she had been at work one week she forgot how she had come there, or that she had ever been away. The work was heart-breaking it was so hard, so thankless, so almost useless. Among the lower classes of Italy a woman who has suffered a loss or a great wrong will turn her hands against herself. Even as she weeps and screams, she will tear her hair out in handfuls, the small, white clot of roots reddened with blood. She will dig into her own flesh with her short, hard, soil-stained nails, scratching long bloody furrows down her cheeks and gouging at her own eyes. Lucy worked hard, trying not to dwell, in her thoughts, on the crowded wards of multilated men and women. In the course of her work she became, to a certain degree, detached —and she thought it was as though all mankind were acting like the peasant women, crying out against some wrong that had come to it, and seeking to destroy itself rather than to correct the wrong. And over and above her fear and sorrow, was a sense of wonder that it could be so.

Every day, new truckloads of casualties were brought in, so that the beds that had held the dead, or those who could be discharged, were made up again without even an interval of airing. Soldiers and civilians, men, women and children, even babies, came in with torn limbs, broken bodies or blinded eyes. Lucy worked hard, in the operating room or in the wards. She assisted the surgeon; she was anaesthetist; she chattered with patients who were in agony, trying in this way to take their minds off their pain, for the little store of anaesthetics had to be saved for operations. The Italian Red Cross nurses were trained to do every sort of work, and Lucy loved it. She loved pinning her hair back sleekly, so that not one strand showed from under her white veil; she loved her nails natural, filed short and kept immaculately clean; she loved the smell of antiseptic, instead of perfume, on her clothes, and the fine, dull shine of unpainted lips and unpowdered nose that she now saw in the mirror. She loved to be called Sister Cavalierre. She felt like a nun, pure and sweet; and when she went home, however tired she was, the kindliness and the decency of a day's work that, in reality, was ugly, carried over and she was not unhappy. The house, and everyone in it, seemed simple and fresh and clean because her own feelings were so. If Alessandro was still austere, austerity in moments of great fatigue can be more relaxing than gaiety, and Lucy was almost glad of it. They spoke sparingly to each other and, at night, when they went to bed, they settled to sleep, sometimes without even saying good night. Yet, more than once, when she awakened before Alessandro did in the morning, she found that she had been sleeping with her hand on his arm or, stretched out, with her arm across his chest. And she couldn't know how many other mornings he might have awakened earlier than she, to find her so and, perhaps, to push her off. If she had been idle, she might have dwelt on his unresponsiveness and been made unhappy by it.

That fall, she spoke to Alessandro about receiving convalescent soldiers for a period of rest in their home. As he made no objection, she filled out the necessary papers and, by Christmas, they already had had two series of men. They were Italian soldiers and well received in the kitchen. Later, they had some Germans. Lucy discovered that the women in the kitchen, who talked very bitterly about the Germans in general, actually got on as well with these soldiers as they had with their own countrymen. When she asked Fortunata how things went, the latter grinned her wide grin, tucked her dust-cloth under one arm in order to free her hands, and said:

"They are just men, Signora! and I would not have believed that Germans could be so useful. This Hans, now! He does not understand one word you say, not one Christian word! But he has got Maria's sink so that it does not drip any more—and the drain, the drain is like a gullet!"

Lucy laughed. "He is certainly useful, then. How about the other?"

"Johann? Do you hear him singing, Donna Lucia? Such noisy songs, but magnificent, no!"

"Yes, I have heard him."

"Well, Donna Lucia, you will not believe it but he is the

magnificent cook. Potato pancakes!" She kissed her finger tips. "A most outlandish dish, but delicious. The raw potatoes grated fine, the juice of an onion, egg and salt and pepper seasoning, mixed to a paste and fried in hot fat. Then you eat it with apple-sauce. It is the most delicate dish!"

"It does sound good. Tell Maria—no, I will," and Lucy left Fortunata to her dusting, and went out to the kitchen.

Maria, small and hunched and homely, stood over the stove and, beside her, a great giant of a blond man towered. His features were thick and his close-cropped hair stood up on his head like pig bristles. He was stirring a pot, and Maria was enumerating on her fingers:

"The oil, a piece of garlic, and some onions. When the onions are cooked, then the tomato: and stew, and stew, and stew! Then, the tomato paste, then the pepper-sausage: and stew, and stew, and stew! Then you take a dish of spaghetti, or of noodles, or of macaroni, put in some pieces of hard-boiled egg, pour the sauce over it, and bake in the oven until the crust comes."

The big man continued to stir and Maria began all over again, as though by repetition he would understand, despite the language. Lucy interrupted them, saying:

"Good morning, Maria, Johann. It is early to be cooking."

"Ah, Signora, Donna Lucia, good morning."

The German swung around and saluted, his wooden spoon in the air. "Heil Hitler" he said; then, noticing the spoon, he turned red and put it back into the pot quickly.

"Are you getting lunch so early?" Lucy asked, hiding a smile.

"No, Signora. This is just a lesson. This pig," Maria gestured towards Johann amiably, "will sit down and eat up the lesson in no time and still have space for lunch."

Lucy looked alarmed. "Maria! With things so scarce, are you crazy?"

"Ah, Signora, it is all right. These pigs bring us all kinds of extra food. I do not waste our supplies—not I, who stand in line half the day."

"Well, in that case. I came to ask you to have Johann"— Lucy smiled at the man and he grinned back sheepishly, recognizing his name—"make these pancakes that Fortunata has told me about, for all of us."

Maria nodded eagerly and turned to Johann. "Kartoffel, Kartoffel," she cried, and made a wide, round gesture with her hands and then clapped them together. Then, gathering her fingers at the tips, she made a motion of stuffing food into her mouth, ending up by rubbing her stomach, with an expression of delight.

Johann beamed and said, "Ja, Ja!" with enthusiasm.

Lucy left them then and went to find her coat, for it was getting late and she was due at the hospital.

Ever since the men had come to the house Pia had been moved downstairs to sleep in a corner of the nursery. Lucy could hear Clara and Pia whispering, or giggling, or singing, in the evenings. She was amused that Pia should be able to step down to Clara's age-level with such ease. Then, one evening, she came quietly into the room in time to hear Pia say:

"The new German, Emil, he's no use at all. He doesn't know about things to do or things to cook or things to sing; all he wants to do is to get up close to you."

"What for?" Clara asked.

"I don't know; just because it feels good, I guess."

Clara said, "How does it feel good, Pia?"

Lucy took another step into the room. "Get your bed things, Pia. And go back to your old room."

Pia, half woman, half child, her braids falling over full breasts, commenced to cry loudly, "No, no, Donna Lucia; please no; for the love of the Virgin, no!"

"No, Mommi, no," Clara joined in. But Lucy would not be moved. She stood in the door until Pia had gathered her things and, sobbing and protesting, stumbled out of the room. Then she tucked Clara in and sat on the edge of the bed to hear her prayers.

Later, she explained to Alessandro: "I hadn't really forgotten how she was but I thought she might have acquired a little sense of proportion——"

Alessandro nodded. For a moment, he didn't speak; then he said:

"Under the circumstances, it's not the best thing for her to be upstairs with all those soldiers. Of course, we can try locking her up again."

But Lucy was angry. "You will only wear yourself out, trying to save her against her will. Let the soldiers have her."

Alessandro shrugged. They would talk about it again. But he had other things on his mind and did not. Nor did Lucy. So that, although Maria locked Pia up at night, there was no one to watch or care whether she went forth on a broomstick after the lights were out.

30: *P*IA STOOD at the window, braiding her hair. She had washed it the day before and it glistened like pale topaz in the sun. She leaned across the sill. Johann was walking up the path to the kitchen; he had been emptying the garbage. Pia liked Johann. He was the first person she had ever told about Leone and the house they were going to have. Johann didn't understand, but she drew him a picture of the house and he said "Gut," many times, and smiled at her. He was a big man and simple, and everything about him made Pia feel clean. Once, when they were all in the kitchen, she tried to kiss him. He only laughed at her and slapped her on the buttocks in a friendly way. The German, Emil, had laughed too, but with a difference. He had grabbed her by the arm and pulled her onto his knee and kissed her hard, at the same time fumbling with her breasts. Johann bellowed something in German and Emil let go of her mouth and laughed again, pulling Pia back when she struggled to get away from him. There was the sound of a chair grating, and Johann had hold of both of them. Pia he dropped unceremoniously to the floor, from where she watched him propelling Emil toward the door. They made the guttural sounds which never ceased to fascinate her. She would have followed them, but now Maria and Fortunata turned on her, wishing her every sort of bad luck, and warning her that if she made any more trouble they would tell the Signore. Reminding her too

that the Signore was a good hand with a belt. Pia called them
as many names as they could think to call her, but she paid
attention all the same. She never held it against Alessandro
that he had beaten her, but she did not readily cross his path.

That night, she saw that Johann had cuts and bruises on
his face, and that Emil was no longer there. After the lights
were out she went to Johann, climbing out of her window and
across the gentle slope of roof to the window of his room.
Johann had been asleep. He was not an easy one to waken,
and when he did waken he did not seem glad to see her.

"Ach, Pia!" he said, and "Nicht gut, nicht gut!" shaking
his head at her. He put on the light and sat staring at her for
a while. Then suddenly he found a pencil and paper and,
propping it against the wall, he sketched a house. It was not an
imposing, block-like cement house such as Pia had drawn, but
a low cottage hugging a rounded hillside, and by it two quick
lines towered and spread to suggest a rooftree.

Pia sighed and said it was beautiful and Johann put down
his pencil and cradled his arms to rock an imaginary baby.
Then he took up the pencil and paper again and drew a ring
and pointed to Pia's hand. He said, "Gut, gut, Pia," and Pia
nodded and got up from the bed.

That had been last night. Watching Johann now, Pia
thought of Leone and wondered what sort of a man he had
grown into. It was hard for her to think of how he would be.
She always imagined him short, as he had been, but very
broad, with a thick, strong neck. She remembered his black
hair and his black-brown eyes. He had been beautiful. But Pia
remembered only that she had thought him beautiful and
could not actually see his features as she could see his wide
shoulders and his neck and his hair and eyes.

She hurried with her braids and flung out of the room to

give Johann his breakfast. Leone was something established, dimly in the past and definitely in the future. Pia was rarely introspective. She did not often wonder what Leone might have grown into or what their lives would be. The cement house of Titto Scalpi, the polished linoleum floor, the radio and the babies, were facts which needed no dreaming, and Pia was too busy living, day by day, to think much about them. Life, for Pia, was like a ball of yarn unrolling along the floor; the thread, once unrolled, was not so big nor so important as the ball still rolling, nor was the thread about to be unrolled of any importance. Today, Johann's breakfast was important, tomorrow Franco was coming home but that would not be important until tomorrow came.

When Emil and Hans left, they were gone. But it was not so with Johann. Pia did not easily forget Johann. For one thing, she had the picture of the cottage he had drawn, stuck in the corner of her mirror, next to the letter she had had three years ago from Leone. Though the cottage was not so elegant as the cement house she was going to have, it was a simple, kindly place and made her think of Johann, and she liked it. For another thing, Pia had been unhappy since Lucy's return, and Johann had made her forget to be unhappy.

That spring, Pia was eighteen. There was money for her in the bank, and she was free to go. Alessandro turned her over to Lucy.

"If you want her to go," he said, "you may send her away now."

But Lucy would not, saying, "I shall be glad to see her go— but it's a bad time for a girl like Pia to be on her own. I should be anxious about her. Let her stay, if she will."

And Pia was glad to stay, for the Cavalierres were her

family and, until Leone came, they were all the family she had.

The summer of 1943 feeling ran high and Alessandro spoke more than once of Lucy's taking the household into the north. It already seemed unavoidable that there would be fighting in Rome. But Lucy would not leave, saying that they would be well enough off if they stayed together. She said it crisply, but she agreed to give up her work, so that she could keep her hand on the household and so that Alessandro could find her readily if need be. Actually, she was not sorry to give up the work, for she was tired and nervous. She would rest, and could always go back in the fall.

Pia was torn between disappointment and relief at this decision. She was disappointed when Lucy stopped working, for now no more soldiers came to the house and Pia was lonely, thrown all day with Maria and Fortunata and Little Doll. Maria's Ricco Polanzari was there only at night and, despite their mutual love of music, he did not think highly of Pia but said that, as the father of twelve, he would like to see her beaten with some regularity, if indeed it was not too late. Nor did Pia care for Ricco Polanzari. She considered him old and sour and decidedly ungrateful. As to Little Doll's man, who used to haunt the kitchen door, he had gone away to war. The three women were poor company. Marriage had not sweetened Maria, but rather entrenched her disagreeable ways, giving them aim and reason. If Ricco snored too loudly during the night, or complained of her too much, that she did not save enough wine for him or that she had not put away a spoon or so of olive oil for him from the Signore's rapidly diminishing stock or, more personally, that her ugly face depressed him to look upon, then Maria turned upon Pia. For was it not all Pia's fault? Maria talked angrily of her happy spinsterhood.

Little Doll was no better company; she who had never been one to talk, was surly now, worried about her man. In her free moments, she knitted all the wool that the Signora Zia would give her, being careful to ignore all the standard regulations and knit things that would fit her man.

"He is compact and little, the great German pigs will not be enjoying these sweaters."

She would mutter these words, over and over, as she worked. Johann and Hans had done little to change the temper of the kitchen. Now the women said, "They can be good men, the Germans." But when they thought of their own men, or of their own relatives, then they became sullen again and forgot Johann and Hans.

Only Fortunata continued to grin, but now she had more wrinkles in her face, and deep lines pulled her eyes down in a perpetual droop, and she too was not talkative. She worried about Cato, from whom they had not heard in a year, and whom she had not seen in three years.

Ill temper is more easily borne if one can find an outlet for it, and Pia was ready at hand. So that Pia was in disgrace most of the time. To be yelled at, to be slapped or pushed about, were ills that Pia was well equipped for. She could yell herself, and certainly she was far more inventive as regards invectives than any other woman in the kitchen. She had never yet dared to slap back, but she was quick to dodge, and she was not afraid to stamp her feet and storm.

However lonely Pia felt, she was grateful for one thing. They were not going north, they were not running away from the Americans. Since the arrival of the money-order Pia had not heard again from Leone, but she had not needed to. The dream was crystallized. If she could not visualize him, still Leone was as real to her now as he had been the day they sat on the rocky shore of Valombra, when he first talked of going to America. With the Americans coming nearer and nearer, Pia's excitement grew, for Leone would surely be among them. She checked off each town as it was taken. She remembered how the public square lay, and what the church was like, and where the trattoria was. Of some of the towns, she could even tell what colors the women wore on feast days, whether red cotton, or black or brown taffeta, or heavy gold lace. Pia was lonely, she was jealous of the governess. But deep within herself she was excited and on the verge of happiness, just as a child awakening Christmas morning is aware of a great sense of pleasure without, for the moment, remembering what it is for. Leone was surely coming.

31:

*7*HE SUMMER of 1943 was hot and sultry. During the course of the summer, Lucy discovered how many and how odd an assortment of people were watching eagerly for the arrival of the Americans. The vegetable man, whose one green for the past eight months had been grass, dreamed of the broccoli and Brussels-sprouts that the Americans would herald in. "You wait!" he said, adding, with what Lucy considered an amazingly far-sighted piece of thinking for the ragged little vendor that he was, "with the Germans, the war will never have an end—with the Americans, you will see, Signora, it is a very big BOOM and it is over. Can you not imagine the vegetables we shall then have, ah!"

And Ricco Polanzari, who was a barber, had many tales to tell of people who looked to the Americans. There was the music teacher who came to him regularly to have his mustache trimmed, never his hair! And this music teacher assured him that, despite Bach and Beethoven, the Germans had the souls of cows. They went where they were herded, they never complained, and they gave all the milk that was required of them. He himself would be glad to see the Americans chase them straight through Rome. He himself would sit at his window and enjoy the sight. Ricco said that this same music teacher was planning to teach the American soldiers to play the piano, free. Besides which, as soon as the war was finished he was going to America. He had a cousin who lived in the Bronx, which was a part of America, and who said that in America they needed many music teachers.

Then, Ricco said, there was the soldier who came in and had his hair cropped short like the Germans. While all the others were talking of the Americans, and where they had arrived at, and were laying bets as to how long it would be before they reached Rome, this man kept interrupting, saying, "They aren't going to arrive anywhere, worse luck," and "Nobody can beat the Germans, worse luck." "The Germans are strong," somebody conceded. The soldier grunted, and said, "They have black-iron guts. A friend of mine tried to kill one of them, a German Master Sergeant, who had machine-gunned ten pigs on a village street, just because the pigs kept getting in the way! My friend shot the German, the bullet going through him from front to back and hitting the ground behind him with a plunk that made the dust jump quite into the air. But do you think the devil died? I am telling you not—he turned around and looked at the ground for a minute, and then he leaned down and picked up that bullet and put it in his pocket. Then he called a soldier and told him to lock my friend up, and the next morning they shot my friend with a machine gun in such a way that the bullets left the letter S on his body, S for Swine. Well, my friend died, my friend being a Christian. But these Germans," he shrugged, "even the Pope cannot do anything with them." He tossed Ricco a coin and went out and he did not come back again. But there were others like him.

Lucy heard the stories and the rumors, and she was relieved to find that so many little Italians wanted the Americans. Her own desire for the end of the war was not acute, it was a controlled numbness. It was necessary to be numb in order to stand it. It was necessary to look closely at each day as it passed and never to lift one's eyes to the next.

Early in the fall, an armistice was signed with the Americans. Hard on its heels, Rome was occupied by the Germans. And now the women in the kitchen said: "We shall see what kind of allies we have had," nodding their heads sagely or shaking them with a great show of foreboding. Actually, the foreboding was not justified. Once the Germans broke into a church to sieze and murder three of Badoglio's generals, who had taken refuge there. The Germans considered these men traitors, who must be shot. If they had been surrounded and starved out of the church, or shot as they sought to escape, even their friends, while they mourned them, could only have said—"That was the chance they took—it is the fortunes of war, you cannot blame the Germans."

As it was, all Italy looked upon the Germans with horror. This they would not forget, either Fascist or anti-Fascist. Sanctuary had been violated. Even the honest atheist will not willingly commit sacrilege against another man's God. All over Rome, men and women crossed themselves and waited in terror for further atrocities. But, after this deed, the new enemy took to humor, their own peculiar, Teutonic humor. The first week of the occupation, barracks upon barracks of Italian soldiers were robbed of their trousers and turned out into the streets in their underwear. Then, for the moment, the Germans settled down to the rôle of conqueror. They were as disciplined as automatons. They transgressed in no way on civilians unless in strict pursuance of the war. There were Italian partisans who helped escaped prisoners, did sabotage and sent information out of the lines. From time to time, these men and women were found out and, when they were, they were taken away. Nobody knew where they went or what happened to them. Within a week, a neat little bundle of clothes was returned to their family and the matter was closed.

The day of the armistice, Alessandro left his office and did not go back again. Lucy worried about him, but she would not tell him so. Ever since she had returned from America she had gradually awakened to the discovery that she had a peculiarly impersonal but real faith in him. Whatever he did, he would be right. She wished that she could let him see how she felt, that he would tell her what was in his mind, sharing his dangers with her. But Alessandro remained aloof.

After Christmas, Franco came home to stay. The Germans were picking up whole queues of schoolboys for labor, and Alessandro and Lucy were worried for him. Franco himself wanted to fight. In June, he would be eighteen and he saw no reason for waiting. But he could not go before then without his father's permission, and Alessandro would not discuss the matter, saying flatly:

"You're not coming home for a holiday. You have work to do. If you are feeling patriotic, you would do well to prepare yourself to think. Italy is emotional enough as it is, and will not be further helped by another seventeen-year-old boy rushing off to fight. You cannot, at this point, even decide which side Italy needs you to fight on."

Franco said, "But I am a Fascist."

Alessandro threw his arms in the air; then he said with studied calmness, "Franco, I have been too busy to notice greatly, but now I see that you have become sullen and—yes, even unfriendly. I realize that these have been hard times for you. You are trying to judge the world and you don't know enough to do it. That is why I don't want you to talk about it or think about it. Just keep on with your studies, and work seriously. There is one thing, however—you are not a Fascist just becaue you belong to the Party. Every boy and girl in Italy belongs to the Party. That is a routine that you were forced into, and you cannot be bound by any routine but only by what is in your own heart. Now, no more of this glowering."

And Alessandro dropped the subject as quickly as he had taken it up. He had made his decisions and it never occurred to him that Franco would disregard them even by so much as thinking of something which he had been told to put out of his mind.

Franco did not speak to his father again until he knew what he was going to do and was old enough to follow his own counsel. In the meantime, he studied. Sometimes he talked to his mother for long hours, but they did not talk about the war. They talked about things that Franco read, about America and what it was like. They talked about other wars that Franco found in his history, the American wars, their Civil War, their Revolution, and about Italy's own civil war. They talked about Galileo, who had said that the earth revolved around the sun, and of how he was persecuted for heresy. They talked of courage and of how men always had to pay for courage but that, having paid the price, the whole world shared in the profit. Sometimes Lucy read aloud to both Franco and Clara, and sometimes Franco read aloud in Italian and then Pia would come in to listen. If Lucy were not there, Pia would curl up on the floor at Franco's feet, letting her head rest against his knees. Franco would put his hand deep into her hair and twist it about his fingers as he read. But if Lucy were there, Pia would sit on a chair by the door. Franco would occasionally look over at her and wink, and she would smile back. Understanding ran between them like something that was solid. But Franco never questioned his mother's attitude. Now that he had grown up, he had not spoken again of marrying Pia. He loved her, but he would never marry her unless they could be happy. If he could go to America after the war, he knew that they would have a chance; if he could not go to America, there would be no chance. Now he couldn't talk about it; he could only watch Pia and have her by him as often as possible.

The months that followed, whatever the strain they all lived under, were happier than any the Cavalierres had known in years. They were together and safe. For the first time, Lucy saw how complete was their unity. Maria and Fortunata grumbled, complained and prayed, but if they saw her looking troubled even the sour Maria would burst into the widest grin she could produce and cry:

"Why it is nothing, Signora Donna Lucia. Have courage and you will see how quickly it is done with! Poof, and over. And think of the fine life we shall have when the Americans arrive! Coffee! Spaghetti! Enough for everybody!"

Lucy would look up from the work that she was doing and smile; whether it was planning a new way to cook grass, or the small piece of unidentifiable meat they had from the black market, or counting the grams of bread which were allowed each of them. She might have been inspecting the laundry that Little Doll turned out without soap. Although there was a pretense of rationing, it had to do with reams of papers, of forms and certificates, and with stores that were empty. The butcher, who had not had a piece of meat to sell in four months, was selling hats and shoelaces; the hat stores were selling bric-a-brac. And not a few stores refused to sell anything, for merchandise was more precious than inflation

money! A hat was, after all, a hat, and with a little redecorating would always be a hat, but a lira could easily be less
than a penny tomorrow, and a paper bill nothing but kindling.

Lucy saw another evidence of loyalty when she found that
Pia saved her bread for Clara. She discovered this when Maria
came upon Pia's cache. There followed a fight in which Pia
received a black eye and several body bruises and came away
with a handful of Maria's sparse gray hair, leaving a goodly
scratch or two behind her. Only after the fight, was the
matter cleared up. Maria thought that Pia was stealing from
the family. Pia was, in fact, saving her own ration to feed
Clara between meals. Lucy said, as gently as she could:

"You must eat your own bread, Pia; you need it. The
Signore and I are already giving our bread to the children.
Clara has plenty."

Actually, they were all thin, and there was a long series of
colds for all the household. In January, Zia Margherita took
to her bed. There she remained until the first hot days of
June, when she went into the garden and sat in the sun, with
one blanket about her shoulders and another about her knees.

Lucy watched her, thinking it strange that she had never
complained when she had so much to complain about and
that now, when the sun was hot and the Americans were just
outside of Rome, she moaned all of the time. And Lucy
thought, 'She is old,' and felt sorry for her, though the Zia
was one person for whom she could have no liking.

On the fifth of June, the Americans entered Rome. The
city went wild with joy. As soon as the boom of guns had died
to some extent, Lucy took Franco and Clara and Pia and ran
down through the garden to the street.

Clara was short for her nine years. Her dark-brown hair
was cut in a Dutch bob and her eyes snapped with pleasure

and excitement. Even from a distance, she looked the personification of all the little sisters in the world, and the American soldiers, who drove by them, looked twice, and the second time they waved and grinned and many of them threw chewing gum and small packages of candy to her. Franco and Pia and Clara scrambled to catch the packages and, as they accumulated, Lucy took off the handkerchief she had been wearing on her head and let them use it as a sack. At noon, they went home.

After lunch, Franco went out again and did not come home until the curfew hour, and the next morning he went out before he had had his breakfast. He was gone all day, and Lucy and Alessandro were half worried and half angry. When he came in, Lucy's anger died away at the sight of his face, for he was white and old in a way that had nothing to do with age. It was as though something had taken shape within him and he had come of age. She said: "Your father has gone to look for you. What has happened to you?"

Franco didn't answer, but only looked at her unhappily.

"He is very angry," Lucy said. "I am afraid that I cannot blame him."

Franco shrugged. "Let him be angry, it is nothing to me."

"Franco!" Lucy cried, a sense of horror rising in her. And then, knowing that he was hurt, she overcame her outrage and tried to reach him, saying softly, "I have never heard you speak this way before. I don't know what is wrong with you, but I am not very proud of your manners."

"I am sorry, Mommi. I have decided what I have to do, and Papa, I know, will be angry. But it doesn't matter. You have told me that in America a boy does not respect his parents because he has to but only when he is able to. And that he can love them without respecting them. Well, I don't love Papa, and I don't respect him. Papa is not going to like what I am going to do. But if he leaves me alone, I will be polite."

"Papa will not leave you alone—and you will still be polite!" Lucy took his arms, as though seeking to feel the reality of him, and she thought wildly that it was as though he had changed into someone strange and unpredictable and her child was lost in the changing. "I don't understand you," she said; "you have always loved your father, and you have every reason to respect him."

"Mommi," Franco asked, as though he had not heard her, "what do they think of us in America?"

"Of us?"

"Of Italians?"

"I don't know," she said slowly, puzzled now. "What do we think of the Americans?"

"No, it's not the same thing at all. The Americans think that we are cowards and traitors, and they have reason to."

"I don't believe that. You have listened to the talk of some drunken soldiers. There are times to be sensitive, Franco— and there are times to be deaf."

"It wasn't one soldier, it was many. And they weren't drunk, they were tired. Most of them hadn't slept in forty-eight hours. They are right, Mommi. I have known it for a long time— we chose our ally and we stayed with him as long as it was convenient. We didn't help him very much, at that, but we would have been right there to share in the profits. The ally is losing now, but that's no good reason to change sides."

"It's not as simple as that, Franco. Your father will explain it to you when he comes in. A world war is not cut out on the straight lines of a fight between little boys."

"I am sorry. It is simple to me. I shall be eighteen in two

from his chair but leaned forward a little. Lucy thought his eyes were not unsympathetic, but he too had tightened his lips and she knew that he would make no concession.

"You've never liked the Germans," Lucy said, to forestall the heavy discipline that she saw in Alessandro's face.

"It doesn't matter, I like Italian honor."

"That is enough," Alessandro said again. "Go to your room, Franco, and stay there until I tell you that you may leave it."

Now Franco turned to look squarely at his father, and he shouted loudly and his voice, between bitterness and anger, was near to tears.

"What do you know about honor?" he cried. "I know about you—you can't tell me what to do, ever again."

"You have gone crazy."

"Maybe you think it was honorable to take Pia into your room at night and then beat her up. Maybe you do!" Franco's voice welled up beyond his control. Lucy listened, for a shocked moment, and then she slapped his face. She had never slapped him before and she was almost as stunned, as hurt, as he. Alessandro pushed back his chair and took two steps towards them, then he stopped and said with a control that made his body tremble visibly:

"There is nothing in the world for which I owe you any explanation. Get to your room, Gian Franco, before I take a whip to you."

"You don't owe me anything and I don't owe you any-thing—I don't want an explanation—" Franco turned to his mother. "Ask Zia Margherita if I'm so crazy." And he ran from the room, stumbling at the doorsill. They heard him go towards the front door, and Alessandro went quickly after him. The door slammed twice, in close succession.

Lucy stood there listening. There was a faint sound of clatter from the kitchen and Zia Margherita had commenced to weep again. "He has gone quite crazy," she cried between her tears, "quite crazy."

Lucy left her there. She didn't know what Franco meant by saying, "Ask Zia Margherita—" but she remembered her feelings at the way the Zia had brought Aurelio up, so unclean and so unhealthy. With a surge of horror, she realized for the first time that, knowing what she did, she had yet gone away and left Franco to that influence.

She went into her room to wait for Alessandro and Franco. The room was dark; the electricity was off all over the city. She lay down on the bed without any intention of trying to sleep. Remorse and fear tore at her. She had betrayed Franco by her own selfishness. She listened to the sounds of the night. Emphasizing the little intimate sounds of the house, and making the moments of stillness vibrant, was the sound of firing somewhere to the north. People didn't violate curfew without knowing that they risked their lives. There was no personal vengefulness about it; it was a discipline necessary in wartime. They were necessary, the white flash and the dead prowler. Lucy closed her eyes. She thought, 'If I think of this I'll go mad before they ever have a chance to come back. I'll think of Crotone—perhaps we can get down there this summer.' She wondered whether the villa had been bombed. And then she thought of the Toccis, and that it was the lawyer's nephew who was to have gone that night with Franco, and terror spread again like thin ice in her veins.

It was midnight before Alessandro came in. He carried a candle which he put down on the desk, and came towards her. In the sudden yellow light, she could not see the look on his face, but she had no need to. He sat on the bed beside her and ran his hand across his face and through his hair. Then he sat forward, resting his arms on his knees.

"I couldn't find him; he must have hidden in a doorway while I passed. I went everywhere I could think of, even to the Toccis. The old Signora was screaming and crying. Nino had already gone."

Lucy sat up and took his hand.

"I'm sorry, Lucia, but at least I am sure the patrols didn't get him—we couldn't have been far apart and I should have heard that—but I'm sorry."

"No—*I* am sorry. The blame goes a long way back and it is mine."

Alessandro didn't move, but his shoulders hunched a little. It was as though he were afraid of what she might be thinking and that, beyond this slight physical gesture, he would not protect himself from it.

"Knowing the Zia, knowing her for so long, I shouldn't have left Franco to her influence—Oh, don't interrupt"—she gripped his hand tightly as he started to speak—"in all the years before I went away I treated Franco as though he were growing up in America. I took away all his defenses, and then I left him with a woman like that."

"Have you talked to her?"

"No, I don't want to."

"Lucy, I don't mind his going so much as his going with his mind in this confusion. I don't know what the boy is thinking. Whatever it is, I am greatly to blame. I need not have worked so hard that I had no time for him. If I had watched him, as I should have, I would have known when he started brooding over this matter and it could have been straightened out right away."

"Could it really, Alessandro? Do you remember what you said to him tonight, 'I owe you no explanation.' "

"Yes. I am sorry. I was angry."

"No, it is more than that," Lucy said, letting go of his hand, but speaking gently; "the Italian father demands a biblical respect from his sons. You would never have explained any action of yours to Franco, partly because you could not, and partly because it would never have occurred to you that there was any need for it. If you had been home often enough to notice that Franco was moody, or perhaps that he was avoiding you and not coming home himself more than he could help, you would have put it down to the war, or to his studies, or even suspected a girl. You would never have dreamed that he might be upset because of something that you had done. And he would never have told you—it took an important emotional crisis to bring it out even now."

"I am still at fault, Lucy."

Lucy was silent, watching his hands pressed hard together, the knuckles white and the long, thin fingers still.

"We are both to blame," she said at last; "you, because you followed the old ways you had been brought up to. You were feudal with Franco. And I, because I was too modern with him, and then left him alone in a feudal world, with his mind half formed and torn between two worlds. I am more at fault than you, for I wasn't blinded by background."

They sat in the semi-dark of candlelight and listened to the sounds of fighting. The house was still now, except for the small noises that awaken in any house after its inmates have settled for the night. Alessandro said, his voice loud against the night: "Would you like me to tell you about Pia —or do you know?"

"No. There's no need."

"Because you don't care?"

"No, because there is something of the Zia in this. If it's ever necessary to clear it up, for Franco, we will. But I don't even want to understand unless it is necessary."

"Lucy, you know that I can't ask her to leave—you know that we'll have to have her with us until things are more settled."

"Of course, my dear; it doesn't matter now."

They fell asleep at last, lying down on the bed and pulling a cover over themselves. When she awakened in the morning, Alessandro had already gone and Lucy was surprised for a moment to find that she was still dressed. When she remembered, she got up from the bed quickly and went to wash and change, afraid to stay by herself. Whatever happened now, she must move towards it. For what was to happen lay ahead, and Lucy, who had once thought to run away, saw that there was only one way to shorten agony. Let the moment come; she would not project herself, but she would not hide. In the meantime, there were the minute-by-minute details of living. There was no water in the bathroom. In the kitchen there was no water, and the servants were already out marketing. Lucy's tray was ready on the kitchen table and a pot of coffee simmered on a small charcoal brazier.

Pia came in at ten o'clock, followed by two American soldiers each carrying two demijohns of water. They put the water down, and Pia took them into the salon, where she turned them over to Lucy, saying, proudly, "American soldiers, Signora. The water pipes have been bombed and there is water only at the public taps. They brought mine home for me. Ask them if they know Leone, Signora Baronessa—Leone Pontevecchio, who lives in the Bronx."

Lucy shook hands with the men, thanking them. "Pia is

going to give you a glass of wine in a moment," she said, "but first she wants me to ask you whether you know a boy from the Bronx whose name is Leone Pontevecchio?" She didn't feel silly; rather, she felt sorry. She would have liked to say, "When you go north, if you see a young boy who is taller than most Italians, who is very thin, with a loose wave in his black hair, who has a high proud nose—if you see a boy whose eyes are suffering for all the wrongs of the world, that boy is mine. He's fallen like a burning branch from a tree and I, the tree, must stay rooted to my place and watch him while the fire that started in me consumes him. If you see him, soldier, please understand, please don't shoot him."

The smaller of the two soldiers spoke shyly. He said, "I don't just happen to know this Leone, I'm from Texas myself." And the other soldier said, "But there's lots coming after us, plenty from the Bronx too, I guess. Is he a relative, Ma'am?"

Lucy smiled. "Pia's fiancé—they've been engaged a long time."

"Oh, well——"

"Sure hope he turns up—" The soldiers looked embarrassed. In a moment, they said good-bye and Pia took them out to the kitchen. Lucy thought for the first time consciously of Leone, and wondered if he would turn up and if he would still be Italian enough to understand Pia, as Alessandro did and Franco. And, as on the first occasion when she had seen her, a ragged little waif by the lake at Valombra, Lucy was sorry for Pia.

33: $\mathcal{D}$AY AFTER day went by and there was no word of Franco. The Zia wore black all the time now. She spoke little and spent most of her time in her room. Lucy felt sorry for her, thinking that it was as though she had been staving off old age for a long time only to have it overcome her now without any resistance. Her eyes had the look of much weeping and her skin was sallow and wrinkled. Despite Aurelio's death, she had always been deeply devoted to Franco. Lucy tried to cheer her, but when she would not be cheered she left her to mourn, for this was something Lucy would not do, saying: "Franco is not dead. I have nothing to give him but my faith; but that I will give him, no matter how difficult it is."

The consciousness of faith was in itself a strain. Added to the years of hunger and malnutrition that had made her thin, now she developed a white, transparent look—the look of her concentration. She never forgot for a moment, but believed that there was some mystical tie between herself and Franco that she could keep alive only by being constantly aware of it. If she was writing a letter, or reading a book, or entertaining friends, there were always moments when she would pause, imagining Franco in a Fascist uniform that would not fit him because he was so thin, and issued uniforms never fit, anyway. She would imagine him lying in a hole in some field, with bullets and shrapnel churning the mud around him, and other men dying. And she would hold tight to her faith, and think 'He will not be killed. He is meant for something. He is the new Italy. Italy is going to need men like him.'

Once she looked up from such a moment to see that Alessandro had been studying her. Something in his eyes, which at once became guarded, hurt her. For she saw that he had not her faith but that he would not, for her sake, permit himself to show this. Ever since the night that Franco had gone there had been this understanding between them. It was something which they had never had before, and it was as though they saw each other for the first time. And they saw that it was not only for their children that they wanted the same things but for themselves and for society: a simple life that was peaceful, a life dignified by integrity. If she had been able to relax the sentry which her battle for faith in Franco's return had set over her every emotion, Lucy would have been happy.

In the kitchen, they watched the Donna Lucia, who had always seemed so robust, turn into a frail-looking woman. They watched Don Alessandro become white and still, his own eyes always on the Donna Lucia. Their warm hearts ached and they talked among themselves of the heart-breaking pity of it. Once, Pia said: "I will go and bring Franco back myself."

But they laughed at her. "If you took time off from running around with those American soldiers to get your dusting done it would be surprising, let alone running off up-country looking for Franco," Maria said sharply.

Pia looked injured. "I'm not playing around. I have to look for Leone."

"You'll find him better if you sit still and let him look for you," Little Doll said.

Pia shrugged. They couldn't understand. Why bother with

them? She didn't say anything else but she didn't forget. Two ideas fought within her. The coming of Leone, who must be near, with so many Americans come to Italy—who would surely come soon. And Franco, who had gone so wildly into danger, leaving a house of sorrow—and not even saying good-bye to her. Sometimes Pia thought of Franco sadly, because she loved him, and sometimes she thought more of the Donna Lucia and Don Alessandro. Their sorrow was strange to her because it was so silent and unexpressed, and more than anything in the world she wanted to stop it. Gradually, the thought took hold. There was something that she could do. "Leone," she thought, "will still be here—maybe when I get back, he will be sitting in the kitchen waiting for me." She was pleased with the idea, smiling to herself, and Leone was easily dismissed. He had been a dream for a great many years, while the need to bring Franco back was as real as housework, as dusting under the beds, as going to the Piazza for water. There was talk in the house now of going south. Pia grew sullen, not wanting to go and yet afraid, suddenly, of her own plans. The family would be far away, and Pia began to think that she had never been away since coming to them and that it would be easier if they would stay in Rome.

Less than a week after the Americans took Rome, people had commenced to talk of returning to the country. All who had their living from the land were anxious to see how their estates had come through the war. Alessandro was especially anxious, for Crotone had been severely bombed. What they would find there, he had no way of knowing. There was no means of transportation, mail service was slow and uncertain, and there was only official telephone communication. But Alessandro was anxious to make the attempt and Lucy's philosophy would not permit her to believe that it could make any difference whether she waited for Franco in Rome or in Crotone. If he should turn up in Rome while they were away, a dozen or more friends would take care of him until he could come south to them. On the other hand, Alessandro was anxious to go and it would be good to get Clara away to the country. A city without water or electricity, which is occupied by a great army, is not a healthful place for a child. It would be good for all of them to get away. The servants were impatient to go, the moment the possibility was mentioned, except Pia. And Lucy was glad to take Pia away. Her old fear and dislike of Pia were lost somewhere along the line of her own years of unhappiness. Lucy found that she now understood more readily and wanted to protect Pia from something which was, at its worst, no more than nature. Rome was teeming with soldiers who didn't know Leone Pontevecchio but who were glad enough to talk about him, their eyes on Pia's amazingly unpretty but voluptuous figure. Perhaps some of them looked into her big, green, childish eyes and did no more than talk of Leone. Lucy was sure that there were not many of these.

Alessandro had offered his services at once to the Allied command but, when they made it plain that they neither needed nor wanted him, he turned his mind to his own affairs. He made application for some form of conveyance, explaining that unless the landowners of the south were not only permitted but were, in fact, urged to go back to their estates and reorganize them, unless they were given transportation to go back and transportation to bring their produce to the central markets, Italy was going to have to be fed by the Allies or surrendered to famine.

A colonel at the Allied Military Government Headquarters,

whom he at first approached, muttered certain unforgivable things about bloody Eyeties trying to make money out of somebody else's bloody fighting and dismissed the whole matter. Others shrugged and passed him on; it wasn't their job. There were officers, tied to the written word, who would neither help nor hinder. Alessandro filled out innumerable forms for them but his heart was heavy. He knew that these men didn't care. They would file his applications according to regulations, and from that moment they would cease to think of him. An infinite number of clerks, drawing impersonal salaries for a day's work and with no consciousness of their own relationship to the problem on the application, would perform their task on this piece of paper. And that would be the end of it. It took a human ear to hear a human voice. Early in July, Alessandro walked into the offices of the AMG and asked to see Colonel Brown. Colonel Brown had filed three applications for him. He was told that Colonel Brown had been transferred. Major O'Hara would see him.

Major O'Hara was a small man with a ruddy complexion. His hair, which against a white skin would have seemed red, was like singed straw. If his father was Irish, out of County Cork, Major O'Hara had been born and raised in Flemington, New Jersey. Like most Americans, he had given generous thought to subjects about which he could not possibly know anything, and he had not in any way suffered by so doing. He knew nothing about the Italian farmer, but his method of translation was simple. He thought in terms of New Jersey. If the farmer couldn't get to the Flemington market and the buyer couldn't get to the Flemington market, what the hell was going to happen to the little woman who was trying to feed her family in Newark? Major O'Hara was not an idealist. He didn't care whether the farmer or the buyer made money by performing their functions. He wanted to see the machine in order. He wanted the little woman to have food on her table. Rome was not much different from Flemington, N. J. Translated into terms of Flemington, Major O'Hara saw the possibility that that little woman back in Newark might have to sacrifice a good part of her table to the woman in Rome. Major O'Hara figured that some fellows were over there to kill, and some fellows were over there to file paper. But that he, John Francis O'Hara, was there to see that this didn't happen. These Eyeties had their own farmers and the land was good enough, and they had their own merchants. He didn't believe in sending memorandums to Washington. He looked Alessandro in the eye, and said: "You'll get your transportaion, sonny." And, in his own mind, he finished— "and, for God's sake, see to it that you feed your own people."

Within a week, they were notified to be ready to leave on the 9th of July. This gave them two days in which to prepare themselves. For two solid days Maria cooked and wept, preparing food for them to take with them, and bemoaning the fact that she must remain in Rome, where marriage now held her. While Maria wept that she must stay, Pia wept that she had to go. Fortunata and Little Doll alone were satisfied, screaming their delight from room to room as they helped Lucy to pack and put things away. The Zia, after changing her mind five times, decided that she would remain in Rome. Maria would look after her, and she would be there if Graziano or Franco should return. Lucy tried to dissuade her, forcing herself to enthusiasm. When the Zia finally refused to change her plans, she was relieved. The job of packing only the essential clothes and provisions became a work of joy.

The south country was as old as any country in the world and as long as it had been inhabited Alessandro's people had lived there. Lucy used to feel as though she had been planted atop a civilization that was old, where danger and decay awaited her once she pushed down her roots into its depths. She had been frightened and unsure. But now she knew that any pioneer goes into the old seeking a place for the newness which he carries in him. Whether the villa were still there or the property damaged, this is what she and Alessandro were about to do. They would rebuild, they would make a new world possible on top of the old.

Then the day before they were due to leave, Pia took her courage in her hands. She would not go. She would go north instead. She said nothing to Lucy or Alessandro, afraid that they would stop her, though she knew herself to be of age. In the kitchen, she said frankly:

"I am going. Some American soldiers have offered me a ride. I will go with them as far as I can and then I will walk."

"There will be fighting," Fortunata said fearfully; "you had better come with us."

"No, I am going. I have decided."

When they saw that she had indeed made up her mind, they stopped arguing and commenced to ply her with advice. Maria prepared a bundle of food for her to take with her. There was a loaf of bread and the can of American meat which one of Pia's soldiers had left as a present and which had been saved for a special occasion. There was also a dish of baked noodles done up in a napkin. Pia wrapped up the food, together with a change of clothes, a stub of lipstick and a half-emptied box of face powder which she had once taken from the waste-basket and treasured ever since. Little Doll found her an old pillowcase to carry her things in and advised her to stop at Fortemino, where a relative of her man's would be sure to help her and, in any case, would know all the gossip.

"Gino Buozzi," Pia said, "I will remember to go to him if I am at Fortemino." And she thanked them and they all kissed her and wished her a safe trip. It was night when she left and no one thought to speak to Lucy or Alessandro of her going, thinking that she would have taken leave of them.

It was not until six o'clock the next morning, when a two-and-a-half-ton truck pulled up in front of the house that Lucy and Alessandro discovered that Pia had gone. Then it was too late to do anything about it. Lucy was distressed but there was too much to be thought of to dwell long on the girl and it was not until much later that she awakened to a sense of anxiety for her.

The entire household rushed to the window of the living room to look at the truck. Lucy said: "Oh no, that's not for us!"

"But yes, but yes, Donna Lucia," Maria and Fortunata cried together. Maria explained that the man who was going to drive them, an Italian soldier by the name of Stefano, was in the kitchen that very minute.

Clara said, "Wait till Pia sees!" jumping up and down in her excitement.

"Why, Pia's gone," Fortunata said, surprised. "Don't you remember, she went last night?"

"Pia gone!" Lucy looked quickly over Clara's head at Alessandro.

"Gone where?" he asked, looking at Fortunata sternly. "Why was I not told?"

Maria commenced to wail, "Ah, the bit of bad luck. We thought surely she had spoken to you—and now she brings down displeasure on all of us. Ah, it was an evil day we ever saw that girl."

"Be still," Alessandro said to her, and to Fortunata, "Well?"

"She has gone north," Fortunata hesitated unhappily. "She has gone to find the Signorino Franco," she blurted out at last.

Lucy put her hand to her throat quickly. Alessandro put an arm about Clara, who was still now. "We shall have to go," he said slowly. "There is nothing that we can do."

"Perhaps we could wait," Lucy suggested. She looked out of the window at the truck. "We can find out something about Pia—and perhaps get a car."

Alessandro shook his head. "We may not be given another opportunity. We can't afford to wait."

Lucy nodded. "Well then, we must start."

Within an hour the truck was packed, they had had their breakfast and were ready to leave. The Zia wept and kissed them all, over and over again, declaring that she never expected to see them alive. Or that if they did return, she would certainly be dead, very likely raped and murdered by the Americans. Lucy, scarcely listening, murmured conventionally, "That would be too bad. Better change your mind and come with us."

"In that!" the Zia cried. "No, no, I'll be quite all right here, quite comfortable. Now, you mustn't worry." And she kissed them all again and hustled them towards the door, Maria weeping and imploring the heavens, kissing Lucy's hand and the hem of her skirt.

The road from Rome to Naples was shelled and torn up almost beyond recognition. In more places than one, where the road was impassable, they turned onto dirt-packed detours, the heavy truck digging into the earth and going so slowly that they could have walked beside it. They went by field after field marked off with white tape, where the mines had not yet been cleared away or exploded. They went through towns that were half destroyed and towns where not one small hut still stood. They saw children, not so old as Clara, who were blind or crippled and more than half-naked. As the truck passed, apathy faded from the children's small bodies, and in an instant they were running and stumbling, hobbling and hopping in their wake, their hands outstretched crying: "Caramelli, caramelli!"

Lucy thought that she would never cease to hear their voices. And she was austerely glad of her own discomfort. The hard wooden bench, the springless truck that jolted them until they could feel every bone in their bonies, the swirl of fine dust that eddied about them, settling on them, and the burning heat of the sun were some slight salve to her conscience. She could not have borne greater comfort, in sight of these children.

The first night, they spent at San Jacimo, at the house of a friend of Zia Margherita's. It was the last night, for a week, in which they were to sleep in comfort. They started out early the following morning and, by nightfall, they had reached Lago Negra, seven hours from Crotone. The small hotel was in process of being taken over by soldiers, and there were only two houses intact in the entire village. Alessandro went into the hotel and in a few moments he returned and spoke to Lucy.

"I know you're tired," he said, "but it would be better if we went on."

"Are there no rooms?"

"It's not only that. We can have a room which has not yet been processed for the soldiers. The servants can sleep in the truck—I don't think it wise to accept. The place is very dirty."

Lucy shrugged. "We must, Alessandro. It's impossible to do this road at night. If I am exhausted, think of the driver! In the daytime, in an ordinary car, these mountains are bad enough." She shuddered. "I shall be so glad to see the last of this truck."

So they stayed for the night. They unpacked their own bedding, giving two blankets each to the women in the truck and taking what was necessary to cover the one broken-down bed in the room which they had been given. Lucy had never before slept in a village hotel in Italy and now she discovered why Alessandro had not wanted her to. Despite turning the mattress and covering it tightly with their own clean sheets, there were bedbugs. Lucy couldn't sleep, and Clara commenced to thrash about restlessly in her sleep. After that, they wrapped up in their blankets and sat up in two straight-backed chairs, with Clara stretched over their laps. Through the night they slept intermittently, and intermittenly they awakened, because they were uncomfortable, or because the laughing and singing and cursing of the soldiers in the salon below and out on the piazza had pierced their dreams. Then they would look at each other and Alessandro would take her hand without smiling and Lucy would feel soothed by the strength that was in him, and she would sleep again.

34:      $\mathcal{D}$ESPITE heavy bombing, there was remarkably little damage done to Crotone. The bottom floor was shot out from the hospital, so that it stood like a Romanesque house on stilts. The main stair was almost completely undamaged, and the second floor was still in active use. There were shell-holes in the streets, and heaps of rubble, and several other buildings had gaps in roof or wall. The truck approached Crotone in the early afternoon. In spite of their state of exhaustion, the entire family stirred with excitement. To all of them, except Little Doll, this was home. Fortunata waved and screamed at people whom she recognized in the streets, who waved and screamed in turn and then ran off to spread the news. By the time they came to the Villa a small crowd of old friends had gathered.

"You can't go in there," they cried, pointing to the house, "you can't go in there! The Allied Military Government is living there. Ah, Don Alessandro, Donna Lucia, what changes, what tragedies!"

Cato appeared, followed by his old dog, neither looking a day older. Fortunata fell upon his neck, weeping and laughing in a breath. Emma was there, with three of her own children, who had been born since the beginning of the war, and another child whose parents had both been killed. Louisa, who had worked at the house as a young girl, was there, with one baby at her breast and another beneath her girdle. Fortunata grinned at her and said: "You were caught for good, without a doubt."

Louisa commenced to cry, her young face breaking into deep creases, and aging her in a second.

Emma said, "Shut your mouth, Fortunata, until you know what other people have had to suffer." Her arm pointed at Louisa, and she turned to Lucy again. "There's not a young husband left in Crotone. Louisa's is rotting in Africa without even an inch of Christian soil to lie in. My Luigi is gone, and Tomaso has come back without a leg. Old Mateo, from Valombra, is without either arm."

Lucy said, "I am sorry," and she thought of the hospital she had worked in. And that in war there are so many casualties that you cease to think of them as individuals—five thousand men are maimed, ten thousand, a hundred—it doesn't mean anything until you come home and find out who those thousands are. Mateo, who had a way with wild things, who could lay a hand on the head of a crazed mule and quiet it, who cut the trees for grafting as delicately as a surgeon cuts human flesh, and himself supervised every growing, living thing at Valombra. Those thousands were Mateo, they were Louisa's husband and Emma's sons. Lucy said softly, "I am very sorry," feeling sick and tired. They came up to kiss her hand and the hem of her skirt, and to kiss Clara on the forehead. And when Alessandro came out of the Villa to announce that the house was indeed Allied Military headquarters, and that there was neither room there nor at the hotel, they offered their homes and their beds. These were old friends.

Alessandro thanked them and said, "No, they would go on to Valombra. They could stretch their legs now and talk a while, and then they must go on. They left Clara to go with Fortunata to Emma's house, while Little Doll and the driver went with Louisa to her mother-in-law's house for a glass of wine. Lucy and Alessandro went onto the terrace of the Villa, where they were greeted by a British colonel in command of the post. He sent for chairs for them and told them that tea was being brought. They talked of local conditions for a few moments and then the colonel left them, saying to Alessandro:

"We've heard from Major O'Hara. We'll try to let you have trucks when your harvest is ready. There is no communication up to your place, and I'm afraid that both of your cars and your truck have been requisitioned. But send a messenger down when you're ready and we'll take care of it."

When he'd gone, Lucy turned to Alessandro anxiously, "The cars and the truck. That's bad!" But he only shrugged.

"I'm surprised that they were still here to be requisitioned. We're lucky that the house is still standing—and Valombra."

They waited for their tea without speaking, but searching with their eyes: the façade of the house, the weed-grown garden, the terrace and the pale aquamarine of the bay. The balustrade of the terrace was smashed in several places, and the small beach was littered with dirt and rubble. Alessandro's eyes were veiled, not telling anything. Lucy thought how only the past could really hurt you. The present could be insecure and unsettled, the future had always to be full of hope, but the past, however happy it had been, was separated from the present by a film of sadness. Franco had been a skinny little boy here, running along the beach or pushing out his boat to go fishing in the day. Here, on the terrace, Clara had learned to walk, and they had all laughed so to see her waddle and tumble like an overstuffed duck. And here Pia had first come, so thin and ragged, flinging her curses at the world in general, a half-drowned kitten spitting at its rescuer. Even the memory of Aurelio was shorn of any bitterness. Lucy wanted to weep, thinking of his broken young body being carried across the terrace.

She said, her eyes searching the beach for those little flecks of gold that the children used to collect and carry around in matchboxes, "Do you know, I think it would be my idea of Heaven to be able to live always in the past but from the point of view of the present."

"The past is something you can never catch up with," Alessandro said softly. "It is not well to think of it too much."

Lucy nodded. "But you can't escape it, either."

"You can if you keep your mind on the present."

Lucy wanted to say, "It hurts you as much as it does me—share it with me, Alessandro, and we will both feel it less." But instead she said, "Where shall we live at Valombra?"

"There is a house there which my grandfather built. In his day it was not easy to get from Valombra to Crotone in a day, and during the season he used to take his family there to live."

Lucy frowned, for a moment, and then she said quickly: "Of course, you told me once, the storage house."

"Yes. We'll have a few rooms cleared out for our use, and then we'll see. Perhaps before winter we can get the Villa back."

Their tea came and, when they had finished, they went out to the truck. They had hoped to spend the night at Nimpha, but they had not left the orange grove five kilometers behind them before the truck broke down. The driver told them that he could repair it in a couple of hours, so they built a fire and prepared supper. But when dark came, repairs were not yet completed. Alessandro decided that they would sleep where they were, for the village didn't know that they were coming, and peasants go to bed with the sun. They wrapped themselves in their blankets again and, this time, Lucy and Clara stretched out beside the two servants on the floor of the truck. Alessandro and the driver wrapped themselves up well and slept underneath the truck.

In the morning, they rebuilt the fire and had breakfast. When they had cleaned up and packed the things that they had used back onto the truck, Lucy took Clara and Fortunata and commenced to walk. Little Doll remained behind, saying that she was too fat to walk, and Alessandro remained to help with the repairs on the engine. From where they had stopped the night before the road was steep and winding and dark. It cut through the forest, where chestnut and pine met overhead, leaving only occasional pieces of sky visible.

By noon, the car had overtaken them and they rode up the mountain to Nimpha. As they went by Valombra, Lucy thought that she had never seen anything so lovely as its wild waters. And she thought that if she could undress here and walk down the rocky shore until the waters closed over her head she would come out not only cleansed of the mud and grime and fatigue of the trip, but somehow refreshed in spirit. She looked towards the small village, among the rocks high above them, and was glad to be there.

35: *I*T WAS early June when
Franco, Nino Tocci, Giuseppe Bruno and Antonio Ronni fled
Rome. It was easy enough, in the confusion. They walked out
of the city, avoiding the roads where the army thundered by.
They went down back alleys and along streets that led far out
of their way. Once outside of Rome, they hid in the hills for
almost a week, for they were afraid that the roads would be
watched, not yet realizing their own unimportance or the im-
potence of their parents to reach out an arm for them in a
world at war.

They had a little money, a thousand lire between them, and
Giuseppe and Antonio had packages of food. They wore black
shirts under their coats but they had no other uniforms or any
arms. From the hills, they watched the roads and saw the
American army moving steadily out of Rome. Towards the end
of the week, they decided to go on, whatever the cost. Their
nerves, between impatience and excitement, were taut and they
thought that if they did not hurry, the war would have been
fought out and they still hiding in the hills.

There was nothing for them to do but to go on foot. If they
had made their decision soon enough, they could have ridden
with the rear guard of the German army—or had lifts from
any number of Fascists fleeing Rome. But in those last days,
there had been too great a confusion. No one had known what
was happening, and their decision was born of this confusion.

They went across country, avoiding the highways. Antonio Ronni was a Tuscan and knew the country to some degree. His memory was not always accurate and they had, on occasions, to retrace their steps, finding that they had gone too far afield. They slept on the ground at night and talked briefly of the things that were in their minds. They never spoke of the thing that they were doing, but of the little things that they would do when they came home again, of the places they would go to and the food they would eat. They thought of honor and of the faith that they kept, and when they slept their lips were tight and their eyes were sometimes wet. For they were proud and they were secretly afraid. They went by day, climbing the hills and cutting across fields and through woods. They got food and, sometimes, wine from the peasants. For the most part they paid for it but now and again some peasant refused any pay, seeing their black shirts and their wild young faces and thinking that there was trouble enough in this world without inviting any more.

Twice they came through the woods, led on by the sound of guns and the heavy jar of bombardment, only to go back and hide until the air was still again. They knew that they would get short shrift from either side if they tried to slip through the lines during action. They became depressed, afraid that they would never catch up. Then, on the 8th of July they came back onto the main route and ran into the rear of the German army, at Arezzo. They stood on the crest of the opposite hill and saw the line of trucks, like gray ants, moving up the hill and into the town. The green fields were mottled with shell holes and the skies overhead were vibrant with small, black fighting planes, covering up the retreat.

Nino caught his breath audibly. Antonio Ronni said: "I guess it's now."

"Yes." Franco could feel the sweat on his hands. He wiped them on the seat of his trousers and started down the hill. At the foot of the hill, and across a wheatfield, they came to the road. Now they saw that the trucks were crowded with soldiers or bristling with guns and mechanized gear. Most of the soldiers looked through them, their eyes blank with weariness and the shock of retreat. Now and again, some soldier would wave or call out to the boys, offering them a ride. The trucks never slowed down but they moved slowly enough, in any case. The boys separated, running beside them and jumping on where they could.

Headquarters in Arezzo were not hard to find, for the Germans had taken over the Grand Hotel, an old palace on the main square. Sentries guarded the massive doors and a steady line of officers and soldiers moved in and out across the threshold. Trucks thundered through the square, rumbling over the cobbles like the clatter of a thousand drayhorses. Franco and his friends jumped off as their trucks drew abreast of the hotel, and they sprinted quickly to the safety of the small garden in the center of the square. They stood for a moment, catching their breath and watching the door of the hotel. Nino said: "I'd give my head right now to be home."

Giuseppe laughed nervously. He was small and slight for his seventeen years and, like Antonio and Nino, he had soft, brown eyes. "You'll probably do that, or the equivalent, for being here," he said.

"Go back if you want," Franco said scornfully, "there's probably time still," and he plunged across the square without waiting for an answer.

The lobby of the Grand Hotel had formerly been the hall of an old palace. A warm, red rug covered the stone floors, but scantily, while imitation Renaissance furniture and worn, red plush upholstery, of later pretensions, had some effect on the size of the room but none whatsoever on its comfort. The walls were hung with painted tapestries. In the center of the largest of these, over the hotel desk, a picture of Hitler had been posted.

A soldier accompanied the boys to the desk, saluted the sergeant behind it and said something in German. The sergeant looked at the boys, saluted and said, "Heil Hitler!"

The four boys raised their arms silently. Giuseppe explained what they wanted. The sergeant, who was fat, red-faced and disinterested, asked for their papers. When he had them, he tapped them until their edges were precisely aligned and pushed them away from him to a corner of the desk.

"Go over there," he said, pointing to a bench along the wall. "Wait until you are called."

It was morning when they crossed the square and it was four o'clock that afternoon before they were called back to the desk. They were tired and out of temper and hungry. Antonio and Giuseppe had decided three times to leave; then, seeing the look of the squat, red-faced sergeant, they had changed their minds. Now it was over. They went eagerly and when the sergeant handed them safety passes and said, "Come back tomorrow," their faces clouded angrily.

Franco and Giuseppe knew German, and Franco protested for them. "We want to fight," he said. "Why do we have to wait? Why do we have to come back? Our papers are in order, aren't they? We've all had good records with the pre-military and the Avanguardisti."

"Come back tomorrow," the sergeant said stolidly. Then, as though taking pity on them, he unbent so far as to explain. "The army is a big thing. It is consolidating quickly for heavy offensive action. It can't stop to consider your feelings. You will be taken care of. You will be taken in where you are needed. Maybe you will have to come back several days. We are keeping your papers until it is decided where you are to go. If we have to move from Arezzo quickly, you will have to come along and report when we set up HQ again. Now, come back tomorrow."

They went out in search of food and, when they had eaten, they wandered nervously about the town. When night fell, they went across the fields to sleep, for the town was crowded and the air was close and restless with movement. They went back to Headquarters the next day, and the next. Then, on the 11th of July, three days after they had stood on the hill opposite Arezzo and watched the retreating army move up the long road, a month and a week since they had left Rome, they were called up.

They went eagerly, grinning at the squat sergeant with a feeling almost of triumph. They followed a soldier down a narrow hall and into a cell-like room. There was one table in this room and behind it sat a young Oberleutnant. They saw that their papers were on the blotter before him.

They saluted and the soldier went out. The Oberleutnant took up the first small stack of papers. "Antonio Ronni," he snapped.

Antonio stood forward, saluting again.

The officer gave him his papers. "You'll find your orders there," he said in fluent, but precise Italian. "You proceed to Rimini—" he looked at his watch—"Company C.s977 leaves in forty-five minutes. You go with them."

Antonio's mouth was open to protest, when the German cut him short. "Giuseppe Bruno." He handed him his papers. "You leave with the same convoy. At Montevarchi report to

H.Q. and they'll trans-ship you to Milano. Gian Franco Cava-lierre and Ferdinando Tocci, you remain here, for the time being. That's all."

The boys fingered their papers nervously, their eyes on the German officer.

"Well! Go on, get out," he said when they didn't move.

"Couldn't we—stay together," Antonio blurted out suddenly. The others were still, their faces hopeful.

The Oberleutnant's head snapped up and he stared at them as though he were seeing them for the first time. He was a young man, with an old face and faded brown hair. For a moment, his gray eyes were warm.

"We wanted to fight together," Nino explained.

"You want to serve your country," the German said at last. "That's good. We're trying to help you. We're putting you where you can do that best. You're a Tuscan," he pointed to Antonio, "and you," his finger waved at Giuseppe, "Venetian. We're putting you where you're needed. Where you know the country and the dialects. You two Calabrians—we'll have to see." Suddenly, the sorry look went out of his eyes. He jumped up from his chair, leaning across the table towards the startled boys. "Why the devil should it matter to me?" he stormed, "I went into Poland when I was sixteen. I've been fighting ever since. Gott! Why should I be called on to be sorry for you— just because you're young!"

The boys were embarrassed. The Oberleutnant sat down and grabbed up a stack of papers. Franco said: "Well, thank you anyway." And they all saluted and went out.

Franco and Nino went with the other two to help them find their Company. They didn't talk. There was nothing that any of them could think of to say. They hadn't pictured the war this way. They wanted guns, and a field with men fighting and dying in plain sight. They stayed together as long as they could. When they had to part, they kissed each other and then turned their backs, Giuseppe and Antonio walking towards their truck, Franco and Nino going towards the square. They wanted food, though they had eaten already. They were nervous and excited. For they were in it, as they had dreamed of being for the past four years.

"Something will happen now," Franco said and Nino nodded. "Bound to!" And they went off in search of the trattoria, talking fast so that they need not think of Antonio and Giuseppe.

36:

*P*IA WAS alone on the road. The other roads, the road from Rome to Cortona, the road from Cortona to Fortemino, had all been crowded. There had been an unending line of trucks and jeeps and army tanks coming out of Rome. Pia, a little cramped but happy, had travelled hidden away in the back of one of the trucks. She had giggled and chattered and sung songs and the soldiers had talked slowly and very loudly as though by this means to overcome the difference in language. In two nights she had covered more than half the distance that it had taken Franco and his friends almost a month to cover. Another half day, and she could have been as near to Arezzo as the British were going to get for the moment. But before Cortona they put her off, sadly but firmly. They were too near the fighting area. They tried to explain, gesturing with their guns and making a pantomime of bombs bursting and men dying. They went off down the highway, waving as they went and singing the songs she had taught them, the sometimes lilting, sometimes two-toned and formless songs of Calabria.

Pia watched them, for the first time frightened. Those soldiers had made her feel so safe. They were nice boys, like Johann and Hans. Some were like Emile, the German soldier whom Johann had thrown out of the house because he had held her on his lap and kissed her.

Truck after truck rolled on to Cortona and down the highway. They all looked alike and they all left Pia feeling more and more alone. The road into Cortona was asphalt, it was the highway to Florence. The way around the town was unpaved and this road was as busy as the highway, for it was crowded with refugees from Arezzo and Morra, from Fortemino and the battleground villages to the north. Carts and people afoot, and overburdened mules, trudged up the road. Pia went by them, going in the direction they fled from. No one gave her a glance, for these people were too heavy with their own troubles to care.

Once she stopped to speak to an old man who was resting by the way. "Are the Germans far from here?" she asked.

The old man only dropped his head a little lower and had no answer. A woman, with a great bundle on her head, called out without pausing, "They're near enough, all right. There's not a room left in my house, that was fine as a palace and the cleanest house in Fortemino."

"Fortemino!" Pia cried, suddenly remembering Little Doll's instruction to look up Gino Buozzi at Fortemino. "Is it the Fortemino where Gino Buozzi lives?" But the woman had gone beyond hearing.

Perhaps he was on this very road and she had passed him, or would pass him, without knowing that she did so. She called out to a woman who walked beside a cart laden with bundles and household goods.

And the woman called back, "Who asks for Gino Buozzi and walks herself into trouble?"

Pia turned and walked beside the woman, going back towards Cortona.

"Is he on the road?" she asked.

"He has not moved from his farm. He does not need to," the woman said, and spat in the dust. Now there were voices breaking the apathy of the people nearest them, and each of the voices cursed Gino Buozzi and warned Pia against him.

"He will bring you a harm," they cried; but Pia would not listen. She had to go on, and this was the only way she knew.

"Where does he live?" she begged of them. When they saw how it was, they shrugged and one of them told her:

"Follow the road to Fortemino. Go straight through the town, where you will see that the church no longer has a roof and the houses no longer any walls, and that the Germans are great pigs. Go out of Fortemino, straight along the road, until you come to the bridge to Morra. Do not set your foot on the bridge unless you wish to die very quickly. To the right of the bridge is a footpath. It will lead you to Gino Buozzi."

Pia thanked them and went down the road to Fortemino. The nearer she came to Fortemino, the smaller was the stream of refugees. In the village itself, a few old people and children picked through the ruins futilely. Nobody looked at Pia and she hurried through the town, half afraid of the derelicts who hovered there, with bleakness in their eyes and strange noises on their lips. Beyond the town, on the now deserted roadside, Pia sat down to eat. She opened her pillowcase and took out the dish of noodles. It was cold but still intact, for the soldiers had refused to taste of it, or to let her do so. They had put it firmly away when she took it out, making her share their rations instead. For all its coldness, it tasted good and Pia thought sorrowfully of Maria's fine cooking and she commenced to cry, the tears making black furrows through the white dust on her face.

The sun had gone down and the soft July dusk gave the throbbing land a sinister air. Coming from Rome, the noise of trucks and the buzz of planes constantly overhead had seemed a warm and friendly sound. When they had come within reach of the far-off, thudding sounds of war these had not seemed important, for Pia was among friends and safe. On the road from Cortona the feeling of fear had started but, even then, surrounded by people, these sounds were still impersonal. Now she was alone. There was not a creature on the road, that she could see. Somewhere ahead of her, beyond the hilly horizon, night crouched—and a terrible pounding and coughing came from that place.

Pia tied up her bundle of food, dried her tears and hastened forward. Whoever Gino Buozzi was, she must get to him, for she was afraid to stay on the empty road.

It was dark when she came to the bridge. She was singing aloud to herself to keep her mind from the thoughts that crowded in on it. "Tornerai—" Because it was a love-song, she thought of Leone and how far away he was, and that perhaps she would never see him at all. Then she thought of Franco and her heart was warm and maternal and she hastened on, thinking how glad he would be to see her, and how surprised. The bridge loomed suddenly and Pia stopped dead, remembering that the people had warned her not to touch her foot to the bridge but to turn to the right and look for a footpath.

She had no trouble in finding it, but some difficulty in following it. It was a narrow path, and crooked. For a way, it went beside the stream; then, abruptly, it bent, going through an olive grove. It was dark here, darker even than the night, and Pia stumbled off the path more than once. Then, out of the black, a dog barked. Pia stopped, dropping her bundle and grabbing at it again. Blind panic seized her and she turned and bolted but, missing her way, ran into the low branches of an olive tree. She moaned crazily, turning again; this time, she ran into the arms of a short, thick-set man who stood on the path. The man held a storm lantern, so shuttered that only a single ray of light escaped it. He lifted it now, catching her by the throat with his free hand.

He studied her for an instant, then he grunted, lowering the lantern. "Who are you and what do you want?" he asked. Behind them, the dog was still barking excitedly.

Pia moaned, "Madonna, Madonna, Madonna, protect me!" She couldn't see the man as anything but a short, black mass. At her throat his hand was as rough and hard as wood. Terror ran through her, turning her body to water, and she commenced to whimper.

"Shut up," the man snarled and he gave her a quick push, twisting her around at the same time so that her back was towards him and his hand was on the back of her neck. "We'll see about you," he said, pushing her ahead of him.

Fifty paces ahead of them the path ended in a clearing. As they came into it, Pia saw that they were before a small stone building. A large dog was chained to a stake in the ground. At sight of the man, the dog gave two short barks and was quiet. The man said something to the animal that was at once gruff and gentle and, at the words, Pia could feel her own muscles relax. The dog lay down. The man let go of Pia, thrusting her towards the house and saying, "Get in."

An oil lamp hung from the ceiling of the room that they entered. The man kicked the door to quickly and put the lantern down without turning it out.

"Now then, we can get a look at you." He pointed to a bench by the wall and Pia sat down, still trembling. In the yellow light, she could see that he was not the black ape that her terrified imagination had conjured up, but a red-faced peasant. His hair was white and grew like a thatch to his head, and his eyebrows were almost as big as his mustache.

"Are you Gino Buozzi?" Pia asked, her fear suddenly gone.

"Who asks?" the man growled.

"I am a friend of Bambolina Cresca, whose husband is your relative."

"Ah, and what does the friend of Bambolina Cresca want?"

Pia giggled nervously. "Nothing, I don't think," she said. "I am on my way to the German army, to look for a friend. The Little Doll told me that Gino Buozzi would likely give me a place to sleep for the night, or perhaps some food."

"She did?" The peasant studied her, his black eyes like gimlets.

Pia started up, angry now. "Well, if you're Gino Buozzi then I don't like you, and I think I'd as soon sleep out in the night."

"Yes, I'm Gino. Sit down," he said. And Pia sat down, her courage gone out of her at his tone.

"How did you expect to get over to the German army?" he asked.

"Walk. I'll go tomorrow, if you'll let me sleep here tonight."

"Walk! You'd blow up in two seconds. Like that, poof!" and he whistled so that his mustache whirled up in the air to flop over his lips when the "poof" was done.

"Oh," Pia said, thinking uncomfortably of the bridge that she had been warned about.

"You could be spying on me." Gino Buozzi scowled at her and Pia was glad that she was not spying, and wondered secretly what there was to spy about. "Have you got any money?" he asked.

Pia shook her head.

He went to her bundle and emptied it out on the floor. He fingered through the clothes carefully, squatting down and examining each thing separately. He even ran his hands through the remains of the noodles, which had spilled out onto the floor. Then he pushed them back into the bowl and wiped his hand on the pillow-slip. Pia watched him and the fear commenced to choke her again. The light of the storm lantern played directly on him, making his shadow grotesque. He seemed to be only a foot tall, with a head so big that it spread out across the floor, turning a sharp angle to climb the far wall. When he had finished going through her things, he sat back on his haunches.

"Take off your shoes," he demanded.

Pia stared at him, but when he started towards her she bent quickly to undo the shoes and toss them to him. He took a long, thin knife from his pocket and prodded the lining up from the shoes, felt inside with his hands and then looked along the edges of the soles carefully for new stitching. When he was through with them he went to her, pulling her to her feet and running his hands over her body. His square, hard fingers hesitated along seams and hems, searching diligently. Pia was sobbing now, thoroughly frightened. If his moving fingers had had another meaning she would not have been so frightened, but this was something which she could not understand. When he was through with her, he said:

"No money, no papers. It is a good thing for you that you spoke the truth." He retrieved his knife from the floor and kicked at her things. "Pick them up," he said. "I'll take you through the lines tonight."

"You will!"

"Yes, if you are good. If you are not—" he made a gesture with his knife. "I have business. I can't have you hanging around. And I can't have you going back full of talk as a magpie. I will take you tonight."

While Pia picked up her things, Gino Buozzi brought out a piece of black bread from a cupboard by the wall. From an iron kettle he dished out two plates of beans. Then he pulled the bench that Pia had been sitting on close to the table and sat down to his meal. When they had finished, he let Pia clear the plates away.

"Do we go now?" she asked. But he shook his head, pointing to a far corner of the room, where she saw a bed of straw.

"The moon must rise and set first. Go and sleep."

Pia went gratefully, suddenly aware of a great fatigue. She lay down, wondering if he would come to her, half nauseated at the idea, for she thought him a dirty old man and terrifying. Then, even as she wondered, she slept.

Pia was awakened by a kick. She stumbled up, with a cry on her lips. But the wooden hand was pressed down over her mouth and she swallowed the sound.

"It's time," Gino Buozzi said. "Be quiet—I've locked the dog up but he's got good ears and I don't want him barking. Now, listen to me."

Pia nodded, shuddering a little as she brought herself back to earth. The room was pitch-black now except for the single ray of the lantern.

"You must keep close to me," he went on. "When we come to a certain place I will close the shutter of the lantern. After that, it will be quite dark—and very dangerous. You must watch me closely and see to it that you put your feet only where I have put mine. If you walk anywhere else you will be killed. Do you understand?"

Pia nodded mutely.

"Then, come!"

They went quickly while they had the lantern. After that, they went like snails and the slow pace was harder to keep than a fast one would have been. For Pia, it was torture. She discovered that Gino Buozzi, for all of his short stature, took steps that were hard for her to put her feet into. But she followed him religiously, for every boulder and every blade of grass spelled terror to her, and certain death. Gino, who was ugly and unkind and strange, became by contrast everything that was secure and lovable.

They went through the woods and across two fields and up a hill. At the summit, Gino Buozzi stopped.

"This is as far as I go," he said, pointing to a white ribbon that was a road, in the valley beneath them. "They've only just finished with the mining behind us—they have done nothing ahead yet. You are five kilometers from Arezzo. You'll probably get shot. Well—good luck!"

Pia tried to thank him but already he was going down the hill, a black mass hardly to be distinguished from the boulders about him. She turned towards the valley, putting one foot cautiously before the other. Now that she was alone, the black of the night seemed solid to her and she stretched out her hand as though by so doing she could feel where she was going. She stumbled once and fell, bruising her leg and her elbow. Then, instead of getting up, she lay there, thinking:

"I will get up when the morning comes. I am too tired now. Now, I will sleep." And she groped for her bundle and put her head on it.

In the morning, she awakened stiff and aching. She lay there for a moment, thinking that the world was not so pleasant a place and that she wished she were back in Rome. Then she got up and took her bundle and went down the hill to the road.

Pia approached Arezzo from the west three days after Franco and his friends had first stood on the hill to the southeast of the town. In the valley, the road was deserted but, over the next hill, it was joined by the main highway. On this road the straggling rear of the German army moved northwards. Arezzo itself was crowded with soldiers and trucks and tanks. Pia thought that she had never seen such movement.

"It is like lice on the body of a dead cat," she thought—and again she wished that she were back in Rome. In Rome, there had never been so many soldiers. In Rome, the soldiers would talk to you too. Here, they went by you as though you were not there, knocking and jostling if you were in their way, even by so much as the measure of a thumb. The people of the town who were on the streets hurried, and they went with their heads down.

At the corner of the Corso and the square, five trucks stood in line, preparing to leave. Pia approached a group of soldiers who were climbing into one of the trucks and asked where she would find the Fascist army. Two or three of them made harsh sounds and slapped at the air to show their disgust at the word Fascist; but one, who understood, answered her in halting Italian:

"They are in the north—Florence maybe. Not here."

"Are you going to Florence?" Pia asked, encouraged.

"None of your business," the soldier said coldly.

Pia smiled at him and her green eyes went from one cold face to another. "Please take me with you," she begged. But the only one who understood her, looked at her so hard and so suspiciously that she shrank away, slipping past the trucks quickly and going down the street.

It was mid-morning and Pia was hungry. She had bread and cheese left in her pillow-slip and a can of rations the soldiers had given her. It was not much and it had to last until she could find soldiers friendlier than these, or perhaps a farm where she could work in return for a dish of beans. She hurried down the road leading out of Arezzo. When the sun had passed the center of the sky, she would eat. At the bottom of the hill, a road-post marked the kilometers to Solfermino, Montevarchi and Florence.

Pia had scarcely reached the sign when she heard the rumble of approaching trucks. She stood aside, waving at them and hoping that one of them would relent and stop for her. There were five, and they went steadily by. The dust whirled backwards from their great tires, encircling her. She choked and put her bundle quickly to her face, peering over the top of it. From the first truck the soldier she had talked to surprised her by waving, but the truck did not stop. Nor did the others. The smile had died unhappily from her face when, as the last truck thundered by, Pia recognized the small, dark face of Antonio Ronni among the horde of bleak, gray soldiers. She sucked in her breath, stunned for an instant, and then rushed towards the truck, screaming: "Signorino Antonio! Franco! Franco!" But the truck was already a hundred yards away and, before she could reach the middle of the road, it had turned a bend and was gone. Pia ran on, alternately screaming and panting. From the bend in the road, she could see the line of trucks already topping the hill ahead of her.

Pia threw down her bundle and stamped her feet and cried aloud. She hadn't seen Franco, but she had no doubt that he was with Antonio. In that small instant all her hunger and fatigue and fear had seemed at a sudden end. Now they were here, to begin all over again. She pulled herself together at last and trudged down the road. She would follow them. Perhaps they would get a flat tire. Perhaps they would stop to eat. Perhaps they were only going to the next town, Solfermino. Pia thought of the road-sign and tried to remember how many kilometers it had said.

Early in the afternoon she came to a place where the road forked, joining a hard road to the east while the western fork was small and dusty. Trucks and tanks had passed her on the way but at this moment there was nothing in sight. Pia looked from one to the other. In the bed of the dusty road there were tire marks and, by it, a post read: "Solfermino." The hard road led to Montevarchi.

Without further hesitation, Pia chose the road to Solfermino.

37: $\mathcal{F}$OR TWENTY-FOUR hours of the day the German army moved in and out of Arezzo. There were Companies and Divisions, under order, that went straight through toward their destination. And there were others that stopped at Arezzo to pick up orders. Every day, for a week, Franco and Nino reported to Headquarters, and every day they were turned away with instructions to stay where they were and report again the following morning. The days crept by and the rumble over the town and through the town did not let up for an instant.

At first, the two boys stood about on the street corners and watched the army coming through. Their eyes were fixed eagerly on the trucks bristling with guns and the slowly moving mechanized equipment. Occasionally, they looked at the soldiers and once Nino said: "They're mostly about our age."

Franco nodded. The trucks were full of young men gray with dust, their faces without any expression. "It can't be such fun," he said slowly.

After that, they went into the trattoria and sat for long hours over a bottle of red wine. They talked with soldiers and with the slow heavy woman who served them. There were rarely any townspeople there. One day, two farmers came in and sat at a table in a dark corner. Franco and Nino stopped talking and tried to listen to them, for they were hungry **to** talk to Italians again. But the farmers were old men and their voices ran together in a long, low mumble. Once, Franco pushed back his chair and went over to them but they only bent their heads closer together and went on talking, as though they had not seen him. Franco thought that out of the corner of their eyes they had seen his black shirt and were afraid of him. He shrugged and went back to Nino.

"A couple of stupid peasants," he said, and then was sorry he had said it.

Nino said, "They're not stupid, they're simple. They don't like war—or they don't like the Germans—so they don't like us. They don't understand what we're doing. They have probably heard fabulous tales of the fortunes we're making. They also, probably, have a cellar full of partisans."

"Well, the honor of a country isn't the responsibility of their class," Franco said, but his voice lacked conviction. He poured himself another glass of wine and slid the bottle across to Nino.

"I wish we could get out of this place," Nino said, taking the bottle.

"We could ask to be sent up to join the Fascist army."

"It wouldn't do any good. Might as well wait. They're consolidating now, and fast—it won't be long. The fighting is all in the rear, anyway; in a couple of days it'll be here, so what good would it do to move on?"

Then, the next day, they were moved on. They were attached to a damaged tank proceeding northwards to rejoin the Goering Panzer Korps. They were to leave the tank at Florence and report at Fascist Army Headquarters.

They left before dawn, going northwest of the main highway by small roads through the country. The tank was limping badly, and had been purposely detoured to keep it off the main route. The boys climbed on eagerly, anxious to be off and delighted that it was a tank rather than a truck. Within the first hour, they were plodding along in the dust of the road with the twelve soldiers who were attached to the tank. For they were moving at three miles an hour and any place you could find to sit was hot metal. The pilot and Sergeant Baumer, the NCO in charge, sat inside, with the hatch thrown open.

When they were tired they rode, moving about uncomfortably trying to find a spot that was even slightly cooler than the one they were on. The metal was rough under them and the tank rumbled and slithered. The fine dust of the road rose and covered them, biting into nostrils and eyes, and cracking lips already dry with the sun. There was little conversation; an occasional joke or song broke the monotony only to die on the air where it was born. Franco, who knew German, soon gave up trying to talk with the soldiers and turned back to Nino.

"They're sour as seaweed," he complained. "But you can't blame them; they've been in this thing for the whole war."

"It probably went faster, once."

"Madonna! Three miles an hour. Florence is how many miles?"

"We'll get there in a day."

"If it doesn't break down to a quarter of a mile an hour."

"Why don't we travel at night?" Nino asked suddenly, "it would be much cooler."

"It probably wouldn't be efficient or something."

Nino cupped his hands and yelled towards the hatch, "Sergeant Baumer!" The soldiers stirred a little, looking at him. "When he pops out," he said to Franco, "you tell him.

We can all go and rest under that tree that we've been passing for the last half hour, and when the metal cools off we can go on. Sergeant Baumer!" he yelled again.

This time, the Sergeant appeared over the hatch. He was a man of medium size, with a square-cut face. The whiteness of his skin contrasted unwholesomely with the bloodless shadows under his eyes, beneath his cheekbones and at his temples. His hair was black, he had a short, thin nose and beneath it surprisingly fat lips.

"What is it?" he asked in a flat voice.

Franco kicked Nino. Nino gave him a hurt look and rubbed himself. "Go on, tell him—he'll never get a good idea like that all by himself."

Franco said, apologetically, "My friend—thought it might be a fine idea if we stopped for the day and went on at night—" When he saw the German's incredulous expression, he went on quickly, "When it's cooler."

The Sergeant stared at them, until they stirred uncomfortably and there was a faint rustle of movement on the tank, as though the German soldiers were being made uncomfortable too. Finally, the Sergeant said: "You Italians are always joking!" Whereupon he snickered as though, having decided that the matter was funny, it was his duty to laugh at it. And he disappeared beneath the hatch without further comment. The rustle on the tank turned obediently to a snicker, and then to a loud guffaw. Franco shrugged, smiling a little. Nino said, impatiently:

"With this wounded tortoise, they could take two weeks to turn up and nobody would question it. I'm not sure that I believe in all this efficiency."

"Shut up," Franco said pleasantly. "The next bright idea you get, bite your tongue out. I'm going to sleep."

At noon precisely, Sergeant Baumer directed the pilot to stop and the men to eat their rations. They could go for a five-minute walk but they must remain in sight of the tank. They were behind their own lines, but there were the Partisans. They were due in Florence by nightfall. They would make it if they could pick up gasoline at Solfermino.

After lunch, the tank picked up and went ahead at a seven-mile-an-hour lurch. The soldiers cheered at this burst of speed and everyone scrambled to get aboard. Half an hour later, they approached a bridge. The tank came to a stop, its end swinging out into the road, so that the dust rose like a tidal wave. Sergeant Baumer appeared over the hatch and issued a sharp command. The soldiers dropped like locusts from the body of the tank and fanned out across the countryside.

"You too," the Sergeant said patiently to Franco and Nino. "The ravine is deep here, we must find a ford. Don't be more than ten minutes."

Nino and Franco went westward, climbing over the edge of the ravine and going downstream. It was a small stream, often not more than half a yard wide, cutting through a dry and rocky bed. Here and there, isolated pools were hidden among the rocks. As far as they could see, the banks were high and steep on either side.

Franco said, "I guess we go over the side."

Nino watched a frog jump into a small, green pool. "Do you remember the wildcat?" he said unexpectedly.

"That we never saw?"

"Yes. Then you wanted the war so badly. Do you still?"

"Oh, I don't know. It's not wanting war. I'd like to be up in the Sila now. But you have to feel right before you can go back."

"Yes. You have to feel right."

When they got back to the tank, the big machine was already moving towards the ravine beside the bridge. The soldiers were all back and had reported they could find no easier ford on either side for a quarter of a mile. Only the pilot and Sergeant Baumer remained with the tank. The rest of them hung over the side of the bridge and watched the tank go over the ravine. It swung and rocked and then steadied itself, gripping the sides of the ravine and going down with a crash that shook the frame of the small bridge beside it.

It was an hour reaching the road on the other side. When it did, it no longer proceeded at seven miles an hour but resumed its old limp and went forward at three miles an hour and sometimes less. Then, three miles out of Solfermino, it came to a complete stop and would not move.

Sergeant Baumer hovered over the two mechanics unhappily.

"It is seven o'clock," he complained. "We should have been in sight of Florence by six. How long are these repairs going to take?"

One of the mechanics sat back on his haunches. "If we can get this broken valve to a blacksmith, it will take ten minutes. If we cannot, it will take over an hour."

Sergeant Baumer snapped out an order and ten soldiers came to attention. One of them took the valve from the mechanics and listened to a brief explanation.

"Get on as fast as you can," the Sergeant instructed. "And keep alert for Partisans. You're not on the main route and you haven't got the tank. We'll follow you, if we can patch up sufficiently. If we're not there by the time the blacksmith is through, return on the double."

Nino said, "I'm going too." He pointed at himself and up the road. Sergeant Baumer shrugged and turned his back on him.

"He means he doesn't care," Franco said. "Personally, I'm going to look for water and stick my head in it."

Nino hesitated. Then he went after the soldiers, at a lope. Franco turned off the road and started up a grassy slope from whose summit he hoped to catch some glimmer of water in the gathering dusk. He had not gone ten paces when Sergeant Baumer called him.

"You stay with the tank or with the soldiers," he ordered. "We have to be ready to proceed. We can't have you roaming around."

Franco came down the hill slowly. He was annoyed at being called back, but he could see the reason for it. He threw himself on the ground, in the shade of a tree, and tried to think of something cool. A bath, with lots of soap. A plunge into the lake at Valombra, or running across the hot sands at Crotone to the cool, still waters of the bay. He thought of Pia in a green dress, of Clara with her square bob and her quiet ways. He thought of his mother and father, not for the first time but in a way that had become a habit with him. For he thought that he was going to fight and die, and he was sorry that he had left them as he had. While he lay there, a sharp sound broke the evening air—and then another, and another.

He was on his feet in an instant, running towards the tank where Sergeant Baumer, the pilot and the mechanics were talking excitedly.

"They've run into trouble," the Sergeant explained briefly. "Get on and we'll try and overtake them."

One of the mechanics shook his head but the other said: "If it's not more than a mile—maybe."

They went onto the tank, closing down the hatch and manning the gun. It was hot as an oven inside, and close. An age seemed to pass while the starters whirred and the big engine coughed impotently. Then the tank again came to life and moved forward in a series of jerks. Franco thought that they were going even more slowly than they had before and he thought of Nino and wished that they would move faster.

They came upon the scene of the fighting three-quarters of a mile farther on, and around a deep bend in the road. From the angle of their approach, they could see the rear of a small stone building, where a group of men were firing from cover. On the road side of the building, two hundred yards up a still-curving road, were their own men. They lay flat in the dirt, firing at short, irregular intervals.

Sergeant Baumer issued a sharp order and opened fire on the men behind the building. Taken by surprise, the Partisans whirled. One man jerked and fell over. In the instant of silence, they saw their disadvantage. The house was no longer a protection but a stone wall against which they stood out, plain as targets. They threw down their guns and came on, with their hands in the air.

As suddenly as it had begun, it was over. There were cries from the road and the thudding sound that men make running. The hatch of the tank was thrown open and Franco and the two mechanics climbed out. The pilot stayed at his place and Sergeant Baumer still trained the gun on the approaching Partisans. Nino came back slowly. He was streaked with perspiration and on his face the dust was smeared black. It was darkest around his eyes, and his eyes were red. He joined Franco without speaking and they watched the Partisans coming in. Franco looked at him hungrily and wondered what it would have been like to be fired on, to fling yourself down in the dirt, regardless of bruises and of the dust in your mouth and in your eyes, to aim your gun and watch for the figure of a man, to pull the trigger. Nino's lips were tight and grim. Franco felt a wave of sickness. He focused his eyes quickly on the Partisans.

There were twenty of them, ranging in age from fifteen years to sixty or so. They were shabbily dressed and without uniform. Franco saw that blood was on the face of one of them, and that it streamed down the arm of another. His eyes hardened, determined not to be sorry for them. For the Germans had carried in two dead. If the dead men had been dull, meaning nothing to Franco, still they had shared the road that day— and then it might so easily have been Nino. The Partisans still held their arms up, while two soldiers searched them quickly. When this was done they were lined up under guard. Picks and shovels were brought from the tank and five of the Partisans were set to work, at the point of the bayonet, to dig the two graves. One of the men turned to Franco, seeing that he was Italian, and said: "We have left a friend by the house. He is dead too. We should like to bury him."

Franco translated quickly but Sergeant Baumer only shrugged. "There are probably others of the kind around who will bury him. We haven't time."

Franco explained to the Partisans, unhappy and embarrassed. He thought that they looked at him strangely, but nothing more was said.

When the graves were dug and the mechanics had completed the repairs to the tank, they went up the hill to Solfermino. The Partisans went first and the guns that the soldiers carried, and the big gun on the tank, were trained on their backs.

There was no garrison at Solfermino; but the tank was sufficient protection in itself. They went down the narrow Corso to the blacksmith's forge, which boasted a solitary gasoline standard. The blacksmith, warned by the first visit of the soldiers on foot, had gone into hiding with his family and his prized possessions. Sergeant Baumer gave the order to break open the standard and fill the tank with gasoline. Then he took Franco and Nino aside.

"I am under orders to proceed immediately to Florence," he said. "I can't take these prisoners with me, and I can't turn them loose. I can't take the responsibility of shooting them. Tomorrow, a Company is coming by this route. There'll be an officer who can give the order. They should be shot, pigs!" He spat the words out. Franco and Nino looked at him expectantly. "You two, you're Italians—I leave you in charge of the prisoners. Tomorrow you turn them over and go on with the trucks. You can hold them in the blacksmith's house."

Franco saluted. Sergeant Baumer turned away briskly and yelled at his men, who commenced to herd the Partisans through the narrow door of the blacksmith's house.

Nino said, "'They'll be shot tomorrow—maybe we'll see it."

Franco shuddered. "Maybe they'll just be sent to a concentration camp."

"When you have seen how they fight—the Germans—you won't think that way. They shoot at a man the way we used to shoot at targets. They like it." Suddenly he was silent, as though he were sorry he had spoken. They stood there for a moment. Then they went towards the house where the Partisans were being locked up.

38: *7*HE ONE room of the blacksmith's house was dark and cool, despite the heat of late July. A blackout shutter closed the solitary window on the street. Franco had moved it, for an instant, to find that the window was barred with elaborate grillwork, a work of love and artistry. It was perhaps a form of advertising, for it was not usual for a poor man to bar his windows. Two doors led from the room, one onto an alleyway in the rear and one into the forge, through which Franco and Nino had followed the Partisans. On the far wall, under a picture of the Madonna, an oil lamp burned. It made fantastic shadows of the arms and legs of the many men in the room, so that on the floors and walls there was a constant writhing.

The prisoners lay about in various degrees of comfort and the lack of it. Five of them were stretched out on the great "matrimonial" bed. The two straight-backed chairs were occupied, the solid wooden table, and the floor. Two of the younger men hovered about the end of the room that boasted a charcoal stove and a cupboard. But the cupboard had been stripped by the departing blacksmith, and not a crumb remained. Franco and Nino sat on the floor, each with his back to a door. They had their guns across their knees and they were nervous and alert. The tank had gone and, outside, the night was still. Franco said diffidently, feeling sorry because the men before him were so dirty and so tired: "Is there anything we can do for you?"

A quick murmur ran through the room. One of the young men near the stove said: "We are hungry," and then he shrugged, "but what can you do?"

An older man, who sat stiffly in one of the chairs, stood up now. "My name is Luigi Tosso," he said. "We have not eaten tonight. Perhaps the townspeople would give food for us. Perhaps they would lend us blankets for the night—it would be more comfortable." There were murmurs of assent.

Franco looked across at Nino. "Want to go out and see," he asked, "or shall I?"

Nino got up. "I'll go." Franco moved over for him to pass. As he passed him, Nino whispered, "Remember what Baumer said. They may try to jump you."

"Don't be a fool. I know these people."

Nino shrugged and went out, and Franco resettled himself by the door. The man who had called himself Luigi Tosso was still standing; he went back to his chair and sat down.

"Thank you," he said; "may I ask your name?"

"I am Giovan Franco Cavalierre."

From the shadows beside the bed a voice said, "From Calabria?"

"Yes."

"Ah," the voice went on, "I too am from Calabria. I am Vitalli from Catanzaro." Vitalli came out from his dark corner and sat down again at the foot of the bed, leaning against the frame. "I should not have thought that a Cavalierre would fight for the Fascist." He was a small man, dark and quick as a viper, with the bandit blood of Calabria plain in his face. When he smiled, a black gap showed in his mouth where four teeth were missing.

"I am not fighting for the Fascist," Franco said stiffly, "I am fighting for Italy."

Luigi Tosso said, "Well now, and so are we. It is strange that we should be fighting one another."

The young man who had asked for food came now and squatted on the ground before Franco. "If you do not love the Fascists," he said, "if you love Italy, let us go."

A short, plump man on the bed raised himself on his elbows and said, "Giovanni speaks well—let us go, if you love Italy."

"Come with us," someone called, "we will show you how to fight for Italy."

"We fight to free Italy," Luigi Tosso said. "You cannot think that you fight for Italy when you fight to keep the Germans here, or to keep the tyrants in power."

"I don't care about the Germans, or even about the Fascists," Franco said slowly, "but a country, like a man, has its honor and, without it, there isn't anything to fight for—freedom wouldn't taste good or last long. If the Fascists are tyrants it's our fault, the country's fault. The country didn't want the responsibility and it was greedy—it took the handouts—the roads and the hospitals, the glory and the doles—and it paid with power. When the power was misused, it whimpered; but it didn't do anything about it. It allowed the treaty with Germany—so long as it thought it was convenient—as soon as it stopped being convenient, the country just backed out."

Vitalli said softly, "There were some of us who were never Fascist. Must we also fight for the honor of those who were?"

They were interrupted by a loud banging at the door. Franco moved aside and kicked the door open, keeping his gun over his arm but turning his back to the room. Luigi Tosso turned to Vitalli:

"There is reason in what he says. I can see that. He is, at least, not one of these Fascists who will make great fortunes out of our corpses."

From the doorway, Nino said, his voice quick with excitement, "Half the town is out here with food and blankets. How do we get the stuff in, without letting them in—or the prisoners out?"

"Let them drop the things there and go away. When they have gone, you and I can take turns bringing the things in."

Nino didn't move. "Pia is out there," he said softly. "She wants to come in."

"Pia!" Franco's gun slipped for a moment, so that the muzzle pointed to the ground. He recovered it quickly. "How did she get here? Who is she with?"

"She is alone. She was in Arezzo last week—while we were there. She saw Antonio Ronni leaving that day but she couldn't get near enough to talk to him, so she followed, because she thought you would be with him. She got here and they told her that no fleet of trucks had been through, so she's been waiting for a ride back to try the other road."

Franco hesitated. Then, his mouth tightening, he said, "Tell her she can't come in now. Tell her to come back tomorrow morning early—as soon as the Germans get here. I'll see if I can arrange to have her sent north."

Nino went out, closing the door. In the silence that followed, the men in the room could hear the rustle and hum of people moving outside. There was the soft, shapeless sound of whispering that people use in the presence of illness or death. Twice, a woman's voice protested loudly. Franco listened, thinking that it must be Pia. Once he moved impetuously towards the door. He couldn't leave her out there. He had to see her. He had to make sure that she was all right. As he moved, the door flew open again and Nino appeared, with his arm full of blankets.

"They've gone," he said, dumping the blankets on the floor. Franco went out to get another armload.

The men took the blankets and the food, thanking them and then settling down to some degree of comfort. Franco and Nino sat at their posts once more and each of them accepted a cut of bread and a thick slice of goat cheese. Vitalli waved his bread in the air, pointing out the band of Partisans: "It is good to eat once more, is it not?" he said. "Tomorrow we shall be dead."

Franco stopped chewing and put his bread and cheese down on the ground beside him. It had tasted good, at first. Now he thought that it was like eating rubber.

The boy Giovanni said to Nino, "We have asked him to let us go."

Nino looked quickly at Franco. "Why should you let them go?" he asked.

"They say they are fighting for Italy—that they can do more for Italy than we can."

"No, no," Luigi Tosso said soberly. "I was saying when your friend came in—there is great reason in what you have said. A country must have honor—and responsibility. But Italy has lost the first through lack of the second. Now we have to decide which must be mended first——"

The plump man on the bed cried excitedly, "The responsibility, of course! Are we going to be responsible to the Germans and the Fascists?"

"Or to Italy!" someone cried.

"You can't patch up honor, anyway," Luigi Tosso said; "you have to remake it."

Nino nodded. "I think they're right about that, Franco."

Luigi Tosso said, "I am the only old man here. I am sixty-seven. I love Italy. I have thought a lot about Italy, in the course of a long life. My father fought with Garibaldi. I was with the Black Shirts in the march on Rome. Well, I was wrong. I know it now. That is why I am here. I wish that I had known the things I do now, many years ago. That is why I say, Don't just let us go—come with us. You will learn, and you will be glad because you will be doing the right thing."

Franco put his head in his hands, ruffling his hair in his perplexity. His gun had slipped from his knees, so that he was no longer protected. It was characteristic of Italians that none of the men in the room thought of jumping him. They would argue all night, but they had fatalistically accepted the situation, and they left it to fate to reverse it.

They argued half the night until, finally, Nino jumped up.

"They are right," he said softly, "and I'm going with them. How about you?"

"No—go if you want—I won't stop any of you—but I'm staying."

There was a murmur of protest. Luigi Tosso said, "In three hours it will be dawn. That sergeant will have sent a report back. The Germans who're coming will shoot you if they find you alone."

"That's my affair," said Franco.

"No, we can't let you."

"Franco—why are you letting us go? If you believe it's right, you should come; if you don't, you shouldn't do it." Nino went over to his friend and put his arm about his shoulder.

"I believe what they say—they're serving Italy—so let them. Perhaps my way is wrong—but there's still my own honor. I'm staying."

Vitalli said, "The Calabrians are always stubborn. I ought to know."

Suddenly the boy Giovanni started to cry, ugly sobs racking his thin body. Luigi Tosso said, "We mustn't wait any longer—if we are going."

Nino gripped his friend tightly and his face was white beneath the streaks of dirt. Then he kicked the door open and went out. Franco turned away to the window, avoiding the words of the men who went by him, the warning, urgent words. There was fear enough in his heart, and bitterness, but he couldn't go.

He pulled the heavy blackout blind back and watched the men separate themselves from the stone building, going into the street boldly. It was black night, black as it always is before dawn—a black that is solid, not cast by shadows. In less than a moment, the men were gone, though the sound of their feet was still on the street. He closed the blind again and went to the bed and threw himself down on it. It wouldn't be long. He shuddered and the hot tears welled to his eyes. He brushed them away fiercely. It was his decision. It was still his decision. As he lay there, he heard the sound of running feet, soft but clear on the still night air. They came down the Corso towards him and when they had reached the blacksmith's house they stopped. He was on his feet facing the door when it burst open and the dark figure of a woman stood for a moment confronting him.

"Pia!" he said gently.

She threw herself on him, sobbing, "Oh, I couldn't see you in the light. Oh, Franco, what are you doing? Why don't you come away! They said——"

"Who said?"

"The Signorino Nino, and all of those men—Franco, you

must come away at once. They are waiting for you at a barn near here. I will go with you."

The elation which he had stifled at the sound of her footsteps, at the sight of her, welled up in him and he held her tightly for a moment. Then he let her go.

"I can't," he said slowly. "I said I would guard those men. I let them go, because I believe in them. But I can't run away. It would be cowardly, it would be dishonorable."

"But the Signorino Nino——"

"He never really cared. I persuaded him to join the Germans. It never really meant anything to him. So, you see, it's all right for him to go."

Pia said, "I don't understand. Think of your poor mother. Ah, the poor, unhappy one. And Don Alessandro. He is like a specter; my heart bleeds for him!"

Franco's face tightened.

"Why did you come, Pia? Did they send you?" he asked, looking hard into her eyes.

"I came to find you if I could. I left two weeks ago and I was lucky. Some English soldiers hid me in their truck. They took me to Cortona. They were very nice men."

"Then what?"

"I came through the woods, and across two fields, with a peasant who is a relative of the Little Doll's man. Ugly! A most ugly man. I had to put my feet where his feet went, so that there would be no explosions. It was very difficult. He took the longest steps of any man I ever did see. Then, just beyond Arezzo, I saw Antonio Ronni. I thought surely that you were with him, and I followed; but I came the wrong way."

"You walked all the way from Cortona?"

"Yes. It has been very easy. Now that I have found you, we can go home and I shall find Leone too."

"Leone?—Oh, yes."

Franco made her sit down. He stood over her and held her face in his hands. In the flickering light, her eyes were dark and colorless and lines of fatigue were etched in her skin. Even with the dust and grime of the trip her hair was bright and beautiful. In his heart he said, 'All of that for love of me? Or for love of my father? Or just to satisfy her conscience, so that she can go hunting that peasant!'

He let her go and straightened up. "Did they send you?" he asked again.

"No—I came because it broke my heart to see them so."

"You love them very much?"

"Of course. They have been very good to me."

"Even my father!" he said, his voice harsh.

She looked at him curiously. "But, of course."

"But, Pia, he beat you!" he cried, voicing the feeling that had been in him so long, the protest that she had been so little affected by what had happened.

"It was all right," Pia said simply, "he thought that I stole the robe. He had to."

"He thought that you stole! What are you talking about?" He grabbed her wrist, pulling her to her feet.

"The red robe. Your mother's. But really, the Donna Zia gave it to me." Pia looked at him, half frightened. She hesitated, and then she went on, the sordid little story unfolding as she talked. When she had finished he let her go, pulling his hand away from her as though she were indeed unclean.

"Zia Margherita," he said slowly. "I might have known." Then, suddenly, he was beating the wall, rubbing his head against it, tears wetting his cheeks and wetting the wall, so that the one smeared blackly against the other. With the flat of his hands he struck the wall again and again, and his sobs shook him and would not be stopped. He thought of his father and the years that he had hated him and wronged him, and how, in so doing, he had also wronged himself. Pia went to him and tried to put her arms around him but he turned on her fiercely, hating her in that moment, even as he hated the Zia, even as he had hated his father.

"Listen," he said, catching his breath to still the sobs, "you get out of here. Go back to Rome. Tell my mother and father that I am sorry. Tell them that I know I was wrong. Tell them that I love them. Tell them that I am proud to be their son." A dry sob convulsed him and he rubbed the wet from his face, where it had congealed with dust. His black hair curled damply on his forehead.

"They've gone," Pia said; "they're not in Rome. When I left, they were going the next day to Crotone."

"Well, go to Crotone, then. Madonna! Have you understood me?"

"Yes."

"Well, repeat what I have said. Tell my mother and father —'Franco is sorry.'"

Pia's eyes pleaded with him but he only stared back at her coldly, waiting.

"Franco is sorry," she said.

"He was wrong. He knows it now."

"He was wrong. He knows it now."

"He loves them. He is proud to be their son."

"He loves them. He is proud to be their son." Pia was weeping. "Then, you aren't coming—oh, Franco—come and tell them yourself! Only that will make them happy."

"No. I've talked a lot. Now I'm going to do something."
He took her elbow and guided her out, across the dark forge,
to the street.

Dawn had already broken the sky with its first faint gray.

"You haven't much time. Are you sure you know where
the barn is?"

"Yes—" Pia clutched at him suddenly, a sense of despera-
tion and incredulity swelling within her—"you can't stay,
you can't—they will kill you, Franco. I won't let you stay——"

He tried to shake her off, but Pia was no weakling. She
only clung tighter, urging him wildly the while, until finally,
freeing an arm, Franco struck her across the side of her face.

Pia gasped. Franco could hear the sound of her breath as she
sucked it in convulsively, and he was flooded with a hot wave
of shame.

"Run," he said softly, "and stay with Nino! He will take
care of you."

He grabbed her then, kissing the top of her head before
pushing her from him. "Poor Pia," he murmured as she ran
sobbing and stumbling up the Corso, "you can't blame her:
she is caught between us all." And he found himself hoping
that she might find her Leone and wondering pityingly
whether he had gone too far away ever to come back to her.
America would have changed him, and Pia was the old Italy.
He went back into the house to wait. He turned down the
light under the Madonna until it was a faint flicker and threw
himself on the bed. He had not long to wait. And then, as he
lay there, the exhaustion of his body and his heart and his
mind crept into his bones and he slept heavily and completely.

*7*HE HOUSE which Alessandro's grandfather had built for his family at Nimpha was a massive stone structure two doors away from the church. In the succeeding generation it had been adapted for purposes of storage and for the processing of olives. The living room, a long, low room with a stone floor, was equipped with machinery for crushing olives. Three other rooms, on the same floor, were lined with oil vats and fruit bins. The entire building was permeated with the acrid smell of various degrees of oil, of fermentation and of decays. The stored wheat and fruit had been cleared out of the second floor when Alessandro arrived with his family in the middle of July. Lucy chose five rooms for their apartment.

When the first truck came for the harvest, she went to Crotone and brought back some pieces of furniture from the house there. In the meantime, they managed as best they could with the two beds which were already in the house and with the rustic furniture which the peasants made. Fortunata and Little Doll slept in the village, for there were no beds for them at the apartment.

While Lucy worked over the apartment, using an army of old women and children to scrub and scour and make the place livable, Alessandro went down into the valley. The wheat was ready for harvest and every able-bodied woman and boy or girl, and the few men whom the war had returned to the village, were gathered in the valley. Alessandro went with Mateo and the boy Carlo, who took care of his grandfather. They went on horseback, Carlo riding on the pommel of his grandfather's saddle, and holding the reins, for Mateo was without arms. They took blankets and provisions with them. They were gone a week, and when they came back their faces were hard with the look that foretells trouble. Alessandro came into the house, talking to Mateo. Lucy could hear them arguing. She heard Mateo say, "It came from the city—and it will eat through every estate in the country."

When Mateo and Carlo had gone, Alessandro came to her. There were black smudges of grain-dust on his face but, aside from a certain look of strain, he showed no signs of fatigue.

"Pancrazio Tregatti, one of the farmers, and Cromo and Tornati, two of the older goatherds, have moved onto the land," he told her. "We're going to have trouble. They have taken the best of the wheat land."

Lucy said, leading him to the bedroom and making him sit down, "I heard Mateo say something—I was afraid there was a disease. He said it came from the city——"

"And would eat through every estate in the country. It *is* a disease! Mateo says that men have come from the cities and talked to the peasants, telling them that the land is theirs, that the law permits them to take it."

"What will you do?"

Alessandro leaned down to unlace his boots while Lucy poured water for him in the china washstand. "It's illegal. They'll have to get off. The law allows the peasants to occupy unused lands. None of these lands have been unused, in my time."

"And if they don't get off, Alessandro?"

"They will." The muscles on the sides of his cheeks tightened. Then he shrugged and said, "Except for Pancrazio they are not even good farmers. Cromo and Tornati have ruined the year's crop and damaged the fields as well. They did no ditching and they plowed down the hill, so that the spring rains have washed them out and left the fields eroded. They should have stayed with their goats."

The next day, Alessandro talked to Padre Pasquale and then he took his horse and went to Crotone. He was gone another week. While he was away Lucy was anxious and went halfheartedly about the tasks she had set for herself. A strange feeling of unfriendliness hovered over the village where there had always been the strong security of generations of good feeling. One day, Fortunata came in crying with excitement. A child of the Corte family, whose estate lay in the south of the province, had been killed in a fight with a peasant. Lucy felt the color wash from her face, leaving her skin cold and moist.

"No, no, it's not possible!" she cried. But Fortunata was very sure.

"There is fighting down there. It is like another war," she said. "The landlords have taken up arms—though it is said that the child was not intentionally killed."

"Do you know how it happened?" Lucy asked. In the kitchen doorway behind her Little Doll appeared, wringing her hands and moaning.

"We'll all be killed now. You will see. Ah, how horrible, how terrible!"

Lucy hushed her, and Fortunata said, "The child was sitting on the horse, in front of the Barone, and the Barone had a gun on his saddle, though he had not drawn it. He went to the peasant's house to tell him that he had to get off the land and the peasant shot. Only he hit the boy instead of the father."

"Horrible," Lucy murmured, and then she said slowly, "Do you know which child it was?"

"The youngest, they say. The one who was born the year that Clara was."

"His name was Guido," Lucy said. "He was cross-eyed." And she turned away that they should not see the fear that she knew must show even through the distress on her face.

When Alessandro came back, he already knew of the shooting. He told her that the trouble in the south was being settled by arbitration. "As soon as we can we also shall call a meeting of the landlords," he said. "There are not enough of us here now to serve any purpose. In the meantime, I'll do what I can and hope that our trouble may stop. The authorities in Crotone won't help. They say that this is happening on a small scale all over the country. The AMG won't interfere, but are leaving it to the Italian Government." He shrugged.

"Alessandro," Lucy said, "I'm afraid. There is something so ugly in this. The Corte child is not the trouble—but merely a symptom. Please—oh, let the peasants have the land! We have the groves and the vineyards, and some wheat too. We have enough."

"I don't think that you understand what is happening," he said, walking across the room to look out of the window and then coming restlessly back to her.

"I do. But let them have it."

"No, Lucy, this is much too big a thing to let the death of one little boy make a difference—or my death, or even yours. If Pancrazio can take my land, tomorrow Cromo can take his. And then what?"

"You are looking far ahead."

"I am looking at something that is happening under our noses." He ran his hand through his hair, and turned from her, and went to the bed where he lay down without even removing his shoes. While she stood watching him he fell asleep, the look of strain and fatigue remaining on his face. Lucy covered him and left him.

Alessandro slept the evening through, without awakening

for dinner and only stirring restlessly when Lucy came to bed. The next morning, he was up at dawn and down in the valley, this time going without Mateo. In the days that followed he came and went, and Lucy watched him anxiously, but did not question him again. He told her, after it was over, that he had called a meeting in the village and had told the people that there were certain lands he was willing to sell to those who proved themselves good farmers. If they hadn't the ready money he would arrange terms and do everything to help them. The law had been informed and, in time, when things were more settled in Italy, the carabinieri might be expected to take a hand with those who did not listen to his words now. He asked for volunteers to form a village police force. The boys and the men kept their hats in their hands, but they made no move to show that they understood. They stood twisting their hats and staring at their own bare feet. No one volunteered for Alessandro's police force. And the next day the signs which he had had posted were torn down or defaced.

For the time, Alessandro let the matter go. Lucy thought that he looked tired, but he would not talk about it, saying only:

"Whatever men say to the contrary, these people need to lean. They must lean on their landlord, or on the law of the land in the person of its representative. The law is a distant thing to them now, so, whether they like it or not, they must lean on me. And you will see, Lucy, that they will do so."

Towards the middle of the month, the Signora Odilia took her household goods and her children and moved down from the village to the wheat fields, where Pancrazio had built her a straw hut. Alessandro moved Fortunata and Little Doll into her house. The women of the village watched silently. Lucy found that they were still quick to kiss her hand or the hem of her skirt. But they were quiet with her now, where once they had been garrulous, full of their talk of births and illness and death, of plants that grew or plants that failed, of animals that were barren or otherwise. She laid it to the trouble in the valley. It had affected them all, leaving them uncertain and nervous.

Until the harvest was over, Alessandro was away most of the time. He went to the fields, or he went to Crotone, for, after the first truck was delivered, the promise of others had not been fulfilled and there was an anxious time as regards the grain. A portion of the crop was forfeit to the state granaries. As there was no way of transporting it, rude huts had to be constructed for shelter, and much of it rotted. Alessandro did well with his harvest, and Pancrazio with his. Cromo's and Tornati's had washed out. Now, Cromo came to Alessandro and said: "I have lost everything, Signor Barone. Will you give me work?"

Alessandro scowled at him, giving him no sympathy. "And where are your goats?" he asked.

"But, Signor Barone, I sold them to buy the grain to plant, and my plow."

"Go to Mateo. We have goats that need tending. Tell him that I sent you and he will see to it."

Cromo went humbly, touching his forehead. Tornati would not come to Alessandro for help, but went instead to Pancrazio. There was great talk in the village, for Pancrazio would not help him, saying: "If you cannot work your own field you cannot work mine." And Tornati went across the valley to the sea road. There he turned towards Crotone and, whether he found work one place or another, he did not come back.

With this turn of events, there was a slight change of feeling in the village. Lucy thought that now Alessandro might have found help to evict Pancrazio. But he would make no move.

"They have not forgotten what I said. In the course of time the law will either force Pancrazio to move out or to pay me. They are more anxious at my silence than they would be if I should show a sudden lack of faith in the law and ask their help. To tell you the truth, Pancrazio is a good man misled by a very confusing issue. In the long run, I am not worried about him."

Lucy was not sure that he was right, but she could give him no advice. She was still more than a little afraid of the bleak village, with its half humble, half black-humored people. But she had found security in Alessandro and she didn't care greatly whether he was right or not. 'He grew out of this place,' she thought, 'he has his own times of being as black-humored as any of them,' and she thought also, 'in him it is a strength.'

In late August, Florence fell and anxiety took hold of Lucy despite her self-imposed faith. Her eyes now no longer saw the mountains about them, or the high, far heavens that were always blue, or the fleets of white clouds ever sailing before the endless sirocco. The lonely lake in the valley and the towering spruce and fir were there, but Lucy's eyes were not for these things, nor even for people, but sought only the road, the winding white road. However much she looked, there was never anyone new on the road, and there were still no mails.

That fall, they commenced to get letters from the north. The Zia wrote precise and detailed letters about the life in Rome, which she said was immoral and unclean in the extreme. But there was never any word of Franco and never any word of Pia. The days grew shorter and there was suddenly more time to rest. Lucy and Alessandro commenced to read aloud to Clara in the evenings. Sometimes they would sit and talk. Clara loved to talk of the things they would do when

Franco came home, and Pia. It gave Lucy a warm feeling of certainty, for Clara was so sure when she planned things. Once only she said, "*If* he comes home." Alessandro had looked at Lucy quickly over Clara's head, and the understanding in his eyes was such that she had felt at peace. She had smiled at him, putting her hand out to tell him so.

In the fall the grapes were pressed and the olives commenced to ripen. All that winter, there was the harvesting of olives and of lemons and oranges. There were not enough hands to work the crops that year, though every man, woman and child who could stand on two feet went down to the groves. Lucy and Fortunata and Clara went too. Alessandro came, and went to Crotone to beg for trucks. Sometimes he was successful, and then he would ride back in the truck, his horse in the van, and he would be jubilant and filled with a new energy. Sometimes there would be no truck, nor even a promise. Then he would come back slowly and he would be white and silent and he would let work go and stand, his hands in his pockets, staring across his lands.

Some fruit they put down in sand, for the use of the village, but the best went north in the trucks. During one long period, when there were no trucks, the produce was taken to the local markets by oxcart, or by mule, or on the heads of the women. The small markets were gutted with food, and the big cities in the north were threatened with famine.

That winter, more than half of the fruit crop was lost. Alessandro said nothing, but stood looking for a long time at the heaps of rotting fruit. When he turned away, Lucy's eyes went after him, afraid that now he would become discouraged.

He had worked that year as perhaps he had never done before in all his life, taking Mateo with him and using his own hands under the direction of the old man. More than once, Lucy had seen tears spring to the peasant's eyes. For it is a painful thing for a man who has loved the feel of his trees, or the stroking of a dusty-furred burro, to be without hands in the sight of a man who is clumsy. But Mateo only said, "Bravo, bravo, Signor Barone; I could not have done it so well myself."

By the time that winter had passed, Alessandro was not as clumsy as he had been.

In December, the pigs which were to be butchered were put into pens and fed for a month and a half on chestnuts and acorns and small chick-peas. In late January, they were butchered, and everyone who had two hands joined in the preparation of the meat.

Then, before there was a chance to rest, the processing of the oil commenced. The winter was long and cold, and in the house where the Cavalierres lived the cold penetrated so that nothing that they did could keep them warm. They burnt charcoal in braziers and kept hot stones in their pockets, and hot bricks in their beds, and they wore coats and heavy scarves in the house. The peasants kept warm by living in one room, with the fire going constantly, and as often as not with animals to add their body heat to the atmosphere.

"I can't regret the animals," Lucy said once, "but it is too bad that our dignity does not permit us to move into the kitchen."

Alessandro laughed at her. "Fortunata and Little Doll would leave on the instant," he said.

"And we must maintain our dignity for their sake?"

"Yes, because our dignity is tied up with theirs, and so, in a sense, it belongs to them."

Then, in the spring Pia came. She came on foot, slowly, as though she had grown accustomed to long and never-ending roads, and to the thought that there was no use in hurrying.

Whatever pace you set, you didn't reach the end of the road.

The villagers who saw her didn't know her, but they stopped in their work to watch her coming. A stranger was an unaccustomed event. Once Pia would have called out to them, naming each one of them, delighted with her advantage and making game of it. Now she went by them dully, as though she did not see them.

She went to the priest, who did not know her and had to be told who she was.

"I am Pia," she said. "I have come back. Will you tell me where I can find Don Alessandro?"

"Pia?" Padre Pasquale looked at her hard and said her name as though he did not understand.

"Do you not remember? They chased the devil out of me once," she said gently, for she saw that he was old. She had remembered him as a tall, gaunt man of no particular age but of a rigid strength. Now he was old, and it hurt her strangely to see it.

"Ah, Pia, the little Pia who was a witch!" he said now. "What trouble we did have with you!"

"I must see Don Alessandro," she said again.

"Yes, yes, you shall see him. Let me get my shawl and you shall see him." He shuffled away. When he came back, he had a dark shawl over his shoulders and he took her arm and they went out of the church.

"You're tired," he said, "and you don't look well. It's a bad time for travelling. But, of course, a good bath will help. And the good God will make it up to you, if you're not well; He always does."

Pia shrugged impatiently, but she said nothing. As they went up the short street, the priest interrupted himself to call out to the people they passed, "It's Pia. Do you not remember? —with whom we had so much trouble."

And the people came running, and some of them welcomed her and some of them stared without speaking. They all followed her to the stone house, and they hovered in excited groups about the entrance long after she and the priest had disappeared inside.

Pia was thin, with gaunt hollows beneath her eyes and cheekbones. Her hair was entirely covered with a black handkerchief, her clothes were ragged and dirty. What remained of her shoes was tied to her feet with a heavy wadding of burlap. She stood before Lucy, and there was no color in her face, but only shadows and dirt, and no expression but that of fatigue and hunger.

Lucy recognized her, where nobody else had. She stared at her for a horrified instant and then she had the girl in her arms.

"Pia, my poor Pia! My poor Pia!" she cried over and over again. At their back, Alessandro exclaimed, tossing aside the book that he had been reading. And Clara came running from her room to join in the embrace. From the kitchen door Fortunata and Little Doll wrung their hands and called on the Saints. Pia, who had never felt the safety of a woman's arms, commenced to tremble violently.

When she would have spoken, Lucy put her away from her, saying, "No, you must bathe and eat and rest. We are glad to have you home, Pia. Later, we shall want to hear everything."

"I must tell you," Pia said dully, almost stupidly. "I have come to tell you, I must tell you."

Lucy's face was suddenly white and she drew away, stiffening. Alessandro came now and put his arm around Pia, turning her towards the kitchen. "The Donna Lucia is right, Pia. You shall tell us. But not now." And he raised his voice to Fortunata and Little Doll, telling them to fill a tub of water and to take care of Pia, and admonishing them that there was to be no talk.

Later, Pia came to them. She stood in the doorway, wrapped in a bathrobe of Clara's, her hair done up in a towel. From the center of the living room the charcoal brazier threw patterns on the ceiling; on a white wood table an oil lamp burned, giving the room a golden look.

"I saw Franco," she said and, without giving them a chance to interrupt, she ran on. "He said to tell you that he was wrong——"

Lucy sat stiffly on her chair by the table. On her lap her fingers wove a needle meaninglessly in and out of a piece of work. On the other side of the table, Alessandro had risen, but now he did not move.

"—He said to tell you that he loves you. That he is proud to be your son. But he—oh!" she cried, breaking from the monotony of a learned lesson, from a pattern of phrases which she had lived with for many months, "he would not come away—I could not make him. Nobody could make him. He would not come."

Lucy still said nothing and Alessandro went to Pia, drawing her into the room. He brought a chair close to theirs, so that she should sit between them. When he had settled her, he sat forward in his own chair, taking her hands in his.

"Now," he said, "when did you see him? Tell us slowly, everything."

Lucy cleared her throat nervously but still she did not speak. Pia's eyes were on Alessandro's. She kept them there, wide and intense, as though in him there was escape from some dread. Slowly and stiffly the words came and she told her story: there was no sound to interrupt her, her words were like islands in a sea of stillness.

When she had finished, Lucy drew a deep breath. "But you don't know, you don't really know," and there was a sound almost of fierceness in her voice.

"That morning early, when the Germans had just come, the bombers arrived." Pia repeated her words of a moment before. "When they flew away, Solfermino was still going up in flames, crumbling and burning and screaming. Nobody could know about anybody. The blacksmith's house wasn't hit. When we went to look, the Germans had gone and there was no one."

"But you said that they went in their trucks, they were not blown up. They could have taken him a prisoner—or perhaps they understood and forgave him——"

Alessandro stood up. Pia hung her head and her words were soft. "There was blood in the blacksmith's house," she said, and she said it without emotion, as though the tears had long since been dried out of her.

"Someone was wounded?" Lucy said urgently. "One of the Partisans was wounded—you said so yourself——"

Alessandro went to the door and called Fortunata.

"Take Pia to bed," he ordered her, "and see that she stays there for a few days. Then we'll see how she is." He made Pia go, taking her face in his hands and saying to her:

"We are deeply indebted to you, Pia, and this is something which the Donna Lucia and I shall not forget as long as we live. Now, go and rest."

Lucy came to stand beside him and said, "Yes, Pia," softly as though there was nothing else that she knew how to say. When Pia and Fortunata had gone, she turned to Alessandro quickly, putting her hands flat on his chest.

"He could have got away," she begged; "he could have, couldn't he?"

"No," he said deliberately, looking into her eyes.

She tried to turn from him but he caught her wrists and held her. "He has to be all right," she cried. "It is what we live for, it is what we are working for, it is what we fight to save all this for."

"He is all right," Alessandro said slowly. "He is all right because he did right. He died proudly, which is the greatest thing that any man can do. He didn't do it to satisfy someone else, but for himself. What we are doing is not for someone else either, not even for our children. We do it to satisfy ourselves. It came to him to die. It comes to us to live, to save our lands, and to fight for a sane life that is honest and peaceful and productive."

"Oh, Sandi!" Lucy cried, unconsciously calling him by the nickname that she had dropped many years ago. Suddenly she was in his arms, clinging to him as though she thought that any moment some wild and terrible thing might come and tear him from her. He smoothed her hair and held her quietly.

"Is it that you want me to believe it?" she said at last. His hand was still for a moment. Then he took her by the shoulders, pushing her away so that he could look at her.

"Yes," he said and his voice was strong, and it was as though he invited her to live.

Lucy drew a deep breath, for she saw agony in his eyes. Her sorrow leapt to meet his and she understood that they both mourned their boy, their mistake towards him, their lack of awareness of every moment in which they had had him. Over and above this, she knew that Alessandro mourned the last of his race. She said to him, her dark eyes making no attempt to evade his, "I cannot. But—I am proud of him too."

He took her gently and she put her head against his

shoulder and wept the fierce, shuddering tears that had been pent up too long. While she wept, her hand felt for his face, caressing it.

The next morning, the village hummed with the news that the girl Pia was dying of a black fever. Groups gathered, screaming that she had brought the pest to them. They burnt fires before their doors and they would not go near the servants' house, where Lucy and Fortunata had shut themselves in with her. And they would not go near the house where Alessandro was, for had not the girl gone there first, had not Don Alessandro talked with her? Only Padre Pasquale escaped their fear, for he went under the protection of God and no harm could come to them through him.

Four days passed. Nobody came down with illness, and Pia did not die. Every day, Lucy sent Fortunata to stand in the doorway and shout up and down the apparently deserted street: "There is nothing but fever here. It is not the pest. Pia is better."

Then, on the morning of the fifth day, the flush was gone, and the bright, wide look from Pia's eyes. Lucy sent Fortunata quickly to tell Alessandro.

"Tell him that it was fatigue," she said. "She will be all right now."

Pia was hungry and, now that the fever was gone, she wanted to be up. But Lucy would not hear of it. She would have to rest for a long time, she said. And she sent Clara to talk and read to her. Do what they would, they could not keep Pia in bed longer than a week. And, once she was up, she commenced to talk of going.

"There is Leone," she said. "I must go and find him. Perhaps he looked for me in Rome and Maria told him that I had gone north."

"But we can write and find out about that," Lucy pointed out.

Pia only shook her head.

Lucy worried about her. Franco had loved her and Lucy began to understand that part of his love had been a possessive thing—something protective—and she too felt it. Pia was theirs, tied to them by infinite invisible strings that had to do with their lives together and with Pia's own position. She could not be turned out on the world. She could not be allowed to wander, any more than Clara could be.

Then, one evening, as suddenly as she had come, she was gone. Alessandro took his horse and went after her, but already he was many hours late. Lucy had little hope that he would find her.

He was away for a night and a day, and when he came back he came alone. Lucy met him at the door, anxiously.

"It's all right," he said quickly, "I found her."

"But where is she?"

"You couldn't have held her," he said, "she had the right to go. I took her to the AMG, who gave her a letter to take with her and the promise of a ride to Naples. I don't see that there is any reason to believe that Leone is in Italy—but if he is, she stands a reasonable chance of finding him through the authorities—none, if she just walks the streets."

"She is so young," Lucy said, "I should have liked to see her settled."

He shrugged, but he put his arm about her. "You have begun to understand, and it makes you suffer," he said. "You were too young to have come to such an old country to live your life. We can stand it, because we have age in our blood. We have seen so many centuries of unhappiness that another story like Pia's doesn't matter. Perhaps she will find her American. I hope deeply that she will. But she may not. She may come back, or she may be killed. She may become a professional prostitute, or she may merely go into service in some other house."

"But you said, yourself, that she stood a chance of finding him."

He smiled at her. "You want the happy ending, Lucy! That's not real."

"It can be," she protested, "I'm sure." And then her eyes dropped away from his, thinking of Franco.

"Completion is what you are searching for," he said slowly. "It is more than the happy ending."

Lucy nodded, understanding that he too thought of Franco.

Fortunata stood in the doorway, announcing dinner. "Go and wash," Lucy said to him. "You smell of horse."

He caught her and kissed her then and, when he let her go, he strode across the room to the bedroom. Lucy thought, 'My life has been full of the sound of his footsteps, coming and going, quick and slow, and I'm only beginning to realize what they mean to me.' And, suddenly, every sound in the house, or that came through the open windows from the village, had a new meaning. In the kitchen, Little Doll scolded in a high shriek and Fortunata giggled loudly. Outside, people worked and the sounds of their work were the splashing of water at the pump or the slap that it makes when slewed from a doorstep onto cobbles; and the sounds were the striking of metal on metal or the bump and rumble of wood against stone as some cart went down the street. Voices called to other voices, or cried out at some animal, or sang a song that was gay or a song that was sad. Lucy thought, 'These are the sounds of life, and its meaning.' And, in her moment of awareness, she listened for the footsteps again, and was happy.

DUNCAN   **MYSTERY**

Duncan, Alice
Lost among the angels

$ 25.95

LOST
AMONG THE
Angels

ALICE DUNCAN

Five Star • Waterville, Maine

MYSTERY

This novel is a work of fiction. Names, characters, places and incidents are either the product of the author's imagination, or, if real, used fictitiously.

First Edition
First Printing: June 2006

Published in 2006 in conjunction with
Tekno Books and Ed Gorman.

Set in 11 pt. Plantin.

Printed in the United States on permanent paper.

Library of Congress Cataloging-in-Publication Data

Duncan, Alice, 1945–
    Lost among the angels / Alice Duncan.—1st ed.
      p. cm.
    ISBN 1-59414-363-3 (hc : alk. paper)
    1. Young women—Fiction. 2. Secretaries—Fiction.
  3. Private investigators—California—Los Angeles—Fiction.
  4. Los Angeles (Calif.)—Fiction. I. Title.
  PS3554.U463394L67 2006
   813'.6—dc22   2005036763

To Anni & Robin, as ever

ONE

July 1, 1926

I hadn't anticipated the heat. As I carefully positioned my high-crowned felt cloche hat and stuck a pin in to hold it to my neat bun, a trickle of perspiration ran down my cheek. My sister frowned at me.

"You need to get your hair bobbed. I don't know why you persist in keeping your hair long. Bobbed hair is ever so much cooler."

This was undoubtedly true, but I hadn't had my hair cut in my entire life. "Mother and Father would disown me if I had my hair bobbed," I said.

"Mother and Father aren't here."

Even as she stated the obvious, my heart soared. I told it to stop doing that. Such behavior on its part was extremely unfilial and in very bad taste.

Nevertheless, Clovilla, my sister, had a good point. Mother and Father were on their figurative thrones in Cape Cod (this being the summertime and all), Massachusetts, and I, Mercedes Louise Allcutt (named after a fabulously wealthy aunt and an engraved silver tea service, although the latter fact is seldom mentioned in the family) was here. In Los Angeles, California. Living with my married sister, Clovilla Adelaide Nash and her rich husband Harvey, who did something important in the motion-picture industry, although I wasn't sure what.

7

"I couldn't do it, Clovilla—"

"*Don't* . . ." She sucked in air. ". . . call me Clovilla." She was angry. I could tell.

Wincing in sympathy—I mean, what young woman in her right mind would want to be called Clovilla?—I said, "Sorry. Chloe. I meant to say that I wouldn't dare cut my hair. If Mother ever found out, she'd crucify me by mail, if she didn't hire a gangster to come out here and do it in person."

Clovilla—I mean Chloe—shrugged her slender shoulders, barely covered this steamy July morning by a filmy silk wrap of Chinese design that came to her mid-thigh. I wasn't sure I'd ever get used to the styles ladies wore out here in the Wild West. "Who cares? You're here now. You're free, white, and twenty-one, and you're in Los Angeles. And *I*, the sister who is charged with your keeping, say you need to get your hair bobbed. And," she added, looking with distaste at my skirt, which hung down a few inches below my knees, "you definitely need new clothes. I never expected to see an Allcutt looking dowdy."

I frowned at my reflection. "I don't really look dowdy, do I?"

"Yes." She spoke firmly.

"I wouldn't look dowdy in Boston."

Reflected back at me in the mirror, I saw Chloe's rolling eyes and sighed.

"Well, maybe I'll get something more fashionable after I have a couple of paychecks in the bank."

"And that's another thing. Why in the name of goodness do you want a *job?*" She said the word as if it had been rolling around in mud and she'd been assigned the unpleasant task of picking it up and cleaning it off. "For God's sake, Mercy Lou—"

It was my turn to interrupt. "Don't call me that!"

"Sorry. But, Mercy, you don't need to work! Harvey and I are happy to have you living with us."

"I don't want to impose."

"It's not an imposition!"

Although I regretted the frustration I heard in my sister's voice, I wouldn't be dissuaded from my purpose. Turning away from the mirror, I picked up my handbag and the marked-up copy of the *Los Angeles Times* I'd perused during breakfast, and smiled at her. "I know you mean that, but I really want to get a job. Just to see what it feels like. Other people do it all the time."

"Not Allcutts," she said with emphasis.

Tilting my head in a gesture of agreement, I persisted. "And I want to be able to support myself if ever I need to."

"Gawd." Chloe uttered the word in the exaggerated drawl she'd adopted since moving to the West Coast and marrying money. Not that she didn't come from money to begin with, but Boston money was old. Los-Angeles-moving-picture money was new, and both groups had their distinct accents. For the most part, the newly rich L.A. folks I'd met sounded snobbier than the old-money Bostonians I'd known forever. Or for twenty-one years, which is my own personal forever, since that's how old I am.

I lifted the paper. "It won't hurt me to look. In fact, I think it'll be fun."

"Fun?" She eyed me as if I'd slipped a cog.

She might be right, but I wouldn't let on. "It's something I've never done before. It'll be interesting. A new experience."

"It'll be a new experience, all right." Her frown lifted. "Say! I have an idea! Why don't you go to work for Harvey at the studio? They always need people to run around and do things."

"That's all right, Chloe. I saw some jobs listed in the newspaper, and I think I'll check them out first. But thank you. I may talk to Harvey later if I can't find anything interesting today."

I didn't tell her that I wanted to find a job all by myself, that I wanted to do something on my own for once in my life. I didn't tell her that I wanted to gather new and different experiences. And, most especially, I didn't tell her that I wanted to do those things because I aimed to use my newly gathered experiences in the novels I burned to write.

Which was the whole point, really. You know how people always say that writers should write what they know? Well, I didn't know anything. How can you write novels if you haven't lived? And I don't care what anybody says, living on Beacon Hill in Boston during the fall and winter and then in a mansion (called a "cottage") on Cape Cod during the spring and summer isn't really living. Oh, maybe if you're a *man* it is, because you still get to leave your mansion and go work in the city.

But if you're a woman, all you do on Beacon Hill or Cape Cod is sit in your gilded cage, order your butler around, and look down on the rest of the world. Play tennis occasionally. Gossip. Hire and fire servants. That's not for me, darn it.

Don't tell my mother I said *darn it,* please.

Chloe and Harvey live on what Los Angelenos call Bunker Hill. Our parents had suffered several spasms when they learned that the upstarts in Los Angeles had usurped a name so closely associated with the American Revolution, but nobody in Los Angeles seemed to care what they thought. What I liked best about where Chloe lived was that there was a precious, tiny, almost vertical railroad ride,

called Angel's Flight, that carried people to and from their elaborate homes on Bunker Hill to downtown Los Angeles, where real people did real jobs of real work.

You could hop on a car on Angel's Flight and in less than five minutes you'd go from fabulous wealth to everyday life, something with which I'd had little to do until then, and which I wanted to scoop up and devour like ice cream. Of course, you could also retreat again in the same amount of time, thereby giving those of us who had one an escape. That seemed like cheating to me, so I didn't aim to give up in my quest for the common touch without a good fight.

Until that moment, when I handed my nickel to the engineer and found a seat, I hadn't realized exactly how many people *did* go to work every day, women as well as men. Sure, there were some women on the car holding shopping bags, who were probably headed out to do their marketing, but I do believe that most of those people were on their way to jobs. A thrill at being part of the worker proletariat shot through me. I'd never tell Chloe, who would laugh. Or my mother, who would faint.

The excitement of Angel's Flight aside, by the time I'd traversed Fourth to Broadway and down Broadway on one side and back on the other, I was beginning to question the wisdom of gathering new experiences. So far, I'd applied for jobs at an attorney's office, two life insurance companies, and the Broadway Department Store, and was about to fall down dead from heat prostration and sore feet. It gets warm in Boston sometimes, but Jeez Louise, as my younger brother was fond of saying, the heat here in Los Angeles was downright oppressive.

I promised myself that after I applied for one more job, the one that was listed at a building on—I consulted my very smeary newspaper—Seventh and Hill, I'd find myself a

soda fountain and have luncheon. I mean lunch. Chloe has been trying to teach me how to speak Los Angelese, so that I don't "put people off with my Eastern ways." I suppose that's a good thing for a novelist to do. I mean, I wouldn't want people not to talk to me because they thought I was a snob, would I? No, I wouldn't.

My heart was too weary to soar, but the rest of me was happy when I found the address. Or was I? Good Lord. I peered up at the washed-out gray brick building and had second thoughts about applying for work there. It looked . . . unhealthy.

Actually, it looked dilapidated, and I wasn't accustomed to that. Bucking up slightly, I reminded myself that just because a building was a little long in the tooth didn't mean anything. Heck—I mean golly—in Boston, we're very proud of our old buildings. On the other hand, in Boston we take care of them. This building . . . Hmm . . .

A dull brass plaque declared the place to be the "Figueroa Building." I wondered who Mr. Figueroa was, and if he knew his building had seen better days.

Nuts. Squaring my shoulders, I pushed open the door and walked inside. Because of the glaring sun outdoors and the relative dimness indoors, I couldn't see a thing. However, an electrical rotating fan set up on a reception desk in the lobby blew upon those of us entering the building, and I stood there for a minute, basking in my drying perspiration while my eyes tried to adjust to the darkness. The breeze felt like heaven.

"C'n I help you?" a nasal voice twanged at me from the desk.

With a sigh, I left my spot in the cooling air and walked over to the voice, blinking as I did so in hopes of making my eyes adjust more quickly to the altered light. A girl about

my age lounged behind the desk, using an emery board to shape her fingernails, which were a bright, bright red. She apparently didn't have rigid parents, because not only were her fingernails painted red, but her hair was bobbed and marcelled. It was also an eye-popping white-blond. She looked a little like a younger version of my great-aunt Louise Mae Allcutt, and I wondered what would cause a young woman's hair to turn white like that. My heart twanged in sympathy, just in case she had a debilitating illness or something.

"Help ya?" she asked again. Her lips were painted the same brilliant red as her fingernails.

I swallowed, never having encountered a female who looked precisely like this one. "Er . . . yes, thank you. I would like to speak with a . . ." Again I consulted the *Times*. "A Mr. Ernest Templeton."

The young woman hooted. Honestly, she sounded like an owl. "Ernie? What you done, sweetie?"

I blinked at her. "I . . . beg your pardon?"

"Never mind." She flapped a few blood-red fingernails at me. "Ernie's on the third floor. You can take the elevator. We don't have a regular operator, so you'll have to manage it yourself." She aimed one of the fingers at the far wall. "If you want to get there, though, you prolly ought to take the stairs." She hooked a thumb over her right shoulder, and I saw a stairwell that looked dark and menacing. Unless that was my imagination.

"Thank you." Assuming from the young woman's esoteric remarks that the elevator was out of order, I aimed myself at the stairs. Unwillingly. However, it was my intention to gather unto myself new experiences and, darn it, this was a new experience.

Oh, dear. I said it again, didn't I?

By the time I'd climbed up three flights of stale-smelling stairs, wondering as I did so why people in Los Angeles didn't take better care of their buildings, I was dripping with perspiration and about to expire from heat stroke. After standing with my back against the wall for several minutes while I panted and attempted to dry myself by means of a vigorous fanning with my wilted newspaper, I looked around for something that might indicate where the office of Mr. Ernest Templeton, P.I., might be. I didn't know what P.I. meant but didn't think it mattered a whole lot. I wanted a job and, according to his advertisement, he needed office help.

The hallway was dim, probably because several of the lights that were supposed to illuminate it had burned out and hadn't been replaced. Squinting my way down the hallway, I noticed that there were no signs at all on several of the doors, as if the tenants had left a long time ago and no one else had rented the vacated rooms. Perhaps Mr. Templeton wasn't the best choice for an employer that I could make. Since I was there, however, I decided I might as well speak to him.

About halfway down the corridor, I thought I'd found his office. Chipped paint on the window declared *E nest Te ple on, P.* I guess the *I* had worn off, along with some of the other letters.

It took me a few seconds to decide whether I should knock at the glass or boldly walk inside, but I decided to err on the side of caution. I knocked. The glass rattled, and I jumped back in case it decided to fall out on my feet, which were encased in sturdy walking shoes. Hot sturdy walking shoes.

"Yeah?" a grumbly voice said a moment later.

Yeah? Was that any way to respond to a knock?

14

Knowing myself to be ignorant of Los Angeles manners, I took a chance, turned the dull brass doorknob, and pushed.

And I walked into an empty room. Well, now what? Dirty windows let in some light, but unless the person who had spoken to me was invisible, he wasn't there. Unless he was under the scarred desk, replete with candlestick telephone and typewriting machine, standing in the middle of the room. Four chairs, one behind the desk, two before it, one to its side, and all empty, also occupied the room.

"Um . . ." I looked around, confused, not really caring to march over to the desk and search beneath it.

My confusion ended in a flash when a voice from an adjoining room called out, "In here."

Ah. That explained it. Unaccountably relieved—in the split-second I'd had to think about it, I had considered the possibility that Mr. Templeton had suffered a fit and fallen down dead behind the desk, and I didn't want to find him there—I went to the adjoining room and entered it. I didn't get farther than a foot inside the door, because I was so shocked by what met my eyes.

A man—a youngish man—leaned back in one of those swivel chairs that you often find in offices. This one looked as if it had seen some hard usage. He had dark hair brushed back from his forehead although a strand or two had flopped forward, eyes so blue I could see them from where I stood, and his feet propped on his desk, which was messy and covered with papers. One of his shoes had a hole in its sole.

I think the thing that astonished me the most, however, was the large knife he held in his hand. It looked as if he was cleaning his fingernails with it.

Was it a local fad, this nail-cleaning obsession people in

this building seemed so fond of?

A coat tree next to his desk held a jacket and a hat. He was in his shirtsleeves, which were rolled up. And he didn't rise to greet me, even though I was a woman. I believe I sniffed, reminding myself of my mother and jolting me out of my initial state of surprise.

He said, "Yeah?" again.

I said, "Mr. Templeton?"

"The one and only."

I doubted that. "You have no father?" As soon as the words left my lips, I could have kicked myself. Even though I had little experience with job-hunting, I sensed it was unwise to be sarcastic to a prospective employer.

Evidently he didn't hold my slip against me. Grinning, he said, "He's dead."

"I'm sorry." Embarrassment burned within me. And probably on me, as I felt my cheeks get hot.

"You got a problem, lady?" Removing his feet from his desk, he plopped them on the floor with a clunk—I noticed then that the office was not carpeted—and said, "You need a P.I.?"

"Um . . . I don't know. I'm looking for a job." I waved the newspaper at him. "I'm applying for the position you have advertised in the *Times*."

Squinting, he said, "Where you from?"

"I beg your pardon?"

"You're not from around here, are you?"

"Er . . . no. I'm from . . . back East." Curse it, how could I fit in here if everyone knew from my voice that I didn't?

He nodded sagely. "Thought so. You sound classy."

I wasn't sure, but I think that was a compliment. Figuring it best not to respond to the comment in case I was wrong, I forged onward, pursuing the employment issue. "What sort

16

of work are you offering, Mr. Templeton?"

He waved his hand, the one with the huge knife attached to the end of it, in the air. I drew back, certain that was an unsafe gesture to be making in so confined a space. "I need a girl Friday."

"Um . . . a girl Friday?"

"Yeah. You know. Like Robinson Crusoe had his man Friday."

"Oh. I see." This man was confusing me. He still hadn't risen. Perhaps men only rose when women they perceived as elderly walked into their rooms. Perhaps I'd been more sheltered than even *I* had conjectured. Ghastly thought.

"Can you type?"

"Yes." I said it proudly, too, since I'd defied both my mother and my father, not to mention assorted aunts, uncles, and cousins, when I'd attended a typewriting class at the local Young Women's Christian Association in Boston. I'd justified my astounding action by saying that I wanted to be able to create a book of her favorite poems for my aunt Ophelia. Ophelia was quite eccentric, but she was so rich nobody avoided her because of it. Everybody backed off after that, deducing that if I was nice to Ophelia, Ophelia might leave me some of her money if she ever died.

"What about shorthand? Can you take shorthand?"

"Of course. Pitman system." I'd learned to use Pitman shorthand at the same YWCA where I'd learned to type. I never even told my parents about that, since I couldn't think of a moneyed relative upon whom I could blame my shorthand. I guess my parents had believed me to be a slow typist who had to take several classes in order to become proficient. Huh.

"Can you use the telephone?"

"Of course."

17

He squinted at me. "I don't know . . . You look kind of young."

"I'm twenty-one," I announced firmly.

"Yeah?" His grin made me wonder if he'd been hoping to discover my age without having to ask. Perhaps he was more subtle than he looked. Or I was more stupid than I had hoped.

"You sure you want to *work?*"

"Of course, I do! Why do you even ask the question? Would I be here if I didn't want to work?"

With a careless shrug, he said, "I don't know. I want somebody who'll really work. Sometimes rich girls think they want a new experience and will get a job for the hell of it and then they quit when they realize working isn't as much fun as sitting at home and spending Daddy's money."

The latter part of his speech shocked his *hell* right out of my head. "Rich girls? Why do you assume I'm a rich girl?"

His teeth were extremely white. I noticed them when he grinned once more. "You are, aren't you?"

There went my cheeks again. "Nonsense," I said, although I don't think there was much force behind the word. "If I were rich, would I be looking for work?"

"Like I said . . ." He allowed his sentence to trail off.

It bothered me a lot that he had guessed my status upon first acquaintance. Besides, it wasn't true that my family's wealth was all there was to me. I didn't want to be classified as some mediocre "rich girl" who was only getting a job for the . . . for fun. I truly craved independence.

Didn't I?

I thought about it for the approximately fifteen seconds Mr. Templeton stared at me, squinting, as if he were attempting to crawl inside my brain and figure out my motivations. Standing up straighter, I said, "I assure you,

Mr. Templeton, that I need a job. I will be a good, assiduous, and prompt employee."

"Yeah?"

"Yeah. I mean, yes." Phooey.

At last he stood up and flipped the knife, which landed point-down on his desk. The gesture startled me into a small jump. "Okay. You're hired. Now let's get some lunch."

And he rose from his scruffy chair, which squealed hideously, rolled down his shirtsleeves, buttoned his cuffs, reached for his jacket, plopped his hat on his head, and motioned for me to precede him from the room.

I wavered. "But . . ."

"No buts. Twenty-three skidoo, kiddo."

I'm sure I looked as confused as I felt. Mr. Templeton gave his hat a pat, shrugged into his jacket, slung himself out from behind his desk, and took my arm. He was quite a bit taller than I, who am five feet, four inches tall in the morning. I shrink during the day. I think everyone does. "Come on, kiddo. Let's rip a duck apart. My insides are rubbing together."

"But . . ."

"I'll tell you about the job while we eat. You like Chinese?"

"I . . . I . . ."

"Good. Chinese it is."

As I stumbled along behind Mr. Templeton, I attempted to assess the situation. Was he only taking me out to luncheon? I mean lunch? Or did he have some devious and far more nefarious plan in mind? On the face of it, he didn't appear threatening. Then again, if every villain in the world looked the part, villains wouldn't get away with so much, would they?

"Mr. Templeton!"

19

"Call me Ernie. We're going to be working together, aren't we?"

"I . . . I don't know."

"That's why you're here, isn't it?"

"Yes, but . . ." I'd had enough. Groping for the stair railing—we'd come that far already—I grabbed on to it and set my feet firmly on the top stair. "Stop pulling me!"

I hadn't meant to yell, but it worked. He stopped pulling me. In actual fact, he released my arm, quit walking—he had very long legs—and turned to frown at me. "What's the matter with you?"

I was out of breath, for one thing, but I sensed that wasn't what he meant. "I came here about a job! Not luncheon. I mean lunch."

"Oh, heck, kiddo, you have the job. It's lunchtime, and I'm hungry. So let's talk about the job over a bowl of noodles at Hop Luey's. Hell, I don't even know your name yet."

"Well . . . I don't believe it's proper for—"

It was probably a good thing that he let out a roar of laughter, since I'd started sounding like Boston again. "Proper! Lady, if you want proper, you don't want Ernie Templeton, P.I." He poked my chest with his forefinger. "If you want a job, I'm your guy."

Oh, brother. Rubbing my chest, I said, "Well . . ."

"Good. Let's go."

So we went.

When I got back to Chloe's house, it was about two in the afternoon, and I was feeling slightly giddy.

But, by gum, I had a job!

TWO

The next morning, I awoke to the jangle of the wind-up alarm clock I'd bought at the five-and-dime on the corner of Fourth and Hill, and jumped out of bed with a feeling of renewed purpose in my life. I had a job! What's more, it wasn't just any old job. It was a job working with a private investigator! Mr. Templeton had told me what P.I. meant over lunch.

If ever there was a job suited to a novelist, I told myself, this one was it. I would surely meet people with problems I could borrow for my novels, since I had none of my own that anyone else would give a rap about. Perhaps I might even meet criminals! Bootleggers! Gangsters! The notion made a shudder of delicious anticipation tap dance up my spine.

I dressed in a sober navy blue skirt and white blouse, picked up my matching jacket and cloche hat, and hurtled downstairs to the kitchen, surprising Mrs. Biddle, Chloe's housekeeper, into dropping an egg.

"Sorry, Mrs. Biddle. Here, let me help you."

I grabbed a rag from the sink, but Mrs. Biddle snatched it away from me. "Never you mind. I don't need nobody helping me."

"Well," I said, dropping the help issue since I got the feeling she didn't consider me adequate—which was probably true—"do you have some brass polish I can borrow?"

"What you want with brass polish?" She looked at me as if I were crazy. I guess she wasn't accustomed to the people

21

for whom she worked raiding her kitchen for cleaning supplies before eight o'clock in the morning.

"I'll need a couple of rags, too," I said. "And what kind of paint do you use to paint signs on windows, do you know?"

"I don't have any idea." She backed up a little bit, hunching, and seemed to be sidling toward the knives.

Well, that was all right. I couldn't help it if people thought I was unusual. "And I'll need something to wash windows with, too. What do you use to wash windows, Mrs. Biddle?"

"Bon Ami," she said. "And vinegar."

Before I could muddle through why the woman was trying to speak French to me, I saw in the cupboard a red-and-yellow cardboard box with the words "Bon Ami" stenciled thereon. Aha. I understood it all now. Bon Ami was some kind of window cleaner. Good. "Do you mind if I borrow it? Just for today?"

She didn't speak. When I turned to look, she was shaking her head slowly and staring at me. She'd made it to the knives, and her right hand was hovering over them. In case I made any sudden moves, I guess. Perceiving that it would be better all around if I desisted in garnering unto myself any more cleaning supplies, at least for today, I smiled in a friendly manner, lifting the box of Bon Ami from the cupboard. "Thank you. I'll just run along now."

Mrs. Biddle nodded, but she neither smiled nor left the knife rack until I was out of the kitchen. I suppose my actions might be considered a trifle peculiar, but that was only because Mrs. Biddle didn't understand that I had a *job* now! Or, if she did understand that, she didn't consider having a job anything unusual, since she and probably everyone else she knew also had jobs. It crossed my mind that there might

even be people in the world who wished they *didn't* have jobs—or at least wished they didn't have to have them. Hmmm. I decided to think about that later.

I was so excited, I could scarcely sit down to eat my toast and drink my tea. As soon as I'd swallowed the last bite, I jumped up from the table and assembled my cleaning supplies into a canvas sack I'd found in the basement. I hoped Mrs. Biddle wouldn't need the sack for anything before I got home from work, but I didn't ask. By that time I'd decided I'd best not fuss her anymore that morning. Then I left the house, walking the two blocks to Angel's Flight with a spring in my step, perhaps aided in the endeavor by the fact that the weather hadn't turned hot yet.

Goodness gracious, but Los Angeles was a bustling city. You could see a good deal of it from the top of Angel's Flight. According to Harvey, Chloe's husband, much of the city's wealth sprang from the burgeoning moving-picture industry. I thought that was interesting, but to tell the truth I also thought it was a trifle distressing. Perhaps that's my moralistic Boston upbringing rearing its ugly head, but wealth based upon illusions seems . . . well . . . unworthy, somehow.

My job, on the other hand . . . well, my job was worthwhile. That is to say, it was going to be worthwhile. Uplifting, even. Because Mr. Templeton, a private investigator, assisted people with their problems. I thought that was quite noble, actually, even though Mr. Templeton himself, upon first acquaintance, didn't necessarily strike one as a particularly heroic soul.

At lunch the day before, however, he'd explained to me exactly what kind of work a private investigator did. I came away not merely filled to the brim with good Chinese food, but bursting with enthusiasm.

Oh, boy, if I wanted to gain experience, this sounded like the way to do it. I'd be working with honest-to-goodness *criminals*. Sometimes. Rarely, according to Mr. Templeton, but still, sometimes. I'd never met a real, live, honest-to-goodness criminal before, unless you counted a business associate of my father's, who had been locked up for embezzling funds from the bank he owned in order to support a mistress. That had been a shame, true, and a terrible embarrassment to his wife and family, but it didn't really count as far as experience went, since I didn't know him well and, besides, it was more in the nature of cheating. I mean, he didn't kidnap anybody or anything.

In this job, I'd get the opportunity to meet *real* criminals, like robbers and people who shot other people and that sort of thing. More, I'd learn all about how to investigate things. Like, for instance, insurance fraud. Mind you, that sounded moderately boring, but Mr. Templeton said that sometimes he was asked to find missing persons. That should be interesting, shouldn't it? I doubted that I'd find it satisfying to spy on roving spouses, but that went with the territory, and I decided that I would just cope in cases like that.

Naturally, I didn't see myself as sitting on the sidelines, answering the telephone and typing, at least not in the long run. Until I became fully acquainted with Mr. Templeton's business, of course, those would be my duties. Long-term, however, I wanted to be more than a secretary. I wanted to be Mr. Templeton's assistant!

He hadn't mentioned needing assistance, but I figured I could work up to it.

Before climbing the stairs to the third floor, I stopped by the reception desk to speak to the girl with the blood-red fingernails and white hair. It was slightly before eight o'clock, and she looked as if she'd rather sleep a few more

withdrew a handbag, and began to root around in it, coming up with an emery board. As I headed for the stairs, she began filing away at her nails. I wondered if they'd ever be good enough for her.

It took a while, but I found Ned. I would have found him sooner, but the door to his closet was closed. Persisting in my pursuit—after all, I was working for an investigator now, wasn't I?—I opened every door I saw and eventually opened the right one. Lulu had been right about him: he was inside the closet, reading. Not *Fu Manchu*, but a book called *The House Without a Key*, by somebody named Earl Derr Biggers. I'd never heard of Mr. Biggers, although Ned had been so engrossed that he jumped a foot off his stool and dropped the book when I opened the door. He said something that sounded like, "Argh!"

I smiled sweetly. "Ned?"

He swallowed and slammed a hand over his heart. "I'm Ned."

"Are you the custodian?"

He was regaining his composure rapidly. Sitting up straight on his stool and lifting his slightly meager chin, he said, "I'm an actor. I'm only doing this lousy job until I hit it big."

This seemed to be a common phenomenon in Los Angeles. I hadn't been in the city long, a mere three weeks, but already I'd met waiters and waitresses, clerks, elevator operators, secretaries, laundresses, housemaids, and now a custodian, all of whom were biding their time working at menial jobs while waiting for fate, or somebody like my sister's husband, to tap them on their shoulders and create instant successes out of them. It seemed chancy to me, but what did I know? I was here to gain experience, not pass judgment.

"That's wonderful, Mr. . . . er . . . Ned. But in your

capacity as custodian, may I borrow you for a few minutes?"

He bent over and picked up his book. "To do what?" He didn't sound awfully eager to do the job for which he was being paid.

"I need three light bulbs replaced and a sign repainted on a window." Recalling the windows, the desk, the telephone, and the brass doorknobs, I added, "And I'll need to borrow a bucket and some soap."

Sliding off his stool, he stood up with a sigh. He was a little taller than I and not particularly handsome, and I wondered how soon his star would shine in movie palaces across the country. I didn't harbor too many hopes for the poor fellow, and thought it would behoove him to learn other, more profitable, skills than acting or janitoring. Naturally, I didn't say so.

"Where?"

"On the third floor."

"Whose office?"

"Mr. Ernest Templeton's."

"Ernie's room?" He squinted at me narrowly, as if he hadn't really noticed me as a person before. "Say, you're new around here, aren't you?"

"Yes." I stuck my hand out and smiled brightly. "Mercy Allcutt, Mr. . . . Ned. Pleased to meet you." Where in the world had all the last names of people living in Los Angeles gone?

After looking at my hand as if it were a strange and unusual object for about ten seconds, he shook it. "Happy to meet you, too." He gave me a smile that I think was meant to be seductive, although I'm not sure. "You're pretty cute, Miss Allcutt."

I snatched my hand back. "Thank you. Please follow me." And I marched off.

28

Perhaps there are advantages to being born in the upper echelons of an old and established society and learning from the cradle how to behave as if the world belongs to you, because after hesitating for less than a second, Ned followed behind me as meekly as a lamb. The phrase *born to command* occurred to me, and I wondered if I had been. If so, it might be a handy attribute to cultivate.

Over my shoulder, I said, "I have to pick up some things at the reception desk first."

"Okay."

And that was that. Ned and Lulu greeted each other with tepid enthusiasm, and then he and I walked up the stairs. After we'd scaled the second flight, he said, puffing, "Gotta fix that elevator, I guess."

Aha. Already I'd discovered something in my new capacity as sleuth's assistant—I mean secretary. If one forces the people who are supposed to fix elevators to climb several flights of stairs, they'll get around to fixing the elevators. "Good idea."

After I pointed out to Ned where the light bulbs were to go and where the sign was to be touched up, I went into the office—using the key Mr. Templeton had given me the day before and feeling quite important because of it—and began doing my own chores. First of all, I organized my desk. Made it my own. Wiped it down with Bon Ami, figuring that if it was good for windows, it must be all right to use on desks.

"Gotta go down to the basement and get the ladder," Ned said at one point.

"Fine." It occurred to me to ask why he hadn't just brought it up with him in the first place, but I didn't want to begin our acquaintance on a sour note.

I have to admit to being slightly flummoxed by the Bon Ami at first, because it turned out to be a solid block. I'm

not sure what I'd expected, but it wasn't a window cleaner masquerading as a bar of soap. However, after reading the directions, I soon figured it out, and I scrubbed and polished as if I'd been born to it. My mother would have been appalled.

But my mother wasn't there—hallelujah!—and I rubbed and scoured and had myself a grand old time. After I'd conquered the desk, I washed the window on the door, which I probably should have done first, since it had to be painted. But it didn't matter since Ned wasn't nearly as enchanted with his job as I was with mine, and he was taking his merry old time with the light bulbs. He'd brought up the ladder and hadn't started doing anything that might count as helpful when he next stuck his head into the office.

"Forgot the light bulbs," he said. "Gotta go down and get 'em."

"Fine," said I, thinking it was a good thing moving pictures were silent so Ned wouldn't have to learn lines should fate honor him with fame and fortune. He'd be a total dud on Broadway.

So I washed the window in the door—the Bon Ami worked quite well once I mastered the art of its proper use—then washed the other windows in Mr. Templeton's office and my own, and got out the brass polish, thinking as I did so that I should polish the plaque on the front of the building. If the Figueroa Building looked a little spiffier, more people might rent offices there. It was while I was polishing the doorknob that Mr. Templeton showed up.

I was totally engrossed in making the brass shine and delighting in its gleam, when his voice made me start. "What's going on here?"

Whirling around, I brushed a lock of hair away from my somewhat damp forehead with the hand holding the rag,

thereby polishing my own nose, which didn't need it, and said, "Mr. Templeton!"

He nodded and repeated, "What's going on?"

I glanced at the clean windows and the shiny doorknob. "I'm just tidying up a little."

He looked from the doorknob to the window to me and said, "Uh." With that, he brushed past me and went into his office, tossing his hat at the coat rack from the doorway. He missed, went behind his desk, stooped to pick up the hat, and placed it on the rack.

"There are no messages," I called after him. The day before, he'd been most emphatic about the importance of documenting telephone calls. As I'd arranged my desk, I'd found a pad especially imprinted for the purpose of taking telephone messages, which I thought must be the very height of efficiency.

He said, "Uh. Figures."

I folded my brass-polishing rag, stuck it in the bottom drawer of my newly reorganized desk, straightened my skirt and blouse, tucked my hair back into place, and went into Mr. Templeton's office. I stood there, holding my hands folded at my waist and smiling for what seemed like an hour before he looked up from the newspaper he'd been reading and said, "Yeah?"

Yeah? Somehow or other, that didn't seem an appropriate greeting to one for whom this was a first day at a first job. "Um . . . is there anything I can do for you, Mr. Templeton?"

He thought about it. "Don't think so, thanks."

At least he'd thanked me. That was something, albeit not much. I had turned to go back to my doorknob when Mr. Templeton's voice halted me, and I turned back to face him. I noticed that he was looking at me rather oddly and

hoped I hadn't done anything wrong.

"Say, is that Ned out there on the ladder?"

"Yes."

"Wasn't sure. Don't see him much."

"Oh."

"What's he doing?"

"Changing light bulbs. Then he's going to touch up the paint on the front window of your office."

"Really?" A grin slowly spread across his face. He had an interesting face. Handsome, I guess, in a rangy, craggy way. His eyes were remarkable. They were almost turquoise.

"Yes." For some reason my heart started dancing a lilt in my chest.

"You got him up here yourself?"

"Yes."

"You must have found him before he went into hiding."

"Ah . . . actually, I didn't. I searched him out in his lair." I spoke lightly, but my innards were unsteady, since I didn't know if I'd done the right thing or not.

Mr. Templeton solved that puzzle for me. He sat up straight, slammed his newspaper down on his desk, and smiled broadly. "Did you now!"

"Yes. He'd closed himself in a closet, but I found him."

"Good for you!" Leaving his newspaper squashed on the desk, he rose from his chair (which, I noticed once more, squeaked horribly—I'd get Ned to oil it) and leaned across his desk, holding his hand out to me as he did so. "Allow me to shake your hand, Miss Mercy Allcutt. It's probably only because you're pretty, but you're the first person I've known since I moved into this dump who's ever been able to get Ned to do anything. And I've been here for three years."

Embarrassed but pleased, I shook his hand. "You mean he's been waiting to be 'discovered' for three years?"

Mr. Templeton threw back his head and laughed so hard, I feared he would suffer a spasm. Before apoplexy could overcome him, he grabbed a handkerchief from his pocket and mopped his eyes. "Oh, my God! Is that what he's doing? He's going to be a star?"

"That's what he told me." My heart resumed fluttering again for no good reason, and I folded my hands at my waist once more, hoping to disguise my condition. Could it be reacting to Mr. Templeton? If it was, it was the first time it had done anything of a like nature, and I didn't approve. I didn't even know the man, for heaven's sake, and he was a total stranger. Well . . . almost a total stranger.

He re-sat himself with a flop. The chair squeaked again and then groaned, I presume from being put to such hard usage. "Brother, that's a gag to write home about. Ned and Lulu LaBelle."

"Lulu? You mean she's waiting to be discovered, too?"

"Absolutely. Maybe we could get 'em both discovered by the same talent scout."

"Talent scout?" I believe my sister's husband mentioned talent scouts at dinner once.

"Yeah. God knows why or how they expect it to happen. Maybe they go out and parade themselves at night on the Boulevard."

"On the Boulevard?" It was as if he were speaking a foreign language.

He flapped a hand at me. "Don't mind me. I'm becoming cynical in my old age."

His old age? Squinting, I tried to determine his age, and couldn't do it. He could have been anywhere from twenty-five to thirty-five, I guess. His was one of those faces that last well. Like John Barrymore's would have if he hadn't taken to drink.

33

Just as that thought flitted through my head, Mr. Templeton withdrew a flask from his jacket pocket, uncorked it, and took a tipple. I must have looked as shocked as I felt—after all, the distribution and consumption of liquor was supposed to have been outlawed years before, not that you'd know it from the news or my sister's dinner table— because he tilted his head, lifted his left eyebrow, and gave me a cynical smirk. "Shocked, Miss Allcutt?"

I hastened to deny it, even though I was. Very. "Heavenly days, no!" Then I made a total fool of myself and tittered.

He stuffed the flask back into his pocket, squinting past me and into my room. "I think we've got a client, Miss Allcutt. Better look snappy."

A client? A client! "My goodness!" Forgetting all about the flask, I whirled around and raced back into my own office.

My excitement suffered a slight check when I saw not a veiled, mysterious woman, or a distraught, disheveled man, but a small girl, perhaps about twelve years old. She didn't look much like a client to me.

Nevertheless, I was a professional, and I determined to treat this child graciously. She looked very shy, poor thing. "May I help you, dear?" Because I wanted to appear efficient as well as gracious, I sat myself behind my desk in my very own chair, folded my hands on my desk, and smiled at her. The chair was too tall and my feet didn't reach the floor, and I determined to ask Ned to fix it. Now that I knew where to find him, I'd just hound him until he did his job—or at least until he'd done the parts of it that benefited Mr. Templeton and me.

The little girl gulped. "Um . . . are you the P.I.?"

"I'm his assistant, sweetheart. Do you need a private investigator?"

She nodded. She was kind of grubby, I noticed, and wore

34

a middy blouse that was probably supposed to be white over a dark blue skirt. Both items were quite dirty. Her long brown hair had been braided at one time or another, but not recently. I think the middy blouse probably had once sported a navy blue tie, but it was either lost or I was wrong.

It occurred to me that her clothes might be examples of what I'd heard were termed "hand-me-downs." I'd had no personal experience in wearing clothing that had once belonged to another. My heart was touched.

Patting the chair next to my desk, I said sweetly, "Why don't you sit here and tell me your problem, dear."

She did, exposing holes in her stockings and extremely scuffed and dirty tie-up shoes. No patent-leather Mary Janes for this child. She had brown hair and eyes, and a smattering of freckles across her nose. She was not a prepossessing child, but was appealing for all that. "I need you to find my mother."

I must have gasped, because she jumped up from her seat and said harshly, her brown eyes flashing, "Don't tell me to go to the coppers, because I ain't gonna do that!"

"No, no, dear," I hastened to tell her, thinking the police were exactly what she needed, but not wanting to lose her confidence. Wouldn't you know it? This was my very first case, and I'd already upset the client. "I'm only . . . uh . . . sorry that you can't find your mother." Peering at her closely, I said, "You did say that you couldn't find her?"

"Yeah. She went to work last Saturday and didn't come home."

"But today is Tuesday!" I didn't know if I was more horrified than shocked or the other way around.

She gave me a look she might bestow on a younger and very stupid brother. "That's why I'm here. This here's a P.I.'s office, isn't it?"

35

"Er . . . yes. Yes, it is. But . . . well, what about your father?"

This time, she looked at me as if I were speaking Swahili or Greek. "My father?"

"Don't you have a father?" I was beginning to despair of this poor child.

She shook her head.

Oh, dear. I could feel a lump starting in my throat, and I ruthlessly suppressed it. I worked for a P.I. I was supposed to be hardheaded and efficient, darn it. I didn't mean to say that. "Well, then, are you sure you don't think the police—"

The mere word "police" had a galvanizing effect on her. As soon as it left my lips, she leaped to her feet again, her hands clenched, a look of something indescribable on her face, although I do believe its components were hate and fear. "No!"

"That's all right," I hastened to say. "Um . . . why don't I consult Mr. Templeton. Perhaps he has a suggestion."

"Not the cops," said she.

I nodded. "Not the . . . er . . . cops." I rose, preparatory to going to Mr. Templeton's office, when it occurred to me that I'd neglected to get the child's name. Some kind of assistant *I* was! However, that oversight was easily remedied. "What's your name, dear?"

"Barbara-Ann."

"And your last name?"

"You gotta know that?" She eyed me in what I could only term a suspicious manner.

Well, no matter. Business was business. I nodded. "I'm afraid so."

She heaved a huge sigh. "Houser."

"Barbara-Ann Houser?"

"Yeah."

"Just a moment, please."

36

THREE

"*Who?*"

Mr. Templeton's roar startled me into dropping my pencil. I frowned at him as I stooped to pick it up, glad that I'd taken the precaution of shutting the door behind me when I entered his office. "Barbara-Ann Houser. She's only a child, Mr. Templeton. There's no need to shout."

It looked to me as if he'd been occupied in staring out the newly cleaned window before I interrupted his contemplation of the building next door. Now he shoved himself up from his desk, and bellowed, "The hell there's not!"

"Well, really!" I know it sounded stuffy, but I was vexed. People didn't usually shout at me when I was only doing my job in a polite and efficient manner. Not that I'd had a job to do before that day, but . . . oh, never mind.

Pushing past me as if I were a mere slight impediment, like a feather or a cobweb or a pesky gnat, he heaved himself out of his office without bothering to don his jacket or hat. I rushed after him, worried lest he frighten poor little Barbara-Ann.

He stopped dead in the doorway, and I had to swerve or bump into him. So I swerved, bumped into the wall instead of his back, and banged my shoulder. My irritation with my employer surged. "For heaven's sake, Mr. Templeton!"

I don't think he heard me. He certainly didn't care if I'd spoken or not. With his fists planted on his hips, and his elbows blocking my view of the girl, he said in a voice that I wouldn't want to have directed at me, "It *is* you!"

Barbara-Ann's sullen voice muttered, "It's me. Didn't know you was a P.I. Thought you was still a copper."

During lunch the previous day, Mr. Templeton had told me he used to be a Los Angeles police officer, but that he had left the department a few years earlier.

"No. I'm not a copper any longer."

She said, "Huh."

Furious now, I applied the palms of my hands to Mr. Templeton's back and shoved. Evidently he hadn't anticipated such a maneuver from his new secretary, because he stumbled forward, then turned to glare at me.

I glared right back. I might be an employee, but I was a human being who deserved politeness if nothing else, as was that poor little girl, who didn't need to be cursed at. "You knocked me into the wall," I said, prevaricating a trifle.

"Sorry." He didn't even have the grace to look abashed, but turned back to the girl. "You really are Babs's kid, aren't you? God. How long has it been, anyhow?"

Now that I was back in my office, I resumed the chair behind my desk and watched with interest. It had become clear by this time that these two were acquainted, but what was really fascinating was that neither one of them seemed to cherish fond memories of the relationship. They were eyeing each other as if each suspected the other of hidden and dire motives.

Barbara-Ann shrugged. "I dunno."

Mr. Templeton hooked a knee over the edge of my desk and sat, blocking my view. Irked, I shoved my chair over so that I could still see what was going on. The man was entirely too casual.

"So Babs has gone missing, has she?"

His tone was snide, a circumstance I deemed inappropriate

to the situation. After all, the missing woman was apparently this child's only parent. In order to soothe the poor thing and assure her that at least *one* of us cared about her plight, I murmured, "We're so sorry, Miss Houser."

Both man and child looked at me as if I were a lunatic. Well, really!

"Haven't seen her since she left for work on Saturday," agreed Barbara-Ann, once more looking at Mr. Templeton warily.

"How come you came here? To me?"

Barbara-Ann shrugged. "Didn't know for sure it was you. But if it was you, I know you."

Poor child! Taking a chance on someone she *might* know, even though she neither liked nor trusted him. If I hadn't been so cognizant of my precarious position as a newcomer and a neophyte, I'd have withdrawn my hankie and blown my nose.

"Huh. Babs still working at the Kit Kat Klub?"

The Kit Kat Klub? Good Lord, what was that?

Barbara-Ann nodded.

"She still with Matty Bumpas?"

A shrug answered this question. I wondered who Matty Bumpas was. A gangster? A bootlegger? My experience-gathering antennae quivered in anticipation.

"You don't know?"

"No."

"You got any other uncles coming around to see Babs in her off hours?"

The sneer in his voice was palpable. So was his insinuation. Since Barbara-Ann didn't seem to understand or appreciate either one, I winced in her stead. I think I must have uttered some sort of protesting syllable or murmur, although I don't recall doing so, because Mr.

Templeton turned his sneer upon me.

"You don't know Babs," he told me.

"Of course I don't. I do know that she's missing, however, and that this child wants to find her mother."

I didn't like the smile that overtook his sneer when he registered this sharp sally from me. "Oh, yeah? You think so?" He turned back to Barbara-Ann. "Why do you want your mother to come back, Barbara-Ann?"

Another shrug. "I don't have no money."

"Business off lately or something?"

"A little."

Business? I could feel my brow furrow in confusion. I don't like being in a state of confusion. "What business? Do you mean to tell me that you work, too, Miss Houser?"

She eyed me in puzzlement. "How come you call me Miss Houser? My name's Barbara-Ann."

Mr. Templeton snickered.

Undaunted—I might not want to be perceived as snobbish, but I believe children deserve to be treated as politely as human beings. I mean adults—I said, "May I call you Barbara-Ann?"

"Dunno why not. Everybody else does." She had an entire repertoire of shrugs, I noticed. The one she executed for me this time told me she didn't give a hang what I did. Because I still felt sorry for her at that point, I didn't resent it.

"But what kind of business are you in, Barbara-Ann?"

"Cadging coins on street corners," she said promptly.

Goodness gracious sakes alive. "Don't you go to school?"

Another incredulous look, as if Barbara-Ann hadn't met anyone as stupid as I for a long time. "It's summer. There's no school."

"Ah. Of course."

"You look like you could use a bath, kiddo," Mr. Templeton observed, tugging on one of her mangy braids.

"Yeah. Well, we don't have no hot water."

"You don't need it in this weather," observed Mr. Templeton. "Do you have any water at all?"

Barbara-Ann heaved a huge sigh. "It was turned off a week ago."

"But I thought your mother was still working."

Yet another shrug. "Yeah, but she's got expenses."

"I'll bet she does."

I tutted in sympathy and reproof. Mr. Templeton only sneered at me again. Beast. For such a basically attractive man, he could be remarkably insensitive. Not that the two qualities have anything to do with each other; I just mention it.

"Okay." He unhooked his leg and stood up, again blocking my view of the child.

I foiled this attempt to keep me in the dark by rising and moving out from behind my desk, skimming around Mr. Templeton, and taking myself to Barbara-Ann's chair. I positioned myself behind *that* and put my hands on the top rail of the chair back. Let him try to ignore me *now*. Barbara-Ann twisted to look up at me, as if she wasn't quite sure she wanted me there, and I smiled down upon her with sympathetic understanding. Not that I understood a thing, but I'd be cursed if I'd allow Mr. Templeton to thwart my effort to gain enlightenment.

He smirked at me, but spoke to the child. "Well, I'm sorry about Babs, Barbara-Ann, but I don't know what I can do about it."

I was about to protest, but something in the look he shot me made the words dancing on my tongue shrivel up and die unspoken.

41

"You're a P.I. now, ain't you?" Barbara-Ann said, frowning. "Don't P.I.s find stuff?"

"Yeah, I'm a P.I., but I work for money. You have any money? I doubt it, since you're Babs's kid."

"I got two dollars and thirty-one cents." The child spoke proudly. "That's all I got, and I earned it my own self."

"Sorry, kiddo. I make twenty-five big ones a day plus expenses."

Her shoulders slumped.

I couldn't stand it any longer. "Mr. Templeton! How can you turn this child away like that? She's lost her *mother!*"

"Her mother was lost long before last Saturday, Miss Allcutt."

"But that's not Barbara-Ann's fault!"

"Sorry," he said, frowning at me. "I don't work for free. Can't afford to. Gotta support myself and pay for my secretary. You'd better go to the police, kiddo."

"No police," the girl muttered.

This time it was Mr. Templeton who shrugged. "Well, then . . ." He held his arms out, palms up, as if to say, *too bad.* He'd probably have added an unsavory modifier between the *too* and the *bad.*

Barbara-Ann stood up, looking small and defeated. "I figured as much. Thought it wouldn't hurt to ask."

Before she could get away, I said, "Wait! I'll help you!"

Both Barbara-Ann and Mr. Templeton looked at me as if I were out of my mind. I was beginning to resent this lack of confidence on their part.

"You?" Barbara-Ann said. "What can you do?"

"You?" Mr. Templeton said. "Don't be an ass!"

I tackled Mr. Templeton as the more culpable of the two. Virtually vibrating with indignation, I said, "I can *try!*

42

That's more than *you're* willing to do!"

Mr. Templeton rolled his eyes in overt contempt. Then he walked back into his office and slammed the door. The noise made me jump. Barbara-Ann was made of more impenetrable stuff. She merely looked at the door as if she were accustomed to having doors slammed in her face. My heart went out to her, and I knelt before her. She shrank back. Imagine that. She was unmoved by a man's rage and discommoded by a woman's sympathy. What a wicked world!

"Listen, Barbara-Ann. I don't have much experience with this sort of thing, but I'll be happy to help you."

"How?"

"How?" She had me there. "Well, I'll think of a way. Why don't you sit down again and tell me everything you think might be useful. Is that all right?" I smiled brightly.

In spite of the expression of grave doubt on her face, she sat again. And, of course, she gave one of her characteristic shrugs. "Guess it can't hurt," said she.

It wasn't an overwhelming vote of confidence, but it was enough for me. I grabbed my pencil, newly sharpened only that morning, and a stenographer's pad, filled with clean sheets of lined green paper, which I'd found in the top drawer of my desk, and I set to work.

Barbara-Ann had given me her name and address, the address of the Kit Kat Klub, her mother's description, and I was totally engrossed in jotting down details and pertinent facts—or those facts I hoped were pertinent—when the office door opened. I looked up to observe a middle-aged, slightly overweight man with squinchy little eyes standing there. He hesitated and appeared uncomfortable, and not, if I were to hazard a guess, merely because of the heat.

"May I help you?" I smiled brightly.

43

The man eyed Barbara-Ann dubiously. She slid off her chair. "Guess I'll go now. You want to know anything more?"

"I believe this will do for now. I'll . . . um . . . begin searching this afternoon after work."

The look she gave me shouldn't be available to children her age. It told of too much experience, as opposed to my total lack thereof, and of the kinds of experiences one didn't necessarily ever want to have. My heart, which was entirely too soft, twanged again.

"Come by the office tomorrow, dear, and I'll give you a report."

"Okay."

"Oh, but wait a minute!" I reached into my bottom drawer, withdrew my handbag, found my little money purse, and rooted in it for a dollar bill. "Here, sweetheart. Take this and get yourself a bath and something to eat. Will you do that?"

She eyed the bill as if she'd never seen one, which might have been the case, and muttered, "Gee, thanks."

And Barbara-Ann left, I suppose to cadge coins at street corners, whatever that meant, although I hoped she'd get herself a meal and a bath as well. I turned my attention to the man.

He'd removed his hat, revealing a sparsely furnished head glistening with perspiration, and he stepped aside, wiping his glowing face with a handkerchief as the little girl walked past him, still staring at the dollar bill. I rose and repeated, still smiling, "May I help you, sir?"

"Well . . ." His voice trailed off.

Well what? I wanted to ask. He was visiting a private investigator's office. I assumed that meant he needed our services. I dropped my voice to one of understanding and

compassion. "Are you in trouble, sir? Do you need help?"

Stuffing his handkerchief into his breast pocket and holding his hat in front of him not unlike a shield, he said, "I don't know . . ."

"Would you care to take a seat?" I gestured at the chair beside my desk. He eyed it as if it were a coiled serpent. His attitude was beginning to annoy me.

"Are you the investigator?"

"I'm his secretary. Perhaps I can take your name and find out a little about your case."

He looked dubious.

Just then Mr. Templeton's door opened, Mr. Templeton appeared in the outer office, and the other man's entire attitude altered. From his initial skepticism, he generated gratitude. From wariness, he displayed relief. From a posture of acute discomfort, he visibly relaxed.

He said, "Are you the investigator?"

Mr. Templeton strode forward, smiling and holding out his hand. "Ernest Templeton, at your service."

"Thank God," the other man breathed.

"Come into my office, and have a seat. We can talk in private."

"Thank God," the other man repeated. "I thought maybe she was the P.I." The emphasis he placed on that *she* was most unpleasant. I didn't like his little piggy eyes, either.

And they went into Mr. Templeton's office together. Before he closed the door in my face, Mr. Templeton winked at me.

I looked upon the phenomenon that transpired in front of my very desk with open-mouthed astonishment. As the door to Mr. Templeton's office clicked shut and the murmur of masculine voices started up behind the wall, I realized that *this* constituted my first really and truly

important new experience.

I had learned then and there, and without the possibility of doubt, that men don't trust women to have brains and the ability to use them. Certainly I'd read such contemptible theories before that point in time. And, in a way, my father's attitude of superiority toward his wife and daughters and his attempts to "protect" us were probably born of the belief in masculine superiority. But this . . . this unwillingness of one man to put his confidence in a woman (me), and his palpable relief when a man (Mr. Templeton) showed up to rescue him from said woman, was the first tangible, overt demonstration I'd received thus far in my life. I didn't like it.

And I decided there and then that I would solve the mystery of Babs Houser's disappearance. Even if it meant descending into the depths of the corrupt and putrid underside of Los Angeles society.

I'd feel a lot more comfortable sleuthing in that putrid underside if I had a sidekick. Preferably a large and burly one with a background in boxing. At that point in time, however, *I* was supposed to be the sidekick, at least in my own mind. I'd already deduced that Mr. Templeton didn't consider me anything other than a secretary, curse him.

But I'd show him.

At least I hoped I would.

Later on that same day, after work, I was contemplating an evening of investigative work with a sort of sick pounding in my chest. Before I'd left the office, I'd asked Mr. Templeton about the location of both Barbara-Ann Houser's home ("It's a rat-trap apartment building on Figueroa and Ninth") and the Kit Kat Klub ("It's a low-class speak off of Hill"). The notion of visiting either location all

by myself in my Boston clothes and with my Boston manners and accent gave me a sickish feeling in the rest of my body that went along almost too well with the sick pounding in my chest.

Now, as I sat down to take an informal dinner with my sister and her husband and one of their friends, a gentleman named Francis Easthope who worked with Harvey, I must have appeared troubled, because Chloe asked, "What's wrong, Mercy? Hard day at the office?" She laughed a little to emphasize the fact that she thought I was nuts for actually wanting to work for a living.

"Oh, do you have a job, Miss Allcutt?" Mr. Easthope asked. He was a very pleasant gentleman, although a trifle too handsome for my own personal comfort. He was tall and exceptionally well-groomed, with smooth dark hair, huge brown eyes that I'd heard my sister call "bedroom eyes," and a tidy, clipped moustache. Chloe had told me he was a very nice man, but he made me nervous, due to the aforementioned handsomeness. I don't know what it is, but whenever I'm around a man I find particularly attractive, I get nervous.

Unless it's Mr. Templeton, and then I only want to bash him.

Mr. Easthope also knew everything there was to know about feminine fashion, if one were to believe Chloe, and I saw no reason to doubt her. I thought that was kind of strange, since most of the men I'd met didn't give much of a hang about ladies' fashions, but I guess Mr. Easthope's interest made sense, as he designed clothes for the motion pictures. He'd asked the question out of genuine interest, too, and I discerned not a hint of censure or titillation in it.

Smiling at him to let him know I appreciated him, even though his magnificent physiognomy made my heart go

47

pitter-pat and I'd have preferred speaking to a plainer man, I said, "Yes, indeed. I'm working as a secretary for a private investigator in the Figueroa Building."

His eyes opened wide with interest. "A private investigator? You mean like Sherlock Holmes?"

My mind's eye quickly compared Mr. Templeton to Sherlock Holmes, and I couldn't suppress a chuckle. "I don't believe Mr. Templeton and Mr. Holmes have much in common except their line of work, but yes, I guess so."

Mr. Easthope pressed a finger to his chin, half-closed his eyes, and mused for a moment. "Templeton. Templeton. Now where have I heard that name before?"

I'm sure I didn't have a single clue. To help him along, I said, "He used to be a policeman."

The eyes popped open and the finger shot into the air. "That's it! Mr. Ernest Templeton? Is that his name?"

"That's the one." I was curious now. "Do you know him?"

"Not to say *know* him," Mr. Easthope said. "But I do know that he caused no end of trouble in 'twenty-two, during the Taylor investigation."

"My goodness!"

In 1922, only months after Fatty Arbuckle had got himself into trouble at a party in San Francisco, William Desmond Taylor, one of the finest directors in the pictures, had been murdered, thereby validating the beliefs of many that the motion-picture industry was evil and filled with repellant, vicious, and fallen individuals. Even I had found the incident and its resulting investigation bizarre and rather scandalous. I'd read reports of a bungled crime scene, in which dozens of people had tramped through Mr. Taylor's house even before the police arrived on the scene, and shoddy police work after they showed up. But I'd had

no idea that *my* Mr. Templeton had been involved. This was very exciting news!

"What do you mean, he caused trouble?" Believe me, I was all ears at that point. I didn't even care that Mr. Easthope resembled Douglas Fairbanks.

Mr. Easthope sipped his wine and thought. Harvey always had wine with dinner if there were guests. He claimed that it was wine left over from before Prohibition, but I had my doubts. He'd have had to have another house or a warehouse entirely given over to his wine collection if that were true, since he and Chloe entertained all the time.

"Well, perhaps *trouble* isn't precisely the right word. But he wanted things done right. That didn't go over well with his superiors in the police department or the folks at the studio."

"Really? In what way do you mean?"

"Mr. Templeton was aghast when he realized the investigators had allowed people access to Mr. Taylor's residence, for one thing, and he demanded that all documents that had been removed from it be returned. Of course, that didn't happen. He was all for cordoning off the house and allowing the police to investigate before anyone else was allowed entry. And he scolded the poor butler badly for washing up instead of leaving the crime scene as he'd found it."

"Ha!" said Harvey. "In other words, Mercy's Mr. Templeton hadn't been paid off yet, and he was mad about it."

I bristled immediately, although I stopped myself before I could rush to Mr. Templeton's defense. For all I knew, Harvey was right. I hated to think so.

"Well, I don't know about that," Mr. Easthope temporized. "I honestly don't believe he was causing trouble in order to be paid off. He was young and eager and

wanted to do things right." He giggled. It was an astonishing sound to hear issue from a full-grown man, especially one whose physical attributes fairly shrieked of masculinity. "The studios had paid off the rest of the department, however, and Mr. Templeton was as a voice crying in the wilderness." He giggled again.

I think I must have stared or something, because Chloe kicked me under the table, and I turned back to my squab, murmuring as I did so, "Perhaps that's why he quit the force. Perhaps he couldn't tolerate the rampant corruption."

"Possibly." Mr. Easthope shrugged, reminding me of Barbara-Ann Houser. "I should think any man with two morals to rub together would be uncomfortable in the Los Angeles Police Department."

"I'll drink to that." Harvey suited the action to his words and sipped some wine. Under the circumstances, I decided it wouldn't be prudent to express my shock at having seen Mr. Templeton's flask or to ask Mr. Easthope if he'd noticed that flask four years earlier, when Mr. Templeton had investigated the Taylor murder.

"But tell me, Miss Allcutt," went on Mr. Easthope, "I should think a private investigator's job must be very interesting."

"Oh, it is so far," I assured him eagerly. "Why, only today, a little girl came in to the office, hoping we could help her find her mother."

"Her mother!" Chloe looked at me, shocked, a bite of squab dangling from her fork. "You mean her mother has disappeared?"

I nodded. "Yes. Since last Saturday, when she went to her job at the Kit Kat Klub."

Harvey and Mr. Easthope exchanged a speaking glance. Harvey said, "The Kit Kat Klub? She works there?"

"According to Barbara-Ann, she does," I affirmed, my gaze slipping between the two men. "Do you know the place?"

"Oh, yes," muttered Harvey. "We know it, all right."

"Dreadful dive," said Mr. Easthope.

Oh, dear. More than ever, my insides felt sick, and I carefully returned to my plate the spear of asparagus I'd been about to stick in my mouth. "I promised Barbara-Ann that I'd go there tonight and ask about her mother."

Although I'd spoken softly, all three of my fellow diners turned to stare at me. It was rather as if I'd dropped a bomb.

"You *what?*" Chloe asked, astounded.

"Never!" That was Harvey, and he'd spoken very loudly. His adamancy surprised me, since Harvey was generally an easygoing sort of fellow.

"My dear, you can't!" said Mr. Easthope, his handsome cheeks pink and a look of real distress in his magnificent brown eyes. "It's a terrible place!"

It was the wrong reaction, and Chloe, at least, ought to have known it. Opposition was what had goaded me into taking typewriting and shorthand classes at the YWCA. Opposition was what had impelled me to move to the West Coast. And now opposition was making the sick feeling in my middle recede and a sensation of rage and purpose subsume it.

Because he was a kind man and truly believed in what he'd said, I addressed my first comment to Mr. Easthope. "I know it's an awful place, but that's where the poor woman works. I have to start somewhere, and that seems like the best place."

"But what about Mr. Templeton?" Mr. Easthope asked. Reasonably, curse it. "I thought he was the investigator and

51

you were his secretary. Isn't it his job to do the investigating?"

I felt my cheeks get hot. "Well, yes, but he was unable to attend to this matter." I couldn't make myself tell these people that Mr. Templeton had flatly refused to assist a poor little twelve-year-old girl in her hour of distress and had chosen instead to sneak about, trying to find that fat man's fiancée, who had probably run away because who'd want to be married to that overweight, sweaty man, who was a toad? "So I volunteered." That last was the absolute truth.

My dinner companions looked at each other and then at me. "It . . . um . . . might be an unwise thing to do, Mercy," said Chloe, choosing her words carefully. She had begun to remember how opposition affected me, I guess.

"I forbid it," stated Harvey. Instantly Chloe reached out her hand and covered his. She shook her head slightly.

I smiled at Harvey, knowing he'd only spoken from a feeling of brotherly responsibility. "I'm sorry, Harvey, but you can't really forbid me, you know. As Chloe reminded me this morning, I'm free, white, and twenty-one."

Again, a fairly anguished exchange of glances took place. I felt kind of bad about that. I mean, I didn't want to upset anyone. But I had told Barbara-Ann I'd help her and, by golly, I was going to help her.

Mr. Easthope cleared his throat. Folding his napkin and placing it precisely beside his plate, he smiled at me kindly, rather as if he were a zookeeper attempting to placate a fretful chimpanzee. "I'll tell you what, Miss Allcutt. Since you seem determined to assist this child in distress—"

I nodded and said, "Yes, I am."

"Right. Well, then, why don't I accompany you to the Kit Kat Klub? I'm sure it would look much more natural for a young woman to attend a nightclub accompanied by a

man, even such a one as I." I wasn't sure what he meant by that, but I thought he was a peach.

"Oh, Francis! Would you do that for Mercy?" Chloe gushed appreciation.

"Happy to," said Mr. Easthope nobly.

I was feeling pretty gushy myself. Mr. Easthope's offer of assistance made all my sick feelings vanish in an instant. Nevertheless, I didn't want to inconvenience him. "Are you sure, Mr. Easthope? If you have something else to do . . ."

"Oh, no!" he assured me. "Not at all. I was looking forward to a dreary evening at home after this delightful meal."

"Truly?" I was skeptical and made sure he knew it. I couldn't imagine so magnificent a specimen of manhood as Francis Easthope spending an evening alone.

He patted my hand. "Absolutely. Why, it will be an adventure."

An adventure. Hmm. By golly, I suppose it would be. "Then . . . thank you. Thank you very much."

The gust of air released as they all sighed in relief made the candle flames flicker.

FOUR

Chloe insisted I wear one of her evening ensembles to the Kit Kat Klub. "Even if it *is* a dive, I'm sure there will be people there who know Harvey and me, and I won't allow my sister to go out on the town looking like a librarian from Bean Town."

I squinted into the mirror. "Do I really look like a librarian?"

"Yes." No equivocation. No mitigating adjectives.

Hmmm. The notion didn't appeal, probably because the only two librarians I'd ever known had been old, gray, stuffy and mean. Since then, I've learned that not all librarians are like Miss Hatchett and Mrs. Trevelian, but I knew to whom Chloe referred and, therefore, I submitted meekly. "Thanks, Chloe."

"Don't mention it, kid. Besides, you want to look your best when you go out with Francis, don't you?"

There was a valid point if ever I'd heard one. "Yes."

"Good. Let me see now." She patted her lip with her finger and looked me up and down. I stood before her in my virginal white combinations, feeling a little silly. "First of all, we have to do something with your bosom."

My hands flew to the protuberances on my chest, and I felt even sillier. "What?"

"We'll have to bind them. Don't worry. I have everything we need." She went to her bureau and fished in it, coming away with a band that she wrapped around me, squashing me almost flat. I wasn't overly endowed there, but I didn't like the feeling, and said, "Ick."

54

"Don't ick at me. You'll wear a corset, too."

"Ew."

"Listen, kid, you're going to be a credit to Harvey and me, or you're not going. I'm not going to have my sister's extraneous parts bouncing up and down when she does the Charleston with the most gorgeous man in town."

"Yes, Chloe," I said humbly, thinking that the sacrifice would be worth it if I could help Barbara-Ann Houser find her mother. Even a rotten mother, which I feared Mrs. Houser might be, must be better than no mother at all, if you're twelve years old.

After Chloe had succeeded in all but mummifying my entire torso, she strode to her closet and flung the door wide. I gaped, amazed, never having seen such a large closet or so many clothes. Why, you could walk right in and move the racks! "Aha!" she cried after a few moments of reflection. "This is it. It'll go perfectly with your coloring."

I'd never thought much about my coloring before that evening. I had brown hair with a few red highlights, dark blue eyes, and a fair skin. I'd never thought of myself in terms of coloring, except that I'd rather have been a natural blonde, like Chloe. Her skin was a little fairer than mine, too, but she had the same deep blue eyes. I thought she was beautiful—and that I fell far short of that designation.

I liked our eyes better than any other of our features. They were large and rimmed with dark lashes. Occasionally, when Chloe and Harvey had been going out for an evening's entertainment, her eyes had stood out starkly against her white face. She'd told me she was trying to achieve the "pale and interesting" look. As far as I'm concerned, she did. I hoped she wouldn't want to make me look like that, but I didn't say so, fearing such a comment would provoke a cutting reaction.

Chloe marched back to me bearing a scrap of a dress, sleeveless, with a low, scooped neck that would reveal more of me than had ever been revealed in my life. "Good Lord, Chloe, I can't wear that!"

"You can, and you will," she insisted. "It's perfect for a nightclub."

It crossed my mind to wonder why women who bound their breasts wore such low-cut tops. I mean, you'd suppose that by wearing such tops, they were enticing men to look at their bosoms, but if their bosoms were squashed flat, what was the point? Again, I didn't ask Chloe, since she'd only have given me one of those looks that I so dislike.

Aside from the skimpiness of the dress, it was awfully pretty, with a patterned silk-and-velvet bodice. The colors were kind of wild, being yellow, orange, and brown, but they didn't scream at one, if you know what I mean. An orange velvet sash was threaded through lappets at the low waist, and the dress had a gold-colored, satin under-bodice and skirt with a scalloped hemline. It was lovely, but not exactly me, at least not the me I knew. I looked at the garment askance.

Chloe didn't give me an opportunity to object. She said, "You wear this, or you don't go. I can pick up that telephone and call Boston, you know."

"Chloe! You wouldn't! Anyhow, you can't. It takes hours to make a long-distance trunk call."

She stuck her face in mine, until we were nose to nose. "You're going to wear this, and you're going to be a credit to Harvey. Do you understand me, Mercedes Louise Allcutt? My husband is an important man in the motion-picture industry, and I'll not have people laughing at him behind his back because his sister-in-law is a dowdy prude!"

"I'm not a dowdy prude," I cried, stung.

"You are, too. And come Saturday, we're going to fix that. I don't mind all that much that you insist on working, but I'll be darned if I'll let you look like a frump. And we're going to get your hair bobbed, too. God alone knows how I'll fix it for tonight."

Humbled—or perhaps humiliated was a better word for it—I decided to bow to my fate. After all, Chloe was really being splendid, letting me come out here and live with her and get a job and all. "Yes, Chloe. Thank you, Chloe. You're very kind to me, Chloe."

She slapped my arm lightly. "Don't be stupid. You've got to wear a pair of my shoes, too. I have some that I had made for the dress.

"You had shoes made to match the dress?"

"Well, I had them dyed to match it."

Good Lord. "Don't you want to save the outfit for yourself? It must have cost a fortune."

"It did, but it didn't become me because I'm too blond for the colors. But I loved the fabric so much, I had it made anyway. It'll go much better with your dark hair."

Boy, I wonder what Lulu LaBelle would think if she could hear my sister talk about expensive clothes as if they were something you could just toss aside if you made a mistake and ordered the wrong color. Anyhow, I'd venture to bet that Lulu bought her clothes off the rack.

If I were to guess, I'd say this entire outfit Chloe was allowing me to borrow probably cost close to a hundred dollars. Maybe more. Some people didn't make that much money in a month. A year even, maybe.

I did look mighty spiffy when Chloe and I walked down the main staircase in her house and Francis and Harvey met us at the foot of the stairs. Chloe had twisted my hair up and stuck some jewelry in it, and it looked good even if it

wasn't bobbed. I felt a trifle self-conscious in Chloe's flesh-colored silk stockings, but Chloe told me I'd get used to them. I had flatly refused to roll them down and rouge my knees.

Harvey grinned and whistled.

Mr. Easthope bowed like the gentleman he was. "You look perfectly charming, Miss Allcutt. It will be an honor to accompany you out this evening."

Chloe had touched up my face with powder and my eyes with mascara, and had dabbed a touch of rouge on my cheeks and lips, and I smiled at Mr. Easthope, feeling shy all of a sudden. "Thank you very much."

And, after Mr. Easthope had led me to his automobile, an absolutely gorgeous Duesenberg that looked large enough for a family of ten to live in, opened the door for me, got in on the other side, and started the engine, and I realized I was being swept away to a real, honest-to-goodness nightclub, I began to understand the lure of the pictures. There was such glamour in them. I mean, who else could afford to live like this? My parents could, I suppose, but they wouldn't do it, because they were "old school," and they'd shun such ostentation.

No. This way of life had been spawned by the so-called movies, and it was being perpetrated by those who made and lived by them. Maybe Ned wasn't such a sap. Maybe there was something to his ambition, although hiding in a closet all day didn't seem like the most effective way to achieve his aim of being discovered and turning into a moving-picture star.

But what did I know? According to my sister, not a blessed thing. And I guess she was right, if this was the way she lived. And I guess it was, since I was wearing her clothes, and she had more where these came from. I began

to look forward to Saturday. It would be fun to update my wardrobe!

My enthusiasm dwindled as Mr. Easthope drove farther into the shabby part of the city. From the glories of Bunker Hill, we drove downhill and through Chinatown, which looked kind of seedy at night, and down some small, dark streets until we got to a place where several large, expensive cars were parked. They looked out of place there on the dingy street.

A big galoot stepped out from the shadows, saw Mr. Easthope and his Duesenberg, and gestured for us to follow him down another dark, narrow street.

"Who's he?" I whispered, although I'm not sure why. Nobody could hear us.

"The parking guard. The speaks hire them so that the neighborhood kids don't steal people's tires."

"Oh." Those speakeasy people were sure organized. Imagine that. They had a man to direct people where to park and to make sure the cars were safe. I wondered if the police knew about this racket. Recalling the conversation at dinner, I supposed they did.

So Mr. Easthope parked his wonderful car, the galoot watching all the time, then he got out, opened the door for me, and I got out, and the galoot said, "Youse guys come with me."

I hadn't realized people actually talked like that. Another new experience! Mr. Easthope took my arm and we followed the galoot down a dark alley to a dark doorway, where the galoot banged on the door with a fist that looked rather like a roasted leg of lamb.

We heard a scratching noise, an eyehole appeared in the door, and an eye appeared at the eyehole. The galoot said, "Guests," and stepped aside, I presume to assist more il-

legal customers to safe parking places.

Someone—it sounded like another galoot—said, "Yeah?"

Mr. Easthope whispered, "Oh, you kid." That must have been the password. He'd told me about passwords on the way to the speakeasy. I didn't quibble that, in this case, entrance was granted by the speaking of an entire phrase rather than one word, because that would have been so utterly Boston, even I could recognize it as such.

The eye disappeared, and the door opened.

Golly, what a difference between outdoors and indoors! Of course, I'd had no idea what to expect, since I hadn't habituated speakeasies in Boston, but this one surprised me. It looked like a bordello designed by a color-blind seventeenth-century French courtesan.

Red-and-black flocked paper covered the walls. Plush red carpeting had been laid upon the floor beneath our feet. The decor was undoubtedly meant to impart the impression of opulence, but it gave me a queasy feeling in my tummy, perhaps because the red clashed with my orange sash. Crystal chandeliers with dangly ornaments were supposed to shed light on all below, but cigar and cigarette smoke was so thick, everything looked merely fuzzy. A jazz band blared away in the main room, which lay straight ahead of us and sported a polished wooden floor suitable for dancing. It was being used, too. A row of dancing girls was executing intricate tap steps and kicks to the evident joy of the patrons.

I'd never seen girls in public in so few clothes. Even at the seashore, women covered up more than those girls did. I tried not to exhibit my state of shock, since I didn't want Chloe to be ashamed of me, but I found the spectacle embarrassing to watch, especially when the girls grabbed the tails hanging from the backs of their skimpy costumes and

twirled them. I guess they were supposed to be cats or something.

The noise was ghastly. While I waited for my ears to adjust, I stared around me in fascination. A long bar had been built against the right wall, behind which stood what looked like a battalion of bartenders mixing and shaking and handing out drinks, all of which I presumed contained alcohol. A huge mirror backed the bartenders, reflecting the revelry going forward in the main room. More girls in skimpy outfits, net stockings, and shingled hair walked here and there with trays loaded with cigarettes and cigars and matchboxes strapped to their shoulders.

Approximately three million people swarmed around the place, dancing to the music, laughing, chattering, and screaming. I think they were screaming because it was the only way they could make themselves heard over the band, which was playing "Baby Face."

Almost everyone who wasn't actively dancing held both a drink and a cigarette or a cigar. Most of the ladies (I use the word loosely) had holders for their cigarettes. I guess that was supposed to be sophisticated. I knew for a sinking certainty that Chloe's beautiful dress was going to smell like an ashcan when I got home.

The atmosphere was supposed to be festive, but it appeared only sordid to me. Maybe that's my Boston upbringing talking, but I don't think so. I doubted that any of those people were truly happy. Then again, maybe I was wrong. Wouldn't have been the first time.

Whatever the mood of the "guests," you should have seen their clothes. I've never beheld so many beads in my entire life. Or so many knees, most of which were rouged. And everybody who wasn't drinking was dancing the Charleston with an air of devil-may-care bravado.

All the band members were dark-skinned. They also appeared a good deal happier than the people dancing and drinking, although that impression, too, might have been colored by my proper Boston upbringing.

"Would you care to dance?" Mr. Easthope yelled politely.

"Um, sure." I needed to question people about Mrs. Houser, but I felt a little uneasy and decided to try to get comfortable first. "I need to put my handbag down somewhere."

"Of course. I'll find us a table." Holding onto my arm, thank God, he maneuvered us through the throng to a table against a wall as far away from the band as he could get, bless his heart.

We danced for what seemed like hours, and I still didn't feel comfortable enough to begin questioning the scantily clad maidens walking around the place hawking cigarettes. Poor Mr. Easthope was perspiring like a lumberjack in August (for that matter, so was I), but he never complained once. I swear, the man's a saint. At any rate, we sat at our table to rest for a while, and I discovered that in my partner, I had a heretofore unrecognized-by-me resource.

Of course, I'd noticed all the ladies sneaking glances at Mr. Easthope. What red-blooded American woman *wouldn't* want to feast her eyes on such a delectable bit of masculinity? But as soon as we sat down, all the cigarette girls in the room seemed to make a beeline straight at him. In other words, it hadn't been necessary to wear us both out dancing. We could have sat at our table and been comfortable (more or less) and let the women swarm to us. Live and learn.

The first woman who appeared before us looked as if she

were a trifle past her prime, and I wondered if it embarrassed her to work in such an outfit in such a place. She looked at me strangely when I spoke to her and asked her name. I honestly don't believe she'd even known I was there until I talked to her.

"Dolly," said she, her squinty-eyed gaze letting me know she didn't think I belonged there, which was moderately discouraging. I mean, I hadn't even really questioned her yet, and she'd already pegged me for a goody two-shoes. More than ever, I looked forward to Saturday.

"My name is Mercy Allcutt, Dolly, and I'm trying to find Babs Houser. Do you know Mrs. Houser?"

"*Missus* Houser?" Dolly laughed a most unpleasant laugh. "Yeah, well, maybe she is. And yeah, I know her. She lost or something? She didn't show up to work."

"Her daughter is worried. It seems she hasn't been home since Saturday."

Dolly whistled. "That's not good." Her eyes, which were heavily made up, popped wide open. "Oh, shoot, I wonder if the white slavers got her."

Her words so shocked me that I pressed a hand to my squashed bosom. "Wh-white slavers?" Good Lord!

"Yeah." Dolly lowered her voice, although that wasn't really necessary. Leaning closer to me, she said, "I heard tell that the Chinks like to capture white girls and ship them to China to work as . . . well, you know." She winked at me.

Actually, I didn't know, but I was too embarrassed to ask. Maybe Chloe would clue me in.

Anyhow, Dolly didn't wait for me to respond, but pointed at another girl, much younger than she. "That there is Gwenda," Dolly said, indicating the girl. "Her and Babs are pals. Maybe you should go ask her."

"Thank you!" I jumped up and hurried over to the girl

Dolly had indicated, only then realizing that Dolly had probably sent me to the other girl so she could have Mr. Easthope to herself. I was learning quite quickly.

I waved at the girl, who had turned my way. "Gwenda!"

She appeared surprised that anyone should be hailing her. Pointing to her chest, she mouthed, "Who, me?"

I nodded, realizing it was no use screeching. I also realized that—and this is hard for me to say, since it speaks of a ridiculous degree of upper Bostonian snobbery—I experienced a great degree of apprehension in approaching a woman who was so skimpily dressed and who worked selling cigars in a speakeasy. I know, I know, the poor thing probably had no choice, and I was only being fussy. I tried to overcome my qualms. Truly, I did, even though I hadn't quite done so by the time I reached her.

"You want me?" Gwenda asked, sounding as incredulous as she looked. "You want a packet of cigs? I've got some clove ones here that sometimes the ladies like."

She'd pegged me as a *lady*, too. I had to do something about that. "Er . . . no, thank you. I need to ask you some questions about Babs Houser. I'm looking for her, you see."

"Oh!" Gwenda's expression of doubt transformed into one of joy. "Where is she, do you know?"

If I knew, I wouldn't be looking for her, would I? I didn't point this out to Gwenda, who gave every indication of being a very sweet, if dim, bulb. "No, I don't know where she is, but I hope to find her. Her daughter is worried."

"So am I. This ain't like Babs." I'm sure that if she didn't have that tray slung over her shoulder, poor Gwenda would have been biting her fingernails.

I stuck out my hand. "My name is Mercy Allcutt, Gwenda. I'm happy to meet you."

After looking at my hand dumbly for a moment or two,

Gwenda took and shook it. It was obviously a new experience for her. "Oh."

"Why don't we sit down for a minute?" I suggested, thinking that might help her relax. Silly me.

"Oh, I can't sit down, Miss Allcutt. I'd get fired." She looked around with apprehension.

"We don't want that to happen," I assured her. "But I would like to know if you can think of anything that might help us find Babs."

Her face fell. "You're looking for her, too?"

"Too? You mean other people have been looking for her?"

"Well, her gentleman friend come here asking for her."

"Her gentleman friend?" I recalled Mr. Templeton saying something snide about an uncle when Barbara-Ann came to the office. "What's his name?"

"Matty Bumpas. I think he's a real stinker, but don't tell Babs I said so."

"I won't," I promised. How could I? "So her . . . uh . . . gentleman friend doesn't know where she is either?"

Gwenda shrugged, almost losing her tray. "Guess not."

"Hmm. Can you think of anything Babs might have said to you that might indicate where she is? I mean, did she seem worried about anything or anyone, or did she say she was afraid of anything or anyone."

"Oh! Yeah! Now that you mention it, she did say she was afraid of a Chink."

I think I blinked. A chink? Why would anyone be afraid of a chink? "Um . . ."

Suddenly, both Gwenda and I jumped about a yard in the air at a roar that came from directly behind me. *"What the devil do you think you're doing in this joint?"*

Gwenda screamed. Fortunately, nobody else heard her

65

due to the aforesaid noise level. I spun around, my heart in my throat, to discover Mr. Templeton! He seemed to be in a rather bad mood, but I was incredibly happy to see him. "Oh, Mr. Templeton, you *do* care!"

Stammering "I gotta go," Gwenda raced away through the swarm faster than I'd have believed possible, dodging and weaving like a boxer in the ring—if what I've heard about the fights is correct.

Although I was thrilled to see him, Mr. Templeton did not seem similarly enraptured. Why, I knew not. He repeated, not quite so loudly, "What the devil are you doing here in this dive."

"The same thing you're doing," I said, feeling bright and cheerful and ever so much more comfortable now that I knew he wasn't the old meanie he'd portrayed himself to be in front of Barbara-Ann. I'd heard before that men are hesitant to demonstrate their softer tendencies.

"I sincerely doubt that," he said. He said it through gritted teeth, too, for some reason. "What the hell are you doing here alone?"

I thought it was sweet that he cared about my welfare, even if I didn't approve of his language. I assured him, "Oh, I'm not alone. A friend came with me."

As if by magic, Mr. Easthope appeared at my side. I saw Mr. Templeton's eyebrows lift until they nearly receded into his hairline.

"Is anything the matter?" Mr. Easthope seemed concerned.

I took him by the arm, feeling very warm and protected. I know women don't *really* need to be protected by men—most of the time—but I have to admit to being gratified at that moment that I had two such staunch and handsome supporters. "Mr. Easthope, please allow me to introduce you to my employer, Mr. Ernest Templeton. I understand

you two may have met before."

Taking in Mr. Easthope and the words of my introduction, Mr. Templeton seemed to grow taller as he stiffened. His face flushed a little, and he didn't look significantly gratified to know I wasn't alone.

Mr. Easthope, on the other hand, appeared a trifle nervous. Nevertheless, he held out his hand like the gentleman he was. "How do you do, Mr. Templeton?"

After scowling at the hand for a couple of seconds, Mr. Templeton shook it. "Easthope." He didn't expound on his comment.

Feeling a little nervous myself, I started to chatter. "Mr. Templeton is here to find that little girl's mother, Mr. Easthope, just as I am. She works—that is to say, she used to work here, you see."

"Say, where do I know you from?" asked Mr. Templeton, ignoring me completely. Really, the man was very annoying at times.

Mr. Easthope cleared his throat. "Ah . . . I believe we met during the Taylor investigation."

"Huh. That mess." Mr. Templeton's voice dripped with contempt, as if the Taylor investigation was all Mr. Easthope's fault.

"Er . . . yes."

"Well, Taylor aside, I don't know how anyone could bring a lady like Miss Allcutt to a dive like this."

Mr. Easthope's eyes opened wide, and he began to look frightened. I didn't like this at all, so I answered Mr. Templeton's veiled accusation.

"He only brought me here because I was going to come by myself if he didn't," I said heatedly. "There's no reason for this rancor on your part, Mr. Templeton."

He said, "Huh," at me and turned to Mr. Easthope.

"You'd probably better take her home now. I'll cover this place."

"That's probably better," I admitted. "You have ever so much more experience than I."

I don't have any idea in the world why Mr. Templeton rolled his eyes and looked disgusted. However, I know for certain that Mr. Easthope was relieved to get out of the Kit Kat Klub. I was too, if you want to know the truth.

FIVE

The next morning, I was pretty tired from my late night, but I chalked it up to experience and didn't let it bother me. I also returned Mrs. Biddle's cleaning supplies to her. She didn't thank me, but looked at me rather as if she suspected me of being the family's skeleton. I think she believed my parents had shipped me west so that I couldn't embarrass them back home.

So be it. In spite of my lack of sleep, I felt buoyant, and I fairly danced to Angel's Flight and to work. The weather that morning was kind of foggy, not, in actual fact, unlike the insides of my head, which were slightly jumbled, notwithstanding my good mood. Chloe had already told me that sometimes Los Angeles weather in June and July was overcast, but this was the first evidence of the phenomenon I'd seen so far.

Lo and behold, I didn't have to track Ned down in his closet that morning! He was there, at the reception desk, talking to Lulu, when I arrived at the Figueroa Building. They both looked up when I entered the building.

"Good morning," I said, cheery.

" 'Lo," said Lulu.

Ned straightened, smoothed his shirt, and said, "Hello, Miss Allcutt. How are you today?"

Lulu stared at him. "You feeling okay, Ned?"

He frowned back. "Fine, thanks."

"Huh." She picked up an emery board and started filing away.

"I'm glad you're here, Ned, because I need you."

He lifted his eyebrows in a suggestive manner, which I found quite off-putting.

"To oil a chair," I elaborated, making my voice stern.

"Be happy to," he said.

"Have you finished fixing the elevator?" I asked pointedly.

"Not yet."

"Too bad. Then you'll have to walk up three flights again, I guess." With a sweet smile, I added, "You might consider bringing everything you need the first time, Ned, so you won't have to climb up and down stairs as many times as you did yesterday."

Lulu said, "Ha!"

Ned shuffled off, and I climbed the stairs.

Although my thoughts were slightly unfocused, I was delighted when I saw that Ned had done a fine job on the door, and that anyone visiting Mr. Templeton from now on would not only be able to find his office, since the hallway lights now worked, but would be able to read his entire name and profession. Well, they could read the initials of his profession, at any rate, since Ned had replaced the *I* in *P.I.* As I put my small handbag in my desk drawer, I breathed a sigh of satisfaction.

I, Mercedes Louise Allcutt, was a working girl. I had a job. An important job. Withdrawing a lined tablet from the top center drawer of my desk, I determined that I should write down all the information I had uncovered the night before while at the Kit Kat Klub.

Before I got started, Ned showed up with the oil can. "What needs to be oiled, Miss Allcutt?" He made sheep's eyes at me. Good Lord.

"Mr. Templeton's chair," I said.

"In that office?" Ned pointed.

70

Where did he think Mr. Templeton's chair was? I only said, "Yes." I said it nicely, too, since I was starting to think poor Ned's stepping stones didn't quite reach his front door, if you know what I mean.

I'd begun my list when Ned appeared before my desk again, staring at me rather like a hungry dog might stare at somebody who was eating a steak in front of it. "I oiled the chair."

"Thank you." Another smile.

"Anything else you need?"

"No, thank you. I don't believe so." I remembered the elevator. "Wait! The elevator. That really does need to be repaired, Ned."

"Yeah, but I meant is there anything I can do for *you*."

"Oh. No, I don't think so." I tacked a "thank you" onto my sentence, because that's the way I was reared. Boston, don't you know.

He seemed a trifle let down, but he left. Thank God, I might add. He was becoming kind of a nuisance. I returned to my pad and my list.

Disappointment had barely begun to overtake my enthusiasm when Mr. Templeton showed up. I glanced from my pad, wishing I'd had more concrete information to write on it, but cheered by his presence. We could discuss the Houser matter, and I'm sure he'd have some valuable suggestions that I could jot down in my almost-empty pad.

"Good morning," said I, noticing as I did so that Mr. Templeton didn't appear as jolly as I felt.

He said, "Huh." Then he went to his office, threw his hat at the coat rack, and plopped into his chair. I know he did those things, because I rose and followed him.

His brow furrowed. He rocked back and forth in his

chair twice. He glared at me. "What the hell happened to my squeak?"

"Your squeak?"

"Yeah."

"I had Ned oil your chair."

"Oh, you did, did you?"

His mood was starting to affect my own. "Yes, I did. It was noisy and sounded most unprofessional. I should think you'd thank me, not growl at me."

"Huh." His furrowed brow did not smooth out. "I kinda liked that squeak. It spoke to me."

"It spoke to everyone," I said sourly, by this time thoroughly disgruntled with my irritating employer.

"I bet it didn't give them comfort on stressful days, though." I couldn't tell if he was joking or not, but he didn't look like it. "I liked it."

"For heaven's sake, why are we talking about your stupid chair? We have more important things to discuss."

"Yeah? Like what?" His glower was really quite magnificent. "Like you showing up at the Kit Kat Klub with that fairy last night?"

With that fairy? What was the man talking about? "What fairy?"

"That Easthope character. Huh!"

"Mr. Easthope was very kind to accompany me to that place." Was Mr. Easthope a fairy? Whatever did that mean? I determined to ask Chloe. It was probably some term specific to Los Angeles, or perhaps to the moving-picture industry, which seemed to have spawned a language all its own.

"He was an ass to take you there, and you have no business in a place like that." He sounded awfully stern. "For God's sake, the joint could have been raided."

Oh, my, that possibility hadn't crossed my mind. I was about to tell him that, in a conciliating sort of voice, when he mumbled, "Of course, they've probably paid the L.A.P.D. not to raid the place."

That comment changed my mind for me. "Well, then, there's no reason for this unreasonable attitude on your part, is there?"

I thought it was a pretty good rejoinder, but evidently Mr. Templeton wasn't buying it. "You damned fool. You were as out of place there as a kitten in a lion's den! I forbid you to go anywhere like that again."

"You can't forbid me to do anything," I pointed out.

"Yes, I can. It's a term of your employment."

I *knew* he was kidding that time. "Oh, for heaven's sake, stop talking about that wretched place, can't you? We have more important things to talk about."

"Yeah?" he repeated. "Like what?"

He had a very effective sneer. It made me want to hurl my secretarial pad with the lined green pages at him. "Like Babs Houser, is what! Whom, I mean."

"Nuts to Babs Houser. I've got to find Mr. Godfrey's fiancée."

That stopped me short. "Who's Mr. Godfrey?"

"The fellow who came in yesterday. He hired me to find his fiancée."

"That fat man with the sweaty face and the piggy eyes?"

"That's not very nice, Miss Allcutt." But he grinned, the fiend.

"Well, I didn't care for his attitude."

"Tsk, tsk."

In spite of my distaste for Mr. Godfrey, not to mention my annoyance with Mr. Templeton, my curiosity was piqued. "What happened to his fiancée?"

"Disappeared. Kaput." He snapped his fingers. "Like that."

I pondered this interesting development for a moment. After recalling my own brief meeting with Mr. Godfrey, I said, "Maybe she did so on purpose."

Mr. Templeton squinted at me. "Eh?"

"For heaven's sake, Mr. Godfrey is a toad. If I were his fiancée, I'd disappear, too."

I know he fought to hide his grin, because I discerned the struggle on his face. He only said, "How unkind you are, Miss Mercy Allcutt. However, he's a paying client, and I'm going to earn my fee."

"Fiddlesticks. Barbara-Ann's problem is ever so much more important than Mr. Godfrey's!"

He shrugged. "He has money and she doesn't."

"Is that all you care about? Money?"

"Some of us have to care about money, Miss Allcutt. We can't all be born into wealth."

His tone was quite snide, but he had a point, the beast. I still didn't believe his heart was as stony as he pretended. "You went to the Kit Kat Klub last night," I pointed out.

"So what?"

"So that's where Babs works. Worked. Works." Nuts. "Anyhow, I know you care about finding her, even if you don't want to admit it, because you went there."

"Maybe I just wanted a drink and a little fun. Did you ever think about that?"

I hadn't, actually, and I didn't particularly want to think about it now, either. I didn't care for the notion of Mr. Templeton dancing with those girls at the Kit Kat Klub and drinking bootleg liquor and being loose and disgusting. "I doubt that. I think you were there to look for information about Babs Houser's disappearance."

"Huh."

"And we need to talk about it."

"We do?" His face had taken on a bland expression that riled me.

Again, I experienced violent urges that were heretofore completely alien to my nature. Ruthlessly repressing them, I said through clenched teeth, "We need to talk about Babs Houser before you go chasing after the poor woman who agreed to marry that detestable man."

"Now what," he said, sneering once more, "is there to talk about regarding Babs Houser?"

"What do you mean *what is there to talk about?*" I regret to say that my voice was quite loud as I asked the question. "She's been kidnapped and sold into white slavery, for heaven's sake, and you can't think of anything to *talk* about?"

He squinted at me. "She's been what?"

I backed off a trifle. After all, I didn't know for a fact that's what had happened to the woman. "Well, that's a theory Dolly propounded."

"Who's Dolly?"

"A lady who works with Babs."

"A lady, eh?" His smile was most unpleasant. "And Dolly claims Babs was kidnapped and sold into white slavery, does she?"

"Well, as I said, it's a theory she propounded."

"Dolly's nuts, and so are you if you believe that wild story."

"Do you really think so? *Really?*"

"Yes."

Darn. And I'd so wanted to know more about white slavery. I still wasn't clear on what the white slavers did to the women they captured. Or what a chink was. In spite of my disappointment, I didn't retreat from what I saw as my clear duty. "Mr. Templeton, *something* happened to Mrs.

Houser. That poor child, Barbara-Ann, needs her mother, and I intend to find her, whether you help or not."

He gave me an unfriendly look, but finally threw up his hands and said, "Aw, hell, all right. I'll talk about it."

My day at once became brighter, even if he still appeared rather gloomy. "Oh, *thank* you, Mr. Templeton!"

"You talked to Barbara-Ann yesterday, didn't you?"

I sat in the chair on the other side of his desk and flipped my notepad to a new page, eager now. "Yes, I did. The poor thing. She was hungry and dirty and I felt so sorry for her."

"Right. I don't suppose you asked her to bring in a picture of Babs, did you?"

"A picture?" I stared at him.

He gave me a look one might bestow upon a puppy who'd just failed to perform a new trick. Kindly. It was a kindly look, and I resented it because I sensed the sarcasm behind it. "You know. To show people. People who might have seen Babs."

"Oh." I frowned as I thought about it. "That's probably a good idea, isn't it?"

"I suspect it is."

His attitude pushed me over the edge. "Now see here, Mr. Ernest Templeton, I may be inefficient—at investigation, I mean. I'm a whiz at secretarial duties." *Whiz* might have been a slight stretch, but I really did think I was going to be a very good secretary. "But that's only because I don't have your experience. There's no reason to be caustic with me. Just guide and direct me, and I'm certain I'll be a tremendous help to you."

"So far you've got me involved in a case that doesn't pay, and you've destroyed my squeak. I'm not as certain as you are."

"Well, really!"

76

"Although," he said pensively, "I have to admit that you did get Ned to put in those light bulbs and repaint my door sign."

I smiled at him.

"I guess I can give you a tip or two."

"Thank you. I really do want to be of assistance to you."

"I'm sure."

That being the case, and since he'd agreed to listen to me, I continued with a theory of my own that I'd come up with that very morning—actually, it had come to me within the last five minutes or so. "I don't suppose it's occurred to you that Babs Houser and Mr. Godfrey's fiancée were kidnapped by the same gang of white slavers, has it?"

He looked at me as if he thought I'd lost what little mind he believed I'd possessed up to that point in time. "Are you nuts?"

"No, I am not nuts! Why do you think it's so far off the mark?"

But he didn't get the chance to answer me because the outer office door opened. With a lopsided grin, he said, "Go greet the client, Miss Allcutt."

Phooey.

However, since he was paying me to do the job, I left his office and entered my own, armed with my nice clean pad and a big smile. One must be cordial to the clients, after all, no matter how irked one is with one's boss. My cheerfulness suffered a slight dent when I beheld the personage who had interrupted us.

There's something about women who dress all in black, pull their hat veils down over their eyes, and speak in hushed and sultry tones that makes me think of Theda Bara. Or Mata Hari and espionage and vile intrigue. The woman who stood before my desk did all those things. I

didn't want to allow her within enticing distance of Mr. Templeton. Not that it mattered to me if he wound up in the talons of a scheming hussy, of course. Only I wanted him to concentrate on the Babs Houser matter.

In my sweetest voice, I said, "May I help you, ma'am?"

"Thank you," she purred, bringing to my mind an image of Mata Hari's cat. If she had one.

I gestured toward my chair, thinking it would be secretarially correct to jot down a few notes before I sicced her on Mr. Templeton. "Please, sit down."

"Thank you."

She slithered into the chair. It looked to me as if her gown were made of silk, which meant it had cost a lot. So. She was pretty good at this seducing-men-out-of-their-fortunes nonsense, was she? "Now," I said, still smiling, "what can I do for you?"

"I need to see Mr. Templeton," she said in her whispery-soft voice. "I need him to locate . . . something for me."

"What?" That was probably a little curt, but curse it, she didn't have to whisper at me. I was a secretary, for Pete's sake, not another man to be rendered helpless by her charms.

It occurred to me that I might possibly be judging her too harshly and too soon, but I doubted it. Therefore, I didn't soften my abrupt question.

I saw her sultry smile through that stupid veil. "Perhaps it would be better if I spoke directly with Mr. Templeton."

Ha! What did I tell you? "Well, ma'am, if you could give me your name, that would be a good start."

"Esmaralda," she purred. "Esmaralda Von Schilling."

And if *that* wasn't a name made up out of whole cloth, I don't know what was. "If you would please wait here for a

moment, Miss Von Schilling?"

"Missus," she murmured. "It's Mrs. Von Schilling."

I just bet it was. But I only said, "Mrs. Von Schilling," and went into Mr. Templeton's office. I closed the door behind me.

He'd been reading the *Los Angeles Times*, but he looked up when I stood before his desk. "Got a live one out there?" he asked mildly, as if we hadn't just been having words about Babs Houser.

"I believe she's alive, yes. A woman who calls herself Mrs. Esmaralda Von Schilling wishes to speak to you."

" 'Bout what?"

"She says she wants you to find something she's lost."

His grin implied all sorts of scandalous things. I pretended not to notice. "She's lost something, has she? Well, see the lady in."

"As to that," I said with a sniff, "I'm sure I couldn't say."

"You couldn't say about what?"

"The lady part." I turned and opened the door.

I heard him chuckling as I retreated from his office. Because I intended to do my job properly, no matter how much I didn't want to, I smiled at Mrs. Von Schilling. "Please come right on in."

She wafted past me, leaving the scent of some exotic fragrance I'd never smelled before in her wake. I saw Mr. Templeton rise from his chair, a courtesy he'd never extended to me, look momentarily bedazzled, and hold out his hand before I shut the door. I didn't slam it, either, and was proud of myself.

I was still fuming internally when Mr. Godfrey showed up.

Six

Mr. Godfrey's smile was sheepish when he removed his hat. "Hello. Is Mr. Templeton available?"

"He's with a client at the moment, Mr. Godfrey. May I assist you?"

"Oh." His face fell. "Well . . . I . . . Say, you know my name, but I don't know yours."

And I'd have preferred to keep it that way. Sensing it would be unprofessional to say so aloud, I said, "I'm Miss Allcutt, Mr. Godfrey."

Holding out a hand that looked soft and damp, he beamed at me. "How do you do, Miss Allcutt? It's a pleasure to meet you."

"Likewise, I'm sure." I meant it not, but I shook his hand, still smiling.

Being pleasant to the clients was beginning to tax my internal resources, and it crossed my mind that this was a good lesson for me to learn in my life. I'd never had to be polite and friendly with people I didn't care for, since I'd always been able to avoid them. Well, unless you count certain members of my family, but I suppose one encounters those types of people in any family. Unfortunately, the oddballs in my family were primarily the most wealthy of its members, and my mother would have locked me in my room and fed me bread and water if I'd dared be rude to any of them. That was before I got myself a real job of real work. Now, as part of the worker proletariat, I had to abide by the rules set down for those born into circumstances less

fortunate than mine or suffer the consequences.

Therefore, I continued smiling at Mr. Godfrey, even though he took the liberty of sitting in the chair beside my desk without my asking him if he'd care to be seated. It then struck me that, since I was Mr. Templeton's secretary, perhaps it was commonplace for people to feel free to do things in my office without my permission. I hadn't considered the possibility that I might have to do or put up with so many things I found distasteful before I decided to get a job. And to think that most other people in the world had to do this every day, and not because they wanted to gather experiences, but because they needed the money they earned in order to survive. It was a sobering realization. I vowed I'd be kinder to Mrs. Biddle from now on—although she might not appreciate it. Was this having-to-kowtow-to-people-one-didn't-like nonsense what drove anarchists to heave bombs at bureaucrats?

Well, I'd think about all that later. At the moment, I had to concentrate on Mr. Godfrey, who seemed to want to chat. Drat Mr. Templeton and that beastly woman!

So I endured. Mr. Godfrey had been talking at me for what seemed like a week, at least, when another interruption occurred—and it wasn't the opening of Mr. Templeton's office door. I kept envisioning Mr. Templeton and that slinky female becoming ever so cozy with one another, and felt as if I had indigestion, which was probably not so since I'd eaten breakfast much earlier in the day.

However, that's not the point. The point is that Ned entered the office after Mr. Godfrey had been droning on for a century or two about his life and his work and his childhood cat Zenobia, as if anyone cared, when Ned interrupted. Ned had not become an especial favorite of mine in the short while I'd known him, but I must say I welcomed him then.

"Ned! How nice to see you." And I smiled at *him,* even though he wasn't a client.

He didn't even glance at Mr. Godfrey. "Is there anything else you need done, Miss Allcut?" He held his cap in his hands, and his watery blue eyes held a fixed stare that made him appear peculiarly feeble-witted.

Mr. Godfrey swiveled—if such a corpulent fellow might be said to swivel. It was actually more like a lumbering rotation—in the chair beside my desk, and his own piggy eyes opened wide. "You!"

That caught Ned's attention. And mine, too.

Ned looked at Mr. Godfrey, and his idiot expression transformed into one of outraged astonishment. "You!"

Well, I guess I didn't need to make introductions, which was probably a good thing since I still didn't know Ned's last name.

"What are you doing here?" Ned demanded.

"What's it to you?" Mr. Godfrey demanded back. "For that matter, what are *you* doing here?"

"I work here." Ned's voice had gone all cold and stony.

"Oh, yeah? Well, what I'm doing here is none of your business." So had Mr. Godfrey's. He stood up from the chair, too, and looked as if he might just launch himself at Ned.

"Gentlemen, please," I said in my most aristocratic of Boston accents. "Let's not have any unpleasantness." Since Ned seemed smitten with me, I addressed him next. "Ned, I appreciate your offer of assistance, but there's nothing that needs to be done at the moment. I'll let you know if there is."

"But . . ."

"I'll *let you know,*" I repeated in my mother's very own voice. I'd have been appalled with myself if it didn't work so well.

Mr. Godfrey sat with a whump that shook the floor.

Ned's attitude of defiance and belligerence vanished. He slapped his cap on his head. "Well . . ."

I presume he'd have left the office then in compliance with my wishes, but I didn't get to test my assumption, because Mr. Templeton's door opened—finally—and Mrs. Von Schilling, assisted by Mr. Templeton, not that she needed help, slithered from his office in her silk and her veils and her black. All attention focused on her. It would.

Ned instantly whipped off his hat again. Mr. Godfrey's mouth fell open and his little eyes goggled. Mr. Templeton, noticing the reaction of the two men, grinned a catlike—or perhaps it was more weasel-like—grin and winked at me. I almost forgave him. For what, I wasn't sure.

Mrs. Von Schilling, also noticing the men's reaction to her, dipped her head coyly, ignored them, and turned to Mr. Templeton. Holding out a limp, black-gloved hand, she whispered, "Thank you *so* much, Mr. Templeton. You don't know what this means to me."

"It will be my pleasure to handle the matter for you, Mrs. Von Schilling."

I sensed that wasn't all he'd be happy to handle for her, the fiend. And he saw her to the door.

Mr. Godfrey and Ned, both still staring, watched her sway out of the office. I wanted to hit them both. Mr. Templeton turned after ushering out the vamp, and grinned at Mr. Godfrey. "Come into the office, Mr. Godfrey. I might have some information for you."

"You do?" As Jane Austen might have said, Mr. Godfrey was all astonishment.

A disgruntled part of me, the part that had been buffeted about quite severely that morning, wondered wryly why he'd plunked down good money to Mr. Templeton if he

hadn't expected him to earn it. Turning to Ned, I asked, "How do you know Mr. Godfrey?"

"That son of a . . . er . . . gun. He stole the woman I loved."

Now this was interesting, if somewhat unbelievable. Mr. Godfrey didn't seem the type to win any woman's heart away from another man. A further perusal of Ned's tepid features made me revise my opinion only slightly. I suppose, all things considered, that if a woman had the bad taste to admire Ned, she might as easily be persuaded to admire Mr. Godfrey next. Personally, I wouldn't allow either man within fifty yards of me—except at my place of employment. "Really?"

"Yeah." Ned frowned, his brow beetling, and his pale blue eyes narrowing. "He's a real piece of work, that guy."

"Hmm."

It looked to me as if Ned planned to hang around some more, and I was trying to think of a nice way to get rid of him, when the front door opened again and my salvation appeared in the form of little Barbara-Ann Houser.

"Barbara-Ann! I'm so glad you came in today."

She gave me an odd look. "You told me to, didn't you?"

Had I? I couldn't remember. But I was still happy to see her, and even happier when Ned clapped his cap on his head and left. I heaved a sigh of relief.

Hooking a thumb over her shoulder, Barbara-Ann said, "That guy's peculiar."

"Is he?" My novelistic tendencies surged to the forefront. Could it be that this twelve-year-old girl, the child of a mother who worked at a speakeasy called the Kit Kat Klub, the child the water in whose flat had been turned off due to lack of payment, the child who earned money by cadging coins—blast! I'd forgotten to look that word up in

the dictionary—had developed instincts honed by a hard life that allowed her to determine the mental or moral soundness of those around her? What a fascinating notion.

She shrugged. "Maybe not. I dunno."

Hmm. Well, I'd keep my new idea in mind, just in case Barbara-Ann's first impression of Ned turned out to be correct. Personally, I hadn't pegged him as especially peculiar, only lazy and somewhat unrealistic. I hoped Barbara-Ann would stick around long enough to give me her impression of Mr. Godfrey. *He* was the one I considered peculiar.

Leaning closer to the girl, I gave her a sympathetic smile. I saw that she'd cleaned herself up, and she didn't look hungry, although, due to lack of experience, I'm not sure how to tell when a person's hungry unless he or she tells you so. Anyway, she looked a little less like an orphaned child of war than she had the prior day. "Did you get a bath yesterday, Barbara-Ann?"

"Yeah. And some dinner."

"Good, good. I'm happy to hear it."

"And I still got fifty cents left from that buck you give me."

"That's wonderful, dear." Good Lord in heaven, where had she eaten that she'd spent less than fifty cents? I presume she'd paid for a bath at one of those bathing establishments that still remain from the days when Los Angeles was a simple little western outpost of the nation. Chloe had told me about them. I'd been shocked to learn that some people actually had no running water in their homes, but she told me I'd been too sheltered. And she was right, but it was a flaw I was attempting to rectify. Besides, she'd been sheltered, too.

"You want it back?" She held out the coin to me.

I was impressed that a girl so far gone in poverty would relinquish money. "No, dear, you keep it." Ruthlessly, I

swallowed the lump in my throat. "Thank you."

"Did you figure out what happened to my mother?"

Oh, dear. At least Barbara-Ann had faith in me. Us. "Um, not quite yet, dear, but Mr. Templeton and I went to the Kit Kat Klub last night. I spoke with a lady named Dolly and another one named Gwenda. They work with your mother there."

"Yeah. I know 'em."

It didn't look to me as if she was especially fond of either woman, but I'd noticed before that Barbara-Ann wasn't wildly demonstrative.

She reached into the pocket of her skirt, which was different from the one she'd worn the day before. Her hair had been washed and inexpertly braided. The knowledge that I'd helped the child, even in a small way, gave me a warm glow in my bosom.

"I brung a picture." She showed me the small photograph she'd retrieved from her pocket.

"Thank you, Barbara-Ann. I was going to request a photograph." I took the picture and squinted at it.

The image wasn't awfully clear, but it depicted a blandly pretty woman in what appeared to be her working costume, only without the tray of cigarettes slung around her neck. It looked to me as if she were wearing more makeup than was generally considered proper. On the other hand, she did work at the Kit Kat Klub, and I suppose she didn't deem it odd to be photographed in such a scandalous outfit and with her face painted like one of those Japanese women who walk on people's backs that I'd read about in an issue of *National Geographic*. Or maybe the photograph only seemed scandalous because I'm from Boston. With a sigh, I laid it on my desk. "Can you give me the names of any of your mother's other friends? Perhaps I could talk to them."

"Yeah. Sure, I guess." Her juvenile brow furrowed as she thought. "Well, there's Matty Bumpas. I guess Mr. Templeton knows about him."

I dutifully wrote down the name, pausing over the surname. "Do you know how to spell his name?"

"Uh-uh."

I gave it my best shot.

"And there's Dolly and Gwenda, but you already talked to them."

"Yes."

"Um . . . oh, yeah! There's Pauline. My mother and her are good friends."

"Do you know Pauline's last name?"

"Um . . . I think it's Richards or Richardson or something like that."

Big help. "Do you know where she lives? Her address?"

"Naw. Her and my mother always meet at our place."

"Do you know if she has a telephone in her home?"

"I guess so. Her and my mother yakked all the time on the wire." She concentrated for another few moments. "Then there's Gladys Merchant. That's her last name, Merchant."

I dutifully noted the name on my pad. "Do you know where she lives?"

"Naw."

"Do you know her telephone number?"

"Naw."

Oh, dear. Peering at my pad, the task of finding Babs Houser with only the information I'd written down seemed rather overwhelming.

"Um . . . that's the only names I can think of."

"I'm sure this will be a big help. But do let me know if you can think of any other names. Will you do that?"

"Yeah, sure."

"And while I'm at it, why don't I jot down your telephone number?" I realized I should have done so the day before. I might be new at this, but I was learning.

"Broadway four nine three two."

"Thank you, Barbara-Ann."

"Uh-huh."

Mr. Templeton's office door opened at that point, and both Barbara-Ann and I glanced at the two men exiting. Barbara-Ann frowned at Mr. Templeton, who returned the favor. I was very curious to know why the two of them didn't care for each other and, since it was clear they didn't, why Barbara-Ann had still chosen to come to him for help.

Returning his attention to Mr. Godfrey, Mr. Templeton said, "Please keep in touch. I'll work on the leads I have."

"Thank you." Mr. Godfrey pressed Mr. Templeton's hand, glanced at the chair beside my desk as if he wished he could sit in it and chat some more, saw Barbara-Ann there, sighed, and left the office.

I leaned closer to the little girl. "What did you think of that man, Barbara-Ann? Do you think he's peculiar, too?"

As I might have expected, she shrugged. "I dunno. Looks pretty dumb, I guess."

Hmm. So far, my idea that she might possess cognitive powers honed on the mean streets of Los Angeles remained unproven, but I determined to keep working on it.

Turning at the front door, Mr. Templeton stood there, resumed frowning, rested his fists on his hips, and glanced from Barbara-Ann to me, and back once more. "You're here again, I see." Grumpy. Very grumpy.

"Yeah." Sullen. Very sullen.

"Barbara-Ann brought me a photograph of her mother and has given me some names of people whom I can question about her. Her mother, I mean," I told him brightly.

"That's just dandy." And Mr. Templeton disappeared into his office and closed the door.

"Well!" I stared at the door, furious.

"He don't like me much," said Barbara-Ann, voicing my own thoughts. I glanced at her and she gave yet another shrug. "It's okay. I don't like him much, neither."

"And why is that, Barbara-Ann?" I spoke eagerly, hoping to clear up at least one muddle in my mind.

"He tried to lock my mother up a couple of years ago."

"Good heavens! Why ever did he do that?"

Another shrug. " 'Cause of that guy she hangs out with. Matty Bumpas."

"My goodness. Is Mr. Bumpas a criminal?"

"I dunno." Hooking a thumb over her shoulder, as she'd done when Ned left, she said, "The P.I. thinks so. Maybe he is. He wears flashy clothes and struts a lot. Always has money, but he's been in trouble with the law more than once. He's pretty dumb."

"Hmm." Mr. Matty Bumpas sounded like an unpleasant character. I was sorry Barbara-Ann had to suffer his presence. Children are so much at the mercy of their parents. As much as my own parents annoyed me, I realized at that moment that I could have had a much more difficult time of it. Money may not buy happiness, but it's probably the next best thing.

"I gotta go," Barbara-Ann announced, rising from the chair. "Gotta get to work."

"All right, dear. I'll see what I can do with the information you've given me."

"Okay. See ya."

"Oh, wait a minute, Barbara-Ann!"

She'd opened the front door, but she turned and looked at me warily. I reached into my desk drawer, withdrew my

handbag, and took out another dollar bill. Why not? The notion of that young child being on her own tugged at my heartstrings. "Take this, dear, and . . . well, get something to eat or something. New stockings would be nice." The ones she had on today were probably the same ones she'd worn the day before. If they weren't, they were every bit as ragged.

Her eyes grew huge. "Gee, you mean it?"

"Yes. Please take it."

"Well . . . I don't need no charity." But she eyed the dollar bill as if she were afraid it would vanish.

"This isn't charity, dear. You need help. I'm only trying to help a little bit. You needn't think of it as charity."

"Well . . . thanks." She took the bill and darted out of the office as if she feared I'd think better of my offer and snatch it back.

It occurred to me that if I could discover how it was done, I might pay the Housers' water bill so that she could have running water again in her apartment. Mr. Templeton could probably tell me how to go about it. I'd heard of utility companies. Perhaps water was a utility. There was certainly a lot about life away from Beacon Hill that I didn't understand.

But that would have to wait. First I needed to go over the information I had collected and see if I couldn't get a hint as to the whereabouts of Babs Houser. The possibility that she might be no longer living had occurred to me more than once, but I preferred to look on the bright side, the notion of Barbara-Ann being bereft forever of the only parent she possessed being too dismal to contemplate.

Therefore, I looked at her photograph. Then I looked at the list of names on my pad. The list was very short. And it contained no addresses or telephone numbers. In fact, only one of the women listed there had a last name I was sure of.

Blast it, why had I neglected to ask Barbara-Ann for Dolly and Gwenda's surnames? Because I was new at this, was why. But collecting people's full names was only sensible when one was bent upon investigation. I wasn't very good at it yet, but I had confidence in my abilities. I'd learned to typewrite, hadn't I?

It then occurred to me that my desk held, besides my handbag, a telephone directory for the city of Los Angeles. So I retrieved the directory and looked in it for the name Pauline Richards. No luck. So I tried Pauline Richardson, and lo and behold, the name was there! In black and white. In front of my very own eyes. Marking the number, I lifted the receiver . . . and paused.

Never in my entire life had I telephoned a perfect stranger out of the blue, without being properly introduced beforehand. To do so was in shockingly bad taste. My mother would never let me live it down if she ever heard about it. I put the receiver back on the hook.

But why would she ever hear about it? And anyhow, the restrictions about not telephoning and not speaking to strangers had been delivered with Boston in mind. This was Los Angeles! This was the new world of the West, where motion pictures were made and life was different! And, Mother aside, if Chloe ever found out that I'd hesitated to telephone somebody because I was worried about bad manners, *she'd* never let me live it down. To fail now, in the name of manners, would prove my sister right about my silliness in wanting to have and hold a job. And about my being a prude, if not a dowdy one.

Worse, it would prove Mr. Templeton right, and he'd go to his grave believing me to be a shallow rich girl who couldn't handle a job of real work. I picked up the receiver again and dialed.

Los Angeles was a large-enough city to have established a direct-dialing system that allowed you to reach people without going through a telephone exchange and an operator. So was Boston. So this (dialing a telephone number), at least, was one thing I didn't have to learn. It felt good to be doing something I knew how to do.

Somebody answered the wire! I was breathless when I spoke in my turn. "Pauline Richardson?"

"Yeah, this is her."

It had to be the right person. Nobody else talked like that, except Barbara-Ann. "My name is Mercy Allcutt, and I'm helping Barbara-Ann Houser find her mother, who hasn't been seen since last Saturday. Are you acquainted with Mrs. Houser?"

A gasp on the other end of the wire told me that Pauline hadn't realized her friend was missing. "Babs is missing? How'd that happen? Where is she?"

The inability of people to think things through before they asked questions amazed me. "I don't know how it happened, and I'm trying to find her," I said gently. "And Barbara-Ann said you and Mrs. Houser are friends. I hoped perhaps you could assist me."

"Yeah? How?"

"Well, perhaps you can give me the names of other friends that I might be in touch with. Or maybe you know if Mrs. Houser has been under any particular strain, or if she seemed worried about anything. Any little bit of information might help."

"Well, there's the Chink. She's been all in a stew over the Chink for a few weeks now. Personally, I think she oughta toss out that louse she's seeing, but that's just me."

I hesitated before speaking again. There seemed to be a rather large language barrier between Miss Richardson and

me, and I wasn't sure what to do about it. Her speech had contained another reference to a chink. And she'd introduced a louse into the conversation. If I saw a louse, I'd most certainly toss it out, although I'm not sure I'd recognize one if it crawled across my desk. I'd read that sometimes a segment of society will create and use its own form of cant or argot. Perhaps this was the argot used by women who work in speakeasies in Los Angeles.

"Um . . . a chink?"

"Yeah. Owns one of them trinket shops in Chinatown."

"The chink owns the shop?" This was terribly confusing, but I swore I wouldn't give up until I'd decoded Pauline's message.

"Yeah. Third one in from the west arch off Hill. Little place."

Nuts. I decided to go ahead and ask. "Miss Richardson, what exactly is a chink?"

Laughter pealed over the telephone wire. "Sweetie, where you been all your life? A Chink is a Chinaman!"

Ah. Illumination at last. "I see. And . . . um . . . the louse?"

"Matty Bumpas, of course! He's the slimiest slug in the neighborhood."

More illumination! I felt as if I were getting somewhere, although I wasn't sure exactly where that was. The argot was commencing to unfold, however, and that was a good thing. I think. "I see. Yes, I understand he's not an admirable character."

"Admirable? Honey, you got a way with words."

How gratifying. "You wouldn't know the name of this Chinese man, would you?"

"Naw. But like I say, it's the third shop in from the west arch. A little ways from that water garden thing with the

funny writing that you throw pennies in. On the plaza there. You can't miss it."

I was writing as fast as I could, and only hoped that reading my notes would prove more edifying than listening to Miss Richardson's directions. "And you're sure you don't know the name of the man? Or the name of his shop?"

"Naw. Anyhow, them Chinks have screwy names. Even if I heard it, I prolly wouldn't remember it."

I'm sure they thought the same of us, although I didn't say so. "Thank you very much, Miss Richardson. Please call if you think of anything else that might help us find Mrs. Houser." I gave her the telephone number to the office and told her that I worked for Mr. Ernest Templeton.

A full-blown shriek on the other end of the wire nearly deafened me. "Ernie? You work for Ernie Templeton? That's rich!" And she hung up the receiver on her end, leaving me staring at mine and rubbing my ear.

There was only one other person on my list whom I could attempt to find, since I knew neither Dolly nor Gwenda's surnames. I turned pages in the Los Angeles telephone directory until I got to the M's. Merchant . . . Merchant . . . Aha! But there was no Gladys Merchant. There was a G. W. Merchant who lived on Figueroa, which was the same street that Mr. William Desmond Taylor had lived on, if I remembered correctly. Hmm. It seemed unlikely that a good friend of Babs Houser would have the wherewithal to live in a fancy neighborhood. Perhaps it wasn't the right G. Merchant.

With a sigh, I decided there was only one way to find out, and I dialed the number. I'm ashamed to say that I was more pleased than not when nobody answered the telephone on the other end of the wire. If I expected to be successful in my new endeavor as a working person, I had to get over my fussy ways.

Still and all, I'd dared, and I'd succeeded, at least with Pauline Richardson. I contemplated the information I'd jotted on my pad. So. Babs Houser had been worried about a Chinese man. Of course, I'd read all about opium dens and so forth, but not in connection with Los Angeles. What was it Dolly had mentioned last night at the Kit Kat Klub? Something about . . .

Good Lord! It suddenly dawned on me what white slavers must be, and I gasped aloud. Could this Chinese person of whom Babs was afraid be involved in the kidnapping and selling of white women into . . . the notion was so shocking, I could scarcely make myself even think the word . . . *prostitution?*

My heart started racing, and I stared at my list, aghast. Shoving my chair back on its little rollers, I stood up and grabbed my pad. I'd taken a step toward Mr. Templeton's office door, when I recalled the events of the morning. And that woman. And how friendly he'd been with her. And how coy she'd been with him. And how much he'd seemed to enjoy it. Hmm. The office door was closed. For some reason, I got the impression it was closed against *me,* in particular.

But that was asinine. Clutching my pad to my bosom, I marched up to Mr. Templeton's door and knocked. Softly, just in case the bear in the lair was grumpy.

"C'm in," he called.

So I did.

I'd expected to find him sitting in his chair with his feet propped on his desk, reading a newspaper, but by gum, he actually seemed to be working on something. About time. He'd been hunched over, writing on a pad of his own, but he shoved it aside, sat up straight, stretched, and said, "Ow. Been writing too long." As if to prove it, he wiggled his fingers and rolled his head to get the kinks out of his neck and back.

"What are you working on?" I hoped he'd tell me. If he considered me a mere secretary, he might not, but if he considered me an apprentice, or something similar, he might.

"Figuring out a way to get Mrs. Von Schilling's lost property back."

That woman again. "Oh. And have you?"

"I think so." He gave me one of his cocky grins. "You wanna be my partner in crime, kiddo?"

"I . . . I beg your pardon?"

"I might need help."

"Oh!" My heart soared like an eagle. "Yes! Oh, my, I'd love to help you!"

"Don't get so excited, kiddo. You won't be doing much."

My enthusiasm suffered a slight check. "No? Well, I'd still like to be of help, Mr. Templeton."

"Ernie." He rolled his eyes.

I didn't appreciate the eye roll, but I decided it would be better not to get huffy, mainly because I needed his help. "May I ask you a few questions? I got some information from Barbara-Ann Houser this morning, and have been doing some investigating on my own."

"Yeah?" His grin faded. "Like what? If you're going to start hanging out in speakeasies to find that—"

"No! No, it isn't that kind of investigating. I was only telephoning people who know Mrs. Houser. Friends of hers."

"Like who?"

His eyebrows had dipped over his startlingly blue eyes, and it was difficult not to succumb to a feeling of intimidation. However, I hung on to my courage and sat in the chair in front of his desk as if I had every right in the world to do

so. Which I did. Although it didn't feel much like it right then. I didn't need to, but I referred to my pad, mainly because his piercing stare was making me fidgety. "Like Miss Pauline Richardson. Barbara-Ann said she's her mother's best friend. Miss Richardson said that Mrs. Houser has been afraid of a Chinese man lately."

"Yeah?"

"Yes. And she also said that Mr. Bumpas, Mrs. Houser's particular male friend, is a louse." I think I had that reference correct.

"Hell, I already knew that."

"You know Mr. Bumpas?" I recalled his mentioning the name when Barbara-Ann first appeared in the office.

He straightened in his chair and frowned at me. "What's this *Mister* and *Miss* stuff? Matty Bumpas is a small-time hoodlum who wouldn't appreciate being called *Mister* any more than I do. If you won't call him Matty, call him Bumpas, okay?"

I took a deep breath and expelled it, thinking he was right, curse it. I was too proper for my own good, especially in this profession. Humbly, I said, "I beg your pardon. I'll try to be less formal. Ernie."

"Good." His grin was back. It was really quite charming.

"Anyhow, Miss . . . er . . . Pauline said that Babs was afraid of a Chinese man." Not even for Mr. Templeton—I mean Ernie—would I call a Chinese man a Chink. "And she said that this man has a trinket shop in Chinatown."

"Yeah? There are lots of trinket shops in Chinatown. Did she say which one?"

Again I referred to my pad, although I remembered the directions perfectly well. "No, but she said his is the third shop in from the west arch, across from the water garden."

"Hmm."

Excitement overcame my dignity and my trepidation, and I leaned forward in my chair. "Oh, Ernie, do you think it really *is* possible that Babs has been kidnapped by white slavers? Or that she's sunk in depravity and languishing in an opium den?"

From the look he gave me, you'd have thought I'd asked him if I thought Babs had jumped out the window. "Don't be stupid. Babs has probably run off with some guy. She'll be back when he kicks her out."

My mouth fell open, but I shut it again instantly. "No! Not even a mother like Babs Houser would run off with a man, leaving her little girl alone in the world to fend for herself!"

"Shows how much you know about the world." He stood up and grabbed his coat and hat. Plunking the latter onto his head, he said, "But, what the hell. It's time for lunch. Let's go to Chinatown and see this trinket shop character."

"Oh, Mr. Templeton—"

He glowered at me, and I amended my sentence.

"Oh, Ernie, *thank* you!"

"You're welcome, kiddo."

I remembered the photograph, which I'd stuck in my pad. Retrieving it, I said, "Barbara-Ann gave me this, too." I handed the picture to Ernie.

He frowned at it. "That's Babs, all right." He stuck it in his pocket.

"You don't like her much, do you?"

"Perceptive of you."

"Why don't you like her?"

"Because she hangs out with bums."

"What's that to you?"

"I think mothers ought to be mothers. If Babs Houser wanted to be a gun moll, she shouldn't have had a kid."

That made sense to me, although I wondered how much thought Babs had put into her career choice. Or motherhood, for that matter. Actually, had anything in Babs Houser's life been a choice? Perhaps she'd perceived no alternative to the things she'd done. At this point in the investigation, however, speculation was only a time-filler. I knew nothing at all about the woman except that she was missing and her daughter wanted her back.

With luck and help from Ernie, though, I was on my way to having my curiosity satisfied! Grabbing my own hat from my desk drawer, I put it on and headed out the office door.

SEVEN

And once more I found myself hurrying beside my employer as we headed out the Figueroa Building on our way to luncheon, waving at Lulu as we passed the reception desk. I noticed Ned there and waved at him, too. He didn't wave back, although I considered his presence in the lobby, instead of in his closet, a step in the right direction. Perhaps my bullying Boston ways were getting him to perform his duties. Perhaps the possibility of that was small, but one never knew, did one?

At the moment, I felt like an explorer venturing forth on a daring escapade. Not only would I get to see how a real private investigator interrogated people, but I might just be going to help find a missing person! Not only that, but Ernie had told me he needed my help to locate missing property! I was so excited, I could scarcely keep from chattering away like a magpie. Sensing that Ernie preferred action to words, I used my breath for locomotion.

The streets were crowded, and I could have sworn I saw Mr. Godfrey when Ernie hurried me past the Broadway Department Store on Fourth and Broadway. I wasn't able to turn and look, because Ernie would have left me in his dust. The morning fog had lifted, and by the time we got to Second and Hill, I was panting and about to faint dead away. It wasn't until we were approaching Chinatown that Ernie noticed my state of perspiring exhaustion.

"Hell, kiddo, you should have told me to slow down."

Slamming my hand over my thundering heart, I said, "I

didn't want to annoy you."

"Nuts. You gotta stick up for yourself in this life, kid. Sure as hell, nobody else is going to do it for you." He slowed down, though, and I appreciated him for it.

"That's a depressing philosophy, Mr. . . . Ernie."

"It's the way the world turns, kiddo."

By that time we were in Chinatown. So far in my life, I'd visited Chinatowns in New York and San Francisco and Los Angeles. The one in San Francisco is the largest and most appealing, I guess, and it had a lot of history behind it, what with the gold rush and the railroads and everything, but this one in Los Angeles was pretty nice, too. I liked the arches and a couple of buildings that were built like Chinese pagodas. Hop Luey's, where Ernie had taken me to dine . . . I mean eat lunch . . . after he'd interviewed me, was one of the pagoda-type buildings. We didn't eat there today. Instead, Ernie led me to a little hole-in-the-wall place on the other side of Hill.

He shoved the door open and stood aside for me to enter, an indication of good manners I hadn't expected from that source. Not that I thought Ernie was a barbarian or anything; it's only that he hadn't thus far in my experience of him demonstrated any particular attachment to the rules of polite society. Enticing aromas met my nostrils as soon as I entered the place, which was small and dark. Several men sat at a long counter. I saw no tables and chairs, and wasn't sure what to do.

Ernie knew. He strode up to the counter, and gestured for me to sit on a high stool. It was a fairly daunting prospect, since I'm not especially tall, but I managed, denting my dignity only slightly. I looked around with interest. I'd never been in a place like this. Ernie and I were the only white people there, and I was the only woman. I'd have felt

uncomfortable were it not for my companion. To a man, the Chinese gentlemen sitting at the counter were holding bowls and scooping food into their mouths with chopsticks. I wasn't accustomed to seeing people eat in exactly that way, but I allowed for cultural differences so as not to seem priggish.

"Howdy, Charlie," Ernie said to the man behind the counter.

" 'Lo, Ernie. Whatcha gonna have today?"

"The usual."

"And for the lady?" The man named Charlie lifted his eyebrows at me.

"She'll have the same." Ernie grinned at me.

I wasn't sure what to do, but I smiled at Charlie, then leaned closer to Ernie and whispered, "What's the usual?"

"Pork and noodles."

Pork and noodles? Well, I'd been eager for adventure. I guess this counted.

It turned out to be more of an adventure than I'd counted on. When Charlie set out bowls in front of us, he set a pair of chopsticks on the counter beside the bowl. I looked at the chopsticks in dismay.

"You can do it, kiddo," said Ernie. I heard the laughter in his voice.

"I've never used chopsticks before," I whispered.

"They're easy. Just hold 'em like this." He demonstrated.

I picked up my chopsticks and, after a little initial fumbling, managed to hold them in the prescribed manner.

"Practice on your napkin, kid," Ernie suggested.

So I did, and one of the chopsticks slipped and fell onto the counter with a clack. How embarrassing. But Ernie picked it up and handed it to me, and I tried again. "Um

. . . now what do I do?" The bowl seemed awfully far away from my mouth. I was sure to slop food all over myself unless I leaned over so far my nose would be in my bowl.

"You can do it. Just pick up your bowl like this." He demonstrated, lifting his bowl in the exact same way as all the other men in the restaurant. Then he dipped his chopsticks into the bowl and shoveled some pork and noodles into his mouth.

"Um . . ." I almost made the mistake of telling him I considered what he was doing incredibly unmannerly. Then I recalled yet again that this wasn't Boston. My mother was thousands of miles away, on Cape Cod, and she'd never, ever know how I spent this particular day's luncheon time. So I picked up my bowl with some reluctance and hoped I wouldn't dribble on myself, the counter, Ernie, or the floor.

I sniffed the steam rising from my bowl with some degree of nervousness. One sniff was enough to calm my nerves, at least about the savoriness of the meal, thank God. It smelled wonderful, and I saw that, along with the pork and noodles, there were plenty of vegetables, so not even my mother could object to this particular luncheon, except for the manner in which the food would be transferred from the bowl to my mouth. She's a stickler for eating vegetables, my mother.

So we ate our luncheon, and then Ernie ordered some more tea. Charlie brought some wonderful almond cookies to go with the tea, and we lingered over dessert. We lingered quite a while, actually, and I was unsure why we were taking so long over our meal. Then the delay became clear to me. As soon as most of the other diners had left the restaurant, Ernie gestured for Charlie to come to us.

"You want something else?"

"No, thanks, but I have a question for you."

"Question?" Charlie frowned a little. "I don't know nothing, Ernie. You know that."

"Don't worry, Charlie. This question won't come back to bite you."

Whatever that meant.

"Well . . . what your question? I might not answer it."

"It's not hard. Have you ever seen this lady around Chinatown?" Ernie pulled the photograph of Babs Houser out of his pocket and laid it on the counter.

Charlie squinted at the photograph for several moments. "I dunno," he said at last. "All you white people look alike to me."

I was shocked, but Ernie laughed. "Yeah, I know, Charlie, but I'm trying to find this woman. You ever see her? She might have hung out in one of those shops across the street."

Charlie glanced up from the photograph. "Why you want to know?"

"Nothing dangerous to you or anybody else in Chinatown. Her family is looking for her, and they came to me to find her."

"Yeah?" Charlie perused the picture again.

"Yeah."

I saw from his expression that Charlie had remembered something. "Wait a minute. Yeah, maybe I seen her once or twice." He transferred his squint from the photograph to Ernie. "What you going to do if you find her?"

"Don't worry, Charlie. I'm not a cop any longer. I don't want to mess up your Mah-Jongg racket or anything. I'm just going to take her home again."

Charlie grinned slightly and nodded. "She do something wrong?"

"You bet," said Ernie without giving the matter a thought. "She does wrong stuff all the time. She's a real

104

loser, but I still gotta find her. Her daughter needs her."

"She got a daughter?" Charlie's expression was far from inscrutable, as I'd heard Chinese faces were. At the moment his countenance registered overt disapproval.

"Yup. And don't ask me why, but the kid wants her back."

Shaking his head, Charlie said, "You might want ask Han Li. I think I see her in his place."

"Han Li? The guy who runs the numbers?"

"You don't care about that." It was a question, although Charlie's inflection didn't designate it as such.

"I don't give a rap about Han Li and his numbers-running racket. I only want to find Babs Houser."

"Yeah? Well, maybe you talk to Han Li."

"Thanks, Charlie. I appreciate it."

To prove it, he laid a ten-dollar bill on the counter. It disappeared so fast, you'd have thought Charlie was a conjuror. "You bet."

Ernie again pocketed the photograph of Babs and helped me down from my stool. My head was buzzing with questions when we left the small restaurant. "What's numbers running? What's a racket?" I didn't get to ask any of the other questions, because Ernie shushed me.

"I'll tell you when we get back to the office. Just shut up and listen for now."

Well! However, in spite of the rude way the request had been phrased, I decided to honor it, since I was such a neophyte at the investigation business. We walked across the plaza from Charlie's noodle shop, and Ernie pushed a door open and gestured for me to enter. So I did, my heart beginning to speed up with the knowledge that I was on an honest-to-goodness investigation of an honest-to-goodness missing-person case.

The place was crowded with trinkets and Chinese bowls and plates and statues and it had an interesting, sweet smell, sort of a combination of sandalwood and roses. I liked it. It smelled very . . . well . . . Oriental, I guess. My gaze was captured by some gowns of silk brocade hanging against a wall, and I wanted to inspect them. Ernie, however, was on a mission. He walked straight to the dusty counter, behind which sat a Chinese man on a tall stool, who'd been smoking and doing nothing else that I could determine.

"Han Li?" said Ernie.

The man bobbed his head.

"I'm Ernie Templeton, and I understand you might know this woman." He slapped the photograph of Babs on the counter.

Han Li gave a start of alarm and hopped off his stool. "Ay! What you mean?"

"Just what I said. I'm trying to find Babs Houser, and *you* know where she is. So, tell me."

I thought he was being a trifle precipitate. After all, we didn't really *know* that Mr. Li—or perhaps he was Mr. Han . . . I forget how Chinese names work—had any knowledge of Babs's whereabouts. But, as I kept reminding myself, Ernie knew what he was doing, and I didn't. And I have to admit that his direct approach was having a definite effect. Whether it was the right one or not, I guess we'd find out.

"No! She bad! I not know her. She bad!"

Mr. Li had started babbling in an incoherent mixture of Chinese and English. He hurried out from behind his counter and made flapping gestures at us. "You go now! I gotta close for lunch. You go!"

"Wait a minute. Where's Babs Houser?"

Another spate of Chinese and English followed Ernie's

106

question. The only words I could clearly distinguish were "Don't know" and "No" and "Bad." They didn't give me a whole lot of hope for a successful conclusion of our afternoon's adventure.

"I'm coming back with the coppers, Li," Ernie warned. "If you know where Babs is, you'd better tell quick, or you're going to be in a whole lot of trouble."

That statement shocked me, since Ernie had promised Charlie that no one would come to harm if he cooperated and told us what he knew about Babs. I was slightly disappointed in Ernie.

Nevertheless, we left the trinket shop. As soon as the door slammed behind us, I heard the key turn in the lock. Ernie put his finger to his lips and drew me aside. Mr. Li was pulling the shades down over the windows when we slipped down a very narrow alley beside the shop.

"Follow me," Ernie commanded in a whisper.

"Why did you threaten him? You promised—"

"Shut up!" Ernie warned. "Scold me later. I've got investigation to do now."

So, fuming inside, I shut up, although I also began to think that perhaps I wasn't cut out for the private investigation business. Honesty had always seemed to me to be an important virtue, and I didn't like to see people I admired—sort of—being dishonest, even if it was in pursuit of a job.

Or a missing woman.

All right, so perhaps I was being a little bit prissy. I'd have to think about it all later, because Ernie grabbed me by the hand and dragged me behind him down the alleyway.

All three of the Chinatowns I've visited have had the same distinct aroma about them. I suppose the same thing could be said for fishing docks and lumber mills and libraries. This Chinatown smell was comprised of rotting

vegetable matter and some kind of incense. At least, I guessed it was incense. It wasn't an unpleasant odor, only distinctive. And strong, at least in that alley.

Ernie moved like a cat. I was most impressed with his silence. I tried to emulate him, although I had fairly sturdy shoes on and they clopped a bit. I attempted to tiptoe. He kept hold of my hand as we exited the alley onto an open, paved space behind some stores. The odor of strange, past-their-prime vegetables became stronger, and it wasn't mitigated by the mingling of incense. I figured out why when Ernie led me past a line of garbage cans. I also realized I ought to have expected detective work to entail some back-alley work.

Mr. Li was almost running. I could see him through the throng, making a beeline for a street north of Chinatown, called Yale. Ernie made sure there were always several people between Mr. Li and us, but he never lost sight of him. Once, when Mr. Li glanced over his shoulder, Ernie shoved me into a doorway and turned so as to appear to be looking in a window. I didn't offer a complaint, even though he'd shoved me pretty hard. One must become accustomed to the vagaries of one's employment, I suppose.

Foot traffic thinned slightly when we turned right on Yale. Ernie hung back a little. When Mr. Li darted into a building which, I presumed contained flats, Ernie sped up some.

"What are we doing?" I whispered, my heart racing with excitement.

"What are you whispering for?"

I frowned at Ernie. "I thought you told me to be quiet."

"Yeah, but that was when Li might hear us. He just went inside this building. Didn't you see him?"

There was still much I needed to learn about the detec-

tive business. Slightly disgruntled, I said more loudly, "What are we doing?"

"Following Li. I think this is where he lives. Let's see." And he pushed open the door and entered the building, bold as brass.

Sure enough, it looked like a rooming house. Or an apartment building. Or something along those lines. The area into which the door led was more of a hallway than a room. Long and narrow, it was lit but dimly. The carpet was shabby, the paint on the walls was peeling, an odor of dust and must prevailed, and I'd have been happier if I weren't there. A bank of mailboxes had been built into one wall, most with handmade cards tacked over the boxes designating which apartment number belonged to which box. There were some names written on the cards, too, but more often than not they were in the form of Chinese characters. I guess the Los Angeles postal service employed some Chinese mailmen, since nobody else would be able to read them.

"How can you tell which one is his?" I asked.

Ernie said, "Shh."

Curse it, I'd never figure this out! I repeated, this time in a whisper, "How can you tell which box is his?"

"I copied down the characters when we were in his shop."

He'd copied down the characters? "How did you know which characters were what?" That didn't make a lot of sense, but Ernie understood.

"You come to know these things when you work in Chinatown long enough."

Oh.

But, sure enough, he withdrew a slip of paper from his pocket and held it up to the mailboxes. And blamed if we didn't find one that matched the artistic scratchings on

Ernie's piece of paper. He whispered, "Li's in number eight."

"Are we going to his apartment?" He looked at me as if I'd just asked him to climb a tree, and I resented it. "Well, what are we going to do, then?"

Without answering, he headed back out the door of the apartment building. Although we hadn't been indoors very long, the sun nearly blinded me. Squinting, I asked again, "What are we going to do now?"

"I think it's time we paid Matty Bumpas a visit."

"M-Matty Bumpas?" He was moving too fast for me. Not physically, since he seemed to recall that my legs were considerably shorter than his and was matching his stride to mine, but mentally.

"Babs's *gentleman friend*." The way he said the words *gentleman friend* gave them an emphasis that belied their intrinsic meaning.

I digested this, or tried to. "Then you're really going to be working on the case?"

"It doesn't look like I have much choice in the matter." He heaved a sigh. "Can't have you poking your nose into these things alone. You're liable to get it punched in one of these days."

He grinned, but I fingered my nose before I could stop myself. I hope he hadn't really meant that, although I didn't ask because I didn't want to be the recipient of any more sarcastic comments or complaints. "I'm glad you've decided to help Barbara-Ann," I told him humbly.

"Huh."

"Where does Matty Bumpas live?"

"Near Fourth and Spring." He sounded so sure of himself that I bridled involuntarily.

"And how do you know that?"

"I have my sources."

110

Hmm. I sensed he'd only make a joke or be sarcastic if I pressed the issue. Since I knew very few street names in Los Angeles at that point in my investigative career, the information that Matty Bumpas lived near Fourth and Spring didn't help me pinpoint his residence in my head. However, since Ernie didn't hail a taxicab or mention driving to the location, I presumed Mr. Bumpas lived within walking distance. For once, my presumption was correct. After we'd been walking for a few blocks and my feet were in danger of either catching fire or falling off, he said, "Here we are." I didn't understand how he could be so cursedly cheerful in such hideous weather. Again I didn't ask, this time because I didn't want him to consider me a whiner.

"Oh?"

"Yeah. Right here." He led the way up a walkway to another dingy building. It struck me that investigative work might entail lots of drab buildings and unpleasant characters. I wasn't going to pass judgment yet, but perhaps I might enjoy another line of work better.

That was neither here nor there at the moment, though. Ernie climbed a set of rickety outside wooden steps, and I dutifully followed after him, limping a little. He opened a door that led into yet another dingy hallway. Next time, I kind of hoped we'd get a client with money. Not that I'm a snob or anything, but when you get used to cleanliness and sanitation, buildings like this one and the one Mr. Li lived in can be depressing.

As if he knew what he was doing, which I presumed he did, Ernie walked right up to number fifteen and knocked hard on the door.

After a pause, a nervous, nasal male voice from inside said, "Who's there?"

"Ernie Templeton, Matty. You remember me, don't you?"

"Shit!"

Ernie grinned, but I was shocked. Silly of me, I know.

"Come on, Matty. I'm not a copper anymore. You can talk to me."

"I *can,* but maybe I don't want to."

"I just want to talk to you about Babs Houser, Matty."

"Babs? What the hell's wrong with Babs?"

The door was flung open to reveal a short, chunky individual with a face like a chipmunk. Mr. Bumpas hadn't shaved for several days, and he definitely wasn't dressed to receive company. To my inexperienced eyes, he appeared to be wearing an undershirt. The garish pattern on his trousers, which were being held up by suspenders, made me blink. I guess he'd outgrown his belts. He looked as if he hadn't bathed in a while, and the stubble on his chin and cheeks went well with the bloodshot nature of his eyes. An altogether unprepossessing specimen, Mr. Matty Bumpas. I couldn't understand what Babs saw in him.

"Hey, Matty. You don't look so good."

"To hell with you, Templeton. What you want with Babs?"

"Not a damned thing. But her kid wants her back."

Frowning from Ernie to me, he stepped aside and said, "Youse two might as well come in. Who's the dame?"

"This, Matty Bumpas, is no *dame,*" Ernie said firmly. "This is my secretary, Miss Mercy Allcutt. You can call her Miss Allcutt."

"Yeah, yeah. 'Lo, *Miss* Allcutt."

I looked around the tiny room into which Mr. Bumpas had led us, and decided I'd just as soon stand while we chatted. It hadn't been dusted in at least as long as Mr. Bumpas hadn't bathed, and newspapers and magazines lay

scattered everywhere. A scarred table and a couple of chairs had been shoved up against a wall, but they were filled with clothes and more newspapers. "How do you do, Mr. Bumpas?"

He didn't answer me, but started in on Ernie again. "So what you doin' here, Templeton?"

"I already told you. We're trying to find Babs Houser."

"Where the hell is she?" Mr. Bumpas's eyebrows, which were thick and bushy and reminded me of caterpillars, drew down sharply over his eyes. His chin jutted out at a defiant angle. He strutted to a chair, yanked off a shirt that had been draped over its back, and shook it out. As he scowled at us, he lowered his suspenders until they hung down around his large waist and shoved his arms into the shirt's sleeves.

"I thought maybe you'd know."

"How the hell should I know?" Matty shifted from one foot to the other as he buttoned his shirt. I sensed he was lying about not knowing where Babs was. He was also as jumpy as my mother would have been if she'd been forced to get dressed for a ball without assistance. A car backfired outside on the street, and he jumped several inches and swore.

Ernie noticed this evidence of discomfort with interest, but he only said, "I thought you and Babs were old friends, Matty." His voice was as casual as casual could be. I was terribly impressed that he didn't let the blustery little man discompose him. "If anybody knows where she is, it's you."

"Babs and me go back a ways, it's true," Bumpas said, tucking in his shirt. "But I don't know where she is. I ain't seen her in a while."

"I don't suppose you have, since she's been missing since last Saturday."

"Says you," said Bumpas, snapping his suspenders back into place. He didn't look much better with his shirt on, but I didn't feel so much as though I'd stepped into a dressing room containing a half-naked man. "Maybe she took a vacation or something."

"Unlikely. She didn't mention a vacation to her daughter."

"Huh." Lifting up a stack of newspapers from the sofa, Bumpas said, "Wanna sit down?"

Good heavens, I certainly didn't want to sit on that filthy thing! Fortunately, neither did Ernie.

"No, thanks," he said, sneering at the sofa. "You sure you don't want to help me out here, Matty? I have a feeling you're in over your head and could use some help."

"Hell, you don't know nothing, Templeton. Go chase yourself, see?"

"A singularly fruitless activity." Ernie's grin reminded me of the Cheshire Cat.

"Huh?" I got the impression Matty Bumpas wasn't a master of English usage.

"All right, Matty. If you won't help us, I guess there's no way we can make you."

"Yeah, that's right." Matty's chin jutted out another couple of inches, and he drew himself up in an effort to appear impressive. All he looked like to me was a cheap imitation of one of the gangsters whose photographs regularly graced newspapers and post-office walls.

"This is your last chance," Ernie told him mildly. "Something's wrong here, and you know what it is. If you want my help, you're going to have to ask now, because I won't ask *you* again."

"I don't need no help," Matty insisted. "And I don't know where Babs is, see?"

"I see. Very well." Turning, Ernie gestured for me to go

to the front door. He's the one who opened it for me, since Matty didn't rush to do his gentlemanly duty. I was just as happy he didn't, since I didn't like being near him.

The door had just slammed behind us when I opened my mouth. I noticed Ernie's finger pressed to his lips before any words leaked out. He took my arm and headed to the staircase, which we descended rather loudly. I got the impression Ernie was making as much noise as he could for some reason beyond my ken. As soon as we reached the bottom of the staircase, Ernie yanked me underneath it. Then he did something inexplicable. He stamped his feet, loudly at first, and then more and more softly, until he stopped stamping altogether.

I couldn't contain myself any longer. Whispering, I said, "What in the world are you doing?"

He whispered back, "Making Matty think we've left."

Oh. I'd have liked to ask why, but Ernie's countenance had assumed a stony cast, indicating to me that he would prefer to entertain further questions at a later time. So I stood there under the staircase next to Ernie without a notion on earth why I was doing so and felt pretty ridiculous about it if you want to know the truth.

A few minutes later, I began to get a glimmer of understanding. A door opened slowly upstairs. I couldn't see anything from where I stood, but several seconds passed before any further noises ensued. Then they were the sound of a door closing softly, and footsteps. When I leaned out and glanced up to the balcony railing over my head, I thought I saw the shadow of a circular head. Was that Matty Bumpas looking over his balcony? Was he looking for Ernie and me?

Ernie hauled me back a little when footsteps began to descend the staircase. Sure enough, pretty soon the

roundish form of Mr. Matty Bumpas appeared. He paused on the bottom step and glanced around furtively, as if searching for something he feared might be lurking in wait for him. Not Ernie and me, surely! We meant him no harm. Maybe Ernie hadn't just been exaggerating when he'd told Matty he sensed he was in trouble.

There it was again: the notion that someone with a lot of experience with crime and the mean streets of the big city might develop a sixth sense about people. So far it seemed to me that both Barbara-Ann Houser and Ernie Templeton might possibly share the trait. I would have given a good deal to be able to develop it, but I wasn't sure how to go about it. I don't suppose gaining insight into the shady side of life could be done without a good deal of practice, and I'd only had two days' worth at that point in time. Besides, getting that type of experience might entail danger, which didn't appeal to me a whole lot. It was kind of discouraging.

Matty Bumpas scurried away from us, toward Chinatown, looking around suspiciously every few seconds. After he was about ten or twelve feet and several people away, Ernie nudged me, and we followed him. I kept my eyes peeled for something that might prove to be a threat to Matty, but since I hadn't a clue what I was looking for, I had no luck in spotting it. I remained silent, even though I was again bursting with questions I wanted to ask.

By that time traffic had thinned a bit, I presume because people had taken their luncheons and returned to their jobs. Therefore, we had to stay farther back from Matty than we had when we followed (I believe the private investigatorial term for it is "tailed") Mr. Li. But we never lost sight of him. Leastways, Ernie didn't. I have to admit that my attention was diverted once or twice when I noticed someone I considered suspicious hanging about in a doorway or wherever.

116

Ernie apparently didn't experience the same doubts, because he didn't take his focus from Matty Bumpas.

As for me and my investigative techniques, I thought I spotted Ned once, but I was probably wrong. Certainly Ned was back in his closet reading and waiting to be discovered by this time. Discouragement piled upon discouragement.

After a few minutes, I was surprised to realize that Matty was retracing the same path Ernie and I had followed from Chinatown! What did this mean? I was pretty sure Ernie didn't have second sight, so he must have figured out something that had eluded me as regarded Babs Houser, Chinatown, Han Li, and Matty Bumpas. I felt quite stupid, and didn't enjoy the sensation one little bit.

There was no time to fall into a melancholy, however, because we arrived at—ta-da!—Mr. Li's souvenir shop at that very moment. Again, Ernie put a finger to his lips. Then he strolled up to one of the shop's windows, all of which were crammed with merchandise. He'd chosen the window closest to the open doorway, and he struck a casual pose, leaning against the building. He stood so that only his profile could be seen by anyone inside the shop, and that was disguised when he pulled his hat brim down low on his forehead. His casual attitude and appearance gave an observer the impression that he might be a tourist waiting for a friend. In truth, as I soon perceived, he was listening for all he was worth.

Pretty soon, even I, who was nowhere near the front door, heard loud voices indicating some kind of quarrel was going forth within the shop. Straining my ears, I could distinguish Mr. Li's voice and Mr. Bumpas's, but I couldn't make out what they were saying. I heard several swear words, and a long string of Chinese syllables that might also have been swear words but didn't sound as bad as the same

words would have in English, probably because I didn't understand them. Chinese is quite a musical language when you're just listening and don't have a notion what the words mean.

Once I heard an entire sentence: "Give her back," spoken very angrily by Matty Bumpas.

Mr. Li said something that sounded like *dough*. My novelistic instincts vibrated as I recognized a slang word for *money*. Ha! I *hadn't* been wasting my time when I'd read all those detective novels, in spite of what my mother claimed!

Matty Bumpas shouted a long string of swear words that proved he was more inventive than I'd heretofore given him credit for being. Mr. Li responded with an equally long string of Chinese words. I heard a loud noise, as if one of the men had slammed his hand on the counter, then Ernie slid away from the wall and hustled me behind a potted plant. Our backs were to the door of Han Li's shop when Matty Bumpas stormed out.

Chuckling, Ernie said, "I guess that takes care of that. We can go back to work now, kiddo."

"I thought that's what we'd been doing since lunchtime." By then I was totally confused and my tone of voice was rather sharp.

"Aw, this was nothing. You oughta see me when I'm really working."

If this was nothing, why was it I was about to fall into a heap from being run off my feet? Before I moved here, I'd been led to believe that people in Los Angeles weren't big walkers, which once again showed how much I knew about anything. I'd never walked so much in my life. I regret to say I borrowed from Mr. Templeton himself when I said, "Huh."

He chuckled merrily. By that time, it was approximately

2:30 p.m., and I'd been on my feet since shortly after noon. I was tired and thirsty and feeling abused and mistreated. I hadn't realized how much physical endurance the private investigative business took. If I hadn't wanted to cling to my job, even though I'd begun to wonder about the real merits of regular employment, I'd have struck him with my handbag for laughing at me.

I guess he sensed my mood because he said in a conciliatory tone, "Say, kiddo, I didn't mean to wear you out. Let me make it up to you. How's about an ice cream soda?"

Oh, my, that sounded good! Since I didn't want to admit how exhausted I was, I said, "Well, if you're sure we don't need to get back to the office right away."

"Hell, what for?" His expression altered slightly, and he looked glum. "There's not that much work to do."

The offer of an ice cream soda had perked me up a little, and I was sorry that Mr. Templeton didn't consider his business a thriving one. This was especially true since he was my employer, and if he didn't have enough work, I wouldn't have any work at all. "What about Mr. Godfrey's missing fiancée?"

"I think I found her."

"Really! Why, that's wonderful, Mr. . . . er . . . Ernie! Where is she?"

"According to a source I consulted, she's in Pasadena."

"Pasadena," I repeated, the word conjuring up images of roses and big mansions and lots of money. I'd heard a lot about Pasadena, even before I moved to Los Angeles. It's where the rich people lived—not new-money rich people like those in the motion-picture industry, particularly, but rich people from back East who wanted a warm place to spend their winters. Pasadena hosted a Tournament of Roses Parade every year, on January first, of all unlikely

119

times of year to find roses blooming. "I'd love to go to Pasadena someday," I murmured.

As we talked, Ernie had been guiding me through Chinatown. We crossed Hill and went through the arch on its other side, which looked pretty much like the one we'd just left, except that this side had Hop Luey's in a red pagoda. My mother would have called the architecture tacky, but I thought it was swell. It looked really Chinese. Evidently Ernie knew Chinatown inside and out because his footsteps didn't waver as he marched along.

"Hell, you can go there with me tomorrow, if you want to."

"To Pasadena?" My attention swerved from my dry mouth and sore feet and landed in a bed of roses. "Really?"

"Sure. In fact, I wish you would. The lady might be more comfortable if you came along. You know, another woman's presence, and all that."

"I'd be helping you with another case?" The word *assistant* did a pirouette in my head. He was actually using me as his assistant! After only two days at work!

"Yeah, I guess you could say that."

"I would," I said firmly.

He chuckled again. "I figured you would. Here we are."

Opening the door to another hole-in-the-wall place, I saw that it was in reality an ice cream parlor. It looked just like an ice cream parlor in Boston might have, except it was occupied solely by people of Chinese descent. That didn't bother me any. Ernie guided me to a little white wrought-iron table for two and held a chair for me. He was being quite the gentleman all of a sudden. I sank wearily into the chair and murmured, "Thank you."

"You're welcome."

A young woman with bobbed hair, a short skirt and lots

120

of makeup came up with a pad to take our orders. I don't know why I should have been surprised to see a Chinese flapper, but I was. She flirted shamelessly with Ernie, too, who lapped it up, the dog.

Still and all, it had been an interesting, if exhausting, day, and I was well on my way to becoming a P.I.'s assistant!

EIGHT

"You're doing what?" Chloe looked at me through bleary blue eyes and blinked several times. She wasn't usually up at this early hour, but she and Harvey were hosting a dinner party that night, and I guess she wanted to make sure the arrangements were up to her standards. I was looking forward to the party, because Mr. Easthope would be there along with a few motion-picture actors and actresses. I'd never met anyone who worked as an actor in the pictures, although I'd met plenty of behind-the-scenes folks, starting with Harvey.

I adjusted my hat. "Mr. Templeton is taking me to Pasadena to meet a woman a client hired him to find."

"Hmm. I like Pasadena."

"I'm glad we're going there. I've always wanted to see it."

"Pretty place. One of Francis's best friends lives there."

"Francis Easthope?"

"Yeah." She yawned hugely and frowned at me. "I'm glad tomorrow's Saturday. I'm going to take you to the barbershop and get your hair bobbed if I have to tie you up and have Harvey carry you there."

"Tomorrow's Friday, Chloe."

"Oh. Well, day after tomorrow, then."

I laughed. "You won't have to do anything so drastic as tie me up. I'll be happy to get rid of all this. It's too darned hot here to have long hair."

"We're going to get you some clothes, too," Chloe said,

eyeing my knee-length green skirt and plain white shirtwaist and man-style green tie with what looked like mighty close to loathing.

"I don't know why you're picking on my clothes. I think a working woman should dress soberly."

"There's sober and then there's sober," Chloe said wryly. "You'd look right at home in a Salvation Army band."

That was slightly daunting, mainly because I couldn't feature Ernie Templeton anywhere near a woman in a Salvation Army uniform. It occurred to me that he might actually prefer a rather more casually attired secretary. Perhaps I'd work up the courage to ask him as we drove to Pasadena. I presumed we'd drive, since even he wouldn't try to walk twenty-odd miles. I hoped.

I scowled at my reflection in the hall mirror. "I think I look suitably attired for a professional working woman." My voice echoed my doubts.

"Professional working woman, my foot," said Chloe. "I need coffee." And she wandered off toward the kitchen where poor Mrs. Biddle was undoubtedly well under way with her daily chores. When I'd asked to borrow cleaning supplies earlier in the week, I got the impression Mrs. Biddle didn't care for interruptions to her working schedule.

But that was nothing to me. Giving my hat a brisk pat, putting on the green jacket that matched my skirt—and that had a fashionably lowered waist, turned cuffs, and a jaunty belt, curse it—and picking up my handbag, I hurried out of the house and strode briskly to Angel's Flight. There I handed the engineer my nickel and sat myself in one of the little seats. I just loved that little railroad.

For a fleeting second, I thought I saw a familiar face, but

when I whipped my head around, it was gone. I'd probably been mistaken. There was no reason I could think of why Mr. Godfrey would be standing on the Angel's Flight platform. Then again, there was no reason I could think of why he shouldn't be there. I reminded myself that just because my first impression of him hadn't been favorable, he still had every right to go any old place he wanted to go in the Los Angeles area. And out of it, for that matter.

I felt particularly perky that day because Ernie was taking me to Pasadena to help him on a case. And he'd already asked me to help him with another case, that of whatever Mrs. Von Schilling's lost property turned out to be. He hadn't told me yet. It bothered me a little that Chloe thought I looked dowdy. Peering at my tidy but fashionable green skirt and my black-gloved hands folded over my black handbag, I thought I looked quite nice.

When I entered the Figueroa Building and saw Lulu LaBelle filing her fingernails, my self-judgment suffered a slight check. Lulu, who was also a professional working woman, had that morning decided to appear at her job in a frilly dress with short cap sleeves, a V-neck, a dropped waistline and a very short skirt, in a vivid fuchsia color that clashed violently with her blood-red fingernails. The combination was truly eye-popping, especially when you added in her white hair. I blinked, thinking it was fairly early in the morning to encounter that particular color combination.

Nevertheless, I greeted her with my usual enthusiasm. "Good morning, Lulu!"

"Morning." She yawned. I guess she was no more of a morning person than Chloe, but Chloe didn't have to keep a job. My sympathies were stirred, and I hoped Lulu would find stardom—or at least a nice husband who would support her so she didn't have to arise so early in the

morning. "Ned was looking for you."

"He was?"

"Yeah." She grinned like an imp. "I think he's sweet on you, honey. Watch out. Ned's a strange one."

"He's sweet on me?" For some reason, my innards went "Ew."

"Yeah. Until you showed up here to work for Ernie, I wouldn't see Ned for days at a time. Now he's out of his closet all the time." Lulu patted her mouth to stifle another yawn. "Gawd, I hate mornings."

"Really? I thought this one was kind of pretty." In truth, I thought it was spectacular, although I have to admit that the view from the top of Angel's Flight might have something to do with my opinion. I had no idea where Lulu lived, but if it was in an apartment akin to those Ernie and I visited yesterday, I could understand her point of view.

"Ned fixed the elevator," Lulu informed me.

"Really?" Now this was good news. Even though I wasn't thrilled with the prospect of Ned favoring me, I was pleased not to have to walk up three flights of stairs since my calf muscles still hurt from all the walking Ernie and I had done the day before.

"Yeah. We don't have an operator, so you'll have to open and shut it yourself. It's not hard to do. Want me to show you how to do it?"

"Thank you, Lulu. That would be very kind of you."

She squinted at me as she slid out of her chair. "You talk classy, you know that?"

"Do I?" The information did not come as good news. I was trying to blend in.

"Yeah. I like it. You'd be great in a play or something."

I would? Somehow I doubted it, but I appreciated Lulu's endorsement. At least I think I did.

Following her to the elevator, I marveled at her exaggerated strut. Whether she'd ever achieve stardom or not, I couldn't say, but she'd certainly adopted most of the outer trappings of a motion-picture actress. Because I was curious, I said, "What steps have you taken to achieve your goals, Lulu?"

She glanced at me over her shoulder. "Huh?"

"Well, I mean, have you auditioned for roles?"

"Oh, sure. Lots of times. There's lots of competition, though. A girl's gotta put herself forward, if you know what I mean."

"Um . . . actually, I don't know what you mean. I've never thought about it."

She waited for me to catch up with her, which took a couple of steps. Then she lowered her voice and spoke in a confidential tone. "Well, for one thing, lots of girls are willing to do *anything* to get parts. You know."

Again, she had me over a barrel. "Um . . ."

"Geez, kid, are you *that* innocent?"

I hated to believe it of myself, but I guess I was. "Um . . ."

She rolled her eyes. "I guess you are. Well . . ." She stopped walking, took my arm, and leaned close. "You know, some girls will actually even go all the way with a producer or a director in order to get into a picture."

All the way? Suddenly, I understood, and gasped in horror. "You don't mean it!"

She nodded. "I do mean it. It's a crime, the way some girls fling themselves around. Like that girl they say Fatty Arbuckle murdered. She was one of the ones who'd do any-thing—and I do mean *anything*—to get a part."

"That's . . . that's pathetic."

"It's worse than pathetic. It's stupid. It never works. A girl might get cast in one movie, but then the director might not want her anymore. He's prolly moved on to another girl

who's desperate to get cast."

"I'm glad you don't do that, Lulu."

"Well, I seen what happened to a friend of mine, and I decided it wasn't worth it. I'll make it one of these days, but I'll do it 'cause I'm good on screen, not because I'm good in bed."

The notion that Harvey Nash, my very own brother-in-law, might be participating in such low tactics entered my mind only to be thrust aside with vigor. Not Harvey. Never Harvey. He was too loyal. Too much in love with Chloe.

Wasn't he?

Good Lord, I hoped so!

There was more to Los Angeles than met the eye, and some of it had best remain hidden, if you asked me. Not that anyone did.

We'd reached the elevator, and Lulu showed me how to open the door and close the door. She rode up with me to the third floor, and instructed me on how to use the lever so that the car was more or less level with the floor. "That part's important, because you don't want to trip and fall on your butt," said she.

"Right." I'd heard that Mabel Normand used language like that. Perhaps Lulu was aiming to become the next big comic sensation of the big screen. I exited the elevator without mishap, and was pleased with the appearance of the hallway since my interview several days earlier.

Not only had Ned put in new light bulbs, so that one could see where one was headed, but he'd also repainted not only the sign on Ernie's office, but on a couple of other offices. As I paused to take my key out of my handbag, I was pleased that no longer was there room for doubt that this was the office of Ernest Templeton, and that his vocation was that of P.I. The glass was clean, too, although I

was the one responsible for that. Well, Bon Ami and I. It looked and smelled as if Ned had been painting the hall-way's walls, too. I tell you, things were moving right along. I was proud of myself for instigating Ned's renewed sense of pride in his work.

A surprise awaited me when I unlocked the office door. A little bouquet of flowers, daisies and anemones, resided in what looked like a rinsed-out jelly jar on my desk. *Ned,* I thought, and wondered whose garden he'd stolen them from.

But perhaps I'd wronged him. Or perhaps it had been Ernie who'd brought the flowers, which perked me up for a second or two before I realized that was unlikely, since he'd left the office before I had the day before and he hadn't arrived yet this morning.

Well, it didn't matter. The flowers, for all their inelegant container, were pretty, and I resolved to thank whomever had been kind enough to leave them for me.

"Hello, Miss Allcutt."

I glanced up from putting my handbag and hat in my drawer to find Ned, clutching the front door and peering in at me as if he were afraid I'd bite. I smiled graciously. "Good morning, Ned. Beautiful morning, isn't it?"

"Yeah. You want me to do anything for you, Miss Allcutt?"

This, from the man I'd had to pry out of his closet when we'd first met. "Um . . . I can't think of anything right now, Ned. Thank you."

He nodded, but he looked disappointed. "I been painting the hall. Did you see that?"

"Yes, I did."

"And I brought those flowers." He gestured at the jelly glass.

"Thank you very much. They're lovely."

"Picked 'em in the park. Pershing Square."

I'll bet the groundskeepers would be thrilled to know that. I didn't say so. "Well, they're lovely. Thank you."

"You're welcome." He stood there, swaying with the door, which had decided to open wider, then said, "Well, you let me know if there's anything you want me to do, okay?"

"Okay." I do believe that was the first time I'd ever used that word, although it was quite popular at the time.

I have a feeling Ned would have lingered, mooning and swaying in the doorway, if Ernie hadn't arrived just then. As soon as Ned spotted him, he leaped sideways.

" 'Lo, Ned." Ernie's voice was friendly and he nodded to Ned as he passed.

"Hello, Mr. Templeton." Ned didn't sound as if he was pleased to see Ernie, but I certainly was.

As ever, Ernie's stride was long and effortless, and he nodded at me, too, as he passed my desk. "Morning, Miss Allcutt."

"Good morning, Mr. Templeton. I mean Ernie."

He grinned as he stopped in the doorway to his office, reached up and lifted his hat from his head, and flung it across his office at the coat tree. "Ha! Made it." And he went into his office and shut the door behind him.

I wasn't sure what I was supposed to do at that point, so I remained seated behind my desk, opened my top middle drawer, and withdrew my pad. Ned was still in the doorway when I glanced up. "Did you want something, Ned?"

"You call him Ernie?" His frown made him look puzzled, and reinforced my opinion that Ned wasn't the brightest candle in the box.

"Why, yes. He told me to call him Ernie."

"Huh." And Ned disappeared from my sight.

I wished Ernie hadn't shut his door, because I'd wanted to chat with him about Pasadena, and Barbara-Ann Houser, and all sorts of things. Since I was his secretary—his *confidential* secretary (I'd seen that description in an advertisement in the *Times*)—I concluded it was all right for me to interrupt him. Therefore, I rose from my chair and was about to break in on his newspaper reading, when the front door opened, and another visitor appeared. While I hadn't been thrilled and delighted to see Ned this early in the morning, I was even less so to see Mr. Godfrey.

My lack of enthusiasm didn't matter, however. I was Ernie's secretary, and I had to be pleasant to the clients. Therefore, I sat back down and smiled. "Good morning, Mr. Godfrey."

"Good morning, Miss Allcutt." He stood before my desk, shifting from one foot to the other, his chubby face pink, and his little eyes darting glances around the office. Snatching the hat from his head, he whipped his other hand out from behind his back. In it resided a pretty bouquet of mixed flowers tied with a pink bow. "I thought you might like some flowers."

I loved flowers, as a matter of fact, but I wasn't altogether certain I wanted to receive them from two such men as Ned and Mr. Godfrey. Now, if Francis Easthope were to honor me with some red roses or something, I'd be thrilled. Or even Ernie.

Mr. Godfrey's gaze came to rest on the jelly jar. "You already have some flowers, I see."

"Yes. People are most kind." There I went: sounding like my mother again. Ah, well. There's a lot to be said for the rules of society; they can ease one's way through many swampy situations.

"You mean somebody else gave you those?" He looked so downcast and dejected that I almost felt sorry for him.

"Well, yes, but I do love flowers, and you were very kind to bring these to me. Perhaps I should try to find a bowl for them."

Thrusting the bouquet at me, he said, "All right. Is Mr. Templeton in?"

"Yes, he is. Let me tell him you're here." So I took the flowers, set them carefully on my desk so as not to squish them, and finished my interrupted trip to Ernie's office, where I knocked on his door.

"C'm in," he called.

So I went in. "Mr. Godfrey is here to see you."

Ernie folded the *Times*, sighed, and set it on his desk. "All right. Show him in."

So I did that, too. As soon as the door closed behind the two men, I picked up my posy and went in search of a vase. Or at least another jelly jar. It really had been nice of both Ned and Mr. Godfrey to bring me flowers, and I suppose it was unkind of me to wish they hadn't.

Deciding that I probably ought to use the stairway, since exercise was good for one's stamina, I did so, trotting down the three flights and ending up in the lobby, where Lulu still filed her fingernails. She glanced up when she heard my sensible shoes clop across the lobby floor.

" 'Lo, Mercy."

"Hello again, Lulu. Do you have any idea where I might find something in which to put these flowers?"

Her face split into a grin. "So *you're* the one, eh?"

I blinked at her. "I beg your pardon?"

"I saw that guy bring 'em in and wondered who they were for. I kinda hoped he'd give 'em to me. I like flowers."

"So do I." It crossed my mind to give the flowers to

131

Lulu, but then decided that wouldn't be right, and it might hurt Mr. Godfrey's feelings. And *that* would be going directly against my secretarial duty. "But I need something to put them in."

"Sure. I bet Ned has something."

Drat. I'd already considered Ned, but didn't want to offend him or make him feel bad by asking him for a container for another gentleman's flowers. Then I decided I was being too sensitive. It wasn't my fault two men had decided I needed flowers today, curse it! "I guess I'll go down and try to find him."

"Sweetie, all you have to do is whisper his name, and he'll come running."

I'm not sure why that comment made my nose wrinkle, but it did. "Swell," I said sarcastically, and Lulu laughed.

Nevertheless, I tramped down another flight of stairs to the basement. Since I didn't feel like spending hours on my quest, I called out, "Ned!"

Instantly, a closet door opened, and Ned appeared, holding another book. Glancing at the title, I saw it was *The Mysterious Affair at Styles*, by Agatha Christie. I couldn't fault his literary taste, even if he was an annoying sort of person. "Miss Allcutt!" Ned beamed at me.

"Hi, Ned. I need something to put these flowers in, please."

His smile vanished. "Where'd you get those?"

Forgetting that Ned already believed he had a grudge against the person who'd given them to me, I said, "Mr. Godfrey."

His lips pinched into a flat line, and Ned's skimpy eyebrows formed a perfect V over his pale blue eyes. "Godfrey! I should have known."

Oh, dear. However, I reminded myself that Ned's dislike

of Mr. Godfrey, and Mr. Godfrey's dislike of Ned were of no concern to me. Therefore, I merely smiled. "Do you have a vase anywhere around, Ned?"

"Huh?" He jumped a little, as if he'd forgotten my presence in his contemplation of the enemy. I had heard from friends who seemed to know more than I about the subject that men were irrational creatures. If most men behaved like Ned, I believed it.

I lifted the small bouquet. "A vase?" I reminded him gently.

"Oh, yeah. Um . . . I think there's one around here somewhere. Lulu gets flowers sometimes."

"That's nice," said I, meaning it. I'd just as soon give her these.

So I followed Ned around the basement, watching him open doors and marveling at his incoherent (to me) method of organization. What he needed was Mrs. Biddle to come to the Figueroa Building and show him how to put things in order. At last he opened a door to a closet whose contents looked promising. "Knew they were here someplace," he mumbled, and stepped aside. By gum, he was right. Before my very eyes was a shelf with glasses and vases on it. So I picked one out, thanked Ned, and climbed the four flights back to my office, deciding as I did so that, while stair climbing might be good for one's stamina, it played havoc with one's flowers. They were already beginning to wilt in the summer heat. I detoured by the ladies' room to put water in the vase.

Evidently Ernie and Mr. Godfrey were still conferring when I arranged the bouquet on my desk and sat again. I was glad of it, because I wanted time to catch my breath before I had to do any talking.

I hadn't quite recovered from my morning's exertions

when the telephone rang. This was the very first time I'd had to answer the telephone for my job, and my heart sped up when I lifted the receiver.

"Mr. Templeton's office. Miss Allcutt speaking." Chloe had told me that was how Harvey's secretary answered his telephone, so I adopted the method for myself. It sounded very professional.

"Good morning," a husky female voice purred in my ear. Mrs. Von Schilling. Nuts. "May I please speak to Mr. Templeton."

"I'm sorry, but Mr. Templeton is engaged at the moment. May I take a message?" I picked up my pencil and poised it over my message pad, just like a real secretary. Which I was.

"Please have him telephone me, dear."

Dear? Egad.

"Certainly."

"Mrs. Von Schilling," she said, as if anyone in the world besides her spoke in that sultry voice. "Madison six two four nine six."

"I'll certainly do that, Mrs. Von Schilling."

"Thank you so much, Miss Allcutt. You're a treasure."

A treasure, was I? Phooey. However, I dutifully copied the name and number, detached the message from the pad, and set it precisely at the corner of my desk where Ernie couldn't help but see it—and I wouldn't forget it. Not that there was much chance of that, messages thus far being quite unusual in that office.

Because I wanted to take pride in both my work and the room in which I did it, I'd stopped by the five-and-dime to purchase a dust cloth on my way home from work the day before. I'd just finished dusting the office, not a difficult task since there was so little furniture, and decided the

place needed a rug on the floor and a table for magazines and maybe another chair or two and a picture on the wall, when Ernie's door opened and both he and Mr. Godfrey walked out of it. Ernie looked at my dust cloth, then at the new bouquet of flowers on my desk, and gave me an ironic grin that I believed was uncalled for.

Mr. Godfrey saw that I'd put his pretty little bouquet in a vase with water and smiled. When he smiled, his piggy eyes almost disappeared into his fleshy face. It was an unfortunate result of a facial expression that usually brightens a countenance.

Peeved with him and with Ernie, I snatched the message off my desk and thrust it at my boss. "Here. You have a message."

"Thank you, Miss Allcutt," he said so politely that I knew he was making fun of me. He read the message, his eyebrows lifted, and he said, "Ah," in a pleased-sounding voice. And he turned and went back into his office, leaving me alone with Mr. Godfrey.

Drat the man!

Mr. Godfrey pulled out the chair next to my desk and made as if to sit in it. I knew what that meant. He wanted to talk. And talk, and talk. Well, I didn't want to listen. Hoping I didn't sound too rude, since Mr. Godfrey was, after all, one of Ernie's clients, I said, "I'm sorry, Mr. Godfrey, but I must consult with Mr. Templeton now. Thank you very much for the flowers, and have a lovely day." And I held out my hand for him to shake. The poor man couldn't do anything else, thank God.

As soon as he left, I went into Ernie's office. "When are we going to Pasadena?"

"After I return Mrs. Von Schilling's telephone call."

Humph.

However, he'd meant it, I guess, because it wasn't another

ten minutes before he left his office again, this time clad in coat and hat and bouncing some keys in his hand. "Ready?" he asked with a smile.

"One minute, and I will be." I retrieved my hat and handbag from my desk, straightened my suit jacket and skirt, plopped my hat on my head, and said, "Ready."

"Good. Come on, kiddo."

Because I was pleased with Ned's recent industry, I made Ernie take the elevator down. "Don't worry, it's safe," I assured him. "And I know how to operate it."

"I'm not worried. But the stairs are quicker." The elevator groaned to a stop in front of us, and I pulled the lever that opened the doors. "And they're quieter."

"Not when you're galumphing down them," I said, feeling perky.

When the elevator got to the first floor, I had to experiment a couple of times before I got the car level with the floor. I didn't want to trip—more, I didn't want Ernie to trip. I figured it would be bad form to cause one's employer to fall splat on the floor because of something one did.

Again, Ned and Lulu were conferring when we entered the lobby. I waved at them both. Ernie said, "Twenty-three skidoo."

Lulu waved some fiery red fingernails at us. Ned just stared. He wasn't a particularly verbal young man.

I was eager to see what kind of an automobile Ernie drove. I didn't expect it would be a fancy model, like the ones driven by Mr. Easthope and Harvey. Actually, Harvey didn't drive his big, enormous Pierce-Arrow Series 33. He had a chauffeur on staff to drive it for him. I was right. Ernie led the way out of the Figueroa Building and down the street a ways until he got to a Studebaker that looked as if it had been around the block a few times. Around several

blocks several times each, actually. He opened the door on the passenger's side. "Slide on in, kiddo. It's not fancy, but it runs like a top."

"I'm sure," said I, not wanting to make him feel inferior by indicating in any way whatsoever that I wasn't accustomed to being driven around in such dilapidated automobiles.

Which pointed out to me once again that one is constantly bombarded with evidence of prejudices one might not even know one possesses until they figuratively slap one in the face. The truth is that I was inwardly sneering at Ernie's car. And that automatic sneer was mine only because I'd been privileged to have been born into a wealthy family. And being born into a wealthy family had been pure dumb luck on my part. See how silly human beings can be without half trying? I determined not to indicate by so much as a lift of a lip that I considered Ernie's Studebaker beneath me. Well, it was beneath me, in reality, but not in *that* way.

He got in on the driver's side and grinned at me. "Not what you're used to, is it, Miss Allcutt?"

I frowned at him. "If I'm supposed to call you Ernie, you really should call me Mercy, you know."

He pressed the starter button on the floor. At least he didn't have to crank the silly thing. "Mercy. That's short for Mercedes, isn't it?"

"Yes."

"Classy name."

"Is it?" Curses! Now even my name was classy. It occurred to me that I might never be able to fit in with the common herd.

But that was defeatist thinking, and I wouldn't allow it to fester in my bosom.

"I was named for an aunt," I told him. "That's not so classy."

He shrugged as he leaned out the window and looked at the traffic passing by on Seventh Street. "She got money, this aunt of yours?"

"She's dead," I said, not caring to go into *that* issue. In fact, my aunt Mercedes had been wildly wealthy, which is one of the reasons I was named after her.

"But she had money, didn't she?"

Darn it, he wasn't going to let the subject drop, was he? "I suppose she was fairly well to do." I spoke repressively, and hoped he'd catch on to the fact that I didn't want to talk about my family's relative wealth.

" 'Fairly well to do,' you say. Ha! I bet she was rolling in it."

"This is a very unsuitable conversation, Ernie. My family's financial status has nothing to do with the matter at hand, and I don't care to discuss it."

I'd used my lady-of-the-manor voice, the one I'd learned from my mother when she spoke to disobedient servants, and I could have kicked myself as soon as I heard what I sounded like. It didn't seem to faze Ernie, who grinned as he guided the Studebaker out into traffic. He turned north on Hill, slung his right arm over the back of his seat, and steered one-handed.

"All right, kiddo," he said at last. "I won't tease you about your bags of money."

"Bags of money? Nonsense!"

But he was right, and we both knew it. Why was it that every time I seemed to sense a lessening of the social gap between me and the world I strove to enter, somebody like Ernie Templeton came along and ripped out the fragile stitches I'd sewed in an attempt to mend the gap? It was a very annoying problem, but I vowed I'd overcome it or die trying.

Then I decided there was no reason to carry things *that* far.

NINE

We'd been tooling along Figueroa Street, heading vaguely northwards for about twenty minutes, before my temper was under control enough to initiate a conversation. "Whereabouts does Mr. Godfrey's fiancée live?"

"I dunno. But I got some information that she's working at a bookstore on Colorado."

I gaped at him. "In *Colorado?*"

"*On* Colorado."

Oh. "Colorado is a street in Pasadena?"

"Right. It's the main east-west street. It's the street the floats and bands go down on New Year's Day."

"Ah. Yes, I've seen pictures of the Tournament of Roses Parade. It must be lovely."

"It's okay. I saw it once."

"It must have been beautiful."

"Yeah."

"When you come from back East, as I do, you probably appreciate seeing all those flowers in the middle of winter more than you do if you're from around here."

"I guess."

So much for that topic. After about another hour or so of driving through some very lovely scenery, Ernie making an occasional comment of a neutral nature, we reached the city limits of Pasadena. His next comment was not in the least neutral. "I'll take you down Millionaire's Row, kiddo. You'll feel right at home."

It was far from professional behavior on my part, but I

lost my temper again. "Darn it, Ernie Templeton, why do you persist in flinging my origins in my face? I'm trying very hard to be a normal, everyday working girl."

He let out a roar of laughter that nearly deafened me, and he proceeded to laugh so long and so hard, he actually had to pull over to the side of the road, pull his handkerchief from his pocket, and mop tears from his eyes. I glared at him the while, cross as crabs, my arms folded across my chest, unable to see any reason whatsoever for him to have succumbed to such hilarity. After several minutes of that nonsense, he calmed down some and I spoke again. "And what, if I may be so bold as to ask, is so funny about wanting to be perceived as a normal, everyday working girl?"

"You'll probably never understand," he said, his voice weak from the strain of so much laughter.

"I'm sure I can if you explain it to me," I said coldly.

After wiping his eyes one more time, he stuffed his handkerchief back into his pocket, took a swig from that accursed flask he kept in his other pocket, turned in his seat until he faced me, and said, "You don't get it, do you? Don't you know that any other girl in the universe would trade places with you in a heartbeat, if she had the chance? You're the only person I've ever met who's willing—hell, *eager*—to trade a life of luxury and ease for one of toil and care."

"Toil and care?" I'd never heard myself sound so sarcastic. "My, my, aren't we poetic all of a sudden?"

He choked back another laugh, I think, to judge by the noise he made. "I'm a real poetic guy, Mercy. And you'll still never understand."

I only glowered some more, and he went on. "Well, hell, how could you? You can't possibly comprehend the irony of it all."

140

"I understand irony perfectly well," I said, offended. "But I can't discern any in this instance. For your information, there's a very good reason for me to want to become a part of the worker proletariat."

He threw his arms out in an expansive gesture. "See? That's exactly what I mean! Do you honestly think that— oh, take Lulu LaBelle as an example—do you think she considers herself part of your *worker proletariat?*"

Put that way, I guess he had a point, although I'd never admit it. "Not unless she reads a lot. Or takes up with a union organizer, I guess. Which isn't impossible, curse it!"

"No, I don't suppose it is," he said. And with one last gurgle of suppressed laughter, he turned and began driving again.

I sat next to him, fuming, and wishing with all my heart that I could prove myself of use to my employer, who still clearly believed me to be a spoiled rich girl who was only taking a job on a lark. Short of performing some sort of heroic deed that none of my friends in Boston would dream of performing because they'd consider it beneath him, and of forcing Ernie to acknowledge my value afterwards, I couldn't think of how to go about it.

Orange Grove Boulevard, the "Millionaire's Row" Ernie had mentioned, didn't remind me of home one little bit. It was ever so much greener and more fabulous than Boston. Rolling green lawns, huge trees, and gigantic mansions surrounded by enormous iron fences abounded. Boston was much more subdued than this, although most of the wealthy there had palatial homes outside the city. I don't think I'd ever seen so many flowers, either. I remember sucking in my breath at one point and whispering, "Oh, my!"

"Pretty swell, isn't it?"

"I should say so." For a fleeting moment, it crossed my mind to try to persuade my parents to move to Pasadena. Fortunately, that insanity passed almost as soon as it entered my head, and I reminded myself that I was here primarily because my parents weren't.

Even after we turned onto Colorado Boulevard and left Orange Grove behind, Pasadena looked like a pretty nice place. "Is this Pasadena's downtown district?"

"Yeah. Pretty keen, huh?"

It was keen, all right. And ever so much cleaner and tidier than the downtown area of Los Angeles in which I worked. Mountains loomed to the north, looking protective and purple in the late-morning sunlight. The air was clean and fresh—and hot.

"I think we're getting close," Ernie said after a few minutes. "Look for a sign that says Vorland's Books."

"Very well." I scanned both sides of the street, trying not to admire the architecture and shrubbery too much, since I didn't want to get sidetracked. We spotted the building at the same time. "There it is!"

"Ah, there it is."

I guess we'd found it. "What is this woman's name, Ernie?"

"June Williams." He'd stuck his arm out the window to signal for a left turn on a street called Hudson Avenue, and upon which I presumed he aimed to park.

"And she was engaged to marry Mr. Godfrey?"

"So he says." He zoomed into a space vacated by a departing Packard Eight Sedan with a liveried chauffeur behind the wheel. I wondered if that automobile belonged to one of those grand mansions we'd driven past.

I stared at him. "You mean you don't believe him?"

The rubber of his wheels screeched against the curb,

142

making me wince, and he turned off the engine. Glancing at me, he said with one of his sassy smiles, "Hell, kid, I don't believe anybody until I get all the facts."

Ernie climbed out of the Studebaker, and I remained in the passenger seat. It only occurred to me when he'd opened my door that perhaps women in my line of work didn't have doors opened for them all the time. Nuts. There was more to this being-of-the-people nonsense than I'd thought about before I attempted it. Ernie didn't sneer at me or anything, so I guess he was accustomed to opening doors for ladies. Therefore, I continued the conversation as if no unpleasant thoughts had interrupted it in my mind. "You don't think you have all the facts yet?"

"I don't know. We'll see. Let's go find out what Miss Williams has to say."

Sounded like a good idea to me, so I walked alongside Ernie to the bookstore.

Miss June Williams proved easy to find. She approached us, as a matter of fact, with a saleslady's smile on her lips. Eyeglasses perched on the bridge of her nose, making her appear the studious type. Of course, at that moment, I didn't know she was the woman for whom we were looking. All I saw was a pleasant-looking person, probably in her early twenties, wearing a plain blue jersey dress with a high round neckline, a tiny collar, and a dropped waist. She looked very prim and proper and businesslike. I believed my own green suit did not pale by comparison, but neither did it proclaim me as being anyone in a higher social caste than she. Which, naturally, made me happy.

"May I help you?" she said in a pleasant voice.

"Yeah, maybe," said Ernie. I frowned, believing more decorous speech would get him further with this young woman than his everyday casual speech that he used with

people like Lulu LaBelle. Not that Lulu didn't deserve courtesy every bit as much as . . . Oh, never mind.

But her smile remained firmly in place. I guess she'd decided she needed to be polite to the clients, just as I had, whether she wanted to be or not. Interesting. I'd learned something else. Some people had to demean themselves every day of their lives in order to secure and maintain their employment and, therefore, their means of existence. Goodness, but life was different when one stepped down from one's ivory tower.

I decided she deserved better from our interrogation than the casual gruffness Ernie seemed determined upon, so I took over from him. He frowned at me when I began talking. "Thank you for your help," I said before he could continue on in his same vein. I gave the woman a gracious smile. "We're looking for a lady named June Williams. Can you help us?"

As soon as I said the name, I knew we'd found her, because her eyes grew large behind her spectacles, and her smile disappeared from her face. "I'm June Williams," she said. "But . . ."

I'd opened my mouth to say we wanted to talk to her, but Ernie nudged me in the ribs with his elbow and I said, "Ow," instead. Blast him!

"Miss Williams," said Ernie. "Is there somewhere we can be private for a few minutes? This won't take very long."

"Private?" She lifted a well-manicured hand to her collar, and appeared nervous. "But why do you need to talk to me?"

Ernie pulled out his private investigator's license and flashed it at her. It's too dramatic to say that she paled or flinched, but she certainly didn't appear delighted to have

been approached by a P.I. "I guess we can talk back here," she said, turning and making toward the rear of the store. "We're not busy now, but I can't leave the floor."

"That's fine." Ernie gestured for me to follow, so I did, thinking all the while.

Miss June Williams seemed, upon first meeting, to be a perfectly ordinary person, if rather more bookish than some. I couldn't imagine her with Mr. Godfrey. And could this possibly be the woman whom Ned claimed Mr. Godfrey had stolen from him? Impossible! This woman was much too good for either of those second-rate fellows.

We stopped when we got to a far corner of the store, between American History and European History. What I wanted to do was look at the latest detective novels, but I restrained myself. When Miss Williams turned to face us, she appeared grim. "Now, please tell me what this is all about. I'm not accustomed to being questioned by detectives in my place of employment. I'm sure Mr. Vorland wouldn't like it."

"Of course not," I said quickly, not trusting Ernie to be gentle with her. "We only need to ask you a few questions."

She squinted at me as if noticing me for the first time. "Are you a detective, too?" Her tone was incredulous. If she'd been a man, I'd have resented it, but since she was a woman, I figured she was only amazed that I'd been allowed to participate in what everyone seemed to assume was a strictly masculine line of work.

"I'm an apprentice," I told her, praying that Ernie wouldn't say anything snide or cutting. He might have, too, for his mouth opened, and he looked as if he were on the verge of refuting my claim, but I stepped hard on his toe and pretended, "Oh, I'm so sorry, Mr. Templeton!"

With a wry grin at me, he muttered, "Think nothing of

it, Miss Allcutt." He turned his attention to Miss Williams. "Please, Miss Williams, allow me to introduce you to my . . . apprentice, Miss Mercy Allcutt."

Silently blessing Ernie, and with a friendly nod, I said, "How do you do, Miss Williams?"

"How do you do, Miss Allcutt?" she returned. "And I *was* doing quite well, thank you."

Her meaning was clear, and I was sorry that we had upset her. I gave her an understanding smile. I'd already pulled out my lined green notepad and had my pencil poised.

"And I'm Ernest Templeton, Miss Williams."

"Pleased to meet you, Mr. Templeton." She didn't sound as if she'd spoken the truth, but it was still a gracious thing to have said.

"Now, then," Ernie continued. "We'll make this as quick as we can."

"Thank you." Miss Williams hadn't been paying any mind to our antics. Her gaze kept sweeping the store, looking for customers, I guess. I knew she was nervous, and I suspected her state of agitation was only partially due to fearing a customer would walk off without paying for a book or two. I suppose I'd have been uneasy, too, if I'd been approached by a detective who intended to ask me questions.

"We're here at the request of Mr. Hiram Godfrey, Miss Williams."

That caught her interest with a jolt. Her gaze focused on Ernie, and her expression was one of utter amazement. "Hiram? What in the world does Hiram want to be hiring detectives to talk to me for?"

So Mr. Godfrey's first name was Hiram, was it? I decided it suited him since, for some unaccountable reason, it brought to mind a person of squashy demeanor, probably

because the only other person I'd ever met named Hiram was a boy who'd been in my grade-school class in Boston. That Hiram had been a chubby, pink-cheeked individual who cried all the time.

"He asked me to find you."

She remained astounded. "Why'd he do that?"

"He maintains the belief that you and he were engaged to be married, and then you disappeared."

Miss Williams's cheeks flushed. I couldn't tell if she was angry or embarrassed. "Oh, for heaven's sake!"

Ernie and I exchanged a sidelong glance, and I detected a glint in his eyes, as if he were saying, "See? It pays to get all the information before jumping to conclusions." I nodded slightly in agreement. Even though no words had passed between the two of us, I felt we were in communication just then.

With a deep sigh, Miss Williams closed her eyes for only a second. When she opened them again, she had herself under control. "Mr. Godfrey is mistaken."

"You mean you weren't engaged?" I asked, excitement making my voice a trifle shrill.

"No. Poor Hiram. I wouldn't be surprised if he honestly believed that we were. He's like that, you see. He prefers to believe what he wants to believe rather than what actually *is*, if you understand what I mean."

"Yes," I said thoughtfully, recalling the bouquet of flowers Mr. Godfrey had given me that morning. I'd certainly not encouraged him to think I would welcome such a gift from him.

Shooting me a glance that told me to shut up and let him do the talking, Ernie said, "So you never agreed to marry Mr. Godfrey?"

"I certainly did not, although he asked me to often

enough." She shook her head, which was covered in reddish hair that had been bobbed and was sleekly finger-waved. She was quite an attractive woman, in spite of her eyeglasses. I wondered if Ernie thought so. "We never even took a meal together."

"How did you meet him?" I asked.

"We worked together. I was a saleslady at the Broadway, and he worked in the accounting department."

Hmm. An accountant, eh? Somehow I wasn't surprised.

"You didn't let him know where you were going when you moved, however."

Miss Williams's eyes widened behind her lenses. "Well, what of it? I owed Hiram nothing. We were friends, and that's all. I didn't tell anybody where I was going." She hesitated. "And there's a good reason for that." All at once, her defenses seemed to crumble. She clutched Ernie's arm. "Please, Mr. Templeton, don't tell Hiram where I am. Don't tell *anyone* where I am."

His eyes narrowing, Ernie said, "You sound as if you're worried about something, Miss Williams."

"Not some *thing*," she said ominously. "Some *one*."

Ernie or no Ernie, I decided to step in and try to help this poor woman, who was clearly afraid of something. Or someone. "Please, Miss Williams, can we help you somehow? You appear to be frightened." Ernie rolled his eyes, but I pushed onward. "Are you frightened?"

"I'm terrified," she said starkly. "And, no, you can't help. No one can help me now."

She spoke with such dramatic finality, that I was moved to urge her to confide in me. "Please, Miss Williams, we might be able to help you, if you'll only tell us what's wrong. Whom are you afraid of?"

Again she shook her head. "There's nothing you can do.

I've already spoken to the police in Los Angeles, and they said they couldn't help me. If the police can't help, I doubt that you could."

A thought struck me just then or I might have taken exception to this verbal slight. "Oh, Miss Williams, is it Mr. Godfrey of whom you're afraid?"

She blinked a couple of times. "Hiram? Oh, no. Well . . . I . . . I don't dare tell you. I don't dare tell anyone. He said if I did, he'd kill me."

Profoundly shocked, I blurted out, "Good heavens!"

Ernie gave me such a scowl, I decided I'd better be quiet. I suppose it had been slightly unprofessional to react to a subject's statement so strongly, but I wasn't accustomed to hearing people say they'd been threatened with death.

"Was it Mr. Godfrey who threatened you, Miss Williams?" Ernie asked, serious now.

"Oh, what difference does it make?" She was quite upset by this time. "How did you find me? I didn't tell anyone where I was going! If you can find me, *he* can find me!" She'd begun to wring her hands. I hadn't known people actually did that until I saw evidence before my very eyes.

"You don't need to worry about Mr. Godfrey, Miss Williams. I didn't tell him where we were going today."

"Did you tell anyone else?" She gave Ernie a pleading look. I saw panic behind it, and my heart hurt for her.

"Not a soul. Say, has someone been bothering you?"

"Yes!" She spoke the word loudly, then glanced around the store to make sure nobody else had overheard. In an intense whisper, she went on. "You don't understand, he used to follow me around. I'd see him *everywhere*. Every time I went out with a friend, he'd be there. Every time I went to work, he'd be there. I couldn't do anything without

him showing up. If I even spoke to another gentleman, he'd threaten me."

Good heavens again. This time I didn't say it out loud. "That's terrible, Miss Williams. I'm so sorry."

Ignoring me, Ernie said, "Listen, Miss Williams, I wish you'd tell me who it is you're worried about."

She shook her head almost violently this time. "It doesn't make any difference! Don't you see? Even if you knew who it was, you couldn't do anything. The police said they couldn't do anything unless he hurt me. By that time, it will be too late."

This sounded bad. Or maybe she was exaggerating slightly. She might be a young woman with dramatic tendencies. I've known a few of those. I was about to try to weasel some more information out of her when Ernie spoke again. His tone was quite serious.

"If you're really afraid of this person, whoever he is, maybe you'd better try to get farther away, Miss Williams. Do you have relations in another state?"

Her eyes were huge, and she stared at Ernie as if he were her last hope on earth. "Another state?"

"I've had experience with people like that, Miss Williams. If this person is the kind I'm thinking of, you might not be safe this close to Los Angeles. He lives in Los Angeles, right?"

"Yes." Her whisper held a panicky edge, and she fingered the collar of her dress anxiously. "Do you really think so?"

Ernie was deadly serious now. "Yes. We might be able to help you if you'd only take us into your confidence."

She stood there, looking like an animal in a trap, for about ten seconds, her terror-stricken gaze passing from Ernie to me and back again, before she burst out with, "Oh,

leave me alone!" And she rushed off. I saw her lift her hand to her eyes, as if she were wiping away tears.

"That went well," Ernie said acerbically.

"Poor thing. I feel sorry for her. Do you suppose Mr. Godfrey really threatened to kill her?"

He gave me a sardonic look. "She said it wasn't Godfrey, remember?"

"She didn't, either, say that." I flipped a page in my stenographer's pad and checked my notes. "Well, she didn't say it *wasn't* him, anyhow." Ernie started walking off, and I scurried to catch up with him. "I bet it was."

"You just don't like the guy," said Ernie, who gave me a knowing grin. "I swear, women are so fickle. Here the guy gives you flowers, and you still don't like him."

"I didn't ask him to give me flowers," I said indignantly. "I thought it was an impertinence."

He shook his head in mock sympathy for Mr. Godfrey. "Poor guy. Goes out of his way to do a good deed, and see what happens."

"Nuts."

We had luncheon—I wish I could stop calling it luncheon! We had *lunch* at a very pretty little restaurant called Mijare's. It served Mexican food, which I'd never eaten before, but it was quite tasty. I especially liked something Ernie called *guacamole*, which was green and squishy, and into which we dunked fried chips of what he called *tortillas*.

"Ever had Mexican food before, kiddo?"

"No. It's really good. Spicy."

"Yeah, I don't suppose you get a lot of spicy food in Boston, huh?"

My eyes narrowed. "Is that meant to be an insult?"

He lifted his hands in feigned horror. "An insult? How could it be an insult?"

151

I dipped another tortilla thing into the green squishy stuff, still squinting. "I don't trust you."

"I'm crushed."

He didn't look it. Nevertheless, I decided not to pursue the subject, since I wanted to discuss Miss Williams. "So what did you think about what Miss Williams told us, and why did you tell her to move out of California? Do you really think she might be in some kind of danger from Mr. Godfrey?"

With a chip halfway to his mouth, Ernie eyed me critically. "Why do you insist it's Godfrey? Why can't it be somebody else? She didn't say it was Godfrey."

"He's a very strange man, Ernie, and he gives me the creeps."

"He gave you flowers, is what he gave you. Poor guy."

The waiter came with our plates, which he called *platos*, and set them in front of us. "Hot *platos*," said he. Since I could see steam rising from the interesting mounds of foodstuffs contained thereon, I believed him. I also sensed it would be fruitless to pursue the issue of Mr. Godfrey's oddities.

Dipping my fork into a mound of brownish stuff smothered in cheese, I nibbled carefully. "Oh, my, this is good."

"Refried beans," Ernie said with authority. "That rolled-up thing is an *enchilada*, and the folded-over thing is a *taco*."

"This is a lot of food."

"Yeah, and it's good, too." As if to prove it, he took a big bite of the item he'd called a taco.

I stared, amazed. "You eat it with your fingers?" Then I could have kicked myself when Ernie chewed, swallowed, and grinned broadly.

"Think of it as a sandwich, kiddo. It's a Mexican sandwich."

"Oh. I guess that makes sense."

Still and all, I decided to sample my enchilada first, since I was unaccustomed to picking up food at the luncheon table—except for sandwiches, but this so-called taco didn't look like any kind of sandwich I'd ever met before. I was doing my very best to fit into this new West Coast culture that I'd rushed headlong to meet, but sometimes one has to work up to trying out alien behaviors. Everything was so tasty, however, that pretty soon I was picking up my own taco and eating it with gusto.

"Oh, my, I wonder if Chloe's cook has ever fixed Mexican food," I said at one point before I'd thought better of it. I'd told Ernie that I lived with my sister and her husband, but I hadn't mentioned that they had a house full of servants.

"Your sister has a cook?" His eyebrows lifted, and he looked amused as he took another bite of beans and rice.

Me and my big mouth, as somebody said once. I can't remember who or where. "Yes." I didn't elaborate.

"Yeah? How many other servants does your sister have?"

I sighed. "Not that it's any of your business, but she employs a housekeeper and a cook and a maid." I didn't mention Harvey's chauffeur since, technically, he worked for Harvey and not Chloe. The staff at the Nash household didn't seem excessive to me, but that's probably because I'd grown up in a house with a housekeeper, a cook, a kitchen maid, two housemaids, two chauffeurs, one for my mother and one for my father, and a butler. I didn't mention that, either.

"Ah. I see. Your sister has a big house?"

"Yes. It's fairly large."

"She have any kids?"

I wished he'd drop the subject. "Not yet."

"Ah."

"But that doesn't have anything to do with poor Miss Williams. Why did you tell her to leave the state?"

"I didn't exactly tell her to leave the state, but I wish she would." Suddenly Ernie's face lost its perpetual expression of cynical amusement. He looked downright worried.

Startled by this phenomenon, I said breathlessly, "Good heavens, Ernie, what's the matter?"

His brow furrowed as he took another bite of his enchilada, chewed, and pondered. When he swallowed, he took a sip of water and said, "I'm getting a funny feeling about this whole thing. I don't think it necessarily has anything to do with Godfrey, but Miss Williams was honestly frightened, and I'm afraid she might have reason to be."

Forgetting about my luncheon for the nonce, I laid my fork aside and stared at him. "Why?"

"When I was a cop, I saw stuff like that a lot."

"Stuff like what?"

"Sometimes a man will think a woman cares for him more than she does, and instead of leaving her alone, he'll begin to hound her footsteps. If she tries to avoid him or get away from him, he'll begin to make threats. A couple of times in the three years I worked on the force, the end result was a dead woman and a man who thought he'd been justified in killing her."

"Merciful heavens." My gaze left Ernie's worried face and focused on my plate, although I wasn't seeing the remains of my luncheon. I was remembering articles I'd read in various newspapers back home. "Yes. I think I've heard of that." A chilling memory made me suck in a breath. "In fact, I do believe I read about a fellow who killed a woman he claimed had thrown him over, but her family said they'd never had any sort of relationship at all, that it was all in his head."

Ernie nodded and took another bite of his taco.

"At the time, I thought they must have been mistaken. How could a gentleman make up something like that?" I really wanted to know.

A fount of information, Ernie was not, however. He only said, "Beats me. Some folks are nuts, I guess."

My thoughts returned to Mr. Godfrey, and I considered him as I picked up my fork and resumed eating. He was a very strange individual. He'd brought me flowers for no earthly reason. Of course, Ned had brought me flowers, too. Flowers he'd picked from a public garden. The notion made me want to giggle. Ned was an absurd sort of fellow.

Mr. Godfrey, though . . . well, I thought Mr. Godfrey was very strange. Was he strange enough to stalk a woman and then hurt her because he was under the mistaken impression that she had cheated on him? The notion didn't sit well with me, since he seemed to be focusing a little too much of his attention on me these days.

"Say, kiddo, could you go somewhere with me Saturday evening? I've got to try to get Mrs. Von Schilling's property back, and I think you might be able to help."

You can believe *that* arrested my attention, snapping it away from Mr. Godfrey as if it were a rubber band. "You want my help?" I was absolutely delighted he'd asked. "Of course, I can! Where are we going?"

"Place on Sunset Boulevard. Big place. Home of a gent named Horatio Fortescue."

"I've heard of him." Horatio Fortescue was reputed to be a millionaire, although I'd never heard mention of how he'd made his money. Maybe he'd inherited it. Millionaires didn't grow on every tree; they were rare birds. Why, I'm sure not even my father was a millionaire, although I'd never asked.

"He's having a party Saturday night, and Mrs. Von

Schilling got me an invite. It would look more natural if you'd come with me. We could pretend to be friends of Mrs. Von Schilling."

"Is it a formal party?"

"Naw. Just cocktails and people."

"Cocktails?" I shook my head and endeavored to hide my shock. Didn't *anyone* in Los Angeles take Prohibition seriously? "What will we do when we get there?"

"Mingle. Snoop. Case the joint."

Case the joint? I thought I'd read that phrase in a detective novel or two. I think it means to observe and note layouts and belongings. Or something like that. "What are we looking for?"

He shrugged. "I don't think there will be much looking required. Mrs. Von Schilling wants me to talk to Fortescue for her."

"Why?"

"Evidently, he has something of Mrs. Von Schilling's, and she wants it back."

Hmm. Mrs. Von Schilling didn't strike me as the type to let something out of her grasp if she didn't want to. "How'd he get it?"

He eyed me, chewing, for a moment. "She was someplace she wasn't supposed to be, and a maid in that place took her property and gave it to Fortescue. Mrs. V. wants it back before her husband returns from a business trip to New York City."

Aha! So the slinky Mrs. Von Schilling had a living husband, did she? And she was keeping secrets from him, was she? "How do you propose to get the item back for her, whatever it is?"

"Probably pay for it."

"I beg your pardon?"

"She wants me to make arrangements to pay the man to give her back her property."

I thought about that for a second as I chewed. "But isn't that blackmail?"

Ernie pointed at me with his fork. "Bingo!"

"But isn't that illegal?"

His wry grin told me that had been a silly statement even before he said, "It's how millionaires are made, kiddo."

I remained incredulous. "But . . . but why do people let people like that get away with it? Why don't they tell the police?"

"Would you want all your dirty laundry aired in front of the world?" He shrugged. "Mrs. Von Schilling doesn't. The desire to keep secrets from spouses is what keeps black-mailers in business."

After mulling it over, I was struck with a cynical thought. I'd never had cynical thoughts before I started working for Ernie. Perhaps I truly was learning and would fit in one of these days. "You mean she doesn't want her husband to find out whatever it is she's keeping secret because it's scandalous and he might divorce her, and then she wouldn't be rich anymore."

After swallowing the last bite of his luncheon, Ernie grinned at me. "You're learning fast, kiddo. I'll pick you up at eight. Give me your address."

When I did, he whistled. "You really are a rich girl, aren't you?"

He didn't appear pleased to have his assumption proved correct, but I was irked. "My station in life means absolutely nothing, Ernie Templeton. At the moment, I'm your assistant."

"Secretary."

I glared at him.

TEN

Chloe's dinner party that night was fun, but I do believe my happy mood had more to do with anticipation of my Saturday-night date with Ernie than with the glittering company. I was going to be acting as his assistant! Naturally, I didn't tell anyone whom we were going to visit, although I did share with Mr. Easthope my excitement about meeting and dealing with a real, live blackmailer.

His eyebrows arched over his spectacularly gorgeous eyes. I wasn't sure I'd ever get used to treating him as just another friend, although I hoped we were friends. "Are you sure you'll be quite safe, Miss Allcutt? Dealings with black-mailers can be . . . unsettling." He cleared his throat. "At least, that's what I've always understood."

He sounded a little nervous, and it crossed my mind that perhaps he might have some experience in this realm. Had he been pursued by a blackmailer? I suppose anything is possible, but Mr. Easthope seemed like such a fine gentleman, I couldn't imagine what anyone could find to black-mail him about. According to Chloe, he was above reproach in every way.

"I'll be with Mr. Templeton. I'm sure I'll be safe." It was the truth. I couldn't imagine anyone I'd rather be with in the pursuit of danger than Ernie Templeton, P.I. Although his inappropriate amusement sometimes put me off, I did feel extremely secure in his company. Protected.

"I certainly hope so." Mr. Easthope was clearly not as convinced as I.

Nevertheless, I looked forward to Saturday evening with a good deal of pleasurable anticipation. *This* is why I'd moved to Southern California. *This* is what I'd hoped for in doing so. I was going to get real experience. I was going to get to meet a true villain. A man who had made a fortune preying on the misfortunes of others. Why, I'd read a Sherlock Holmes story about this very thing! I wondered if Mr. Fortescue would appear to be as overtly evil as Mr. Charles Augustus Milverton.

Naturally, Chloe disapproved of my proposed adventure. She was almost as annoying as Mother but didn't wield as much authority over me, so I didn't have to pay as much attention. We went out shopping Saturday morning with the express intention of updating my wardrobe and getting my hair bobbed. I balked as she led me toward a barbershop. "A *barber*shop!" cried I. "I've heard about women getting their hair bobbed at such places, but I never thought *I'd* enter one."

"Sidney has a way with bobbed hair and spit curls, Mercy, and he's wonderful. He's cut my hair forever."

"Not forever," I muttered. "Only since you started living in Los Angeles."

"It seems like forever. And it's ever so much cooler to have bobbed hair. Not to mention freer. Why, you won't know yourself!"

"Hmm. Maybe I don't want to be a stranger to myself, did you ever consider that?"

"Mercy." Her voice was quite stern.

"Oh, very well. But if it turns out badly, I'll never forgive you."

"If you don't like it, just wear hats. For Pete's sake, Mercy, hair grows back, you know."

I did know that, but I'd never had my hair cut in my en-

tire life. I know vanity is a sin, but I thought my hair was rather pretty, for all that it was brown, and even though I'd been looking forward to having it cut, all of a sudden I wasn't sure I wanted to lose it. However, Chloe was relentless, and I got to carry my hair home in a sack, so I didn't feel *too* badly about it. And I have to admit that I looked quite nice with short hair. The bob framed my face, and the side curls were quite fetching. I was actually pretty. Fashionable. Smart. Modern.

And light. After losing all that hair, I felt sort of as if I were about to fly up into the sky, I was so lightheaded.

"You don't have to keep shaking your head, Mercy," Chloe told me at one point, sounding slightly peeved. "You look like you're showing off."

"But it feels so different!"

"Different or not, you don't want the whole world to look at you and know you just got your hair cut. They'll think you're a hick from the sticks."

"Nonsense. Anyhow, why should I care what strangers think of me?"

"Nobody's a stranger to Harvey in this town, Mercy Allcutt, and you'd best remember it."

"Oh." When she put it that way, I guess she had a point. I hadn't been living with Chloe and Harvey for very many weeks, but I'd come to understand that Harvey was truly a big shot in the motion pictures. Therefore, for the rest of the day, I attempted to act blasé about my new hair. It felt *so good!* I can't quite explain what it's like to lose a couple of pounds of hair, but it's definitely a freeing experience.

Shopping with Chloe was fun, even if she did carp at me about accompanying Ernie to a villain's home that night. She took me to the best dressmakers in Los Angeles, and I regret to say I splurged extravagantly. Anyone making the

wages I made with Ernie could never have afforded all the clothes I bought. However, I justified the expenditure by reminding myself that, while I was employed as a private investigator's assistant, and I was determined to do an exemplary job while so employed, there was no law prohibiting me from using my own private funds to refurbish my wardrobe.

Then I felt guilty.

Fortunately, the feeling passed. It did so with a jolt when I thought I espied Mr. Godfrey in the crowd of shoppers thronging the sidewalk in front of several fashionable shops on a street called Beverly Boulevard. I took Chloe's arm. "Stop!"

"What is it?" She turned and looked at me as if I'd lost my mind.

But the conversation I'd had with Ernie on Thursday at Mijare's had remained with me. If Mr. Godfrey was a lunatic who had pursued June Williams, could he be transferring his attention to me? I'd lost him—if he'd even been there—in the crowd, however, so I couldn't do anything about him. Not that I'd have been able to do anything about him anyway. How could a person eliminate another person's fantasies, anyhow? I had no idea, but I felt distinctly creepy for several minutes.

And then, wonder of wonders, we ran into Ned. He looked out of place among the well-dressed shoppers along Beverly Boulevard, but he whipped his cloth cap from his head and smiled at us. Actually, he smiled at me. I'm not sure he even noticed Chloe.

" 'Lo, Miss Allcutt."

Since he'd stopped dead in front of us, I couldn't do much but respond in kind. Not that I wouldn't have been polite, but it was slightly awkward to be standing still while

161

the mob flowed like a river around us. "Hello, Ned. Fine day, isn't it?"

"Yes."

"Um . . . Ned, this is my sister, Chloe Nash. Chloe, may I present . . . Ned." Curse it, I wish somebody had bothered to tell me his last name. I'd also introduced him to her instead of the other way around, but nobody present was a stickler for polite forms of address, so it was all right. "Chloe, Ned works in the Figueroa building where I work."

"Oh," said Chloe, bored. "Hello, Ned."

Ned nodded, but he didn't look away from me. "You got your hair cut."

"Yes, I did. Do you like it?"

"You look modern."

I couldn't tell if he approved of my newly attained modernity, but I also didn't much care. "Thanks, Ned. Well, we'll be getting along now."

"Oh. Okay." He stepped aside, and I forgot all about him in the excitement of buying new clothes.

It wasn't merely clothing I purchased that day. I also found a cunning, but tasteful, rug with flowers on it that would look very nice in my office, and a framed picture of a fall scene that reminded me of home to hang on the office wall. Since I didn't want to upset Mrs. Biddle or deal with Ned, I also purchased a small hammer and some nails, with which I aimed to hang the picture my very own self come Monday morning.

After we got home, I sorted through all my newly acquired frocks and suits, and decided upon a fetching outfit for my foray into blackmailing that night. It was a black faille crepe frock whose skirt had three scalloped layers (scallops were all the vogue that year) that came down just below my knee. When I donned black silk stockings and threw a black crepe

cloak over my shoulders, I thought I looked wildly sophisticated. As I gazed at my reflection in the mirror, I decided Ernie would have nothing to object to in my appearance. I was terribly excited about meeting Mr. Fortescue, and knowing I looked my best helped boost my self-regard tremendously.

"I want to meet this Mr. Templeton of yours," Chloe announced when I descended the staircase to wait for Ernie in the living room.

"He's not *my* Mr. Templeton, but you can certainly meet him."

"Huh."

He rang the bell promptly at eight. I'd been poised to answer the door, because I didn't want him to think we in the Nash household were a bunch of snobs, but Mrs. Biddle beat me to it. I was right behind her. I know I blinked when I saw him.

"You're all dressed up!" I cried, and then felt stupid. But he looked very handsome in his black evening suit. We'd look quite well together, I decided.

"So are you," he said, frowning at me.

"I guess you're expected," grumbled Mrs. Biddle, and she stepped aside to allow Ernie into the foyer. It was a lovely foyer, with a floor covered in Spanish tiles and lots of pretty house plants that got plenty of sunlight from the big windows on either side of the double door.

Ernie looked around, a bland expression on his face. "Nice place."

"Yes. My sister and her husband, you know."

"Yeah. Nash. Isn't that their last name?"

"Yes."

He was holding his hat, which was polite of him. I hadn't known what to expect of him. In the office, he was relaxed

to a fault, but I guess he could use good manners when he had to. "Say, your brother-in-law wouldn't be Harvey Nash, would he? The movie guy?"

Drat! I was hoping he wouldn't have made the connection. However, Harvey's profession didn't have anything to do with me, so I owned up to it. "Yes. Come into the living room and meet my sister, Ernie. She's been dying to meet you."

"Yeah?" He didn't believe me.

Undaunted by his doubt, I said, "Follow me," and led him into the living room. Chloe sat in a chair by the fireplace (in which no fire burned, this being July and all). She glanced up, then rose. I could tell she was favorably impressed by Ernie's looks. She sauntered over to us. "You must be the Mr. Templeton Mercy is always talking about." She held out her hand for Ernie to take, which he did.

"I'm not always talking about him," I said with some heat. "I'm always talking about my *job*. There's a big difference."

A flicker of his usual wicked grin passed across his face before he turned it into a normal, everyday smile. He didn't respond to Chloe's comment. "Pleased to meet you, Mrs. Nash."

"Where are you taking my sister, Mr. Templeton? She wouldn't tell me. She only said it had something to do with blackmail. That's a bit worrying to Harvey and me."

"She didn't tell you the name?" Ernie glanced at me with what looked like absolute approval, although I wasn't sure, since I'd never seen that expression on his face. And I'd certainly never expected it to be directed at me.

"No. My kid sister is the soul of discretion." Chloe gave me a sardonic smile. "But I'd feel better about this evening's jaunt if I knew where she was going."

"It'll be all right, Mrs. Nash. There's no danger involved. We're only going to be attending a small party on Sunset Boulevard."

"Sunset. My, my."

"Chloe," I said, irked, "I'm a grown-up now, remember. I'll be fine. Ernie will take care of me."

"Oh, Ernie will, will he?" Her artfully penciled eyebrows arched over her pretty blue eyes. I guess she was surprised to discover that Ernie and I were on a first-name basis, but she shouldn't have been. I'd told her before that evening that Ernie was a very unceremonious individual. On the other hand, perhaps her incredulity was directed more toward what she perceived as my stuffiness than Ernie's easiness. Nuts. I've always gotten along well with Chloe, and I love her dearly, but she did have a very prudish mental image of me, and I don't believe I deserved it.

Ignoring her barbed comment, I said, "Let's be off, Ernie." I turned to Chloe. "You don't need to wait up for me."

"We aren't going to be late," Ernie said.

"Oh, it's not a problem," said Chloe. By which, I knew she meant that she *would* wait up for me, and that nothing I could say would make her alter her intention.

Sometimes it's difficult being the youngest member of the family.

Mr. Fortescue's house was truly fabulous. Sunset Boulevard twists and twines around a woodsy area of Los Angeles. All we could see was foliage for the most part, but every now and then an elaborate gate would loom up from the shrubbery. At one point Ernie turned the Studebaker onto what looked like a side road, but which was, in reality, a private drive that ended at another enormous wrought-iron

gate with scrollwork and all over it.

"Fortescue's," he said.

"Good heavens," I said.

"Blackmail pays."

"I guess so."

A uniformed guard appeared at Ernie's window, which he rolled down. "Templeton," he told the guard.

"Yes, sir." The guard held a clipboard, and he looked at it, probably searching for Ernie's name. He must have found it, because he stepped back, pressed a button, the gate started sliding open, and he said, "Thank you, sir."

"Sure thing." And Ernie drove through the parted gates.

While Sunset Boulevard had been dark, with very few street lamps aglow, Mr. Fortescue's yard was as bright as day. Actually, *yard* is too puny a word to describe the lavish spectacle into which Ernie drove. *Park* is more like it. Ernie turned toward the left, and drew up before two more uniforms, these being worn by young men. As I sat in the car and waited, Ernie got out, handed his keys to one of the attendants (who looked upon the Studebaker with barely concealed contempt), and then came around to my side and opened the door.

"Let's go, kiddo."

So, with a swirl of my black cape to give me courage, I took Ernie's arm, and we walked along a path lined by trellises dripping with roses and overhung with Chinese lanterns. It was a very impressive display. I thought I'd mention to Chloe how beautiful the roses were. I thought the lanterns were a trifle excessive to be considered tasteful. Then again, according to my mother, the words *tasteful* and *Los Angeles* should never be used in a sentence together. She's prejudiced, however.

All the females employed by Mr. Fortescue wore tidy

black uniforms with black caps, white aprons, white stockings, and black shoes. These liveried ladies stuck out against the ruby red of the interior walls like zebras swimming in tomato soup. And the chandeliers! Well, let me just say that the chandeliers were remarkable. Totally tasteless, and absolutely jangling with crystal hangy things. I can't remember what they're called.

Surprisingly, at least to me, was the fact that we were met in the huge black-and-white tiled entryway by a perfectly precious, and very tiny, black French poodle. It danced across the tiles with a tippity-tap of little doggie claws and slid to a stop before us, wagging its poofy tail and yipping. Its bark reminded me of the sound a baby's rubber toy will make when squeezed.

I've always been very fond of dogs, and I knelt to greet this one with at least as much enthusiasm as it met us with, although I refrained from yipping. "Hello there," said I, enchanted.

Its tail wagged harder, and I picked up the dog, heedless of dog hair on my new frock (truthfully, I'd been told by Mr. Easthope, who owns two of them, that poodles don't shed). As I did so, I noticed a butler standing there, impassively watching me.

"May I take your wrap, Madam?"

"Certainly. What's the doggie's name?" I unhooked my cape, and Ernie caught it before it hit the floor. He handed it to the butler with a frown for me. The puppy licked my cheek, and I laughed with delight.

"Rosie, Madam." If he'd told me he was going to shoot the dog in the morning, he couldn't have sounded more gloomy. Perhaps Rosie wasn't the enchanting creature I thought she was. More likely, the butler was an old grump.

"What a charming name for a charming dog."

"Bingo," muttered Ernie, for a reason I was to learn shortly. He scratched the poodle behind the ear and said, "Cheers, Rosie."

I guess because I grew up in a well-to-do family that entertained a lot, I've never been shy about attending parties or other social occasions where I didn't know many people. It didn't embarrass me in the least to carry Rosie into the huge room in which the main party was going on. As Ernie led the way, I whispered at him, "Why'd you say 'bingo'?"

He whispered back, "You wanted to know what Mrs. Von Schilling's property is that Mr. Fortescue has and that she wants back, didn't you?"

"Yes."

"You're holding it."

My gaze flew to Rosie, who was perched in my arms and watching all the people gathered in the front room with sparklingly alert brown eyes. "Oh!"

"Right. I don't suppose your handbag is big enough to hold her."

He was probably joking, but his comment gave me an idea. "No, but perhaps I can arrange something else."

"Eh?" He eyed me, startled, but I didn't respond because we were among the throng by that time.

It was certainly a glittering ensemble. I'd never seen so many famous people all gathered in one place, although Chloe and Harvey had invited their share of picture people to dinner several times. I nearly fainted when I saw Douglas Fairbanks chatting with a couple of women, one of whom looked like Vilma Bankey. While it's true I grew up with money, even rich girls get a thrill when they see famous people who have made their hearts go soft and mushy in the flickers. Theda Bara, dressed in a black dress infinitely slinkier than mine, slouched against a fireplace on the far

wall, holding a cigarette in a long, black holder. Smoke wafted from her cigarette, and she looked bored—or perhaps she was only trying to look bored. Whatever her intent, she looked terribly glamorous and mysterious. Not unlike Mrs. Von Schilling, in actual fact.

Ernie nudged me with his elbow. When I glanced up at him, he leaned over and whispered, "Look over there. It's John Barrymore. I understand he's starring in *Don Juan* for the Warner brothers, and it's going to have sound."

I stared at him, hugging Rosie the while. "You mean, a picture will actually *talk?*"

"So they say. It'll be interesting to see if we can understand what they're saying."

"I always thought the cameras were too loud to permit talking."

"Guess not. Say, there's one of the Warner brothers right there." He indicated a gentleman talking to John Barrymore, whose eyes were half closed and whom, I regret to say, looked rather the worse for drink.

"Do you know him?"

"Naw. I've only met a few of the bright lights in the flickers."

I spotted someone else. "Oh, my goodness, is that Rudolph Valentino?" I almost dropped Rosie, I was so amazed.

"Looks like it from here. But say, I've got to talk to our genial host. Want to meet him?"

I thought about it as I petted Rosie. "I don't believe so, thank you. I think I'll mingle a bit." I was good at mingling. Having money might not be all it's cracked up to be, but it does give one confidence. For the most part. I suppose there are some wealthy people in the world who wouldn't feel comfortable at a party where they didn't know anyone,

but I didn't suffer from that problem.

Although I had formulated what I considered a brilliant scheme and was eager to put it to the test, I waited until I saw Ernie approach a heavy-set man with a pencil-thin black moustache and perfectly elegant evening clothes. Aha. Mr. Fortescue, who had made his fortune by blackmailing people. I wondered how many people in that stellar mob were there because they were afraid not to be.

After pinpointing where Mr. Fortescue and Ernie were in the room, I meandered over to a table laden with all sorts of edible treats. Hoisting Rosie to a position against my hip, I held her firm with my elbow. Then, arming myself with a plate and filling it with liver pâté, a few tiny sausages, some cheese, and two little meatballs, I put her down on the floor and gave her a snitch of liver pâté. She was my friend for life after that.

That being the case, and with an air of perfect innocence, I wandered over to the door to the foyer, where stood the butler, poised to answer the door should some exalted personage—or even another couple like Ernie and me—ring the bell. I stumbled a trifle, and pasted an expression of great pain on my face, dropping as I did so one of the meatballs for Rosie's delectation. She obliged.

"Excuse me."

The butler turned and lifted an eyebrow at me. Probably Lulu would have been intimidated. I'd grown up with butlers stuffier than this one lording it over the house in which I lived, so I wasn't. "Madam?" said he in a snooty voice.

"I'm terribly sorry to disturb you, but I'm feeling ill. Could you please direct me to the ladies' parlor?" The look on my face was one I'd practiced when much younger. Chloe and I used to see which of us could appear more pitiable in an attempt to weasel candy money from our

grandparents. I almost always got more money than she did, although I'm not sure if it's because I looked pathetic or because I was younger and had long brown braids and big blue eyes.

He thawed. I'd figured he would. "Of course, Madam." He gestured at a uniformed footman. "Henry, please show this lady to the ladies' retiring room."

The ladies' retiring room? Merciful heavens.

Henry was a young man with an air of awed interest about him. This was probably his first big party, and it was crammed with famous people. He bowed to me, even though I wasn't famous. "Right this way."

"Thank you so much, Henry." Deciding I might as well pretend to be a starlet, I gave him a glorious smile and his Adam's apple bobbed when he swallowed. I, still carrying my plate of doggie delectables, followed Henry, and Rosie, bless her greedy little heart, followed me.

Her toenails made a clackety noise on the tiles. I hoped Henry wouldn't try to shoo her away or put two and two together. When we got to the ladies' parlor, he made as if to get rid of Rosie, but I forestalled him. "Oh, please, let her come in with me. She's such a sweetheart."

"Very well, Madam." He was so bedazzled, I doubt that he even rolled his eyes as he turned to go back to his post beside the butler. "Oh, Henry," I said as he started off. "I'm afraid I'm going to have to leave the party because I feel so unwell. Would you please fetch my cape. It's a black crepe one with embroidery down the front." I'd already anticipated this sly move with two dollar bills which I thrust at Henry. "And if you could please tell Mr. Templeton that I'm unwell? He'll have to take me home."

The next part might be tricky. However, under the policy of "nothing ventured, nothing gained," I decided to

go ahead and try. Leaving both the plate of goodies and Rosie in the ladies' parlor (I set the plate on a counter where Rosie couldn't get at it), I left the room and stood near the ladies' parlor door, trying very hard to look as if I were in the process of dying, and waited for my cape and Ernie. My cape arrived first, carried by yet a third uniformed lackey. I handed him another dollar bill and another brilliant, but pitiable, smile. "Thank you so much. Is Henry fetching Mr. Templeton? I do feel terribly ill." To prove it, I put a hand to my brow as if checking for fever.

"I'm awful sorry, ma'am," this latest fellow said, goggling at me. The black crepe frock was truly quite lovely, and my newly bobbed hair made me look the picture of fashion. At least, I believe it did. I couldn't think of any other reason for him to stare so, unless he was memorizing my features in case I later got famous.

Making my smile a trifle more pathetic, I said, "Thank you so much," and prayed he'd go away.

"Is there anything I can do for you, ma'am?"

"No, but I do thank you. You're very kind."

My nerves were jumping like boys on several pogo sticks as I stood there, and I wanted to yell at him to go away and leave me alone.

He didn't get the hint. "Are you sure? Would you like something to drink or anything?"

I couldn't stand much more of his attention. "No, thank you. In fact, I feel quite ill." And, lifting my hand to my mouth, I ducked into the ladies' parlor once more. Rosie jumped on me as if we'd been parted for a year or three. I knelt to fend her off—I was wearing new black silk stockings, and didn't want to get a ladder—and listened for all I was worth, praying I'd hear the sound of that pestilential boy's retreat. I did, and I nearly fainted from relief.

"Wait here another little minute, Rosie," I said, and exited the room, giving her a sliver of cheese to keep her company.

And there, thank God! was Ernie Templeton, walking down the hallway toward me, his face like a thundercloud. I didn't care about that.

"What the devil is going on? That guy back there—" he hooked a thumb over his shoulder "—said you're sick. Damn it, Mercy—"

"Stay there," I commanded crisply, and ducked back into the ladies' parlor. There I scooped up Rosie, threw my cape over both her and my arm, wrapped the remaining sausages, cheese and meatballs in my handkerchief, and stuffed them into my pocket, praying they wouldn't stain my gorgeous new frock beyond redemption. From that pocket, I could fetch tidbits and feed them to Rosie under the cover of my cape. Then I left the parlor, jerked my head in Ernie's direction—I didn't dare take his arm for fear I'd drop something—and said, "Let's go."

"Damn it, Mercy—"

Through gritted teeth, I said, "Let's *go!*" I gave him as significant a look as I could under the circumstances, and stepped out smartly toward the front door, still attempting to appear as if I were about to faint from whatever mysterious illness I'd suddenly developed. The two behaviors weren't necessarily compatible, but I do believe I carried them off rather well.

He didn't understand, of course, but he did as I requested. The butler opened the door, and we departed from Mr. Fortescue's party approximately twenty minutes after arriving at it. Ernie grumbled all the way to the Studebaker. I didn't say a word until the uniformed car caddies had opened my door for me, and Ernie started the engine. Actually, I didn't speak then, either, because I was too busy

rescuing food from my pockets and praying my dress wasn't stained.

As I did the above, Rosie crawled to freedom, and Ernie uttered a startled, "Shit!" But by that time we were almost to Mr. Fortescue's huge gate. I threw my cape over the pup as we passed the guardhouse. If the guard happened to glance into the car, and providing he could see anything at all in the dark, he might have wondered why my cape wiggled so much, but he didn't say anything, opened the gate, and we were off.

Ernie drove approximately three blocks on Sunset Boulevard before he pulled the Studebaker to the curb and parked, turned, and stared at me as if he'd never seen me before. "I can't believe you did that!"

I gave him one of my innocent smiles. "Did what? You wanted Mrs. Von Schilling's property back, didn't you? This is her property, isn't it?" I was cuddling Rosie at the time. "I hope to heaven you didn't give that horrid man any money."

"I never even got to meet him. That guy in livery came and told me you were sick."

"Good." I believe I should be forgiven if I felt a sense of pride over a job well done.

Ernie shook his head for about ten seconds before he started driving again. I noticed his shoulders shaking, though, and I was pretty sure he was laughing. My assumption was confirmed when we pulled up in front of Chloe's house, and he had to wipe his eyes.

Turning to me, he held out his hand. "Mercy Allcutt, allow me to shake your hand."

"What for?"

"For pulling off one of the greatest feats of skullduggery in Los Angeles history. You got the better of Horatio Fortescue. I don't think anyone else has ever done that— well, and lived to talk about it."

174

I felt my eyes open wide in alarm. "Good heavens, is he truly dangerous?"

"Well, yeah. Why do you think people are so afraid of him?"

I swallowed, much as Henry's companion had done when I'd smiled at him. "But . . . but I thought he was only a blackmailer. I thought that's why people were afraid of him."

"I suppose that's his main business."

"Then you don't think I'm in any physical danger?"

"How could you be? He never even met you. Hell, he never even met *me*. He doesn't know you took the dog. If he asks, the butler will say the pooch followed some lady into the bathroom, but nobody knows your name and nobody saw you leave with the dog." He chuckled again. "God, that's priceless."

"So can I be your assistant now?" I didn't expect a positive response, but as long as I was on the one-can-but-try theme, I figured the question was worth the asking.

"You're turning out to be a pretty good secretary, but let's not rush things."

I sniffed and thrust the dog at him. "Very well, then, *you* get to take care of Rosie until Mrs. Von Schilling comes to fetch her."

"Hey!"

"Thank you for an interesting evening, Ernie," I said as I opened my own door and exited the Studebaker. "I'll see you bright and early Monday morning."

I heard him holler, "Mercy!" as I tripped up the walkway to Chloe's house.

When I told Chloe what had happened (naturally, she'd waited up for me, although she hadn't had to wait long. I walked through the door of her house at around nine-thirty that night), she laughed so hard she claimed I gave her a stomachache.

ELEVEN

When I arrived at work slightly before eight o'clock on Monday morning, after having greeted the emery board–wielding Lulu LaBelle in a friendly manner, I saw that a note lay on the office floor, shoved there at some point during the weekend, I guess. I picked it up, and was surprised to find it was addressed to me.

My nose wrinkled when I opened it and discovered it to be an epistle of love signed "Your Adorer." I threw it in the waste-paper basket and muttered, "Ew."

However, I didn't let Mr. Godfrey's insanity bother me for very long. I'd done an admirable piece of work on Saturday, and I was proud of myself. Even Ernie had appreciated my ingenuity and daring. True, he hadn't actually said so, but he had shaken my hand and told me I'd done a good job. Although I'm sure it bespeaks a weakness in my character, I was hoping for a little more praise that morning. I spent my first few minutes in the office throwing wilted flowers away and washing out vases.

And then, after taking a careful measure of the office and determining where I should hang my newly acquired purchase, I stood on one of my office chairs, hammered a nail into the wall as if I'd been doing such things all my life, and hung up the fall-foliage picture. It looked quite well there when I climbed down from the chair and scrutinized it. Placing the rug, an oval in muted green and brown with yellow flowers, on the floor, I concluded that the place looked ever so much more inviting than it had. And the

picture and rug hadn't cost all that much, either.

My state of elation lasted until Ernie got to work about three-quarters of an hour after I did. After redecorating, I'd dusted the office, straightened the papers on my desk, and fended off Ned, who seemed inclined to want to use my office as his reading closet, and was still feeling smug. I'd half expected Ernie to be carrying Rosie when he arrived at the office. His arms were empty of poodles, however.

"Good morning," I said brightly as Ernie slouched into the room.

"Yeah," he said, and, after stopping dead in his tracks for approximately five seconds as he surveyed my improvements to my room, he went into his office. I heard his hat land on the floor, heard him say, "Damn," and assumed he was picking it up.

Well, this was no fun. I rose from my desk and went into his office, stopping before his desk with my pencil and secretarial pad clutched in my hands, poised to begin my work week. "Where's Rosie?" I said by way of starting a conversation.

He glanced at me, scowling hideously. I resented that. I was a heroine, curse it, and deserved more than ugly looks and scowls. "Where the hell do you think it is? I gave it back to Mrs. Von Schilling."

This information startled me. "Already? But it was Sunday."

"It was Saturday night," he said with what I can only describe as an evil grin. "Mrs. Von Schilling was most appreciative."

I wasn't sure what that grin meant, but I pursued the subject because it interested me. "I should hope so. You fulfilled your duties to her admirably."

"I sure did."

The grin broadened, and I began to get an inkling of the meaning he was attempting thereby to convey. I gasped and then could have kicked myself. Darn it, I didn't want him to think of me as a spoiled, innocent little rich girl from stuffy old Boston! Lifting my chin, I said, "What do you think of the improvements I made to the outer office?"

"Improvements, eh? Well, I guess." He uttered a bark of laughter, the fiend, but sobered at once. "June Williams is dead."

This information came at me so abruptly and was so unexpected that I couldn't quite take it in at once. It certainly drove all thoughts of redecorating out of my head. "June . . ." Then it hit me, and I gasped again. "Good heavens!" Sinking into one of the chairs facing Ernie's desk, I whispered, "How did it happen?"

"She was murdered sometime between Friday night and Sunday morning."

"Murdered!" I dropped my pencil.

"Yeah. And I'm afraid I might have been the unwitting cause of it, since I'm the one who followed her to Pasadena. Apparently, somebody followed me."

"Oh, surely, it's not your fault."

He shrugged, and I knew I hadn't reassured him.

"Mr. Godfrey," I said in an awful voice.

"You don't know that, and neither do I."

"It must have been he."

"Nuts. I've got a friend on the L.A.P.D. coming in today to talk to me about the case. He's the one who tipped me off that she was in Pasadena."

"Why was he interested in her?"

"He wasn't until I asked him about her. But I guess she filed a report saying somebody was following her." He heaved a deep sigh and leaned back in his chair. Then he

leaned forward again. "I miss my squeak," he said bitterly.

"Nonsense. What can we do about this?"

"About what? My squeak?"

His deliberate obtuseness irked me. "About the murder, of course!"

"*You* can't do a damned thing. I'm going to talk to Phil and see if we can come up with something."

"Phil is your friend on the police force?"

"Phil Bigelow. He's about the only honest cop I know."

That was certainly a depressing observation. "Are you going to ask him about Babs Houser, too?"

Another huge sigh met this question. "Ah, hell, I guess so. He might be interested because of the Matty Bumpas connection."

Silence reigned as Ernie brooded and I tried to get my nerves to stop leaping around like frightened rabbits. That poor woman. And we'd just spoken to her a few days earlier. I'd never met anyone who'd been murdered until then. The knowledge that my world had expanded to include one didn't make me feel very good. "How did it happen?"

The nasty look he directed at me was wholly unwarranted. "I already told you. She was murdered."

I gave him back glare for glare. "Yes, I know you did, but you didn't tell me *how* she was murdered. For heaven's sake, Ernie Templeton, you're an intelligent man. Stop pretending to be dense."

"Dense, am I? Maybe you just can't make yourself clear. Ever think of that?"

What a childish conversation! Nevertheless, I strove to get an answer from him. "How was she murdered, Ernie?"

"Strangled."

"Oh!" I don't know why I was so much more horrified to

179

hear that than I would have been had he said "shot" or "hit by a car," but I was.

"Yeah. I guess it was an ugly scene. She'd been packing to leave town."

"You mean, she was going to follow your advice?"

"I guess. Only it came too late. Maybe I should have wired her to leave town before I went to see her," he added with scathing acidity.

"It's not your fault. The only person at fault is the man who murdered her."

He thought about that, his head cocked to one side. "Yeah, it had to be a man."

For some reason, this statement surprised me. "Was there any doubt?"

"Naw. I doubt that a girl could have pulled the cord so tightly." He eyed me, and for almost the first time since I'd met him, his eyes were serious. "I don't want you wandering out on the streets by yourself, Mercy. One woman has been killed, and I don't want to add you to the killer's list."

"*Me?*" I was so astonished, my voice squeaked. "Why in the world would anyone want to kill *me?*"

"I don't know. That's the problem. I don't know why anyone would want to kill June Williams, either, but somebody did. If we're dealing with a lunatic, and if whoever the lunatic is found her by following us when we went to Pasadena, he might target you next."

Pondering our conversation with June Williams last Thursday—good heavens, that had only been three days before—I murmured, "She was obviously afraid of someone."

"Yeah. Wish she'd told us who."

"Whom," I corrected without thinking.

He only frowned at me.

I remembered that so-called love note I'd found on the office floor that morning, and recalled what June Williams had said about Mr. Godfrey believing against all reality that she loved him and he was engaged to marry her. More shaken than I'd care to admit, I said, "Just a minute. I want to show you something." Retreating to my own office for a moment, I retrieved the note from the waste-paper basket. When I returned to Ernie's office, I held it out to him. "You'd better look at this."

He took the note and read it, his eyes going wide, and that sarcastic grin of his annoying me yet once more. "So you've got yourself an adorer, do you?"

My hand itched to slap his face, but I, being a lady whether I wanted to be one or not, restrained myself. "It's not funny. I think it's from Mr. Godfrey. Do you suppose he's transferred his . . ." I couldn't offhand think what to call it, so I settled on ". . . attentions to me?"

"You don't know it's Godfrey," said Ernie as if he were drumming a lesson into a slow student's head. "For all you know, it could be anyone. That Easthope character, even."

"Francis Easthope?" I stared at him, appalled. "Heavens, no! Mr. Easthope is a perfect gentleman."

"He's a fruit," grumbled Ernie. "However, that probably lets him off the hook in this case."

He's a fruit? Whatever did that mean? I didn't have a chance to ask because the door to the outer office opened. I rose from my chair, prepared to do my duty, but the man who'd entered walked into Ernie's office without secretarial intervention.

"Ernie, you old son of a gun!" he cried out jauntily.

A tall man, he was probably Ernie's age, only his complexion was fairer than Ernie's. He was also a good deal heavier than my employer, who was lean and muscular. I

had deduced the muscularity from what I'd seen of his fore-arms when he'd rolled up his shirtsleeves. This man wasn't wearing one of the police department's blue uniforms, so I deduced he was on the detective force.

"Phil Bigelow, how the devil are you?"

Ignoring me, Ernie surged out of his chair, came out from behind his desk, and grabbed the other man's hand, pumping it heartily. "Killed anybody lately?"

"Not so's you'd notice," the man called Phil said, laughing. Personally, I thought the comment had been in deplorable taste, but nobody'd asked me. "You?"

"No." Ernie sobered as he headed back to his chair. "But I managed to get somebody killed."

There he went again: harping on his responsibility in the June Williams murder. As far as I was concerned, the only person to blame for Miss Williams's demise was Mr. Hiram Godfrey.

Mr. Bigelow tossed his hat at Ernie's coat stand. His aim was better than Ernie's, and his hat landed squarely on a peg. Feeling left out, I cleared my throat.

Ernie lifted his eyebrows, then remembered his manners—if he had any. "Oh, yeah. Mercy Allcutt, this disreputable emissary from the Los Angeles Police Department's detective force is Phil Bigelow. Phil, my secretary, Mercy Allcutt."

"How do you do?" I said politely, holding out my hand for Mr. Bigelow to take.

He did, after tipping a wink at Ernie. I didn't care for that wink, although I sensed it would be better to conceal my indignation, since I didn't want him to think I was a prig. I also didn't want to be left out of the conversation that would certainly ensue between the two men. "I'm fine, Miss Allcutt. And you?"

"Very well, thank you." For some reason, when I was with Ernie and I behaved as I'd been brought up to behave, I felt like an insufferable stuffed shirt. However, as much as I didn't like the feeling, even more did I believe (still do, for that matter) that manners are important and smooth over a good many otherwise uncomfortable social situations. Not that it matters. I only mention it.

Mr. Bigelow took the chair next to mine and directed his next comment at Ernie. "So, what's up? I understand why you feel bad about the Williams woman, but it wasn't your fault. If she'd bothered to tell anybody what was going on, we might have helped her."

"Yeah? How?"

Mr. Bigelow shrugged, but admitted, "I don't know." He shook his head and it looked to me as if this admission dissatisfied him. "You know how it is. If a guy goes nuts and starts giving a broad grief, there isn't a whole lot the police can do about it unless he actually hurts her, and then it's generally too late."

That was more or less what June Williams herself had said, and I was beginning to think there was something wrong with the laws if it was so. Because I was there and an integral part of the office staff—in truth, I *was* the office staff—I felt justified in asking a question. "Aren't there any laws against harassing people?"

Both men looked at me as if they'd forgotten I was there and weren't pleased to be reminded.

I frowned back. "Well? Aren't there?"

The men exchanged a glance. Ernie spoke first. "Actually . . . I don't think there are. Phil?" He made a sweeping gesture, as if he were an announcer at a vaudeville show and was welcoming a new act to the stage.

"None that I know of. There's disturbing the peace, of

course, but you only get that if a guy starts yelling and bothers the neighbors. And it's illegal to break and enter. If a guy hits a woman, it's a crime, I suppose. But if somebody wants to be on the same public street as another person, it's not a crime."

My mind went back to Saturday, when I thought I recognized Mr. Godfrey among the shoppers on Beverly Boulevard. Coincidence? I couldn't be sure, but I didn't much like it. "I should think it would be a crime to . . . to . . . stalk another person. For a man to treat a woman as if she were . . . were his *prey*, for heaven's sake! To follow her everywhere for the purpose of mischief. Or even if the party of the first part only harasses the party of the second part, why isn't that a crime?"

Ernie shrugged. Mr. Bigelow didn't do even that much, but only stared at me, bemused. Ernie said, "We aren't responsible for the laws. The laws are . . . well . . . the laws. And nobody's passed one like that so far."

I was indignant, not so much because these men didn't seem to know much about what I had presumed to be their business, but because apparently there were no safeguards in place to protect women like June Williams from maniacs like Hiram Godfrey. "Do you mean to tell me that Mr. Godfrey can pursue a woman against her will, as if she were a deer in the forest, and kill her, and there's no law against it?"

"There's a law against killing her," Ernie said. "But if a man follows a woman around, it's not a crime."

I thought about that for a moment. "Well, there should be. Mr. Godfrey hounded that woman out of Los Angeles, and then went all the way to Pasadena and killed her! If the police had stopped him from bothering her in the first place, she'd still be alive today."

184

"The police can't enforce laws that don't exist," Ernie reminded me. Not that I needed a reminder.

"There should be," I repeated stubbornly.

"Yeah, maybe. But the fact remains that there aren't. Now we have to solve the poor woman's murder, and I'm afraid I can't take your hunches about Mr. Godfrey as proof of anything, much less that he killed June Williams."

"They're more than hunches, confound you! There's proof!" Against all the lessons in deportment my mother drummed into my head, I pointed at the piece of paper on Ernie's desk.

"Oh, yeah. Take a look at this, Phil." Ernie handed Mr. Bigelow the note from my supposed adorer. "I hope she's wrong, but Mercy here thinks the killer might be after her now."

Mr. Bigelow's face took on a troubled cast. He was serious when he looked from the card to me. "Where did you find this, Miss Allcutt?"

"On the office floor when I came to work this morning. It looked as if somebody had shoved it under the door over the weekend."

"Is the building locked on Saturdays and Sundays?"

"I . . . don't know." I turned a questioning glance upon Ernie, who shook his head.

"No," he said. "Some of the lawyers' offices are open on Saturday until noon."

Mr. Bigelow nodded, and I said, "Ah." I'd forgotten that most businesses were open five and a half or six days a week— if I'd ever known it. The realization made me appreciate Ernie, who allowed me two full days off over the weekends.

"Well, that doesn't help us much then," said Mr. Bigelow.

Focusing his attention on me, Ernie said, "I don't want

185

you to go out alone, Mercy. If—and it's a big if—but *if* the same madman who pursued Miss Williams has transferred his affections—"

"Affections? Ha!" I know it was impolite to interrupt, but I couldn't help myself.

"Yeah, but listen to me," Ernie went on. "Whatever you call 'em, I don't want you going out alone. You hear me?"

"Of course, I hear you. I'm sitting right in front of you." For some reason, I was annoyed. I suppose he had only my interests at heart, but I didn't appreciate being handed down orders from my employer. They reminded me too much of my mother's orders which had restricted me from doing anything at all, ever.

"I know you're sitting in front of me," Ernie said with a perfectly tremendous glower, "but I want you to understand that this is serious. A woman's been murdered, for God's sake."

"There's no need to take that tone with me, Ernest Templeton. I fully comprehend the situation. I will take care never to be caught out alone where Mr. Godfrey can get at me."

Ernie's face took on the same thunderous cast it had taken that night at Mr. Fortescue's house. "Damn it, you *don't* fully comprehend! You keep saying it's Godfrey, but we don't know that. It could be anybody on God's green earth!"

I huffed. "Yes, yes, *you* keep saying *that*."

"He's right, Miss Allcutt," Mr. Bigelow said. I got the impression he was attempting to inject calm into a heated situation. "We really don't know who killed that woman, or if Godfrey or anybody else you might know was involved. For all we know, Godfrey might just be a poor sap who honestly believed his fiancée had run out on him. Ernie just

wants you to be careful." He grinned. "Secretaries like you are hard to come by."

Whatever that meant. However, I perceived that it would do no good to argue with the two stubborn men. And, anyhow, their advice was good, however little I wanted to have it shoved down my throat. "Very well. I shall be careful." I pinned Mr. Bigelow with a sharp look. "You *are* going to talk to Mr. Godfrey, aren't you?"

"Of course. We have to talk to everyone who knew the poor woman or who might have had an interest in her life and death."

"Good."

"And you won't go anywhere alone." Ernie, of course, still glaring.

I glared right back at him. "I will be *careful*."

He heaved a huge sigh and spoke next to Mr. Bigelow. "I'll make sure to see her home after work. And pick her up in the morning."

I felt my teeth grinding together, but I spoke not, sensing it would be not merely futile, but perhaps unwise.

A pause ensued, during which I suppose we were all gathering our separate thoughts. Then Mr. Bigelow spoke. "You mentioned Babs Houser's gone missing."

"Yeah. Her kid wants to find her." Ernie took his flask out of his coat pocket, uncapped it, and sipped its contents. And it was only about nine o'clock! I hope I hid my distress at this evidence of a dependence upon alcohol that I could only deplore.

A funny look crossed Mr. Bigelow's face. "Yeah? Well, I suppose any mother's better than none. The force has been watching Matty Bumpas for a while. Do you suppose he has anything to do with her disappearance?"

"I don't know, but Mercy and I did a little investigating

the other day, and here's what we discovered." Ernie proceeded to lay out what had transpired the day we had visited Han Li's shop in Chinatown. As Ernie spoke, Mr. Bigelow began to smile.

"Han Li, you say?" The smile on Mr. Bigelow's face widened into a wicked grin. "I'm so glad to hear that. And Matty Bumpas was worried, was he? Aha!"

He rubbed his hands together in what looked very much like glee to me. I couldn't account for this reaction, although I suspected it had something to do with Mr. Bumpas's criminal career and a perceived (by Mr. Bigelow, not I) opportunity to put him behind bars. Poor Barbara-Ann! To be saddled with a mother who fraternized with low criminals!

"Do you think Mr. Bumpas was involved in Mrs. Houser's disappearance?" I asked.

"I don't know," admitted Mr. Bigelow, "but we've been watching him for a long time now. We're pretty sure he's involved in bootlegging off the coast. If he's taken to dealing with Han Li, he might be in even deeper sh—er—trouble."

"What kind of trouble?"

Mr. Bigelow shook his head. "Not sure, but the department has been eyeing Han Li in connection with a rash of opium problems that's hit the L.A. area."

Opium! I felt my eyes open in gratified amazement. To think that I, Mercedes Louise Allcutt, from an old and exceedingly—one might even say excessively—proper Boston family, might actually have met a real, live, honest-to-goodness bootlegger and drug dealer and lived to tell the tale! Why, it was positively thrilling.

Since I didn't expect the two gentlemen in the room with me to share my sentiments, I kept them to myself.

Wouldn't you know it? At exactly that moment in time, the outer office door opened, and the nod Ernie gave me told me that he expected me to perform my secretarial duty and greet the customer. So I did, and with alacrity, too, because I didn't want Ernie to become annoyed with me. Besides, I wanted to prove to Mr. Bigelow that I was an efficient secretary, since it had occurred to me that his comment about "secretaries like you" might have been meant as a subtle form of sarcasm.

Gripping my notebook and pencil, I left Ernie's office—and almost ran smack into Mrs. Von Schilling, who was not merely clad in another elegant and expensive costume, complete with black gloves and a veiled hat, but who was carrying Rosie in her arms.

Delighted to see the dog again, if not her mistress, I cried, "Rosie!" and reached out to pet her. She wagged her stubby tail and licked my hand. Mrs. Von Schilling smiled a secret, sultry smile at me, although I don't know why she bothered. I wasn't a man who could be influenced by such a demonstration of her feminine wiles.

Rosie had undergone a transfiguration. Since Sunday—or, more likely, Saturday night, curse it—Mrs. Von Schilling had had her groomed and trimmed, and she wore two tiny red bows in her ebon locks, pinned to the fur beside her ears. She looked the very essence of a rich woman's pet. I felt a stab of sorrow on Rosie's behalf. She was worth so much more than to be an ornament adorning a female seductress! I have to admit she looked happy, though. Rosie, not Mrs. Von Schilling. Mrs. Von Schilling looked merely mysterious. As usual.

However, that wasn't the point. I marched to the business side of my desk and sat in my chair, folded my hands on my desk, and tried my best to look professional. "May I

help you, Mrs. Von Schilling? I'm afraid Mr. Templeton is occupied with another . . . client at the moment." I wasn't sure exactly what Mr. Bigelow was, and I knew very well he wasn't a client, but I wasn't sure what else to call him. An associate, I guess, but I didn't think of that word in time.

"That's fine, dear," she said in her low-pitched purr, taking the chair beside my desk. "I don't really need to see him. I came primarily to see you."

"Me!" My voice registered my astonishment.

"Indeed. Mr. Templeton told me what an integral part you played in getting my darling Rosie back." She buried her painted lips in Rosie's freshly washed fur. Rosie tolerated this indignity with aplomb. There's a lot to be said for breeding, as my mother always told me.

"He did?"

"Indeed. Ernie told me that if it wasn't for you, Rosie might still be in the clutches of that evil man."

Oho. So he was Ernie to her, was he? And just exactly why *had* Rosie been in the clutches of Mr. Fortescue, anyhow? Exactly whom had Mrs. Von Schilling been visiting that had resulted in blackmail? I didn't feel it was my place to ask, although curiosity gnawed at me. "Well, that's very kind of Mr. Templeton. I'm sure he exaggerated." Of course, I wasn't sure of any such thing. In fact, I had been the heroine of the piece, but I was too modest to say so.

"Nonsense. He told me exactly what you did. And I wanted to come here today to give you this token of my appreciation." She opened the handbag on her lap and removed an envelope, which she held out to me.

Taken aback, I didn't reach for the envelope. Rather, I put my hands in my lap and stammered, "Oh, but . . . really, Mrs. Von Schilling, I can't . . . it wouldn't be proper to . . ."

Ernie's door opened at that point, and both Ernie and

Mr. Bigelow emerged. Mr. Bigelow's eyes opened very wide, and he nodded to Mrs. Von Schilling. I guess he didn't even notice me with her in the room.

"Oh, Mr. Templeton, I'm so glad I caught you." Dropping the envelope on my desk, Mrs. Von Schilling wafted to her feet. "Rosie and I came to thank you." She cast a disinterested glance at me. "And Miss Allcutt, of course."

Ernie's blue eyes twinkled. "Of course. That's very nice of you, Mrs. Von Schilling. Please let me introduce you to Detective Phil Bigelow, from the Los Angeles Police Department's detective bureau. If you ever decide to further pursue the matter we just handled, Phil's the guy to go to."

"How do you do, Mr. Bigelow?" She held out a black-gloved hand, and looked up at him through pounds of mascaraed eyelashes and that stupid veil.

"Fine, thanks." Mr. Bigelow gulped. "Here's my card if you ever need me." He fumbled in his coat pocket and managed to come out with a card, which he handed to the lady. I use the term loosely.

"How kind," she murmured.

Tearing his gaze from the seductress with a visible effort, Mr. Bigelow turned back to Ernie and held out a hand. "Well, I'll see you later, Ernie."

"Yeah, Phil. Let me know what you find out."

"Will do."

Mr. Bigelow forgot all about me, I guess, because he didn't offer me a farewell before he stumbled out of the office, obviously still under the influence of Mrs. Von Schilling. I really hated that woman.

That being the case, and because I didn't want anything she might decide to give me, with the possible exception of Rosie, I picked up the envelope on my desk, stood, and thrust it at her. "I can't accept this, Mr. Von

Schilling. Thank you very much."

She glanced languidly from the envelope to me. "Don't be silly, Miss Allcutt. It's merely a small token of my appreciation."

"I'm sorry, ma'am, but I can't accept it. Mr. Templeton pays me an adequate salary."

"Fiddlesticks. If you won't take it, donate it someplace." And that was it for me. Dismissing me as if I were some kind of lackey, she turned to Ernie, took his arm, and said, "Oh, Ernie, I must tell you what happened."

And they went into his office and shut the door.

Well!

TWELVE

I scowled at the envelope, wondering what to do with it. I didn't want any of her old money. I had plenty of my own money, blast it. I wanted to tell her so. For some reason, even though I knew very well that money didn't equate to moral worth, I wanted that awful woman to know I was her equal in every way. That I recognized the urge to be foolish didn't make it go away. Nuts.

It was money, wasn't it? She couldn't be giving me anything else, could she? Contained within this envelope couldn't be, say, a certificate granting me rights to a little tiny poodle puppy, could it? It seemed unlikely. Mrs. Von Schilling didn't strike me as a woman with the imagination to consider giving anyone such a gift. I'm sure she never thought further than money—well, and protecting herself from the consequences of whatever action had lost her custody of Rosie, which I'm sure was immoral if not illegal. Hmm . . .

The front office door opened, diverting my attention from the envelope and the outrageously annoying Mrs. Von Schilling, to the person who entered.

"Barbara-Ann! How good to see you!" It was, too. After Mrs. Von Schilling, I'd have almost been happy to see Ned, but not quite.

She directed her somber gaze at me. "How come?"

Poor child. She looked as though no one had ever been glad to see her before. "Because I'm interested in your case, Barbara-Ann. Here." I patted the chair beside me. "Take a seat."

"Okay." She did so, and reached a grubby hand into an equally grubby pocket. Really, the child needed parents. "I found this." She held out a piece of paper that had been folded in quarters.

"Oh?" I took the paper, unfolded it, and read the note written on it. "My goodness!"

"Yeah," said Barbara-Ann. "I figured you'd know what to do about it."

Would that it were so. In block letters, the note read, *Cough up the dough, or you're both dead.* I gazed from it to Barbara-Ann, wishing I could offer some sort of solution to her problem, but probably looking as upset and helpless as I felt. "I . . . ah . . . where did you find this, dear?"

"Under my mother's mattress."

Under the mattress? I couldn't help myself. "Why in heaven's name were you looking under the mattress?"

With one of her assortment of shrugs, Barbara-Ann said, "I was looking for money."

That poor, poor child! Instantly, I picked up Mrs. Von Schilling's envelope and ripped it open. Contained therein was a twenty-dollar bill. Without even thinking about it, I held it out to Barbara-Ann. "Here, dear. Use this to get something to eat."

Her eyes were huge, and she clutched the bill as if she'd never seen one before, which was probably so. "Twenty bucks? Wow." Her voice held awe.

Eyeing her frock, a dirty pink-checked number that day, I ventured another question, feeling guilty because I hadn't thought to do something about the situation earlier. "Do you have water yet, dear?"

Another shrug. "Yeah. Mr. Templeton had it turned on a few days ago."

I felt my eyes pop open. "He did?"

She looked at me as if she didn't understand my amazement. "Yeah."

"Um . . . that was very kind of him."

Shrug. "Yeah. I guess."

Again Ernie's office door opened, this time to reveal Mrs. Von Schilling. She stood there for a moment, posing for her audience with her veiled hat and Rosie. Since her audience consisted of Barbara-Ann and me, I guess she didn't get the reaction she wanted, because she slithered into my office after a second or two of that. Behind her, Ernie spotted Barbara-Ann and frowned.

"Good day, Mr. Templeton," said Mrs. Von Schilling, turning and holding out a limp hand. "Do remember what I told you."

"Yeah, sure will," said Ernie, giving her hand one quick shake and dropping it.

Although I know I shouldn't admit it, I was glad he hadn't fallen for her vamp routine. At least, I hope he hadn't.

From the chair beside my desk came a smallish voice. "Is that a dog?"

It was the very first note of interest I'd ever heard in that voice. Not even when she'd come in to report her mother's absence, had Barbara-Ann Houser sounded anything but jaded. My heart was touched. Again. "Yes, dear, it's a dog. Her name is Rosie."

"The dog's?"

"Yes."

"Oh."

Mrs. Von Schilling wafted out of the office. Ernie frowned down at Barbara-Ann. "What's up, kid? Learn anything about your mother?"

She shook her head. "But I found something."

"Yeah?"

"Here," I said, handing the note to Ernie. "Read that. It's very . . . unsettling. Barbara-Ann found it under her mother's mattress when she was looking for money."

Ernie read the note. Then he sniffed it, held it aloft, and squinted at it. I realized he was examining it more closely, using the overhead light bulb.

Made curious by this performance, I said, "Well? Can you tell anything about the note? Or the person who wrote the note? Or anything?"

"I can tell it's Chinese paper. The kind you can buy in Chinatown, I mean. Don't know where it's made."

I didn't believe him. I thought he was showing off. "How in the world can you tell that?"

Tossing the note on my desk, he said, "Hold it up to the light."

I did so. "Yes?"

"You see any marks?"

"Marks? You mean like watermarks?"

"Yeah. See there?" Leaning over Barbara-Ann, he pointed at a spot on the paper. "See that flower there, imprinted on the paper?"

"Um . . . oh. Yes. It looks like a chrysanthemum."

"Whatever it is, that's the kind of paper they sell in Chinatown by the ton."

"By the ton?"

He eyed me with what looked like disfavor. "You've gotta stop taking everything so literally, kiddo. They actually sell it in boxes. You know, like stationery and envelopes in a box."

"Oh." I hoped he wasn't correct about my overall literal-mindedness, since that bespoke a lack of imagination, which would be a poor quality for a novelist to possess. "So you believe this note to have been written in Chinatown?"

"Hell, I don't know where it was written, but I'd lay odds the person who wrote it got the paper in Chinatown."

After thinking about this for a moment, I said, "I don't mean to cast aspersions on your theory, but even if it's correct, I can't see that where the paper came from helps us much."

He grinned, pulled the chair in front of my desk out, turned it around, and straddled it. "It narrows the field, though. Look at it this way." Holding up his left fist, he counted points using his fingers. "We've got a missing Babs Houser." Up went the forefinger. "We've got her afraid of a Chink." Up went the middle finger. "We've got Matty Bumpas having an argument with Han Li." The ring finger shot into the air. "And we have this note written on the kind of Chinese paper Han Li sells in his shop."

"Well . . ." I could see his point. "So where do we go from here? We still don't know where Babs is."

"I think we do. I think she's being stashed in Han Li's apartment somewhere. He sure skedaddled over there fast enough when I confronted him in his shop."

Stunned, I cried, "Do you mean to tell me that you've known all this time where she was being held, and you haven't done anything about it?"

This time he held up both hands. "Hold it, hothead. I didn't say I knew she was there. I said I suspect she's there. And I'm not the L.A.P.D. I can't go around busting down people's doors if I suspect they're doing something wrong."

"But . . . but . . . can't you get your friend Mr. Bigelow involved? Can you get him to rescue the poor woman?"

Ernie frowned at me. "You sure jump to conclusions fast, kiddo. I just told you I don't know Babs is there. And, if you'll recall, this very morning, I *did* get Phil involved. In fact, he's on his way to pick up Matty Bumpas right this

minute. Then he's going after your friend Godfrey. When he gets them, we'll see what we can do about Babs."

First he'd called me unimaginative, and now he was calling me rash. In my own defense, I said, "I didn't know he was going to pick up Mr. Bumpas. Or Mr. Godfrey." I sniffed. "Although I believe it's wise to do both."

"Well, gee. Sorry I don't explain my every intention to you."

That stung. "I'm your secretary, Mr. Ernest Templeton. I should be kept informed."

He rolled his eyes.

Barbara-Ann had been sitting in the chair next to my desk, her gaze bouncing between the two of us as if she were watching a tennis match. At last she spoke. "Do you really think Ma's at the Chink's place?"

With a shrug that would have been right at home on Barbara-Ann herself, Ernie said, "Don't know. When Phil gets back with Matty Bumpas, we'll see what we can find out."

"Okay," the phlegmatic child said. She had folded the twenty-dollar bill into a wad and stuck it in her shoe. While I understood her caution and her desire to protect her cash supply, I didn't envy the merchant destined to be paid with that bill.

The door to the office opened, and we all glanced at it, hoping, I'm sure, that it would be Mr. Bigelow with Matty Bumpas and/or Mr. Godfrey in tow. I don't know about Barbara-Ann and Ernie, but I was terribly disappointed when I recognized our visitor. "Oh, hello, Ned."

He appeared disconcerted, I suppose because he hadn't anticipated that my office would be full of people. "Uh . . ."

"Morning, Ned," Ernie said pleasantly. "We were just having a . . . uh . . . conference."

Ned said, "Yeah. H'lo, Mr. Templeton." He didn't greet Barbara-Ann, probably because he didn't know her name. She didn't greet him, either, I presume for the same reason. "I just brought you some flowers, Miss Allcutt." His cheeks burned with color as he took another step into the room and thrust a bouquet of geraniums at me. I wondered where he'd stolen these flowers from.

Not that it mattered much. I really didn't want any more flowers from Ned. However, I'd been bred from the cradle to be gracious, so I thanked him politely. "I'll put them in water right away," I promised him.

He seemed inclined to linger, although I'm not sure why, since it would be obvious to the rudest intelligence (which definitely included Ned) that I was busy. I said, "We need to confer some more now, Ned. Thank you again."

Shooting a scowl at Ernie, Ned said, "Yeah, sure," and backed out of the office, shutting the door rather hard.

Ernie's grin broadened.

Barbara-Ann said, "That guy's real strange."

I sighed. "Yes, he is, isn't he?"

The door opened again, abruptly, and Ned reappeared.

"Yes, Ned?" My voice was a trifle sharp.

"If you'll give me a vase, I'll get water."

Good idea. I retrieved an empty vase from the drawer of my desk where I'd stashed it, and handed it over. "Thank you."

"You're welcome." He gave Ernie another frown and left with the vase and the geraniums.

"You've sure got an admirer there, Mercy. Lucky girl."

Ernie got another frown, this one from me, for that comment. "Getting back to the problem at hand," I said pointedly, "can we do anything now except wait for Mr. Bigelow to come back?"

"Not that I can think of," said Ernie.

And he dismounted from the chair, turned it around, patted Barbara-Ann on the head, and sauntered back to his office. I heard the newspaper rattle as he separated the sections and figured he was going to read the *Times* until something happened. I don't know what else he could have done, but his nonchalance struck me as being insufficient under the circumstances. I mean, here was Barbara-Ann Houser, dirty and alone in the world, without a mother or father. Ernie Templeton, a private investigator who was supposed to be reuniting her with her mother, was reading a newspaper. With his feet propped on his desk, unless I missed my guess.

Insufficient or not, however, I couldn't think of anything to do, either. Therefore, I smiled a kindly smile at Barbara-Ann and said, "I'm sorry, dear. I wish we could do something useful."

Naturally, the child shrugged. "It's okay. I guess Ernie'll find her one of these days."

Her faith in a man who had thus far shown very little affection for or interest in her touched me deeply. "Do you have enough money, Barbara-Ann?"

She gawked at me. "Enough? I'm rich now, thanks to you."

Rich, was she? With twenty dollars in her shoe? I thought not. "But what about your apartment, dear? Do you need to pay a rental fee or anything?"

Another shrug. "Mrs. Pipkin lets it slide most months. She's nice."

"Mrs. Pipkin? Is she your landlady?"

"Yeah. She gives me food sometimes."

"That's very kind of her." I absolutely despaired of Barbara-Ann Houser. To someone like me, who had grown

up pampered and petted and indulged, even though it hadn't felt like it at the time, Barbara-Ann's circumstances seemed downright pathetic. But fruitful. If she had any novelistic tendencies, she'd be chock-full of experiences by the time she grew up. "Do you enjoy reading, Barbara-Ann?"

"Reading what?" Her expression remained blank. Either she was a mistress at hiding her inner feelings, or she didn't have very many.

"Books. Newspapers. Magazines. Reading anything."

Of course, she shrugged. "I read movie magazines sometimes. My mother has a stack of them. I like going to the flickers."

"Ah."

I'd have pursued the matter and asked her if she'd like to go to the library with me one day, but the office door opened yet again. This time I anticipated Ned, and was pleasantly surprised to espy Mr. Bigelow.

Rising from my chair in anticipation of seeing an irate and perhaps manacled Matty Bumpas and a similarly encumbered Hiram Godfrey enter right after him, I sat again, disappointed. Mr. Bigelow was alone. He didn't look very happy, either, as he nodded at me, ignored Barbara-Ann, and marched straight into Ernie's office.

"I sent some guys out to pick 'em up. They've both skipped."

I heard the newspaper being folded and set aside. "Figures."

My brow furrowed and I glanced at Barbara-Ann, who was, as ever, impassive, as if nothing ever surprised her, not even hearing that a notorious criminal and a vicious murderer had skipped. Which, I believe, means that they'd both run off and left no forwarding addresses. I was about to get up and force the two men to explain the matter to me, when

I heard Ernie's chair being pushed back and distinct sounds of Ernie rising therefrom.

"I'm sick of this shilly-shallying, Phil. Let's go to Han Li's and make him spill it. If we can't do anything else worthwhile today, maybe we can get Babs back."

Mr. Bigelow chuckled. "Sure that's worthwhile?"

I was shocked that he'd say such a thing in Barbara-Ann's hearing, although she didn't seem to mind.

"Naw, but what the hell."

Both men emerged from Ernie's office. Ernie spoke to me. "We'll be back in a bit."

"What?" I couldn't believe he was going to leave me behind in the office while he went off and perpetuated a rescue. I wanted to be involved, curse it! "Wait!" Leaping from my chair, I rushed around my desk and grabbed Ernie's arm.

Both men stopped and turned, frowning. "What?" Ernie's tone was cold and he eyed my hand gripping his coat sleeve with overt hostility.

Nuts to that. "What are you going to do? I'll come along and take notes." All right, I know it sounded weak, but I didn't fancy being left out of any action that might ensue.

"You stay right here, kiddo. There's nothing you can do, and I don't want you to get in the way." He added, as an afterthought, "Or get hurt."

And they left. Well! Scowling at the door, which had slammed in my very face, I made a decision. Turning to Barbara-Ann, I said, "Let's follow them."

For the first time in our brief association, Barbara-Ann's face took on an iota of animation. "Really? You're gonna follow them?"

"Yes."

"Keen!"

So, after I retrieved my handbag and hat, Barbara-Ann and I headed to Chinatown. It was nice to know I had an eager colleague, even if it wasn't Ernie Templeton.

Barbara-Ann and I didn't bother with the elevator, which, while repaired, was quite slow. We pelted down the staircase. As we rounded the last set of stairs, I almost ran plunk into Ned, who didn't seem to want to use the elevator, either. Screeching to a halt, I panted, "Ned!"

He blinked, startled. "Miss Allcutt! Here." He shoved the vase of geraniums at me.

Oh, dear. I didn't want to hurt his feelings, but I didn't want to carry a vase full of flowers to Chinatown with me, either. "Um . . . would you mind putting them on Lulu's desk for a little while, Ned. Barbara-Ann and I have important business that really can't wait."

He didn't like it. "You want me to give your flowers to Lulu?"

"Not give them to her. Just ask her if she'd mind if I left them there until I'm through with my business." Deciding Ned was more trouble than he was worth, I patted his shoulder as I hurried past him. "I truly appreciate the flowers, Ned, but it's vitally important that Barbara-Ann and I be on our way now." And we left him on the staircase. Poor Ned. I was beginning to think of him as a hopeless case.

That, however, was neither here nor there. Eyeing my companion with some concern, I asked, "Do you mind walking there, Barbara-Ann?"

"Uh-uh."

"Good." So we hot-footed it the few blocks to Chinatown. There was quite a bit of foot and automobile traffic, but we made good time. I suspected that Ernie and Mr. Bigelow

had driven to Mr. Li's shop, but didn't believe they could have gotten there very much sooner than we did, owing to the traffic.

I was right. When Barbara-Ann and I barreled into Mr. Li's shop, we saw a sight thrilling enough to gratify any aspiring novelist. Han Li stood behind his counter, trembling from head to toe, staring at the gun Mr. Bigelow held in his hand, and stuttering.

"No!" said he in a terrified voice. "I don't know. Honest."

"Can it, Li. You don't know the meaning of the word *honest*." That was Ernie, who, hearing us new arrivals, swung around, a gun of his own drawn. His face registered an instant of astonishment before it settled into anger. "You! Damn it, Mercy Allcutt, I told you to stay put."

"It's not fair to leave us out," I said, wishing he'd aim the gun elsewhere. I wanted to point out that anyone else might have discovered him there, waving that gun in the air, because the front door of the shop had been standing wide open, but my heart had taken that opportunity to lodge in my throat, so I didn't. I did, however, close the front door.

Ernie muttered, "Christ," in a disgusted-sounding voice. It wasn't a prayer.

In truth, I hadn't anticipated guns being involved in this venture, and seeing two of them wielded in a threatening manner in that confined space made me wonder if I hadn't been the least little bit precipitate in following the men.

But we were there now, and there wasn't much I could do about it but be careful. That being the case, I took Barbara-Ann's hand and backed us both up against a row of cluttered shelves, watching the action carefully, keeping my eye on the door to the shop, and praying it wouldn't open. When we'd entered, both Ernie and Mr. Bigelow had been

facing Mr. Li with their backs to the shop's front door. If it
had been a villain who'd entered instead of the two of us,
they might well have been in trouble. I decided to point that
out to Ernie as soon as he was finished with Mr. Li. It was a
valid argument in mitigation of what he might otherwise
consider my interference.

"Give it up, Li," growled Mr. Bigelow. "You've lost."

"If I do that, they kill me," whined Mr. Li. "You know
they will."

"The L.A.P.D. will protect you."

"Huh." Clearly, Mr. Li didn't believe it.

"What's the score, Li?" Ernie asked. "Where's Babs, and
why are you holding her?"

"I can't tell!"

"You damned well better tell," said Mr. Bigelow. "Otherwise, you'll go down alone for kidnapping."

"But I didn't do anything!" cried Mr. Li in anguish.
"They threaten me!"

"The hell you say. What's it all about Li? Booze? Drugs?
Bumpas has skipped, so you're all by yourself now."

"Skipped? Skipped?" Mr. Li's voice cracked. "What you
mean he skipped?"

"He's gone. Ran out on you. You're on your own, Li.
You going to give up the broad, or do you want to go to jail
to think about it?"

"No! No! He gotta give money to get woman!"

"Who's got to give you money?" asked Mr. Bigelow.

"Bumpas. He got money to get woman!"

Mr. Bigelow disabused him of that notion. "Too late for
that. Bumpas has skipped town, and there won't be any
money. You'd better give us the woman."

"No money?" Mr. Li's voice had gone tiny.

"No Bumpas. No money. No Li, either, if you don't

205

start cooperating pretty damned soon," growled Ernie.

Mr. Li hung his head. For a moment, he was the very picture of despair. Then he looked again at Mr. Bigelow. "If I tell you, you gotta help me. I don't wanna get killed."

"We'll help you if you help us," promised Mr. Bigelow. "Where's the broad, and what's the scoop?"

Shaking his head, Mr. Li said, "They kill me."

Ernie said, "Nuts. We said we'd help you, and we meant it."

"Give it up, Li. What's up? Drugs?"

Mr. Li stood there, indecisive for a moment, before he nodded. Then he said, "Opium," in a defeated tone of voice.

"Figured as much." Mr. Bigelow glanced at Ernie. "Didn't I tell you?"

"Yup. Now, Li, where's Babs?"

"Woman at my apartment." Mr. Li seemed to be catching his second wind because he scowled at Ernie and Mr. Bigelow and said with renewed energy, "You get her out of there! She noisy. She bad. She nuts. She pain in ass."

I wished I'd thought to cover Barbara-Ann's ears before she heard Mr. Li's denunciation of her mother, but I hadn't. I squeezed her hand.

She said, "Ow," and looked at me as if she thought I was crazy.

THIRTEEN

We left Han Li's shop the back way (which, Ernie told me, was the way he and Mr. Bigelow had arrived), so as to prevent anyone who might be watching the front door from following us.

"What? Did you think we marched in the front door, bold as brass, like you did?" Ernie asked with scorn dripping like acid from his words.

I sniffed. "I wouldn't have been surprised. You ought to have closed the door before you pulled your weapons, at least."

Ernie rolled his eyes, a gesture I had anticipated, but which sat ill anyhow.

"Let me lock shop," Mr. Li pleaded.

"All right with me," said Mr. Bigelow. "But I'm going with you." And he did, showing an appalling lack of trust, which, I gather, he'd acquired during his years as a policeman.

According to Mr. Li, the people who supplied him with the drugs weren't due to show up at his shop for another three days. Mr. Bigelow did him the courtesy of not handcuffing him as he led him to the automobile he'd parked in the alley behind Mr. Li's shop. Both he and Ernie held an arm, I presume so he couldn't escape.

When we all got to the car, Ernie looked from it to Barbara-Ann and me, and his scowl deepened. "We can't all fit," he announced in a tone of finality that belied the evidence of my own personal eyes. Mr. Bigelow's automobile was a Ford, and it was plenty big enough to hold the five of us.

Nevertheless, I decided to be a good sport about it. Smiling sweetly, I said, "Barbara-Ann and I can walk."

"Walk where?" demanded Ernie ferociously.

"Why, to Mr. Li's apartment building, of course."

A fulminating silence ensued. Mr. Bigelow, still gripping Mr. Li tightly, grinned at Ernie, who finally said, "Aw, hell," and opened the back door. "Get in, Mercy." Frowning at Barbara-Ann, he said, "You. Get in the front seat." He directed his last statement to Mr. Bigelow. "Li can sit between Mercy and me. You got any cuffs?"

"Do we need them?"

"I don't want him to try anything funny."

Mr. Li shook his head violently. "No cuffs. No funny business. No escape. They kill me if I escape."

"That's true," muttered Ernie. "Okay, I guess we don't need cuffs. Shove him in after Mercy. And *you*," he growled at me, "don't you try anything funny, either. You've pulled enough fool stunts for one day."

"I don't like your tone, Ernie Templeton."

"To hell with my damned tone. Get in the damned car." He opened the door in a manner that assured me he wasn't being polite, and I got in the car.

Barbara-Ann, who had remained silent during the preceding incidents, slid into the front seat after Mr. Bigelow, who had opened the door for her much more gently than Ernie had opened the door for me. Oh, well. It wasn't my fault if my employer was touchy.

Mr. Bigelow drove us the two blocks to Mr. Li's apartment building on Yale before anyone spoke again. Then it was Ernie, and his speech was directed at me. "I don't suppose there's any way you'll consent to stay in the car while we take care of this, is there?"

"No, there is not."

"Figured. All right. Let me get Li out, and then you can get out."

"Is my mother in there?" Barbara-Ann asked in a small voice.

"We'll soon find out," said Mr. Bigelow.

I took the girl's hand, and we followed the three men into the building. Barbara-Ann's grip was tighter than it had been, but that was the only evidence of emotional intensity she displayed as we walked up a dismal staircase to the second floor. The corridor here wasn't as depressing as the one on the first floor, being well-lighted and hung with Chinese pictures. A faint scent of sandalwood hung in the air, too, which gave the place an exotic atmosphere.

Ernie and Mr. Bigelow marched Mr. Li to apartment number eight, and Mr. Li fumbled in his pocket for the key, which he had trouble inserting into the lock. Ernie eventually took it from him and unlocked the door, then shoved Mr. Li inside and followed. I made sure Barbara-Ann and I were hot on his heels, because I didn't want to be left out in the hallway and miss any of the action. I inadvertently bumped Ernie's heel with the toe of my shoe, and he glowered at me. I pretended not to notice.

The apartment was austere, with little by way of furniture, and that shabby. There was a couch and a chair and a table upon which resided some sort of shrine, I guess, in which it was evident that Mr. Li burned incense. For someone in so questionable a profession as drug dealing, this indication of some sort of religious feeling seemed odd to me, although I didn't have time to think much about it

"All right, Li, where is she?"

Mr. Bigelow didn't have to ask twice. And, as it turned out, Mr. Li didn't have to answer. As soon as we were all inside the apartment, loud noises began to emanate from

behind a closed door to our right.

"Watch 'em, Ernie." And, as Ernie shoved Barbara-Ann and me away from the door, and Mr. Li cowered behind Ernie, Mr. Bigelow hurried to the door, stepped aside, and with his gun drawn, threw it open. I didn't notice until then that Ernie had a firm grip on Mr. Li's arm, so cowering was about all the poor man could do.

"Well, I'll be." Sticking his gun in its holster, a shoulder model I never did get to see clearly, Mr. Bigelow put his fists on his hips, and smiled at whatever the room contained.

I heard more noises, including muffled human sounds, as if someone were trying to speak but had something covering his or her mouth. Barbara-Ann suddenly yanked herself free from my grip, ran to the door, and disappeared into the room. Instantly, her cry of "Ma!" rang out. Also instantly, tears filled my eyes. I blinked them back, praying Ernie hadn't noticed this evidence of feminine weakness on my part. They didn't prevent me from rushing into the room, where I saw Barbara-Ann Houser, her arms thrown around a woman gagged and tied to a chair.

"Go ahead, kid. You can untie her," Mr. Bigelow said. Barbara-Ann hopped off her mother's lap and started working first on the gag.

Ernie and Mr. Li joined Mr. Bigelow and me in watching the touching scene of reunification between mother and child. I clasped my hands to my bosom and tried to keep from crying. When I glanced at Ernie, I saw definite signs of disenchantment, and that evidence of his cold-heartedness drove any compulsion to weep away. "How can you be so callous?" I whispered harshly.

"Wait till the kid gets the gag out," he advised, sounding more cynical even than usual.

At that moment, the gag fell away, and I was forced to acknowledge that Ernie had a point, even though I didn't want to. Acknowledge his point, I mean.

As Barbara-Ann stood beside the chair, watching, the woman I presumed to be Babs Houser pinned Han Li with a perfectly hateful frown, and started screaming. "You God damned son of a bitch! You dirty, rotten Chink!" And she went on in that vein until Ernie threatened to replace the gag.

I, naturally, was shocked and outraged that a woman should use such terrible language in front of her child. I had anticipated an emotional and heartwarming exchange of endearments between mother and daughter. Which demonstrated once again how little I knew of the world.

As she screamed and hollered, Barbara-Ann and Mr. Bigelow were working on her bonds. Mrs. Houser was what is colloquially known as a mess. Her blond hair was dirty and straggled around her shoulders; her makeup, which I presume had been slathered on her face two Saturdays prior, was smudged and streaked; her stockings had ladders as wide as my hand, her clothes were crumpled and sweat-stained; and she looked as if she'd not enjoyed her captivity one little bit.

Mr. Bigelow had to use a knife at one point to get her legs untied, and then he had to rescue Mr. Li, since Babs surged from her chair and launched herself at him. Ernie didn't release Mr. Li, so it was up to Barbara-Ann and me to wrestle the woman to a standstill. Any urge to cry I had experienced had by that time vanished entirely, and I was on the verge of asking Barbara-Ann why she'd wanted this harridan back in the first place.

Recognizing that impulse to be unfair, and after peace had more or less been restored, I asked, "Would you care for water, Mrs. Houser?"

She stared at me as if I were a hydra-headed monster. "Who the hell are you?"

Oddly enough, it was Barbara-Ann who leapt to defend me. "She's my friend, Ma. She's Ernie's secretary, Miss Allcutt, and she gave me twenty bucks today."

"Twenty bucks?" Mrs. Houser's hostility vanished, and she took my hand and shook it. "Thanks a lot."

"Is that what was in that envelope?" Ernie whispered in my ear.

I nodded and spoke to Mrs. Houser. "You're welcome. Would you care for some water?" I figured she must be thirsty after having had that gag in her mouth for so long.

"Naw. I just want to get the hell out of here." She turned like a cyclone on Mr. Bigelow. "So are you going to arrest that son of a bitch, or what?" She jerked her head at Mr. Li, who swallowed.

"Let's go down to the station and talk about it," Mr. Bigelow suggested, then turned to Ernie. "You coming, too?"

Eyeing me with an expression of frustration, Ernie hesitated before saying, "I guess I'd better. And I suppose we'll have to take these two along."

"My baby's coming with me," said Babs, belatedly throwing her arms around her daughter. "And you can't stop her, Ernie Templeton." I don't know what history she and he had, but it evidently didn't conjure up pleasant memories.

"I just said they were going with us," he snarled.

It took Babs a few minutes to get her legs working properly. She claimed she'd been tied to the chair, with only very few time-outs for personal hygiene purposes, for over a week. Since she'd disappeared two Saturdays before, I guess she wasn't lying, although I have to admit that my

opinion of her wasn't the highest. It seemed to me that she was setting a very poor example for her child, both with her language and with her choice of associates.

Speaking of which, as we headed down the stairs, she said, "Where's Matty? Did he go to you guys?" She sounded hopeful and, at the same time, doubtful, as if she understood Mr. Bumpas's character too well to believe that he'd done anything so noble.

"He's skipped," said Ernie brutally.

"Skipped?" she screeched. "You're kidding!"

"You know I'm not. And you ought to have expected it."

Through gritted teeth, she muttered, "Son of a bitch."

On the drive to the police station, she and Barbara-Ann sat in the front seat, and Ernie and I flanked Mr. Li, as we had done on the way to his apartment. I was looking forward to this, since I'd never been to a police station before. New experiences were piling up in my life, and I vowed to use them as well as I could. I was pleased to see that Mrs. Houser put her arm around Barbara-Ann in the automobile.

Once we got to the police station, Mr. Bigelow and Ernie took custody of Mr. Li, and I walked with Barbara-Ann and Babs. "Your captivity must have been a terrible ordeal for you, Mrs. Houser," I said by way of getting to know her.

"It was rough, all right."

"Did he feed you, Ma?" Barbara-Ann asked.

"Yeah. Noodles. If I never see another noodle, it'll be too soon for me."

"My goodness, is that all he gave you?"

She shrugged, from which I deduced Barbara-Ann had picked up the gesture from her mother. "It's all he ate. I guess Chinks eat a lot of noodles. They weren't bad, but too many noodles is too many noodles, if you know what I mean."

"Yes, indeed." I shook my head. "Poor Barbara-Ann was very worried about you."

"Was you, sweetie?" She stooped to give her daughter a quick hug. "Thanks, doll."

The urge to give her a lecture on the proper care and feeding of children warred with the knowledge that I had no experience of my own in that regard. That, coupled with my desire not to be perceived as a prig, made me hold my tongue, although I did feel compelled to say, "Mr. Templeton had your water turned on so that Barbara-Ann could bathe."

"Ernie did that?" She glared at Ernie's back, since the three men preceded us into the building. "I'll be damned."

I didn't doubt it for a moment, but I wished she'd kept her prediction to herself. It was then I decided I'd best not talk to her further, since I didn't want to hear any more bad language issue from a woman's lips. And there, if one were needed, was another example of how protected I'd been all my life. From magazine articles I'd read, I'd learned that your average flapper took pride in using as much bad language as she could as often as she could, but until that day, I'd managed to avoid listening to any of them do it.

We entered a big room full of desks and people. Mr. Bigelow handed Mr. Li to another policeman and told him to put him in "holding," whatever that was. Then he threaded his way through the crowded room to an empty desk, where he pulled a chair out for Babs. Ernie hauled up another one for me, which I gave to Barbara-Ann. With a frown for me, Ernie snabbled another chair and shoved it at me. I sat, and dug my pad and pencil out of my handbag.

Babs eyed me slantways. "What's that for?" She gestured at my pad.

"I'm only going to take a few notes," I told her with

what I hoped was a winning smile.

"How come?" Her tone dripped with misgiving.

My goodness, but the woman had a suspicious streak! If she didn't hang out with hoodlums, she might find that the whole world wasn't against her. "Just for my own reference. I'm not going to publish them or anything."

"Publish them? Huh?"

"Never mind that," Mr. Bigelow said sharply. "Forget Miss Allcutt. You're here to answer some questions, Babs."

She sneered at him. "Yeah? Well, we'll see. I don't believe you about Matty. He ain't skipped. He was going to get money to bail me out."

"Yeah?" said Mr. Bigelow in his turn. "How do you figure that, Babs? Matty's skipped, see?"

"Huh. I don't believe you."

"You'd better believe me, because I'm about all you have now. Why was Li holding you, and who was he holding you for?"

Mr. Bigelow must have seen me wince at his grammatical construction, because he glanced questioningly at me for a second. I only smiled, and silently commanded myself not to be so cursedly prim and proper.

"First you tell me where Matty is," Babs said.

"He's gone, I tell you. His pad's empty, and he's flown, sugar puss, so you'd better cooperate."

"Empty?"

"Empty."

Babs pinched her lips tightly together, thereby making quite a spectacle of herself, because a tiny bit of lipstick remained from when she'd last painted her mouth, and when she crinkled her lips like that, pink lines radiated in all directions. It was an odd effect, and I couldn't help staring. Fortunately, she didn't notice.

At last, she said, "Aw, hell. I still don't believe you about Matty, but the bum didn't pay up, so I guess I can't depend on him."

"You've got that right," Ernie interposed.

Babs glared at him, and he subsided, sitting on a corner of Mr. Bigelow's desk, folding his arms across his chest, and observing Babs with his hat set to one side. He looked the very image of a motion-picture tough guy. I was impressed.

"Okay," Babs said then, her tone softer than it had been. I guess she'd realized she had no other option. "There's this guy, see, this man named Carpetti. He's running drugs up from Mexico, and Matty thought he'd get a bite of the action." At the name Carpetti, Ernie and Mr. Bigelow exchanged a significant glance. It was clear to me that they'd heard the name before.

"I thought Matty was strictly booze," Mr. Bigelow interrupted.

"Yeah, well, he decided he wanted a piece of the drug action, see?"

"Good old Matty," muttered Ernie. Babs shot him another hateful glance.

"Anyways, see, Matty likes the horses, and he gambled away some of the money he was supposed to give Carpetti, and Carpetti nabbed me. They've been using Li's shop for the deals, see, and Carpetti's goons made Li hold me. Matty was supposed to come up with the money in exchange for me." Her eyebrows formed a deep V over her nose. "The bum never come. I thought they was gonna bump me off."

"They probably would have if Matty hadn't paid up by the time the next deal was supposed to happen," Mr. Bigelow commented. "Do you know when that's going to be? Li said in a couple of days. Is he telling the truth?"

Again she shrugged. "I guess. That's what I heard,

anyhow. Li told me Carpetti and his goons are supposed to come to his shop on Thursday at noon. If Matty hadn't paid up by then . . ." She shuddered, and I felt rather sorry for her, even if she had brought this misery on herself. "Well, he didn't say, but I got the picture. They was gonna bump me off." She reached out for Barbara-Ann, who took her hand and squeezed it. The image of Barbara-Ann left alone in the world because her mother consorted with low felons made my heart squeeze painfully.

That, however, was irrelevant. Ernie and Mr. Bigelow again exchanged a glance. "So," said Mr. Bigelow. "We've got to figure out what to do by Thursday."

"Yeah," agreed Ernie. "We need some kind of sting."

"That would work. Got any ideas?"

Risking censure, but profoundly eager to understand everything, I said, "What's a sting?"

Both men looked at me, and I sensed annoyance in both faces. Nevertheless, I lifted my chin and persisted. "Perhaps I can help if I know what you're talking about."

"You?" Babs laughed. "What could you do?"

"Not a damned thing," said Ernie in a deadly voice.

"Wait a minute, Ernie," said Mr. Bigelow, putting a hand on his shoulder and eyeing me with a speculative gleam. "Maybe we can use her."

Ernie's head whipped around so fast, I feared for his neck. "The hell you say!"

"Wait a minute. Let's talk about this."

When Ernie opened his mouth and appeared ready to explode, Mr. Bigelow went on, "Hold on a minute, Ernie. Let me get something." He fished around in his desk drawer and withdrew one of those broadsides you find hanging on walls in post offices. "Is this Carpetti?" He showed the broadside to Babs, who squinted hard.

"I . . . I'm not sure. I don't think I ever seen the guy. If you ask Matty . . . oh, yeah. I forgot. The creep ran out on me." She sucked in a gallon or two of air, which was tainted with the smoke of about a million cigars and cigarettes being puffed on by the minions of the Los Angeles Police Department. "I swear to God, I hope the drug guys skewer him. And if they don't, I will."

"Hmm." Mr. Bigelow was clearly disappointed. "Maybe I'll show Li." And without explanation, he rose from his chair and went to speak to a uniformed officer. The officer nodded and walked away, and Mr. Bigelow rejoined us. "Li will be here in a minute," he announced.

"Maybe I'll skewer him, too," muttered Babs.

"Did he treat you badly?" I made sure to sound sympathetic.

Shrug. "I guess not, except that he kept me tied up. He's scared of Carpetti, too. I'd still like to skewer him."

"Wait till we get Carpetti before you do that, okay?" Mr. Bigelow's request was jocular, but his voice wasn't.

As we waited for Mr. Li to show up, Ernie turned to me. "Don't think I'm going to let you get involved in this, Mercy. You're a secretary, not a detective, and you'd better remember that." Turning to Mr. Bigelow, he said, "I don't want her involved."

"But I already am involved," I said indignantly.

"That's not my fault," Ernie announced ominously. "If you'd obeyed orders, you wouldn't be here now."

"Orders! Well, I like that!"

"I'm your *boss,* dammit!"

"You may be my boss, but you can't direct my every action!"

"If you want to keep your job, you'd better do what I say from now on!"

"Hey," Mr. Bigelow cut in—and loudly, too, or we'd never have heard him. "Cut it out, you two. I want to see if Li recognizes this picture."

Mr. Li, in handcuffs and being escorted by a burly uniformed police officer, shuffled up to Mr. Bigelow's desk, his head bent, his expression downcast. I didn't feel any sorrier for him than I did Babs Houser. In fact, of all the people involved in this mess, the only one for whom I had sympathy was Barbara-Ann.

The uniformed officer pulled up yet another chair and shoved Mr. Li into it. Over Mr. Li's head, he asked of Mr. Bigelow, "Anything else?"

"Yeah. Go get the book, Sullivan."

Mr. Sullivan departed (he didn't salute, from which I gathered that the L.A.P.D. and the armed services didn't have all that much in common), and Mr. Bigelow showed Mr. Li the same broadside he'd lately shown Babs. "Recognize this mug, Li?"

Mr. Li glanced at the broadside and winced. "I guess."

"What do you mean, you guess?" Mr. Bigelow said in an ominous tone. "Is this Carpetti or not?"

Mr. Li squinted harder. "Scar on forehead. Yeah, I guess it's Carpetti."

"You guess?" More ominous this time.

"Yeah. That Carpetti."

"Aha!" Mr. Bigelow shot a triumphant glance at Ernie. "So we *are* dealing with Carpetti!"

"Told you, didn't I?" asked a surly Babs, tossing her head, a gesture that would have been more effective if her hair had been clean and neatly arranged and her mascara unsmudged.

Both Ernie and Mr. Bigelow ignored her. Mr. Bigelow handed the broadside to me, of all people. I took it, and I'm

sure I appeared as surprised as I felt. Before I'd had time to do more than close my fingers on it, Ernie snatched it away from me.

"Wait a minute, Phil. What the devil's going on here? Mercy's done enough butting in. She's not doing anything else in this game."

"I will if I want to!" cried I, sounding, I regret to say, like a much younger Mercy Allcutt when denied a treat.

"Wait a minute, Ernie. We really can use Miss Allcutt, and she won't be in any danger, either."

I grabbed the broadside and tugged, causing it to tear a little. Exasperated, I said, "Ernie Templeton, give that to me this minute." It was the first time I'd used my tone of command on him. As I might have anticipated, it didn't work anywhere near as well on Ernie as it had on Ned.

He let go of the pasteboard, but he still scowled. "I don't know, Phil. I don't like this."

"I'll be the one who decides what I do," I said, using my haughtiest, Mother-inspired Bostonian voice.

I noticed Ernie and Mr. Bigelow exchanging another glance. Mr. Bigelow seemed amused, Ernie disgusted. I ignored them both.

After studying the face on the poster, as evil a one as I'd ever seen, I spoke to Mr. Bigelow. "What do you want me to do?"

Ernie muttered something under his breath. This time he was ignored by all of us.

"Not much. But if you could be in the shop on Thursday, looking around for souvenirs, if you know what I mean, you can give us the high sign when you see Carpetti or any of his goons enter the shop. I don't want Li to signal, because it would be too obvious, but none of these guys have ever seen you, and they'd never suspect a nice lady like

you to be working with the law." He smiled, and I guess I was supposed to be flattered by his assessment of my demeanor, but I can't say that I was, mainly because it confirmed me in the opinion that even with bobbed hair, I still looked like a proper lady. Not that there's anything wrong with being a lady. But I was trying *so* hard to fit in that it was slightly discouraging to know that I didn't. Not that I wanted to be mistaken for a Babs Houser type of female or anything, but . . . Oh, never mind.

The officer named Sullivan came back to Mr. Bigelow's desk, carrying with him a very large book, which he placed in front of Mr. Bigelow, who thanked him. Mr. Sullivan subsided to a location behind Mr. Li's chair, his arms at his sides and his legs braced apart, as if to be ready in case Mr. Li tried something desperate. I didn't believe Mr. Li was in any position to try to escape, what with his handcuffs on and all, but I suppose they knew better than I.

"Okay, Li, I'm going to turn the pages in this book, and you're going to stop me when you spot anybody you've seen with Carpetti."

Mr. Li grunted and said, "Dunno. White people all look alike to me."

"Don't give me that," warned Mr. Bigelow. "Look hard. It can't be too tough to pick out Carpetti's goons. They're all Italians." He pronounced the word *Eyetalians*, whether by accident or intent, I don't know. "You take a look, too, Babs. Maybe you'll spot somebody you've seen with Matty."

"Okay," she said unenthusiastically.

With a heavy sigh, Mr. Li turned his attention to the book. It was interesting to see all the photographs contained therein. I understand that these photographs were what are termed mug shots, I presume because they fea-

221

tured the faces and profiles of various criminals, and the lower classes spoke of faces as *mugs*.

Slowly, Mr. Bigelow turned the pages. Each page contained a head shot and a profile of a different man. Mr. Li and Babs both concentrated hard. At one point, Babs pointed at a picture and looked to Mr. Li for confirmation. He hesitated, then nodded.

"You sure?" asked Mr. Bigelow.

Babs said, "I'm sure."

Mr. Li said, "I think so."

"You better be sure," warned Mr. Bigelow. "No mistakes. If you cooperate, it'll go easier on you."

"It's him," said Mr. Li more firmly, if less grammatically.

"Told you so," muttered Babs, who apparently didn't care for shilly-shallying.

The two of them spotted one other face that they claimed was associated with Mr. Carpetti, and Mr. Bigelow closed the book with a satisfied sigh. "Good. Okay, here's what's going to happen on Thursday."

With many grumbled and sometimes profane objections from Ernie, Mr. Bigelow set out a plan whereby he expected to scoop up the primary members of the opium ring that had been operating with relative impunity in the Los Angeles area for several months. And I, Mercedes Louise Allcutt, was going to play an integral role in the action! I can't recall ever feeling such a satisfying degree of excitement, unless you count my first piano recital when I was eleven, but I knew nothing of the world then. This was a much greater accomplishment. Or it would be, providing everything went the way Mr. Bigelow hoped it would.

"You got it, Li? No funny business. You cooperate, hear?"

"I hear," said the melancholy shopkeeper.

And Mr. Sullivan led him away, to be kept in "holding," I presume, until Thursday.

Before we left the police station to go to luncheon, since it was time and I was hungry, I had some questions to which I wanted answers. Directing my attention to Babs, I said, "What are you going to do now?"

She shrugged, as I had expected of her. "Go home, I guess."

I turned to Ernie and Mr. Bigelow. "Will she be safe there? The drug people don't have their hostage any longer, and they might not like it. They might try to kidnap her again, even though Mr. Bumpas has . . . er . . . skipped. Will you give Mrs. Houser and Barbara-Ann some kind of protection?"

Both men gave me looks that I don't believe I deserved. The question was a valid one, and so was the point I had made in asking it.

Babs's eyes popped open wide. "Jeez, I never thought of that!" She slapped Mr. Bigelow's desk in a panicky gesture. "Look, Bigelow, you gotta put guards on me and my kid here. I don't want nothing to happen to either of us."

"Don't you have a friend you can stay with?" asked an unsympathetic Mr. Bigelow.

I interceded. "Wouldn't that just put the friends in danger? I presume these men wouldn't hesitate to use deadly force."

"Which is why I don't want you mixed up in this mess," grumbled Ernie.

I chose not to respond to that inflammatory comment. "Can't Mrs. Houser and Barbara-Ann stay at a hotel or something until after the arrests are made on Thursday?"

Babs turned her big-eyed stare on me. "A hotel? Are you

nuts? I can't afford to stay at no hotel!" She squinted at Mr. Bigelow. "Unless the L.A.P.D. pays."

"We don't have a budget for that sort of thing," said Mr. Bigelow, sounding amazingly like my father.

He glanced at Ernie, who shook his head. "If the L.A.P.D. can't afford her, I sure as hell can't." He gave Babs a sneer that she returned with interest.

I was tired of all of them except Barbara-Ann, who had remained silent and watchful during the entire time. "Oh, for heaven's sake, I'll pay for you to go to a hotel for a few days!" I reached into my handbag and pulled out my little money purse. I was about to snap it open and pull out money when Ernie put his hand over mine.

"Wait a damned minute. You can't just hand over money like that."

I frowned up at him. "Why not?"

"Because Babs Houser isn't a very trustworthy individual."

Babs snorted, but Ernie went on.

"If you give that money to her, God alone knows what she'll use it for." His scowl was magnificent. "But I don't suppose I can talk you out of throwing your money away on her, can I?"

"No," I said firmly. "You cannot."

He heaved an enormous sigh and stood up. "Phil, can Sullivan help Babs and Barbara-Ann get settled in a hotel somewhere? I guess I'd trust the money with him."

"Well, really!" I said, indignant on Barbara-Ann's behalf, if not her mother's. Truth to tell, I'd rather not trust Babs with money, either.

Mr. Bigelow rubbed his lower lip with his thumb for a moment, before gesturing for Mr. Sullivan to join us again. "Yeah. I guess it's a good idea to stash her somewhere."

I don't know why he had to make everything sound so sordid, but I don't suppose it mattered. Babs and Barbara-Ann left with Mr. Sullivan, to whom I gave fifty dollars. I told him to make sure the two females had a nice room and that there was a restaurant nearby.

Another thing I don't understand is why everybody, including Barbara-Ann, looked at me as if I were an alien creature from another planet.

True to his word, Ernie saw me home that evening in his Studebaker.

"There's really no need," I said, settling my hat on my head and picking up my handbag. "I don't mind walking, and I enjoy taking Angel's Flight."

"You can take Angel's Flight after we catch whoever killed June Williams."

"It's Mr. Godfrey."

"Right." He stood at the office door in his hat and coat, grinning at me, and I knew my joy in Angel's Flight was destined to be postponed for a while.

"What about in the morning? May I walk to work?"

"Nope. I'll pick you up. I've got Phil checking on something for me. Until I get an answer, I don't want you going anywhere alone."

"Nonsense!"

"I said I'll pick you up," he said in a measured voice, as if he were dealing with a person of very tiny intellect.

"But I'm always here before you."

"I'll make an effort."

FOURTEEN

All of that happened on Monday. By Thursday, I was about to jump out of my skin with anticipation. I was going to be participating in a real, honest-to-goodness police sting.

The entirety of my anxiety could not be laid solely at the door of fevered anticipation, however. Other things had happened between Monday and Thursday that bear on the final outcome of this narrative. Few of them were enjoyable.

For one thing, Ned seemed determined to haunt me. From a fellow who had a reputation for hiding away from the world, not to mention the work he was supposed to do, he had turned into someone who was so eager to please, Ernie and I all but tripped over him constantly. Ernie seemed inclined to treat this as a joke. I found it quite annoying, although I did my best not to hurt Ned's feelings.

"Are you sure you don't need me to do anything, Miss Allcutt?" he asked Tuesday afternoon.

"No, thank you, Ned. You've done a wonderful job fixing the things I asked you to fix, but there's nothing else at the moment. I'll let you know if we need anything."

"Are you sure?"

"Yes, Ned, I'm sure."

He hesitated in the doorway on his way out. I stifled an exclamation of annoyance. I wanted him to go away. "Say, Miss Allcutt, are you seeing Ernie?"

I didn't catch his meaning for a moment. When I did, I felt my face get hot. "If you mean are Mr. Templeton and I social acquaintances, no, we're not. He's my employer, and

I'm his . . . secretary." I was his assistant, curse it, but not officially.

"You shouldn't be going around with him, Miss Allcutt."

That was enough for me. I pinned Ned with one of my superior Boston stares. "I don't wish to be cruel, Ned, but let me state here and now that neither my movements nor my associates are any business of yours."

He pouted for a couple of seconds. "Sure. I just thought you ought to know that it's not good for you to be going around with him. I don't like it."

I borrowed some more ice from my mother. "Your likes and dislikes are of no concern to me, Ned. Now, if you'll excuse me, I need to get to work." I didn't really have anything to do but hang another picture on the wall that I'd bought the day before, but Ned didn't need to know that.

"All right." He looked as if he'd shrunk a little. "I'm sorry if you're mad at me."

"I'm not mad at you," I said, relenting slightly on the anger but not the hauteur. "But I can't talk any longer. I have work to do."

He left. Thank God.

Wednesday morning: "H'lo, Miss Allcutt. Here are some more flowers for you."

After sighing internally: "Thank you, Ned. Um . . . where did you get these?"

He clasped his hands behind his back and shuffled his feet. "Somebody's garden."

I gave him a severe look. "You really oughtn't do that, Ned. Not unless you ask first."

"They don't need them," he declared stolidly. "Anyway, they're for you."

His reasoning eluded me. "But they weren't yours to

give to me, Ned. Taking things that belong to other people without asking first is called stealing."

After puzzling over that one for a moment, he said, "But you should have them."

"Please don't steal any more flowers for me, Ned. It's not polite to take things that don't belong to you."

"But I wanted to give them to you."

I gave up.

That afternoon another bunch of flowers was delivered to the office by a young lad. I took them with misgiving, wondering if my lecture about theft had registered with Ned. When I opened the card that accompanied the flowers, I doubted it. It read: "To a special lady. Love, Hiram."

After considering and discarding the notion of throwing the flowers in the waste-paper basket, I dug the other vase out of my desk drawer, filled it with water, and plopped the flowers in it, figuring they were in the nature of evidence in a murder case. Or at least evidence that Mr. Hiram Godfrey was out of his mind.

"What was that?" Ernie called from his office. He'd been in there with his feet on his desk, reading the newspaper, ever since he and I arrived at the Figueroa Building in his Studebaker. I have to admit that he was making an effort to be on time now that he insisted in picking me up and driving me to work. If you could call it work. Except for Hiram Godfrey, who had apparently gone away only to re-surface via flowers I didn't want, and Barbara-Ann Houser, who couldn't afford to pay a bill if one were presented to her, Mrs. Von Schilling seemed to be our only client.

"Flowers," I said, wishing I didn't have to because I didn't want to be teased. He'd already ribbed me about my latest contribution from Ned. These flowers, however, were

different. I took them, vase and all, along with the card that came with them, into Ernie's office.

"Ned again?" he asked in a sugary voice that inspired the most violent of impulses in my bosom.

"No. You might be interested in these." I was standing in front of his desk by this time, holding the flowers in one hand and the card that had come with them in the other. I showed him the card. "Is there any way to investigate this?"

He'd deposited the paper without folding it on his desk in order to take the card. When he read the name, he whistled. "Hiram, is he? You two have become better acquainted since he last appeared in the office."

Irked, I said, "We have *not* become better acquainted, and you know it. If I saw the man, I'd have him arrested for murder."

"That might be a little precipitate, although I'd sure like to talk to him. For one thing, he owes me money."

That took the wind out of my sails. "He owes you . . . but I thought that poor woman died."

"She did." He grinned at me. "But I found her first, and that was what Godfrey was paying me to do."

It seemed so callous, hearing a human tragedy being spoken of in terms of monetary compensation. That's probably only because I'd grown up without having to think about how people earn money to buy the bread they put in their mouths.

"Do you suppose the florist would have an idea where he is living now?"

"Who knows?"

"Don't you *care?*" I was growing impatient with my blithely indifferent employer, who appeared to me as though he didn't give a hang about poor June Williams and didn't give a fig about finding her murderer.

With a sigh, Ernie handed the card back to me and folded up his newspaper. "Yeah. Actually, I do care. I'll give Phil a call. He ought to know that Godfrey's surfaced again. Almost. I also want to find out what he's learned about your other suitor."

"My other . . . What in the world are you talking about?"

He grinned at me. "Just a joke, kiddo." Since he reached for the telephone on his desk, I decided I'd get no answers for the nonce, and also that I'd done my duty as far as the flowers went, and returned to my desk. I'd hung the picture, a nice painting of Angel's Flight done by an old man who hawked his pictures in Pershing Square, and was admiring it when Ned showed up again. It was approximately the sixth time he'd come to me in quest of work that day. My temper had become a trifle frayed by then.

"Ned, do you ever do any work for anybody else in this building?" I made sure my voice sounded as stern as I felt.

"Sure, I do. I got my job, you know."

"I just wondered. You're in this office so much, I can't imagine when you have time to perform the rest of your duties."

He didn't reply to that comment. His attention seemed fixed on the flowers I'd received from Mr. Godfrey. "Where'd you get those?" His tone was accusatory, and I reacted negatively.

"Where I got them is of no concern to you, Ned. I'm getting a little tired of you pestering me, if you want to know the truth."

"Did Mr. Templeton give you those?"

"No, he did not." Irked with myself for answering such an irrelevant question, I added, "Not that it's any of your business."

"I don't like you getting flowers from other people."

I'd had enough. Standing and putting on my most intimidating Boston manner, I said, "What you like and don't like is of no importance to me, Ned. Now will you *please* go away. I will let you know if Mr. Templeton or I need assistance from you."

"What's up?" came Ernie's voice from the doorway between our offices. I looked at him, and noticed to my surprise that he appeared very grave. Gravity was such a novelty on his usually flippant features, that I stared.

"I'm trying to convince Ned to do his job and leave me alone."

"I only wanted to see if she needed anything done," Ned muttered, pouting.

"And does she?" asked Ernie sweetly.

"No."

"Then I suggest you take yourself off, Ned."

"I'm going, I'm going." And, thank goodness, he did.

After the door closed, Ernie came over and sat in the chair in front of my desk. "I don't like that guy hanging around here so much, Mercy."

"I don't either. If you have a suggestion as to how to get him to go away and stay away, I'd be more than happy to hear it."

He shook his head. His expression remained troubled, a circumstance for which I couldn't account. "I don't know. There's something wrong with that guy. I wish Phil would show up so I can ask him. He's supposed to be dropping by today."

"Whatever do you mean?"

"I don't know. I just think there's something wrong there." He tapped his head with his forefinger.

I rolled my eyes, an unladylike gesture my mother would have deplored, but I was exasperated. "There certainly is. Not

231

only does he think he's formed a romantic attachment with me, but he claims he's going to be a star in the motion pictures."

That reminder took care of Ernie's state of sobriety. His grin came out of nowhere and would have looked right at home on the Cheshire Cat. "That's right. I'd forgotten old Ned aims to be in the pictures." He leaned back in the chair, balancing it on its back legs and propping his feet against my desk. "I can see it now." He held up his hands as if he were framing a picture. "Lulu LaBelle and Ned What's-his-name, stars for the ages."

"Or the aged," I muttered, still feeling grumpy about Ned being such a pest and also recalling Lulu's white hair. Which prompted my next question. "Ernie, is Lulu ill?"

His chair's front legs clumped to the floor. "Is she ill? What do you mean? I guess she's healthy enough. She hasn't told me if she's sick. You know something I don't?"

"No." I hesitated, then went on. "It's her hair. I mean, isn't it strange for so young a woman to have white hair like that?"

His grin remained, and his eyebrows lifted, giving him a teasingly incredulous expression that told me I'd made another error based on my upbringing. Drat it! Sometimes it seemed as if I'd never learn the ins and outs of West Coast living.

"Do you mean to tell me you've never encountered a bottle blonde before, Mercy Allcutt?"

I was nonplussed. "A what?"

"A bottle blonde. A peroxide blonde."

"Er . . . no, I guess I haven't. Except for Lulu, if she is one."

"*If?* Lady, Lulu was one of the very first. She'd be a regular trend-setter if she wasn't stuck in the Figueroa Building every day. As it is, I think she's only trying to follow in the footsteps of Mary Pickford."

"Oh." I pondered this revelation. "Do you mean to tell me that she *wants* her hair to be white?"

Ernie tutted. "It's not white, sweetie, it's *blonde*."

"It looks white to me."

Standing and stretching, Ernie said, "Me, too, but we're not Lulu. And thank God for it, I say."

It was a mean thing to say, but I have to admit that I agreed with him. The door behind Ernie opened, and Mr. Bigelow walked in. "Hi, you two," he said, smiling at me and punching Ernie on the shoulder lightly, which I took to be a demonstration of masculine friendship. My father's friends never punched each other when they met, but my father was almost as stuffy as my mother.

"Good afternoon, Mr. Bigelow," I said.

"Phil, you old phony!" said Ernie, punching him back. "Got any news for me?"

"Not much." Turning to me, Mr. Bigelow said, "Please call me Phil, Miss Allcutt. Every time you call me Mr. Bigelow, I think my father's entered the room."

I smiled at him, understanding completely. "Certainly. And please call me Mercy."

"Nice name," he said.

"All right, can it," said Ernie, sounding cranky. "I've got to talk to you about something else, Phil. There's somebody I want you to look into for me."

"Yeah? About what?"

"Just a background check. This guy makes me nervous."

Wondering who among all the thousands—or was it millions?—of people living in Los Angeles who could possibly have that effect on so nonchalant an individual as Ernest Templeton, P.I., I suddenly recalled Ned. Could Ernie seriously be worried about Ned's seemingly irrational fondness for my personal self? It seemed unlikely, but I realized my curiosity would have to be satisfied later, because they went into Ernie's office and closed the door.

At least Ned didn't bother me again that day, and I had no less an escort than a detective from the Los Angeles Police Department to safeguard my return home that evening, because Phil went with Ernie and me. I suspect that Ernie had told him about Chloe and Harvey's big house and he wanted to see it for himself, but I didn't ask.

Thursday finally arrived! When Ernie picked me up that morning, I was agog with anticipation, which I hadn't wanted to share with Chloe. After the fuss she made when Ernie took me to Mr. Fortescue's house, I feared she'd call our parents if I told her I was going to be working in an undercover (that's what the police department calls it) capacity that very day in order to trap a group of vile drug smugglers. I fairly danced out to Ernie's Studebaker.

Eyeing me critically, Ernie said, "What are you so jolly about?"

He didn't sound happy, but I try not to allow other people's moods to affect my own. "I'm excited about what we're going to do today."

"Yeah? Well, I just hope it goes all right and nobody gets hurt."

He opened the door, and I slid into the car. "Do you anticipate gunplay?" I asked avidly.

I'd read in the newspaper about hideous gunfights involving crooks and policemen, all armed with so-called "Tommy" guns. I'd also read that many crooks carried these guns in violin cases, in the hopes that nobody would realize what they were carrying. I couldn't quite understand this particular effort at deception. If any of the violin case–toters looked like the fellows in the mug shots I'd recently viewed, I doubt that very many citizens were being fooled by the ruse.

Did Ernie truly suspect that such a gun battle might transpire in that tiny curio shop? The notion, while frightening, was also rather thrilling. Ernie would probably have said I was being naïve, so I didn't tell him the part about me considering the possibility of a gun battle thrilling.

"We're dealing with some very bad guys here, Mercy. I don't like it that Phil wants you to be in on it."

"But I *want* to be in on it," cried I, fearing Ernie was going to change the scheme.

"Yeah, I know, but that's only because you're young and stupid."

"I am not!"

He only gave me a shows-what-you-know look and took off down the street. I was very annoyed with him and, although I sensed it would do no good to complain, I opted to do it anyway. "I may be inexperienced, but I am *not* stupid. If anything happens, I'll be sure to duck."

"Duck? A bullet? It's been tried before, and to my certain knowledge, nobody's ever succeeded."

"Fiddlesticks. Mr. Bigelow said there would be little or no danger."

"Phil doesn't know that, and neither do I."

"Well, I'm going to do it, and that's that."

"Yeah, yeah. I know. I'd have to lock you in the office to keep you out of it."

This time it was I who grinned. "I'd have Ned let me out."

"Ned." Ernie didn't appear to consider my comment funny. "And that's another thing."

"What? Ned?" I stared at him. Ned was a pest and a bother, but I didn't see that he was a threat to anyone, especially me, for whom he'd developed a certain affection. If you could call it that. "Don't be ridiculous!"

"Hmm."

We'd arrived at the Figueroa Building, and Ernie parked the Studebaker close by. We went into the lobby of the building together, and together we greeted Lulu, who was, as usual, filing her long, red fingernails, and who greeted us with, "Ned's looking for you."

"Christ," muttered Ernie.

I said, "Thanks, Lulu. Do you know where he is?"

"Prolly in the basement reading. That's where he usually is."

"Maybe I should go down and see what he wants," I said with a sigh. I really didn't want to, mainly because I was sick of Ned, and also because I was pretty sure he wasn't looking for me for anything truly important.

Lulu shrugged, a la Barbara-Ann Houser. Ernie took my arm and said, "Nothing doing. He can come to the office if he has more flowers for you." He winked at Lulu, who grinned.

Vexed with them both, I shook off Ernie's hand. "Very well. But I don't know why you insist on teasing me about Ned. I certainly did nothing to encourage him."

"Ned doesn't need encouragement," Lulu said.

"I should say he doesn't," said I, heading for the elevator, mainly because I wanted to practice getting the carriage to stop exactly at the right spot. I was getting better at this elevator nonsense. Which made me smile.

"You know, Ernie, if you ever fire me, I bet I'll be able to get a job as an elevator operator."

"That must give you a real sense of security," he said dryly.

I laughed until I remembered how many women there were in the world who could use the skills I possessed—and I'd only come by them because I'd had the time and money to go to school and then move to California. In other words, I only possessed my marketable skills because I

236

hadn't really needed them to earn a living to begin with. If I'd been forced to earn money from the age of twelve (or earlier) like Barbara-Ann Houser, I'd never have had the opportunity to learn the things I knew.

When viewed from certain perspectives, life seemed remarkably unfair.

However, that didn't alter the fact that this particular Thursday seemed destined to be one of the most exciting days in my entire life. Which, when I thought about it, didn't mean much, as my life had contained very little in the way of excitement until then.

Mr. Bigelow—or Phil, as he now was to me—arrived at the office at ten o'clock, and we spent about an hour going over our plan for the arrest and capture of the drug-dealing scum, as Ernie called them. The discussion didn't really seem necessary to me, as the plan was remarkably simple.

I was supposed to browse in Mr. Li's shop until the criminal element entered. In case I didn't recognize them, which was entirely possible since I'd only viewed the men via photographs, Mr. Li, who had been let out of jail for this express purpose, was to give me a signal. The signal might be anything from a nod to a screech of warning. I was to leave the shop, wave at Ernie and Phil, who would be holed up in Charlie's noodle shop across the plaza, and they and the policemen accompanying them would scoot into the shop and arrest the bad guys.

It was rather heartening to know that Ernie worried about me, although if looked at from another angle, I suppose his concern indicated a lack of faith, which I don't believe I deserved. It had been I, after all, who'd saved Mrs. Von Schilling's poodle. If that hadn't proved my overall usefulness in the private detecting business, I don't know what did.

FIFTEEN

At eleven o'clock, the three of us (I'd had to shoo Ned off twice by then) piled into Phil's big Ford and tootled to Chinatown and Mr. Li's shop. Because I didn't want to be weighted down with extraneous things to fuss with, I stuck some money in my skirt pocket and left my handbag in the drawer of my desk. I did, however, put on my hat, since to do otherwise would have been in poor taste since proper women didn't appear in public without hats. Clearly, I needed more practice in California living.

We gathered in the little noodle shop across the plaza from the shop, and Phil escorted Mr. Li and me to the shop, which had been closed since Monday's arrest of Mr. Li on kidnapping charges. According to the plans that were made between Mr. Li and the police, those charges might be lowered to false imprisonment (I didn't understand the difference, to tell the truth) if he cooperated fully in this day's events.

Poor Mr. Li was a nervous wreck, a fact I hoped wouldn't tip off the bad guys to possible police involvement. When I whispered as much to Phil, he said not to worry. Anybody with half a brain would be nervous when faced with an interview with Mr. Carpetti, even when the law wasn't involved. He went on to say that he doubted Mr. Li's state of anxiety would seem out of place to Carpetti or his henchmen.

"He'd have been nervous anyway, since he lost Babs Houser and didn't get any ransom to show for her."

Mr. Li whimpered. Phil eyed him coldly. "You don't get any sympathy from me, Li. You play with fire, you get burned."

"I know. I know," mumbled Mr. Li.

Since his shop had been closed for so long, it was terribly musty and stuffy. I offered to help him dust the place, but Phil nixed that idea. "You're supposed to be a tourist, Mercy. Act like one." His voice was sterner than I'd ever heard it.

"Very well," I said. I said it meekly, too, what's more, since I didn't want him to have second thoughts about my involvement in the day's activities.

That day I had worn one of my sober, pre-bobbed hair suits and a very sensible pair of shoes, since I'd anticipated standing around for an hour or more in that dumpy little souvenir shop before anything of interest transpired, but my feet were aching after about the first half-hour or so. The shop was very small, and Mr. Li had it filled with knick-knacks of one sort and another, primarily manufactured either in China or made to look as if they were Chinese. There were a few silk brocade robes in various colors, and they held my attention longer than anything else.

Some pretty pottery vases and porcelain goddesses, too, caught my eye—for about five minutes. Face it, when you're in a ten-foot-by-ten-foot shop for an hour and a half, unless it's stocked with fascinating books or something equally entertaining, you'll be bored in a very few minutes. I was bored. And I wished I'd brought a novel along with me until I realized that I couldn't just stand there reading, either, because that would negate my pose as a tourist. Nuts.

Ernie had told me that a lot of private investigation work was tedious. I had believed he'd been attempting to

dampen my ardor for the profession, but that day I discovered he'd been telling the absolute truth.

I'd just picked up a tiny porcelain teacup, which went with a tea set made up of a tray, a teapot, and six little cups, for about the seventeenth time, attempting to look like a lady trying to make up her mind, when I heard Mr. Li utter a frightened squeak. I almost dropped the teacup. When I glanced at him, he jerked his head in the direction of the front door.

Acting very relaxed and touristy, I replaced the teacup, picked up another one from a different set, and glanced at the front door. The jolt of excitement that shot through me when I saw two swarthy gentlemen approaching from the direction of Hill Street made the breath catch in my throat.

Out of the corner of my eye, I watched as the men entered the shop. Neither one of them carried a violin case, which was a relief, although I'm sure they had guns tucked away somewhere. Maybe gangsters only carried guns in violin cases when they aimed to "shoot up the joint" (another phrase used by the police and the criminal element). I didn't relax, however, since Phil and Ernie had both warned me that these were genuine gangsters who used real weapons and killed real people. The two men noticed me right off the bat, and one of them frowned, which was rather disconcerting. I guess they didn't want to transact illicit business with Mr. Li as long as anyone else remained in the shop. They both paused a few feet and an aisle away from me and pretended to be interested in some rose-scented soap. I hoped I looked more like an innocent tourist than they did.

It was fine with me if they didn't want me around. By that time I was rethinking my desire to be a part of any action that might involve gunplay. Casually putting the

teacup down—I am proud to announce that my hand did not tremble the least little bit—I made my way to the front door. The man who'd frowned at me continued to do so. I felt his eyes boring into my back as I left the shop, and it was a most uncomfortable feeling, I can tell you. My shoulder blades itched and my breathing was unsteady.

I confess to sucking in a deep breath as soon as I was out the door, although I knew it was too soon to celebrate. My job wasn't over yet. On knees that felt as if they'd been sculpted of aspic, I walked across the plaza toward the noodle shop.

What happened next I couldn't have anticipated if I'd been given a year to contemplate possibilities, although I'll keep it in mind when I start writing my novels. Out of nowhere, somebody rushed up and grabbed my arm. I'm pretty sure I screamed, since I was already in a state of anxiety due to the brutes in Mr. Li's shop, although I don't remember doing so.

I do remember whirling around, sure my accoster would prove to be the frowning man.

You can imagine my astonishment when I discovered Mr. Hiram Godfrey clinging to my arm. The expression on his face looked like one of pain, although, to judge by what he said to me, I guess it was ardor.

"Miss Allcutt! Mercy! You must come with me. I adore you. I love you! We can be married right away!"

Trying to shake him off, I cried, "Stop it! Let me *go*, you murdering fiend!"

I was terrified lest this interruption of our carefully laid plan would spell its failure. If I could help it, Mr. Hiram Godfrey, mad murderer that he was, wouldn't thwart our purpose.

Mr. Godfrey did not release me. He looked mighty puzzled, however, when he said, "Murdering fiend? What do you mean?"

I kicked him hard in the shin with my sensibly shod foot. He released me then. He also clutched his shin and started hopping around the plaza on his other foot, looking rather like an overweight flamingo, since his face had turned a brilliant red by that time. "Why did you do that? Don't you know that I *love* you?"

Forsaking caution as well as an answer, I raced to the noodle shop, hoping that if the criminals in Mr. Li's shop saw me doing so, they'd chalk up the cause to Mr. Godfrey's assault. Which it was, primarily.

By the time I reached the noodle shop, I was in such a panic, I wrenched the door open and practically fell inside—right into Ernie's arms. He propped me up and said, "What the hell?"

"It's Mr. Godfrey!" Reminded of the original purpose of this trip to Chinatown, I added, "And the men went into Mr. Li's shop!"

I know I was being almost incoherent, but darn it, I was in a real state by that time and believe my lapses might be excused. As uniformed policemen poured out of the noodle shop, Ernie and Phil exchanged a look of surprise.

Phil said, "You take care of Godfrey. I've gotta be in on the arrest."

"Right." Squinting down at me as if he suspected I'd lost my mind in the excitement of the moment, he said, "What's this about Godfrey?"

"He's *there*," I cried, pointing in the general direction of the plaza. "He grabbed me! He said we had to get married!"

Ernie's squint got narrower. "Geez, the guy really *is* nuts, isn't he?" He yanked the door open and rushed out.

I wasn't sure how to take that, but it didn't seem to be the right time to ask how Ernie had meant his comment. I hurried after him, eager to see Mr. Godfrey arrested and

locked up for the brutal murder of June Williams.

Fortunately, in the several seconds it took to achieve the above results, Mr. Godfrey hadn't gone anywhere. In fact, he'd sat on a bench in front of the good-luck pond that was in the middle of the plaza, rubbing his shin. His piggy eyes, when he lifted them from his trousers, conveyed an expression of hurt bewilderment until Ernie reached him. Then he looked up and smiled at him. Really, the man was truly mad!

"Hello, Mr. Templeton," said Mr. Godfrey, nodding at Ernie as if he hadn't recently murdered anyone or just assaulted me on a public plaza. "I've been meaning to get to your office. I owe you some money."

"Yes," said Ernie, standing before him and looking down at him, his fists on his hips. I had sort of expected him to grab him, or at least point a gun at him. Instead, he said, "Hiram Godfrey, you've really got to stop expecting every woman you meet to marry you."

Mr. Godfrey's smile faded and the hangdog expression returned to his chubby features. "You mean Miss Allcutt doesn't want to marry me, either?"

"I'm afraid not," said Ernie, much more gently than I believed was called for.

"Ernie," I said, "what are you doing? Do you realize this man just attacked me?"

"Attacked you?" Mr. Godfrey said in a hurt voice. "But I thought you wanted to marry me."

It was my turn to put my fists on my hips, only my voice was anything but gentle when I spoke next. "What in the world made you believe that?"

"But you were nice to me."

"I'm nice to everyone."

"Oh."

I turned to Ernie. "Aren't you going to arrest him?"

"Arrest me?" Now Mr. Godfrey appeared alarmed. Past time, if you ask me.

"Sorry, Mercy, I'm not a cop. Besides, we have some real criminals to pick up now, it looks like."

I realized his gaze was fixed on Mr. Li's shop. "But . . ." I didn't get to finish my sentence because suddenly shots rang out. The front window of Mr. Li's shop exploded, sending a spray of glass out onto the plaza. I said, "Oh!" and covered my head with my hands, although I'm not sure why. Shock, I guess. What I should have done—and what I'll try to remember to do the next time I'm in the vicinity of a gunfight—was to flatten myself out on the ground. Getting one's clothes dirty was a much more pleasing alternative to getting drilled by a stray bullet. Ernie told me that later, and quite sarcastically, too. I didn't appreciate his tone of voice, but I did understand and agree with the sentiment.

He didn't speak in that moment. What he did was grab me around the waist and hurl me to the ground, landing on top of me. He said later that he was covering my body with his so that nobody in my family could accuse him of putting me in harm's way, but I honestly don't believe that. I think he has the instincts of a gentleman, no matter how hard he tries to pretend he doesn't. His first impulse is to protect a person he perceives might be in danger. His impulse didn't prevent me from ending up with torn garments and skinned knees (and you should have seen my stockings!) but I didn't blame him for those minor casualties. I thought he was sweet. I'd have told him so, but I sensed he wouldn't have appreciated it.

Before I had gathered my wits together, Ernie shouted, "Stay there!" and he took off, crouched over and running, toward the shop.

I shrieked, "Ernie! Get back here, you idiot!" but I

didn't mean it. The idiot part. The getting back there part I meant with all my heart.

"Miss Allcutt!" Mr. Godfrey, who, I discovered, was on his stomach on the plaza alongside me, said. "Are you all right?"

"Of course, I'm all right! Stay away from me, you maniac!"

"But . . ."

I'm not a fool. Nor am I stupid. I didn't want to get myself shot. However, I was absolutely *dying* (so to speak) to know what was going on in the shop. And I also didn't want to remain lying next to a man whom I believed to be a cold-blooded murderer. Therefore, I decided not to perform a citizen's arrest on Mr. Godfrey—he was ever so much larger than I and probably would have objected if I'd tried—but crawled on my hands and scraped knees to the shop, trying to stay behind things such as the wishing well, a restaurant sign, a potted plant, etc., on my way.

Before I got there, the shop's front door slammed open, and one of the two Italianate gentlemen, the one who'd frowned at me when I'd seen him entering the shop a while back, pelted out onto the plaza, a gun in his hand. His attention was riveted on the shop, so he didn't see me there on my hands and knees. It was but the work of a second to scoot myself directly into his path.

It hurt like mad when he ran into me, but the result was most satisfactory. He went sprawling, his gun flew out of his hand and went spinning across the plaza, and he said, *"Damn!"* a second before he said, *"Ow!"*

The next thing I knew, I'd been grabbed around the middle and all but heaved out of the way. I feared at first that it was the first man's partner who'd handled me so roughly, but then I saw Ernie hurl himself on top of the fallen man and deduced it had been he.

Hoping like mad that nobody else would fire any more bullets at anybody, I decided the most prudent thing to do would be to secure the first man's gun. When I got to my feet, I was horrified to see that Mr. Godfrey had anticipated me. He held the gun via a finger poked through the trigger guard and was looking at it as if it were a poisonous serpent.

Terror seized me. Then I remembered that, according to Mr. Godfrey, he wanted to marry me. Men didn't shoot women they wanted to marry, did they? Several newspaper articles and June Williams flashed before my mind's eye, but I thrust them aside. Ernie and the police obviously needed help. "Give me the gun, Mr. Godfrey. Please," I added because I can't seem to help myself. All that breeding, I guess.

"But . . ."

Sternly, I said, "Now! That's evidence in a police investigation." I was proud of myself for thinking of that line.

He said, "Oh. Okay."

And, by gum, he handed me the gun! It was very heavy. I'd never held a gun before, and handled it gingerly. I didn't touch the trigger.

"Damn it to hell, Mercy Allcutt, give me that gat!"

It was Ernie, who'd wrestled the criminal to a position of surrender and snapped handcuffs on him.

I didn't understand. "What gat? What's a gat?"

"Damn it, give me the damned *gun*, you idiot!"

"Curse it, Ernie Templeton, I saved you from being killed! Don't you dare swear at me! And don't call me an idiot, either." But I handed him the gun.

He took a deep breath, yanked the criminal to his feet, and said tightly, "Thank you. You helped a lot. And you're not an idiot."

I sniffed.

At that moment, two uniformed policemen exited Mr. Li's shop. Between them, handcuffed and being held in a mercilessly tight grip by the police, was the second man. Phil came out of the shop, holding Mr. Li's arm. Poor Mr. Li, while I agreed with Phil that he didn't deserve much sympathy, was clearly in a state of abject terror and agitation. The poor man was actually shaking with fright.

By that time, we'd drawn quite a crowd, including Mr. Godfrey, who still hung around. I'd expected him to escape ere this, but I guess he didn't have the sense to realize he oughtn't remain where there were police available to arrest him for June Williams's murder. Phil spotted him, and leaving Mr. Li to another policeman, came over to talk to him.

"You're Hiram Godfrey?"

Mr. Godfrey nodded.

"Come down to the station with us. I need to ask you some questions about June Williams."

With a sigh, Mr. Godfrey said, "Yes, I meant to do that sooner. Can I get a ride with you?"

"Sure."

Well, thank God for that! At least *somebody* was going to interrogate the man who'd brutally murdered that poor girl. When I thought that I might well have been his next victim, my blood ran cold.

People were milling around, all talking amongst themselves, mostly in Chinese, although a few tourists were clumped here and there. Mr. Li, still in police custody, spoke to a fellow shopkeeper, I presume about his shop because the man took a key from Mr. Li and went to lock it up. Mr. Li seemed extremely dejected when the police led him away. The two Italian men appeared more annoyed than dejected.

I was about to seek out Ernie and ask him what we needed to do next when he walked over to me. "You look like hell, Mercy. I'm sorry you scraped your knees when I threw you down."

Those weren't exactly the words I'd been hoping to hear from him, but they brought my mangled condition to my mind. Glancing down, I realized that my brown cotton suit's skirt had sustained a rip, probably from when my knee struck the concrete floor of the plaza, and that blood ran down my shins. My stockings were a total loss. Instead of taking Ernie to task, I sighed. "I guess so."

"Want me to take you home so you can get yourself doctored up?"

"Oh, no, you don't! I was instrumental in the capture of that vicious criminal, Ernie Templeton, and I'm going to see him charged. Booked. Whatever the term is."

For a second or two, I thought he was going to blow up at me, but he controlled himself. In actual fact, after his initial reaction to my demand, which entailed tight lips, a hideous frown, and a deeply furrowed brow, he grinned. Then he took that blasted flask from his pocket, uncorked it, and swallowed some of its vile contents. Right there on the plaza in Chinatown, in front of God, half the Chinese population of Los Angeles, and the Los Angeles Police Department. Not to mention me. "Okay. You can wash up at the department, I guess. They have iodine there, too. And bandages."

"Thank you."

I was grateful that Phil had Mr. Godfrey ride in the front seat with him, because I certainly didn't want to sit next to him. Ernie and I shared the Ford's back seat. The drive to the police station took only a couple of minutes, since it was right there near Chinatown. The two gunmen, who arrived in a marked police vehicle, were led into the station by the

uniformed policemen, and we followed with Mr. Godfrey. It seemed to me that Phil and Ernie were treating him with alarming negligence, considering he had murdered an innocent woman. Then again, I knew they both maintained that they weren't sure who had murdered June Williams. I guess they didn't want a suit for false arrest or something filed against them. I still thought they should have been more vigilant.

We went into the same large, busy room that we'd visited before with Barbara-Ann Houser and her mother. People were smoking and walking and talking, and I saw that Phil and Ernie got admiring nods and several comments from other officers present when they spotted the two gangsters. That made me feel good. Evidently the police had been looking for those men before this.

Phil gestured at me to take a chair on one side of his desk, and nodded to Mr. Godfrey to take the one on the other side. Ernie hauled over another chair, set it near mine, and straddled it.

"Take 'em to booking, Sullivan," Phil said to the same man who'd escorted Mr. Li on our prior visit. "Then come back here. I might need you to pick up Babs Houser and the kid."

That caught my attention. "Why do you need Mrs. Houser? You're not going to charge her with anything, are you?"

Phil eyed me speculatively. "You don't think she was involved in this?"

Bridling, I said, "I sincerely doubt it. Why, she was held hostage, wasn't she?"

Ernie took over from Phil. "Yeah, but her boyfriend was in it up to his eyeballs. She was only kidnapped when Matty blew the dough on the ponies."

I believe that meant he gambled the money away on horse races. "But she didn't say she was involved in the crime itself. In fact, she seemed rather irritated with Mr. Bumpas. I mean Matty." Drat my upbringing!

"You expect her to confess to being involved with a dope ring?" Ernie chuckled.

I felt stupid and naïve, but I pursued the subject not because I cared much about Babs Houser, but because I had formed a fondness for Barbara-Ann, a girl with spunk and grit, two qualities I admired and even wanted to emulate. In a way. "Just because a woman has poor taste in men and doesn't have sense enough to leave one when he pursues a criminal life, doesn't mean she's actually *involved* in the criminal activity," I pointed out, believing it a valid argument and worth consideration.

The glance exchanged by Phil and Ernie let me know they didn't share my sentiments. Feeling rather as if my back were to a wall, I said desperately, "But what about Barbara-Ann? You can't arrest her mother! What would the poor child do?"

Ernie shrugged, again reminding me of Barbara-Ann herself. "She does okay on her own, it looks like to me."

Horrified, I cried, "But she's only twelve years old!"

"Don't worry, Miss Allcutt. We don't plan to arrest Babs Houser," Phil said, relieving my mind considerably.

I frowned at Ernie to let him know I didn't appreciate his attitude about what I considered a serious subject. He only grinned and took out his flask again. I watched, disgruntled, as he took a swig. Honestly! Right here in the police station.

Mr. Sullivan came back at that point, and clapped Ernie on the back. "Still sucking on that flask, are you, Ernie?"

Grinning up at him, Ernie said, "Can't seem to shake the habit, Sully."

Mr. Sullivan winked at me, probably because I was gazing at Ernie and him with patent disapproval writ large on my countenance. "Don't worry, ma'am. It's only apple cider."

"Don't tell her that!" Ernie cried, either honestly aghast or faking it very well. "She thinks I'm a lush!"

I'm pretty sure my mouth fell open in surprise. Surprise quickly transformed into indignation. Since Ernie was still holding the small flask, I whipped out a hand and grabbed it from him. He tried to snatch it back, but I was too quick for him and held on tight. When I sniffed its contents, I realized that Mr. Sullivan was right. Ernie had been sipping apple cider out of that blasted flask! I glared at him. "Do you mean to tell me you've been pretending to be drinking spirits ever since the day I first walked into your office?"

Ernie held up his hands, palms out. "Not I. I never told you what was in that flask, did I?"

I tried to remember. Actually, I couldn't recall that he'd ever *said* he was drinking liquor from the flask. But he'd made sure I *believed* he had been. "A sin of omission is no less a sin than one of commission, Ernest Templeton. You led me to believe you were drinking spirits. You lied to me."

"Nuts. I'm not responsible for your evil mind."

Mr. Sullivan winked at me again, and I decided I'd never win this particular argument. It was also past time to take care of my appearance, if I could. My poor skinned knees hurt when I stood up. "May I wash up, please?" My voice was almost as stiff as my knees.

"Sure." Ernie rose, too. He didn't look especially repentant, but I did appreciate it when he led me to a woman who was a secretary, I guess, and asked her to take me to a washroom.

She wanted to know all about Ernie as she did so, probably because she thought he was good-looking and would have liked to get to know him better. Although Ernie Templeton wasn't my favorite person at the moment, I obliged as best I could, deliberately leaving out references to his less savory character traits. I thought that was very nice of me.

SIXTEEN

When I returned to the big room full of people, I was surprised to see that Mr. Godfrey was gone and even more surprised to see that Matty Bumpas had taken his place in the chair next to Phil's desk. Mr. Bumpas was clearly not happy to be there, but there wasn't a thing he could do about it, since his hands were cuffed behind his back, and Mr. Sullivan loomed like a monolith behind him, ready, I presume, to squash him flat if he tried to escape.

I met Ernie at the secretary's desk. It looked to me as if he'd been talking with her for some time—and the cad was making great headway, if I was any judge. When he saw me, he broke off his conversation, and we walked back to Phil's desk together.

"Where's Mr. Godfrey?" was my first question. I'd taken off my stockings and thrown them away, acknowledging as I did so that money was a fine thing to have enough of, if you didn't overdo it. I'd washed my knees and used the iodine, which stung like mad, on the scrapes, then made gauze pads to cover them and stuck the pads in place with the tape the kind-hearted secretary had let me borrow. Since my handbag was in the office and I didn't have an alternative, I'd finger-combed my hair, grateful for my new bob since it fell into place quite well even without the benefit of brush or comb. There wasn't anything I could do about the state of my ripped and stained clothing.

Looking me up and down in a very unprofessional manner, Ernie said, "There was an outstanding warrant on

253

him, so Sullivan took him to booking. You don't look much better, kiddo."

"Thank you *ever* so much."

He grinned. "You're ever so welcome."

I gave up on that topic. There was obviously no making Ernest Templeton, P.I., use the manners his mother had taught him if he didn't want to use them. "When are they going to arrest him for murder?"

Casting a sarcastic glance at the ceiling, Ernie said, "After they book him on the outstanding FTA charge, I expect."

"What's an FTA charge?"

"Failure to appear. He didn't show up in court on an assault charge."

"An assault charge?" My outlook brightened instantly.

"Yeah. I guess he thought somebody before you and Miss Williams wanted to marry him. Only she pressed charges."

"Ha! I knew he was a fiend!"

"Yeah, maybe."

"And you're sure they'll take care of Mr. Godfrey?"

"They'll take care of him, all right," he assured me.

I eyed him closely, not entirely sure he meant they were actually going to arrest the man for the murder of June Williams. However, it was nice to know that Mr. Godfrey would be out of my hair at least for a little while. I lowered my voice for my next question. "Where did they find Matty Bumpas?"

"Train station. Phil's had some fellows watching it for a day or two, in case he tried to skip. He did." Ernie's grin was quite devilish.

"Good for Phil."

"Yeah, he's a good copper."

"Did he send someone to bring Babs Houser here?"

"Yeah. She should be here any minute now if she was at that fancy hotel you put her in when they knocked on her door."

"It wasn't a fancy hotel," I muttered, embarrassed, although why I should have been, I don't know. People are supposed to do good deeds for other people, aren't they? Anyhow, now that the criminals had all been picked up, I suppose Babs and Barbara-Ann could return to their apartment. Their shabby, depressing apartment.

Oh, well. As Ernie was fond of pointing out to me, I couldn't rescue the world.

When we got to Phil's desk, Ernie pulled out a chair for me, and he took the one I'd been sitting on earlier. Matty Bumpas was being questioned by Phil.

"Was Babs involved in this scheme of yours, Bumpas?" Phil asked, frowning menacingly and using a voice that would have scared me if it had been directed at me.

"Babs?" Matty Bumpas had as sour an expression as I'd ever seen on his face. Or "puss," as the gangsters call it. According to Ernie. "Naw. She damn near skinned me alive when she realized I'd lost some of the money." He looked around, as if searching for someone. "She *will* skin me alive if I'm here when she shows up. When they kidnapped her, I knew I'd better leave town."

"Why didn't you just bail her out?" asked Phil.

"With what?"

Ernie decided to join the conversation. "I don't suppose you've ever considered working for a living at a real job, have you, Matty?"

Matty Bumpas shot him a very mean-looking frown. Phil chuckled.

"Ernie's right, Matty. You're apt to get killed if you keep

up your present way of life."

"Go to hell," muttered Matty.

A penetrating shriek rent the smoke-filled air, and Matty leaped to his feet, knocking his chair over backwards, and made as if to escape. Sullivan neatly thwarted that intention, but Matty kept struggling.

"You goddamned son of a bitch!" the same voice that had shrieked cried out. "You lousy, rotten bum!"

Babs Houser had arrived.

Acknowledging the meaning behind Phil's nod at him, Ernie hurried to intercept Babs before she could carry out the will of the State of California by herself and execute Matty Bumpas. She fought like a wildcat for several seconds before Ernie got her calmed down. He did it by twisting her arm behind her back, which I suppose was a brutal tactic, but it worked. I must say that I wished Barbara-Ann Houser had at least one decent parent. It was becoming increasingly apparent to me that life was unfair more often than it was fair, unless I was only becoming jaded.

Shooting murderous glances at Matty Bumpas, Babs settled herself in the chair Ernie had vacated, and unloaded more damning evidence against her erstwhile lover than Phil ever could have got from Matty himself. Babs must have raked up every single sin Matty Bumpas had committed in the past ten years. As for Matty, he sat in glum silence, apparently believing he'd be better off in jail than anywhere Babs could get at him.

It was all very interesting, but I was beginning to feel pretty achy, and I really wanted to go home. I still had to drop by the office and pick up my handbag before I could do so, and in order to do that, I either had to walk to the Figueroa Building on my scraped and bandaged legs or wait until Ernie or somebody else could take me there.

Unless I caught a cab. By George, until that moment, I'd never even considered hiring a taxi to take me to work.

Because I didn't want to interrupt the continuing interrogation of Matty Bumpas and Babs Houser, I quietly excused myself and got up from my chair.

Ernie frowned at me. "What are you doing?" he whispered.

"Don't mind me," I told him. "I'll be fine."

"But—"

Phil asked him a question, diverting his attention from me. I took the opportunity to scoot. As long as Mr. Godfrey was safely in police custody, I didn't fear for my well-being, and Ernie shouldn't either.

It was almost five o'clock when I got back to the Figueroa Building. It had been a busy day, and I realized I hadn't taken time for luncheon. Lunch. Therefore, it was no surprise that my stomach growled when I paid off the cabbie and wearily pushed the door to the lobby open.

Lulu looked up from filing her nails and saw me. Her eyes went as round as saucers and she dropped her emery board. "Cripes! What happened to you?"

So I told her. It was actually fun to narrate the day's adventure, since Lulu was an appreciative audience and made several cries of astonishment during my recitation. Except for rescuing Mrs. Von Schilling's poodle, my life hadn't been chock-full of adventures to date, so I made the most of this one. When I got to the part about Mr. Godfrey accosting me on the plaza, Lulu clapped a hand to her cheek, almost putting her eye out with one of her fingernails.

"That fat man? The one who's always bringing you flowers? He asked you to *marry* him?"

"He didn't so much ask as assume," I said wryly. "He grabbed me by the arm and tried to yank me off. I presume to a registry office or a judge or something."

"For land's sake!"

When I got to the part about Han Li's shop and the gangsters, her mouth fell open and stayed that way until I was on my hands and knees on the Plaza.

"You mean to say, you tripped the man with your *body?*" Her voice throbbed with admiration.

"Yes, indeed. I'll probably have a shoe-shaped bruise on my ribs for a week or more. And then there are my knees." Ruefully, I stuck out my leg to show Lulu my poor battered knees. Not to mention my skirt.

"Lands sakes," she whispered, awed. "I didn't know Ernie did that kind of work. That's . . . that's . . . well, it's thrilling."

"It was pretty thrilling," I admitted. "And the police have Mr. Godfrey, too, so I don't have to worry about going to and from work by myself any longer, either."

She gasped. "You couldn't even walk to work by yourself?"

I shook my head. "Ernie wouldn't let me."

"Oh, Mercy, that's just awful!" She didn't mean it. What she meant was that she considered my being pursued by Mr. Godfrey almost as exciting as my having tripped an armed gangster.

I nodded and decided that memories probably improved with age and that I'd appreciate this one a good deal more after my scrapes and bruises healed. "But I want to go up-stairs and get my handbag and go home now. I'm bushed." And starving to death, although I didn't tell her that.

"I should say you have a right to be," said Lulu, in amazement.

So I limped to the elevator, pulled the lever, and climbed aboard when it groaned to a stop on the first floor. I was

getting very good at operating it by this time, and even though it was slower than walking the three flights to Ernie's office, my knees hurt, my ribs were beginning to ache, and other muscles that I hadn't known about until that day were beginning to make their presence known. In other words, I was stiff as a board.

I had just retrieved my handbag when Ned showed up. I ought to have anticipated this, but I hadn't, and I don't suppose I sounded exactly thrilled to see him. "Ned," said I, not bothering to mask my weariness.

"Lulu told me what happened," he said in a voice that sounded unusually dull.

"Yes, it was pretty exciting."

"Exciting?"

I only sighed. "I'm tired, Ned. I need to go home now."

He shook his head. "She said you're going to marry Godfrey."

"You misunderstood, Ned. He wanted to marry me. I didn't want to marry him."

His head continued to shake slowly back and forth. "I don't like girls to cheat on me, Mercy."

I'd been locking my desk. At that comment, I jerked my head up and squinted at him. "I beg your pardon?"

"It was the same thing with June. She was my girl, and Godfrey stole her from me."

A horrible doubt began to niggle at my consciousness. "J-June?"

His head stopped shaking and began nodding. "She was my girl. Godfrey stole her."

"June Williams?"

More nodding.

Uh-oh. "Um . . . Ned, do you know that somebody killed June Williams?"

Still nodding, he said, "She cheated on me." He took a step closer. "I don't like it when girls cheat on me."

"Um . . . did you happen to follow Ernie and me when we went to Pasadena the other day?"

He nodded some more, and my insides started churning sickeningly at the same time that my brain began to whirl. Had I been wrong about Mr. Godfrey all along? Had Barbara-Ann Houser been right when she'd told me Ned was peculiar? Well, of course, she had been! Ned *was* peculiar. Even *I*, a straitlaced prude from Boston, could tell that. But was he *violent?* Was he *murderously* peculiar? Was he . . . I swallowed . . . *insane?* Frantically, I searched the office for weapons I could use to defend myself in case he was. Unfortunately, the office was barren of protective weapons. *Darn* it!

"Um . . . Ned. Are you the one who hurt June Williams, by any chance?"

"Hurt her? She hurt me."

He'd begun scowling at me, and his face expressed the trouble he was having in trying to decide exactly what to do with me, a woman whom he'd decided had cheated on him. How did these stupid men come to these idiotic conclusions? I decided to mull the matter over later. At that particular moment, I only wanted to get out of there.

I could hit him with a chair. It didn't seem like the best way to thwart a maddened murderer, if Ned was one, but I didn't perceive any other options. First, though, I guessed I might as well try to bluff my way out of the office.

"Listen, Ned, you've completely misunderstood what happened today. In actual fact, I helped to capture both Mr. Godfrey and two drug-dealing gangsters. I'm very tired now, and want to go home."

"On Bunker Hill," said Ned dully.

"Yes. On Bunker Hill."

Good Lord, how did he know that? Had he followed me? But I'd thought Mr. Godfrey was the one who'd been following me. Figuring there was no harm in asking, I did so. "Have you been following me, Ned?"

More nods. "You cheated with Mr. Templeton, too, didn't you?"

Darn it, this wasn't fair! When I'd agreed to be Ernie's secretary, I'd hoped for a little excitement. I hadn't anticipated actual danger to my own personal self. "I didn't cheat with anybody!" I hollered, furious. It had already been a rough day, full of terror and scraped knees and no food. I didn't want to end up dead at the end of it; I wanted to be able to tell my sister and her husband and maybe Mr. Easthope all about it! "Didn't your mother ever teach you that it's not polite to follow people around? How *dare* you spy on me!"

He looked puzzled. "Spy on you?"

Lord, preserve me from stupid people! "Yes! That's what it's called when you follow people around."

His chin jutted slightly, quite a feat for so sparse an object. "You were cheating."

"I was not!"

"Were, too."

"Oh, go away!"

His stupid head began shaking again. "I've got to punish you for cheating on me."

Oh, dear. I presumed this was where he'd whip out a cord or something and proceed to try to strangle me. Well, I wasn't going to sit around and wait for that to happen. I jumped up from my chair, an activity that made my knees silently scream for mercy, and grabbed it by its laddered back. "Get away from me, you murdering fiend!" It occurred to me that I'd told Mr. Godfrey that same thing earlier in the day.

Stupid day.

"No, I have to punish you."

To heck with that. Taking the bull by the horns, so to speak, I rushed at Ned, wielding my chair like a battering ram. He was bigger than I, but not by much, and I guess my charge shocked him, because he staggered back and said, "Whuff!"

Grabbing the doorknob as I passed, I slammed the door as I hurled myself out into the hallway and headed for the stairs.

And there, of all people in the universe, was Mrs. Von Schilling, looking approximately as slinky as Theda Bara on a hot date, carrying Rosie. Although Rosie barked a greeting, I didn't stick around to chat. I raced past them both.

I got to the elevator just as Ned threw the office door open and collided with Mrs. Von Schilling. Both went down as I pulled the lever to open the doors and pressed the "down" button, hoping maybe Ned would believe that I'd taken the elevator rather than the stairs. Slim chance, but I was willing to try anything at that point. Ned was up again in a flash, as was Rosie.

"Sic him, Rosie!" I shrieked, not expecting much from the command, but hoping.

Mrs. Von Schilling started screaming. She would. She wouldn't think of doing anything useful, like tackling Ned or anything, being the type of woman who preferred being rescued to helping rescue others.

Rosie, on the other hand, was not so snooty that she didn't express her resentment at being treated so roughly by a crazed lunatic. She started barking up a storm and snapping at Ned's heels. He tried to swat her away with his hands, but didn't have any luck. She was tiny and quick and thoroughly incensed. She chased him down the hall after

me, leaping at his pant legs with her sharp little doggie teeth and snarling. I saw with shock that Ned had pulled out a knife and was making slashing gestures at her as he hopped around and tried to avoid getting bitten. She was too quick and he was too distracted, I guess, to do much damage, but I wasn't sure how long that could last.

I couldn't allow Ned to hurt Rosie. It would have made more sense for me to run down the stairs, but poor Rosie was in danger, not to mention being a heroine, curse it, and I couldn't allow her to suffer for it. I screamed, *"Stop stabbing at that dog, you wretch!"*

And then, because I figured even Mrs. Von Schilling might pitch in to help a person if there was no alternative and her dog was in danger, I decided to try to trip Ned, as I'd done the other man earlier in the day. Then, if I succeeded, perhaps Mrs. Von Schilling and I could sit on him or something until the police arrived. Provided we could restrain him long enough to call the police. I ducked into the stairwell, but didn't head down the stairs. While Ned seemed to be keeping an eye on me still, his attention was seriously diverted by Rosie, who didn't seem inclined to let him get away with knocking down her mistress and kicking her. Good old Rosie. I vowed that I'd get myself a poodle as soon as I could.

"Mercy! Where are you?" Ned cried, still partially distracted by Rosie, God bless her.

Needless to say, I didn't answer that question. I remained where I was, Ned getting closer by the second, my heart hammering away in my bosom like a pile driver.

The time had come. Hoping to spare Rosie, I bent over—my knees were too sore for me to go down on them a second time that day—and I scooted out into the hallway from the stairwell. Have I mentioned that the stairwell was

about three feet away from the elevator? Well, it was. Ned couldn't stop himself in time to keep from plowing into me. I scooped Rosie up a split second before she would have been trampled by him as he staggered forward toward the elevator.

Holding Rosie close, I realized with absolute horror that I'd forgotten to shut the elevator doors after I'd pressed the "down" button. And then, with what could only be called calculated menace, another idea occurred to me. Ned had just managed to stop himself from falling into the elevator shaft, when I ran up behind him, and shoved. Hard.

The ghastly noise he made as he fell three floors was really quite awful. I regret to say, it was also quite welcome. That terrible man had tried to kill Rosie!

Not to mention me.

When that thought settled into my mind, I started shaking. Rosie licked my chin.

And then, all of a sudden and as if by magic, Ernie was there. I guess I'd heard somebody pounding up the stairs, but I was so busy with Ned and Rosie, I hadn't taken the time to think about it.

"Mercy! What the hell . . . ?"

"It—it wasn't M-Mr. G-Godfrey," I stammered, squeezing Rosie tight and with tears streaming down my face. She was sweet enough to snuggle. Maybe she needed it, too, after her own ordeal "It was Ned."

"I know it was Ned, damn it! Why the hell did you leave the station?"

I stared at him. "You . . . you *knew*? About *Ned*?"

Standing there, his fists on his hips, glaring at me, he hollered, "Why the hell did you think I didn't want you to be alone?"

I tried to take it in. Ernie had known something about

264

Ned that had led him to believe Ned might be a menace to me. Had Ernie told me? He had not. "But . . . but, I thought . . ."

"Thought? You *thought?* You don't think at all, dammit!"

In the face of Ernie's treachery, my panic and terror were fast transforming into fury. "Now you see here, Ernest Templeton. Don't you *dare* talk to me like that! If you'd believed Ned to be dangerous, why the devil didn't you *tell* me?" I'm ashamed to say I was hollering, too.

"Damn it!" Ernie bellowed. "I thought that maniac had killed you! When I walked into the building and Lulu told me he was upstairs with you, I damned near—"

"Stop *swearing* at me!" I shrieked.

"*Damn* it!"

And, by golly, Ernie reached out and took me, Rosie and all, into his arms and squeezed until Rosie yipped. Personally, I didn't mind the embrace. It showed proper managerial anxiety over the welfare of a person in his employ. I have to admit that being in his arms did more to alleviate my terror than anything else up to that moment, even though I was still mad at him.

Furious is perhaps a more accurate word. Irate. Enraged, even.

"What on earth is going on here?" Mrs. Von Schilling didn't sound nearly as sultry as she generally did, although her question effectively inspired Ernie to release Rosie and me from his embrace. I stumbled backward a couple of paces, not, I assure you, because I had in any way reacted to the embrace with anything other than leftover fright regarding the entire incident.

Oh, why not be honest? I'd never been hugged that way by a man, and it felt good.

However, that's nothing to the point. Ernie reached out and took my sleeve to keep me from following Ned down the elevator shaft, and I, demonstrating great presence of mind all things considered, pulled the lever to shut the elevator doors. I didn't want to look down and see what had happened to Ned.

Ned didn't die that day. Or any other day, for that matter, at least that I know about. He was badly injured, but according to the police surgeon accompanying Phil Bigelow and several other members of the Los Angeles Police Department who showed up shortly after Ernie called them, with the proper medical care, he would survive. That was, of course, after they'd brought the car up and scraped Ned off. I shuddered, just thinking about it, and couldn't quite make myself watch the operation. As Phil and the rest of his police friends swarmed in the corridor and hovered around the elevator, Ernie, Mrs. Von Schilling, Rosie, and I went to Ernie's office. I felt very shaky. And I was still madder than a wet hen, as one of my former schoolteachers used to say.

Although the weather that day was hovering around the ninety-degree mark, I was shivering violently by the time I sat on my trusty office chair, which Ernie had righted and set for me behind my desk. Ernie said it was shock, and put his coat over my shoulders. It helped some.

Mrs. Von Schilling, who actually had a sympathetic character trait to call her own, called a nearby restaurant and had tea and sweet cakes sent up to Ernie's office. "Put milk and sugar into the tea, dear," she told me. "It will help you calm down." I didn't ask how she'd come by the knowledge, but I thanked her mainly because she allowed me to hold onto Rosie until sustenance arrived.

I was still mightily peeved with Ernie. After my teeth had stopped chattering, I scowled at him. "Why didn't you tell me you suspected Ned of killing that poor woman?"

"Dammit, Mercy, I'm the detective here, not you."

"But you saw that he had formed a . . ." I wasn't sure what to call it. "Well, he'd started bringing me flowers and that sort of thing."

Ernie wiped his handkerchief across his forehead and took a nip of apple cider from his flask. Apple cider, for heaven's sake. "It was a police matter, Mercy. I can't go around accusing people of murder. Unlike you," he added with considerable bitterness, which I resented. "Anyhow, I didn't know anything. I'd asked Phil to look into his background."

Indignant, I cried, "But he was here every single day, Ernie Templeton. He bothered me all the time. You ought to have told me to be careful of him, at least!"

Lulu had showed up by this time, too. She looked accusingly at Ernie. "Yeah. And me, too. How were we supposed to know the man was a lunatic who killed women for fun? If you knew, you oughta of told us."

I nodded emphatically, even if I didn't agree with her grammatical construction. "Yes. It wasn't fair of you. Not at all."

Mrs. Von Schilling smiled enigmatically. She would.

"Damn it, I didn't *know*. For all I knew, you were right about Godfrey being the one. They both had records of violence against women."

I stared at Lulu, who stared back. "And you didn't tell *either* of us?" I said. Perhaps a little too loudly, because Rosie yipped.

Ernie took a quick turn around the office. There wasn't much room for him to do so, but he managed. "Damn it, I . . ." He suddenly seemed to run out of steam. "I'm sorry. I

probably ought to have warned you both that we considered Ned a viable suspect in June Williams's murder. Evidently, both he and Mr. Godfrey are the type that go gaga over broads for no particular reason and then react badly when the broads don't like it. When you and I interviewed her, she didn't seem scared of Godfrey, but she was definitely afraid of somebody. I guess it was Ned."

A rush of internal coldness flashed through me, and I hugged Rosie and Ernie's coat closer to my body. "I wish you'd told me."

He hung his head. "I'm sorry."

It was quite a victory, actually, getting him to apologize like that.

Phil and the police surgeon pushed the office door open at that point, so I didn't get to gloat. Phil looked glum. "I guess he'll make it, but I'm not sure."

I shuddered again. "Will he have decent medical care?"

Phil and Ernie both eyed me as if they couldn't believe I'd asked such a question. Ernie said, "Why the devil do you care? He was going to strangle you, just like he did June Williams."

"Actually, he had a knife," I said. "He tried to stab Rosie with it." I was embarrassed when a few tears leaked out of my eyes.

"A knife! Then I *really* don't understand why you care," bellowed Ernie.

"It's okay, Ernie," said Phil, patting him on a convenient shoulder.

"Stop yelling at me."

"Damn it, Mercy Allcutt," said Ernie in a softer voice. "The man was going to kill you. You do understand that, don't you?"

"Of course, I understand that. But the poor man must be

mad. Madmen can't be accounted wholly responsible for their irrational deeds, you know. He probably ought to be put into an insane asylum. Psychologists have discovered—"

Ernie said, "Sheesh."

Phil threw his hands in the air. "I don't believe this!"

I frowned at him. "Well, he deserves medical attention, anyhow."

"He'll get it," Phil assured me.

"Good." I thought of something else. "What about Mrs. Houser and Barbara-Ann?"

"What about them?" Phil sounded wary.

"Are you going to put Mrs. Houser in jail?"

He flopped onto my desk, looking quite weary. "Naw. She gave us Matty Bumpas and enough information to put the bast—ah, I mean, she helped us with evidence against him. He and Carpetti and D'Angelo will go away for a long time."

"Are those the two men from Mr. Li's shop?" I asked.

"Yeah." Phil took a handkerchief from his pocket and wiped his face.

"What about Mr. Li?" I asked

"Don't tell me you're worried about his health, too," said Ernie sarcastically.

I glowered at him. "No, I am not worried about his health. I only wondered what was going to happen to him."

"He'll probably be put away for a while. He was helping a gang of drug dealers, you know," said Phil. "So I wouldn't feel too sorry for him, if I were you."

"I don't feel sorry for him!" I cried, stung. "I'm not a softheaded moron, you know!" The glance they exchanged irked me. Because I couldn't see a way to win a war of words with them—I'm sure they'd misconstrue anything I said—I asked instead about the Housers. "Will Barbara-

Ann and her mother have a place to stay now? I mean, one that's free from kidnapping gangsters?"

He nodded. "Babs and her daughter are moving back to their apartment. Babs said she's sure they'll be safe now, and she's got her job at the Kit Kat Klub back, for all the good that'll do her. But they both told me to thank you for helping Barbara-Ann."

"Good. I'm glad they'll be able to return home." Even such a home as theirs. I didn't add that part.

"And don't drop by and give them any more money, or they'll both be on your doorstep for the rest of your life," Ernie said in what I can only describe as an extremely sour tone of voice.

I gave him a look. You know the kind. "You needn't worry about that."

He said, "Huh."

Stupid man.

SEVENTEEN

Chloe had several fits when Ernie took me home that evening, but she calmed down when he told her that I'd been a big help in getting two vicious gangsters (Messrs. Carpetti and D'Angelo), a murderer (Ned, whose last name, I learned, was Bennett), and a general all-around lunatic (Mr. Godfrey) locked up so that they'd be unable to hurt anyone else for a long time.

"*You* did that?" she asked, staring at me as if she'd never seen me before.

"Yes," I said firmly. "And I don't appreciate the doubt I hear in your voice."

"Is that why you look like such a mess?"

I sighed, exasperated. "Ernie pushed me down—"

"Hey!" said Ernie.

"I mean, I fell during a shootout in Chinatown, for heaven's sake! It's not as if I could help it!"

"A *shootout?*" Chloe's pallor owed nothing to makeup that time.

"It was a short one," I assured her.

"Well, but . . ."

"I tried to keep her out of it," said Ernie, I guess in an effort to placate Chloe, but he only made me sound like an idiot, and it annoyed me. "She wouldn't obey me."

We were sitting in Chloe and Harvey's beautifully appointed living room, taking tea, when this conversation took place. The flowery porcelain teacup looked out of place in Ernie's big hands, although his manners were impeccable.

Yet another indication, thought I, that he'd been brought up right, even though he'd evidently decided to eschew manners in his everyday life.

"Obey you?" I repeated, frowning at him. "I will obey you when you give me instructions as my employer. You have no right to—"

He held up his hands in a gesture of surrender. "I didn't mean *obey!* All right? I meant that you didn't take my suggestions. My constructive suggestions," he clarified, as if it made a difference. I knew what he meant. "Shoot, are you touchy."

"You said the wrong thing," said Chloe dryly. "Mercy doesn't take constructive suggestions well."

Darn it, they were both against me! "That's not true! But I saw an opportunity to help, and I helped! I helped the police break a case. I did! You said so yourself."

Ernie stood up. "Yes. You helped. Thank you. Now take care of those knees." He shook his head in feigned sorrow. "Boy, the flapper organization will kick you out, with knees like that."

"I'm not a flapper," I growled.

He only grinned at me.

Mrs. Biddle let him out the front door, mainly because Chloe didn't see anybody to doors because she was mistress of the house. I didn't see him out because my knees hurt and I was annoyed with Mr. Ernest Templeton, P.I. I *had* helped a lot, curse it. From rescuing Rosie Von Schilling to tripping up that gangster on the plaza to sending Ned down the elevator shaft in the Figueroa Building, I'd helped. A *lot*.

I sipped more tea. It occurred to me that I hadn't eaten any lunch, and I was really hungry. "When's dinner?" I hoped Chloe and Harvey weren't having guests, because when they had guests, they ate later than usual.

"Seven."

"Good." I sighed heavily.

"I like him," said Chloe.

I squinted at her. "You like who? I mean whom? At least I think I do."

"Oh, forget the grammar! I like Ernie Templeton. I think he likes you, too."

Astounded, I could only gape.

"Don't look at me like that, Mercy Allcutt," Chloe said. "He's a good-looking guy, he's helpful in a crisis, and he's funny. He's got a wonderful sense of humor."

"He does?" I hadn't noticed that particular quality in my employer, perhaps because his humor often came out as sarcasm that he turned against me.

"You know he does."

"I guess." I really didn't want to talk about Ernie with Chloe. Every time I thought about Ernie I got funny tripping sensations in my chest. I didn't understand them, and I didn't have any inclination to have Chloe explain them to me. Slowly I rose from my chair. Every time I moved, my skinned knees crinkled and throbbed. "I'm going upstairs and take a long, soaking bath."

"Good idea. You might think about washing your hair, too."

I slapped a hand to my head. My hat was still there, but I guess it hadn't protected me entirely from the day's activities. With another sigh, I agreed. "Yes. You're probably right."

It would have been a pleasure to walk to Angel's Flight the next morning if my knees hadn't hurt so badly. As I'd soaked in the bathtub the night before, I'd discovered other wounds, as well. My palms were scraped, my elbows were bashed up, I had bruises on my shins, a big one on my backside where I'd hit the concrete of the plaza, and a huge

273

one over my ribs, which ached madly, where that gangster had run into me. It would take a while to get back to my fighting form, I guessed.

Still, it was fun to take Angel's Flight, even if it was a more painful experience than usual. At least I didn't have any mad killers stalking me any longer.

When I got to work, Lulu jumped up from her desk and came to help me into the building. I didn't really need her assistance, but it was nice of her to offer—even though I'm pretty sure she did it because she wanted to talk about the events of the prior day.

"I guess Ned's pretty badly broken up," she said in a hushed voice.

"Well, he did deserve it, I guess. I mean, he was going to kill me, and he'd already killed that one woman."

"More than that," said Lulu avidly.

"What?" I gaped at her.

"Look at this!"

We'd made it to her desk by that time, and she grabbed a copy of the *Herald Examiner* that she'd been reading, in lieu of painting her nails, I guess, before I got there. "Look! It says he's wanted in connection with the murder of another woman in Texas, of all places!"

"Texas?" Good heavens. If you're from Boston, you don't very often think about people actually living in places like Texas. Texas sounded so . . . so . . . I don't know. Full of cows and armed cowboys. It sounded primitive, I guess. Anyhow, Ned had proved himself to be a primitive, at the very least. "Is that where Ned was from?"

Lulu shrugged. "I dunno, but he musta lived there, 'cause the paper says he might have strangled a woman there, too."

"How do they know that?" Personally, I was skeptical,

mainly because I couldn't feature a police station in Texas and the Los Angeles Police Department comparing notes on a daily basis.

"Look," said Lulu, pointing at the paper with one of her blood-red talons. "It says right here that when the authorities asked Ned where he was from—"

"You mean, he was capable of talking to them?" I hadn't realized until that moment that I'd been feeling faintly guilty about sending Ned down that elevator shaft, although I know I shouldn't have. After all, the man had been trying to kill me.

"I guess. Anyhow, when they asked if he had folks anywhere, he mentioned a town in Texas. Spur."

I looked at her blankly.

"Spur!" she repeated. "That's the name of the town! Isn't that a hoot?"

It was, kind of. "So they called somebody in Spur?"

"Yeah. The police. Or the sheriff. You know, it's probably a sheriff, being Texas and all."

Images of cowboy-hatted men on horses galloped into my brain. I shook my head to get rid of them. "Maybe so."

"Well, they said that Ned was suspected in the murder of a young woman in Spur. He'd thought she was in love with him, and when she got engaged to another man, he— Ned, I mean—killed her."

"So it was a pattern," I murmured, lifting my hand to my throat. "And to think that I might have been his next victim."

"It's enough to give you the creeps, huh?"

It certainly was. As I headed to the office, I paused, discovering within myself a reluctance to take the elevator. When I turned to go to the stairwell, I realized I was reluctant to climb the stairs, too. Something about being in a con-

fined area with no easy escape made my skin crawl. Telling myself to cut it out, I climbed up the stairs. Along about the second flight, I mentally scolded myself for cowardice. The elevator might have been where Ned met the end of his criminous career, but the elevator was a blessed sight easier on skinned knees and an achy body than the stairs were.

However, I made it to the office without mishap, and when I unlocked the door and entered, a feeling of well-being engulfed me. I had a job! And it wasn't just any job, either. It was a job that had promised excitement and actually delivered it! Plots began creeping around in my mind, and I decided that if work was dull that day, I'd jolly well begin to type them out. Why not? My job was my inspiration. Perhaps it could also provide a place for my novelistic outpourings. I was sure Ernie wouldn't mind. If I ever dared tell him.

He showed up a little while later, as jaunty as ever. "How're you feeling today?" was his first question, which I thought was nice.

"Fine, thank you. And you?"

"I'm not the one with the bashed-up knees," he reminded me.

"They're fine. They'll heal soon."

"How about the ribs where that guy fell over you. You don't think any of them are cracked, do you?"

I fingered my sore ribs, aghast. "Cracked? How would I tell?"

"If they were cracked, you'd know it," he assured me.

"Oh. Well, then, they're sore, but I don't think they're cracked."

"Good." He went to his office, stopped in the doorway, and hurled his hat at the rack. I heard it plop to the floor. Ernie said, "Damn," and walked inside. I envisioned him picking it up and putting it on the rack, and taking off his

coat and hanging it up, too, then plopping down in his chair, and putting his feet on the desk. My timing was perfect. At the very moment I expected to hear the newspaper crinkle as he opened it, I heard the newspaper crinkle as he opened it.

Life was good.

It got better a little while later when who should appear but Barbara-Ann Houser. She entered the office with what looked like trepidation. I don't know why, unless she figured I wouldn't want to see her anymore after her mother was back home. Poor child. I'd formed quite a fondness for her, really.

That being the case, I smiled brightly. "Good morning, Barbara-Ann! I'm so happy to see you."

"You are?"

"Yes." To prove it, I got up from my chair, in spite of my knees, and went to give her a hug. Perhaps the hug was a mistake, because she stiffened up like cement setting and her eyes went wide with alarm. Oh, well.

Returning to my desk, I patted the seat next to it. "Have a seat, Barbara-Ann. Did you get to go back home yet?"

"Yeah. Ma and me, we moved back yesterday after the coppers picked up Matty Bumpas and threw him in the joint."

"Ah." I think I'd understood that sentence correctly.

"And Ma, she wanted me to give you this. She don't have money, but she wanted to give you something because you were nice to us." She reached into her pocket and pulled out an ashtray with *Kit Kat Klub* stenciled in gold on its outsides. Inside a picture of a black-and-white cat's face had been painted.

Wondering what I was supposed to do with something like that, I took it from her and smiled. "Thank you so much, Barbara-Ann. That's very kind of you and your mother." Something occurred to me. "Um . . . your mother

got her job back, didn't she?"

Barbara-Ann nodded. "Yeah. They said she could come back to work since she hadn't just up and run out on them, but she'd been kidnapped."

Benevolent of them. "I'm happy to hear it. But you must be rather short of funds since she hasn't been working for a couple of weeks."

"Three," said Barbara-Ann.

"Three weeks?"

"Yeah."

I tried to imagine living on the wage that Babs Houser earned. I didn't know how much that was, but I knew what I was making working for Ernie, and it wasn't much. Even living week-to-week would take some scrimping if I had to depend on my salary for my everyday expenses including food and housing. My heart twanged in sympathy. "Then I suppose you really *are* short of funds, aren't you?"

Naturally, Barbara-Ann shrugged. "I dunno. What does that mean? Does that mean we got no money?"

"Well . . . yes."

"Yeah. We're flat busted. Ma said it'll take a while, and maybe the water will be turned off again."

"Oh, dear." I looked at the child sitting next to me, and decided I couldn't allow that to happen.

I know, I know. I'm softhearted and probably softheaded, but darn it, I'd been born lucky and Barbara-Ann Houser hadn't been. I opened my desk drawer and took out my handbag. Taking out two twenty-dollar bills, I handed them to Barbara-Ann, whose eyes went as round as saucers. "Do you think this will help with the utilities, dear?"

"Forty bucks?" she whispered. "That'll take care of the rent and the water and gas and electric and everything. Maybe even buy some bread and milk."

"Take it, then. It's a gift."

"Gee," she said, awed. "Thanks."

And, to my utter astonishment, she got up, leaned over, and kissed me on the cheek. I was touched. Barbara-Ann herself was clearly embarrassed. She turned red as a radish and beat a hasty retreat, calling out another "Thanks," from the doorway.

After she left, I sat back in my chair and sighed. A feeling of accomplishment and satisfaction suffused my very being.

Until Ernie spoke from the door of his office. "I saw that," said he.

I started and turned to frown at him. "Don't do that. I'm still skittish from yesterday."

"You gave them more money, didn't you?"

I huffed. "You said you saw it."

"I did. And I saw you give them more money."

"So what?"

"You're going to go broke, is what. I thought you wanted to earn money at a job. You keep giving it away. Any normal girl would need her salary to keep going, you know."

With a sigh, I admitted it. "I know. All right, so I spent quite a bit more than I've earned during my first two weeks as your secretary. Still, I learned a lot, it was exciting, and it was a very valuable learning experience." I smiled winningly. "I'm looking forward to working for you for a long time, Ernie Templeton."

He gave me an odd look. "Yeah?"

"Yes."

"Hmm." He fingered his lower lip. "Well, all right, but I'm not sure I can stand the strain." And he turned and went back into his office.

I'm pretty sure he was kidding.

ABOUT THE AUTHOR

In an effort to avoid what she knew she should be doing with her life (writing—it sounded so hard), for several years ALICE DUNCAN expressed her creative side by dancing and singing. She belonged to two professional international folk-dance groups and also sang in a Balkan women's choir. Alice got to sing the tenor drone for the most part. Hey, one does what one can.

In September of 1996, Alice and her herd of wild dachshunds moved from Pasadena, California, to Roswell, New Mexico, where her mother's family settled fifty years before the aliens crashed. Alice loves writing because in her books she can portray the world the way it should be instead of the way it is, which often stinks. Alice started writing books in October 1992, and sold her first book in January 1994. That book, *One Bright Morning*, was published by Harper in January 1995 (and won the HOLT Medallion for best first book published in 1995). Alice hopes she can continue to write forever.